# THE WINTER SUN

## ⊰ THE VAGRANT FAE SAGA ⊱

*USA TODAY* BESTSELLING AUTHORS
### NATHAN SQUIERS & MEGAN J. PARKER

Cover Design by MiblArt Book Cover Design
Interior Design by The Illustrated Author Design Services

Printed in the United States of America
Literary Dark Duo Publishing
First Printing, 2021

ISBN 978-1940634364

"The **wide world** is all about you: you can fence yourselves in,
but you cannot forever fence it out."
-J.R.R. Tolkien

# PROLOGUE

Like strawberries and wheat...
He'd told her that her hair was the color of strawberries and wheat.

It was like looking back at a dream now, as though everything before that moment had been the sweetest, most beautiful lie that could have been told to her. She wanted so badly to convince herself that it was the other way around; that she was in a nightmare and looking back on a life she missed so terribly. The pain was what made it real, though. In her dreams, she never knew this sort of agony—gripping and tormenting spells of regret and hatred and sadness that stirred within her like a mixing potion. She recalled seeing her elders blend potions during her classes and how the ingredients, already in their ether state, would shine with such brilliance as the magic blended into spirals of radiant colors. Eventually the mixture settled, though, and while the potions only ever shone in a single shade, it was always breathtaking. Now, however, the mixture of agony stirring in her belly held no awe for her, and she knew that when it settled it could wear only one hue:

That of a vagrant.

She'd once been told that her hair was the color of strawberries and wheat, but in less than an hour the ancient iron gate leading to the labyrinth would open and the only color anybody would remember Gwen for was brown.

# ONE
## ~Two Weeks Earlier~

"Gwendolyn Clearwater!" the shrill call of Rosalind Clearwater rose up and over the normally impenetrable shroud of the helitrad forest. The patches of pale, papery bark of the helitrad trees rippled on the angry gust of the elder healer's voice and seemed to point like accusatory fingers at the wayward fae. As if the trees were showing her the way, Rosalind's voice grew closer but no less demanding. "IF YOU HAVE NOT FILLED THAT BASKET BY NOW I SWEAR BY THE—"

"Let calmness be you, Mother!" Gwendolyn bound towards her, holding her basket high as evidence that she had not strayed from her errand.

Provided the trees were not truly in league with her, there was no way she would know—

"Hoofmeat!" the elder fae stomped her foot hard enough on the ground to wilt a nearby dreamcap mushroom. "You were trying to track that injured fox you spotted limping off last night!"

Gwendolyn's eyes went wide. "No!" she held out her basket once more, hoping that the contents that nearly filled it might sway the accusation.

Her mother only planted her balled fists on her hips. Long, platinum hair whipped in the lingering breeze as the still youthful yet weathered features wore the fury that only a mother could don. Gwendolyn felt her ears droop under the weight of the elder healer's gaze and, for the hundredth time in that month, wondered what it was like for those apprentices whose masters weren't also a parent. Unfortunately for her, Gwendolyn had the privilege of being birthed by one of the fae nation's highest-ranking healers; probably the best healer the fae had ever known!

A "privilege," they called it. Gwendolyn thought it was a strange word for everyone to use given the burden she felt from it. After all, the relationship between an apprentice and their master was stressful enough without having to *also* sit across from them at the family table every night. And while other young fae had the option of requesting a new master to train under, for Gwendolyn it would have been a great dishonor to her mother. Moreover, such a request would force her to be assigned to a less knowledgeable healer.

At that moment, however, under the scornful and knowing weight of her master's gaze, Gwendolyn found herself curious if "less knowledgeable" might also mean "less insightful."

The long silence stretched on until the young fae girl's drooping ears were nearly touching her slumped shoulders. "Really, I wasn't…" she began before letting out a sigh and lowering her basket. "What gave me away this time?" she asked.

Rosalind's sternness melted away like healing wax under a blue flame and a grin blossomed in its place. Even the swaying bark of the helitrad trees seemed to calm, and with the swaying blossoms no longer blocking out the late-afternoon sunlight the entire forest seemed to brighten with her. Rigidity turned fluid like a thawing stream under spring's kiss and her locked arms reached out to grip her daughter's shoulders.

"You gave yourself away, songbird," she sang.

Gwendolyn lingered, reciting the conversation several times in her head as Rosalind started back towards where her daughter had come. Unable to think of a single way she might have incriminated herself, Gwendolyn turned to follow after.

"You deceive me, Master Healer! I did no such—AHH!"

Catching her toe on a gnarled tree root, Gwendolyn toppled forward. In a mess of twisted limbs, dark green fabric, and wavy red hair, the young fae whimpered at her clumsiness. Detangling herself from her own embarrassment, she looked up and groaned at the sight of her mother studying the overturned basket of dreamcaps and belchberries.

"Gone nearly three hours and nothing to show for that time but *these*?" Rosalind clicked her tongue at her. "And what sort of spell did you have planned with this? Were you going to curse your poor brother with gassy dreams again?"

Gwendolyn jumped to her feet and straightened her dress, giggling to herself as she did. "Actually," she skipped ahead and winked at her mother, "I thought I'd give the potion to Father this time and watch you flee from the bedchamber when it took hold of him."

"Oh, you wicked little monster!" Rosalind feigned shock and hiked up the hem of her sea-blue dress to chase after her daughter. "I've got a right mind to use those belchberries in your breakfast before you visit with the elders for tomorrow's review!"

"You wouldn't!" Gwendolyn gasped, planting her own hands on her hips. "You would cast such poor manners upon an apprentice—and your own daughter—on such an important day?"

Rosalind laughed and tugged on Gwendolyn's ear after she caught up. "To the apprentice *and* daughter"—she mocked her daughter's tone—"who would cast such a dreadful fate upon her master? And her own mother at that!" A single nod punctuated her point, "I think it would be only fair!"

"I suppose you speak fairness," Gwendolyn sighed, rubbing her ear and continuing after her mother. "Make pause! Where are we headed now?"

"To your next lesson, songbird," Rosalind announced. "See now, I sent you out for supplies: herbs and bark and rarities that one could use in creating *useful* elixirs and potions. I sent you out for those supplies *knowing* that the fox, though troubled with an injured leg, still sprinted within your mind. And now, having humility-bringing shame hang over your head, it's important for you to understand the danger of your jilted priorities."

The healer's steps grew longer and swifter then, forcing Gwendolyn to keep up. Their slender bodies darted through the forest, weaving between the trees and over the brush like a feather on the breeze. A herd of star-eyed elk yelped in surprise at the pair as they passed between them, and a clamor of hoof beats sounded behind them. They laughed, knowing that no harm would come to the creatures short of an interrupted grazing and the possible perturbed crow or two that might be forced from the low-hanging branches that their antlers caught. And on they ran. All the while, though sharing in the splendor of the sights and sounds, Gwendolyn noticed her mother's keen, well-trained eyes as they followed unseen clues. They carried on through the forest for a ways, darting and weaving but never straying from the core direction, then, seeing her mother's green eyes flash with recognition like an enchanted gem, they veered off towards the sunset and, in one mighty leap, cleared a ravine that landed them into a sandy cove that bordered the lake, where the fishers' vessels had begun to silhouette the horizon.

"Mothe...er, Master?" Gwendolyn corrected herself, remembering that, during a lesson, her mother refused that title and the coddling that came with it. "There are no supplies for us here! There is only sand and rocks!"

"And *him*," Rosalind Clearwater's pace slowed to a cautious crawl as she motioned towards an upturned length of driftwood that jutted from a recessed nook.

Following her mentor's motions, Gwendolyn strained her eyes against the concealing rays of the setting sun. At first, she saw nothing, only a small well of inky blackness harbored beneath the sea-beaten plank. However, as they drew nearer and the eclipsing rays hid behind the neighboring forest's canopy, she spotted the lone occupant and let out a victorious cry.

"It's him!" she cooed, moving to close the distance between her and the injured fox.

"Let calmness be you, apprentice! Have stillness take you!" her mother gripped her shoulder with a startling strength. "See how pain has scorned him! Look at how he suffers!"

Turning back to the poor creature, Gwendolyn watched as the fox worked to burrow further into his sandy nest, growling and yapping angrily at the two of them as he fought to hide.

"He's... he's *scared* of us, Master," she whispered, nearly driven to tears from the sight. "But... but *why*? We only mean to help him; to *heal* him!"

"Here lies the lesson I must teach you today," her mother continued to whisper. "There is little else in this world that will drive a being to distrust quite so much as pain. A body that suffers seldom holds a mind that can conceive of sympathy or kindness. To him, my loving songbird, we are two that could just as quickly bring him more pain as not, and he would sooner know the pain he holds now than allow himself to invite even more."

Gwendolyn felt a hot well of tears begin to grow. "Then let us show him, Master! I beg of you! Let us show him that we mean to help; let me heal him!"

"And with what will you heal him with?" her mother's voice turned hard with the iciness of truth, and Gwendolyn felt the lesson that her mother meant to teach her take hold of her throat. "You spent the better part of this afternoon trying to find this creature rather than collecting the supplies I asked of you. Those supplies," her voice dipped again, "were the very ingredients that I could have used to calm this creature and mend his leg. I have tracked this creature down, as you sought to for the past few hours and with every bit the same haste you'd intended, but we find ourselves at our goal without the means to help him. Now, my apprentice, we stand here, unable to help and, in fact, allowing his fear and the pain motivating it to further injure him."

Tears streamed down Gwendolyn's face as she saw that the fox, in its maddened effort to dig away from the two of them, was causing his injured leg further harm.

"STOP IT!" she wailed, trying once again to move towards the animal. "STOP! YOU'RE ONLY HURTING YOURSELF MORE!"

"Be calm and still, apprentice! You're frightening him!"

Gwendolyn sobbed and looked away, overwhelmed by the thought of the fox's pain and the guilt of adding to it. "Please..." she whimpered, "Please, Master! Please do something for him! I cannot take this! He's in such pain!"

"Do you understand, my dear, that acting on kindness alone is not enough? Do you see now why your good intentions mean nothing if you are not mindful of everything— mindful of your supply and yourself and your actions?"

"I do..." Gwendolyn's words slipped past her lips like freshly pressed sootheoil. "I will hold this lesson today and forever, Master, just don't allow this creature to suffer any further at the cost of my carelessness. I beg you!"

"Dear, sweet Gwendolyn Clearwater," her mother's soothing song-voice rolled across her ears like the waves over the shore as she reached into the purse within her left sleeve and withdrew three leather pouches. "Your love for all life will carry you further than the mightiest phoenix's wings, but without the wisdom of self—the clarity to see the before, the now, and the after with eyes unclouded by raw sympathy—your distance will have only been in the wrong direction."

Opening the first pouch, she poured a small portion of a light-blue powder into her palm, which she then gently blew in the fox's direction. The air shimmered with the enchantment as it swirled around the creature and, as its frantic breaths drew it in, its body began to relax and the terror in its eyes faded to a dreamy stare.

"Faithmist for stillness," she whispered, drawing a small vial from the second as she crept closer towards it. As she closed the distance, she uncapped the vial and pressed her palm to the opening, upturning its contents and letting it coat her hand. Then, once she was close enough, she gently ran the palm over the top of the fox's head, and Gwendolyn marveled as the once scornful creature looked upon her with love and adoration. "Sootheoil for clarity," she went on as she opened the third pouch, drawing forth a strip of helitrad bark. Unfurling the papery length, she carefully wrapped the bark around the fox's injured leg, and then retrieved the vial of helitrad sap that hung around her neck to seal the makeshift bandage. "And the flesh and blood of the god-tree for mending…"

The master healer chanted then, calling upon words that were not words and a song that no other knew how to sing. This was her personal *sparadikt*, a spell that was all her own. Every healer had their own *sparadikt* that drew out the magic in their potions, but it was known to all in their class that none were as powerful as the master healer Rosalind Clearwater's. As if eager to give truth to all the praise, the words of the *sparadikt* seemed to take a life of their own within the air, resounding and echoing on unspeaking tongues and sparking new life and excitement within the fox's body. Its eyes shone blue with the faithmist and its fur shimmered anew from the sootheoil, and, with Gwendolyn's master still chanting her *sparadikt*, the helitrad bark and sap grew bright as the night's first star before igniting and burning away to nothing.

Then, beneath the pale, flaking ash, there was a newly healed leg.

The fox barked excitedly and tested its limb—licking away a spot of ash and sneezing as he did—before leaping forward and nuzzling Rosalind.

"You did it!" Gwendolyn praised, clapping her hands and throwing her arms around her mother. "You did it, Mother! You saved him!"

Rosalind Clearwater nodded, forgiving her daughter's slip and smiling at the two of them as she freed herself from their combined affections and rose to her feet. Returning the pouches to their place in her sleeve, she watched as the fox redirected its attention onto Gwendolyn, leaping forward and offering his savior's daughter several excited kisses much to the delight of the young fae.

"Do you hold within your heart the truth of today's lesson, songbird?" Rosalind asked.

"I do," her daughter answered in between kiss-induced laughter. "I hold its truths within my heart and will call upon them in times of need."

Rosalind nodded, motioning to the fox. "Then, should he accept you as I see you've accepted him, you may take this one as a companion."

Gwendolyn's eyes sparkled with joy at that and she hugged the creature close to her. "Truly, Mother? No deceptions?"

"No deceptions," Rosalind nodded, "provided you hold true to your oath on this evening."

A pair of crows called angrily behind them as they soared over the vast wall of the fae city. Though Gavrael felt uneasy venturing too close to their world—a world they'd worked very, very hard on dividing from the rest of the world—it was to be the final resting place of Alastair, one of the last grandfathers of their herd. Like Alastair, Gavrael was branded a *vernunt* at an early age, so few, if any, ever felt up to the task of trying to speak with him on topics of any importance.

"There are many in the herd that would trample the ground in a stampede, child of us," one of the father centaurs had told him when he was still a foal. "You are not like this, not like them. You would sooner stampede within your head, trample your mind with a storm of thoughts, and, for this, you are different. But do not let this difference upset or unsettle you, young one, for it is our differences that carry the herd."

Though it was the way of the herd to celebrate the differences of those within it, Gavrael found it irritating—a word that seemed to only hold meaning to those who'd happened across a patch of poison sumac—that he had thoughts and feelings that the others neither shared nor understood. While the other males vied for the attentions of the budding females in their herd and created displays of strength and speed to attract them, Gavrael worried himself over matters of affection. Were he to create a display of strength or speed like the others and catch the attention of a female whom he could not find any connection with, how would such a union hold him? Moreover, what if in his efforts he found himself pining for one female in particular who was unimpressed with his display? The other males, when he presented these concerns, could only assure him that every female had their admirable strengths; that none of them would bear him weak or incapable offspring.

Questions of right and wrong plagued him, as well, and it was these burdens that drove him to run and train. For every meadow he crossed and every tree he toppled with a single swing of his axe, Gavrael felt a sense of control over the unknown. The herd, though blindly supportive of all their children, worried that the long days and nights he spent on his own were driving him away from the One Truth: that, though its parts were many and each operated differently, they all worked towards one end: that of the herd. Like the bizarre machines that gremlins constructed, all of the pieces had their place...

And none of their places was far from the machine, dwelling on its own over thoughts that no other dwelled over.

It came as no surprise to Gavrael that word had reached Alastair of the herd's concerns. Only a *vernunt* understood a *vernunt*, and until the wayward part that Gavrael represented was once more in place in the herd the machine couldn't work.

The young centaur sighed. It was *exactly* those sorts of thoughts that isolated him. He officially had more in common with the wandering elf minstrels that traveled along the East Sea than with his own people.

With the shadow of the fae city wall looming over him, he removed the axe from his back and leaned it against Alastair's hometree before venturing further.

The grandfather centaur—a still-powerful light-brown frame on which the hardened, olive-toned body and grayed, chiseled expression rested—stood atop a great boulder that had been wedged between two mighty trees. From this vantage, Alastair was able to stand over any who sought his guidance while allowing the trunks to support his aging frame. One of the branches, level to the grandfather centaur's chest, held a clay bowl that he was gazing into upon Gavrael' arrival.

The young centaur knelt before his elder and held his right fist over his chest in a salute to all he'd given to the herd.

"Father Stesko told me you had wisdom to grant me," he recited the words that he knew the herd wanted from him.

The grandfather centaur let out a dry laugh. "Father Stesko told me you were in need of granted wisdom." He gave his graying beard a gentle tug and smirked, "Unless one of us can realize what wisdom they mean, I fear we may both find our resting places where we stand." He gave one more thoughtful tug on his beard and tilted his head, "*Do you know of what wisdom Father Stesko speaks?*"

Gavrael sighed and rose from his kneel, still forced to look up at the elder. "I think the wisdom is of anything but, Grandfather Alastair."

The grandfather centaur hummed at this and hung an arm over one of the trees so he could lean forward. "Go on."

Another, much deeper sigh. "I find myself troubled by thoughts," Gavrael confessed.

Another, much louder hum. "Ah, but thoughts of *what?*" Alastair asked.

"Does it matter?" Gavrael shrugged. "It would seem that any are unwelcome."

Alastair's brow furrowed with intrigue, "And which of the fathers or mothers have read your thoughts, child of us?"

"I…" Gavrael shook his head, "I don't understand what you ask?"

"You speak of unwelcome thoughts and the concerns of the herd regarding them, but I've yet to encounter a single one among us with the ability to hear another's thoughts.

Tell me," he leaned further in, "is it Mother Brumank? I've had my suspicions of that one, I have, but not a mind to see her thoughts to be certain."

"No, it's not… I do not believe any in the herd have such an ability."

"Oh, then how is it that the herd knows of these thoughts enough so to not grant them welcome?" Alastair grinned at his own question.

Gavrael groaned and looked down, realizing he'd galloped straight into one of the grandfather centaur's jokes. "They know because I tell them…" he sighed, "I run off to train and meet other creatures, and when I return the others ask where I've gone."

"And then they ask *why*," Alastair nodded.

Gavrael nodded back.

"Well there you have it, child of us. Your thoughts are not just thoughts. You act upon them—those are actions— and you speak upon them—those are statements—and you are a part of a herd that does not understand such actions or statements."

"But why do they not understand, Grandfather Alastair?" Gavrael asked, "Why do my actions and statements confuse them so?"

Alastair shrugged. "For the same reason that you do not understand their reason to act and speak as they do."

Gavrael scoffed, "You think I don't understand their simple ways?"

"You call their ways simple?" The grandfather centaur scoffed back, "Then why, my misguided *vernunt*, have you been sent here to gain their wisdom?"

Gavrael looked down, realizing that he'd been bested by the elder's wit.

"You are strong and with great mind, Gavrael," the grandfather centaur boasted, "but you forget the needs of the many in favor of the welfare of but a few."

"Is this because I've been giving Lysoks an extra portion at mealtimes?" Gavrael demanded. "Am I to let my own sister go hungry?"

"That you call her your sister is cause enough for concern," Alastair's voice grew uncomfortably stern. "She is all's sister, just as you are all's brother, and you both are children of *us*! To favor one over the other is to endanger us all!"

Gavrael narrowed his eyes at the grandfather centaur, "Do you truly believe that to be so?"

"A fact is only as strong as the herd's willingness to accept it!" Alastair stomped his hoof down hard enough to chip the boulder. "What I—but one male of many in the herd—believe holds no more power than what another believes. And when all but one believe something else to be true, who is the one to challenge it?"

"We are the *vernunt*," Gavrael said, "and isn't that what we're meant to do?"

"The herd takes pride in the *vernunt* for their insight to benefit all of them. Many generations ago, it was a *vernunt* who first came to this system, and it has been a system of prosperity and growth and happiness for us ever since!" Alastair stomped again, "But you, young Gavrael, would like to believe that your thoughts—that your actions and statements—should resonate more within all of us when your hooves have yet to travel the distance of an elder?"

Gavrael frowned, shaking his head. "This has nothing to do with Lysoks, does it?"

Alastair smirked at the question, "You are, indeed, a *vernunt*." He glanced down at the clay bowl by his chest, still smirking. "The herd concerns itself with greater things than whether or not a young centaur cannot break the birth-ties to a sibling. It's *irritating*, I know"—he quirked a knowing brow up at him—"but it is certainly not the sort of thing that they waste time discussing. A stubborn *vernunt* who's transformed himself into the fastest and strongest in our ranks, however..."

Realization crashed down on the young centaur like lightning striking a dried-up helitrad tree.

"You speak of the labyrinth?" Gavrael felt his flank tighten and stomped out the cramp with his hind leg.

The grandfather centaur took note of this, neither remarking nor frowning at the gesture, but simply following the motion with his old, brown eyes. Realizing this, Gavrael stilled his leg, only to have his tail slap nervously at the lingering sensation.

"Your body speaks more than your words, child of us," Alastair sighed as he set his palm into the bowl he'd been lingering on. "And what is it about the Labyrinth that you so adamantly oppose?"

"It's a foolish and barbaric fae practice!" Gavrael exclaimed, surprising himself with his own brashness. Clearing his throat, he shook his head, afraid to make eye contact with the grandfather centaur as he continued. "Their justice system is their own to uphold, but to ask us to volunteer ourselves to play the role of a murderous beast for a moon phase in exchange for their moldy bread and fatty meat trimmings is absurd!"

"The offerings the fae bestow upon the volunteers represent a great bounty to the herd," Alastair said calmly.

"Great bounty? They toss their garbage at us and call it a reward! And at what cost! Allowing ourselves to be locked in those tunnels and wait for them to release a fae miscreant so that we can make a show of hunting them down and murdering them? We act like slobbering monsters and butcher their criminals for them in the hopes that they'll offer *more* moldy bread and fatty meat trimmings at the end of the eight-day cycle!" He growled, seething at the idea, "And then we just offer up another. Then another, and another! What sort of an absurd mind agreed to such an ugly and demeaning practice?"

16

"The sort of mind that arrogant, young *vernunt* unknowingly insult in their presence," Alastair voice was cold enough to send a tremor up both of Gavrael' spines.

"You?" the young centaur shook his head in disbelief, "How... how could you possibly...?"

"Because the fae have always and will always live in a walled-off world, child of us," Alastair told him, "But their walls don't just rise from the ground and sink beneath the sea, they're erected deep within their minds, and those walls are the most impenetrable of all. As hard as it may be to get through to you, Gavrael, it is but a simple and quick task when compared to any hope of breaking past one of theirs. They will never *not* believe us to be slobbering monsters or murderous beasts, so to use that bigotry to benefit the heard—to harness their hate and superstition so that we might have plenty and cause to celebrate each victor's successes—is a means by which we turn something awful into something wonderful. And you, Gavrael, are the fastest and strongest of us all. If any could enter the labyrinth and emerge not only victorious, not only the bringer of the largest bounty the herd has ever seen, but as the most celebrated victor to ever set hoof within those tunnels, *then*, child of us, you will take your place and understand your role within the herd."

Gavrael trembled at the grandfather centaur's words, feeling a curious pull that just as quickly turned into a nauseous regret.

"I'm sorry," his voice shook as he carried the weight of the disappointment he knew he was earning, "but any prize or glory that can be won within the Labyrinth isn't worth the blood of a fae I have no quarrel against staining my hands."

Alastair's weathered features wore a frown at the end of Gavrael' words, but the young centaur had doubts that what he saw was actually disappointment. The grandfather centaur drew in a slow breath through his nostrils and, after

17

holding the air within his lungs for a long moment, blew it out through parted lips.

"Words of peace from a warring mind," he mumbled to himself, lifting his hand from the bowl and reaching towards Gavrael with a hand dripping crimson.

Not wanting to dishonor the elder by pulling away, the young *vernunt* allowed the only likeminded centaur in his herd press the sticky, wet hand against his chest. A moment, more than just one of awkward silence or mysterious contact, passed between them, and a sense of clarity and respect hung like a heavy, waiting raincloud. Finally, Alastair withdrew his hand, leaving a red, seven-fingered imprint upon his predecessor's chest.

"You wear the mark of our herd, child of us," his voice carried more pride than Gavrael felt he deserved, and the young centaur felt that something within him might break at any instant, "and you wear the blood of a *vernunt*, blood I shed solely for you upon this meeting. Whether you choose to believe it or not, your path and the answers you seek begin within that labyrinth."

# TWO

Gwendolyn knew she should've been collecting herbs and supplies for her mother, but Bren had other plans. Though she'd only had the fox for a few days, the young fae had already discovered a stronger bond with the animal than she could have guessed. That first night, with the fox curled up beside Gwendolyn and her tail draped over the young fae's shoulder like a scarf, she'd dreamt of running alongside the fae city's wall. It was in that dream that the name had come to her. Bren, though without words, had seemed appreciative of the name when Gwendolyn had spoken it allowed; meeting the call with a series of excited yips.

Each day since, though she was certain that her mother had noticed that her daily quota of supplies wasn't being met, Gwendolyn and Bren had continued to go out together. She was certain that the day would come when her mentor would tire of letting her training come second to her new pet, but until that day arrived Gwendolyn was set on having as much fun as possible. So, though the days were counting

19

against them and collecting herbs and berries was supposed to be her first priority, Gwendolyn decided to shirk her duties for one more day before returning to her studies with a refreshed vigor.

"Come on, Bren!" Gwendolyn raced ahead, leaving her basket hanging from the branch of a helitrad tree near her favorite gathering site. "I want to show you a secret place!"

The fox barked happily as it chased after her across the meadow, heading closer and closer to the massive wall that surrounded the fae city. Like in her dream, Gwendolyn and Bren raced alongside the structure, allowing only what distance was needed between them so that they could pass around the trees and shrubs that grew alongside the stone wall. As she ran, Gwendolyn traced the path of the wall beside her before letting her gaze follow it as far ahead as she could. From there, she let her memory of the great wall continue the unseen path around the full area of the fae city. With the exception of the lake, which extended out and fed into the eastern sea, the wall surrounded the entirety of the massive fae city. And while the wall followed, for the most part, a direct path, there were, for those keen enough to seek them out, irregularities to be found. When she'd been young, Gwendolyn and her close friend had found one of these irregularities and declared the awkward curve of the wall to be their secret place—a place that Gwendolyn had never shown anybody else. After a short while, where a shallow pond and a pair of willow trees forced the wall to break its straight path and snake around the water, they stopped. The wall, for the most part, followed as direct a path as nature would allow.

This was it: their secret spot.

Gwendolyn, still panting from her run, stared at the willow trees' reflection in the calm waters of the pond, and remembered. As they often did, a well of emotions flooded up as memories filled her mind. Life had moved forward since, and though she didn't want to admit that she'd allowed herself to forget or even move forward from those days, they were, in more ways than one, days that had been lost. The memories of this spot *were* happy ones—she couldn't think of a single one that wasn't, in fact—but, be that as it may, that she'd built memories here that were doomed to be unmatched was a haunting fact she couldn't ignore.

It was Hawkes' spot first, and he'd been the one to show it to her so many years back. Even then, with the innocence and ignorance of youth, they'd known the rules surrounding the wall, but her friend was too curious even then to let such a mystery stay hidden. He'd found this place while exploring the wall's strangely irregular path—boldly declaring that it was not as straight as the elders claimed—and, after showing it to Gwendolyn, he'd confessed that he wondered what it was like on the other side.

Even then, Gwendolyn had known better than to dwell on such a thought for very long.

As Bren continued to trot towards the gate, Gwendolyn allowed the memories to continue to sweep her away. She didn't allow herself to think of Hawkes too often due to the sadness it brought to her. She had once believed that she and Hawkes were in love, and though her mother would later say that she'd been too young to feel such things, she remembered when she and Hawkes would overhear their parents conspiring about their future wedding over tea. On one occasion, Gwendolyn had even caught her mother discussing what sort of flowers Gwendolyn would wear in her hair on the day they were married. When she'd gone to Hawkes with this news, he'd smiled and looked out towards the wheat fields that his neighbor grew on the outskirts of a vast meadow. Though the owner of the vast stretch of land had been careful to clear the field for the crop, a set of spring storms earlier that season had allowed a patch of wild strawberry vines to cover the western side of the hillside and begin to choke the outermost stalks of wheat. Gazing at the red-and-yellow spectacle in the afternoon sun, Hawkes had told her that she didn't need any flowers in her hair on the day of their wedding. It was on that day that he'd told her that her hair was the color of strawberries and wheat.

And, like the scarlet berries and their tight embrace against the golden lengths of grain, nothing more was needed to spotlight the beauty than the right lighting.

Earlier that year, while recounting that story with her mother, Rosalind had denied ever planning a wedding between the two of them. This had caught Gwendolyn off guard, not because she believed her mother and doubted her memories, but, rather, because she *knew* that the memory was true. Her mother was never one to lie, even in instances that might have been better for it, but at that moment, over a memory that had been an otherwise joyful one, she did just that. The pain from that denial cut Gwendolyn deeper than she'd ever let on, but only because she understood that the pain of Hawkes' fate was not hers alone to bear.

That denial, like Gwendolyn limiting her memories, was her mother's only way to cope with the truth of the crime Hawkes had committed and the penalty he'd been forced to pay.

Gwendolyn needed that memory, though. Knowing that he loved her—that there could have been a life for them—allowed her to forgive him for his crime. Even if he hadn't wanted to leave her, his actions had forced him out of her life. In some way, believing Hawkes loved her...

A tear burned a path down Gwendolyn's cheek and, as she reached up to wipe it away, she heard Bren whimpering up at her. Looking down, she caught sight of the fox's titled head as she gazed back up at her.

"You can tell I'm sad, can't you?" she crouched down to pat her friend on the head. Gwendolyn sighed and nodded, sniffling as she looked back at the pond. "There's a lot of good memories here, but the one I made them with is gone now. He died."

Saying the word aloud awoke the old heartbreak, and Gwendolyn buried her face into the fox's fur as the tears came.

For a long time Bren allowed Gwendolyn to hold her and stain her fur with her tears, but as the sobbing carried on the fox began to match the tormented whimpers with her own. Thinking that she'd grown impatient with the tight embrace, Gwendolyn dropped her arms and let the fox scamper off. But the whimpering continued. Looking up, the teary-eyed fae watched as Bren hurried around the pond to the base of the stone wall and began to frantically dig. Perplexed, Gwendolyn stood, drying her eyes and beginning to follow after her friend.

"What's gotten into you, girl? We can't go out there! Nobody's allowed out there!"

More whimpering. More digging.

"Bren!" Gwendolyn stood over the fox and looked down at her, "What are you doi—"

A sharp sob echoed through the canopy of trees then. Gwendolyn's ears perked and she looked up towards the top of the wall where the sound was still spilling over.

Somebody on the other side was in terrible pain...

Gwendolyn's heart lodged in her stomach as the sounds of struggle and agony became that much greater and she realized that whoever was in pain was only on the other side.

Were it not for the wall she could have reached out and touched them!

Bren barked and continued to dig.

"I... I know. I know."

Gwendolyn's body tensed as another cry of agony rolled over the wall and she felt it stab into her stomach like a toxic blade.

She couldn't let whatever that was out there suffer any longer, it wasn't right.

A shiver.

A jump.

Just a short way to fall…

"I know. I know it hurts," she heard herself whispering. "It'll be okay."

A cry of terror brought Gwendolyn back to herself and she looked up into the wide eyes of a little girl.

She was on the other side of the wall.

She'd jumped over in response to the sound of pain.

It scared her how easy it was; she could barely even remember doing it.

The awe of her own bravery was short lived. The little girl—a young centaur with the thin, frail-looking legs of a newborn mare—struggled against the binds of a fae deer traps. Though her people went on regular hunts around the proximity of the wall, it wasn't uncommon for them to leave traps after a hunt to ensure a few easy catches during their next outing. These traps, a simple set of wooden bars lined with sharpened bits of bone and teeth, rested around a spring-loaded pad and "bit down" on the leg of any unfortunate creature that stepped on them. A dark enchantment kept anything caught in the traps from freeing itself, and while this was a clever way to keep a deer from pulling free it also appeared to be a cruel way of keeping an unfortunate child from escaping its clutches.

Though she already had mixed emotions about those sorts of enchantments, Gwendolyn found herself loathing them all the greater at that moment.

"It's alright," she assured the young centaur, "I'm here to—AH!"

A small, hoofed foot lashed out at her as the little girl cried out and fought against the trap's tight hold to put additional distance between the two of them.

She was terrified of her, Gwendolyn realized. Just like Bren had been.

Recalling her mother's lesson, Gwendolyn reached into the pocket in her sleeve and retrieved a familiar set of ingredients before laying them out in front of her. Opening the first pouch, she poured a small portion of a light-blue powder into her palm, which she then gently blew in the centaur's direction. The air shimmered with the enchantment as it swirled around the little girl and, as her frantic breaths drew it in, her body began to relax and the terror in her eyes faded to a dreamy stare. "Faithmist for stillness," Gwendolyn recited, drawing a small vial from the second as she crept closer towards her. As she closed the distance, she uncapped the vial and pressed her palm to the opening, upturning its contents and letting it coat her hand. Then, once she was close enough, she gently ran the palm over the centaur's forehead, and she watched as the once terror-stricken child looked upon her with trust. "Sootheoil for clarity," she repeated, awestruck by her own work. With the centaur finally calm, Gwendolyn kneeled in front of her and began to carefully open the trap. The magic reacted to fear and panic, so she was careful to keep her mind focused as she pried the makeshift jaws apart and pulled it free of the centaur's leg. With the trap out of the way, she caught sight of the wound and winced. The trap had dug too deep, and blood quickly began to pool across the ground. Seeing this, the centaur cried and covered her eyes, whimpering that her leg was broken and she'd never be able to run again. Gwendolyn shook her head and shifted herself so that the little girl wouldn't be able to see the blood. "No, no," she assured her, tearing a portion of her right sleeve to mop away some of the blood. "You're going to be alright. I promise!" When she was finished cleaning the wound, Gwendolyn tied the length of fabric above the wound to slow the bleeding. As the knot tightened, she heard the centaur yelp and felt her shift slightly at the pressure, but she otherwise stayed quiet and allowed her savior to work. Retrieving the next parcel, Gwendolyn opened the third pouch, drawing forth a strip of helitrad bark. Unfurling the papery length, she carefully wrapped the bark around the girl's injured leg and then retrieved the vial of helitrad sap that hung around her neck to seal the makeshift bandage. Calling upon the memory of her mother's steps, she whispered "And the flesh and blood of the god-tree for mending…"

The bark began to glow as she applied the sap, but, though she could see the magic working, Gwendolyn found herself regretting that she'd yet to unlock her own *sparadikt*. The bark and sap of the helitrad tree would, in time, allow the centaur's leg to fully heal, but without the boosting spell to unlock its full potential she'd be forced to wait days for what a better trained healer could do in seconds.

Though it was far from a perfect healing, Gwendolyn felt the centaur's body relax. Looking up at her young patient, she was met with a smiling face.

"Th-thank you," the centaur whispered.

Gwendolyn could only nod.

She'd done it.

She'd actually done it!

"You'll be just fine," she said, standing up and beginning to put away her supplies. "Just be careful not to put too much weight on it for—MMPH!"

Gwendolyn watched the panicked centaur turn to race off as several pairs of hands seized her all at once and she was dragged back over the wall.

# THREE

"Gwendolyn Clearwater..."

The elder fae's voice was an icy trickle over Gwendolyn's reddened ears. She'd barely taken a breath since she'd been found in the woods. The sight of the little centaur girl racing into the thicket had captured her attention so much that she hadn't heard the other fae descend upon her. Even then she couldn't be certain how many others there had been; one moment she'd been relishing in a moment of pride and the next...

Gwendolyn had always known that the fae warriors were fast. It was one of their most admirable traits, after all. Their speed was legendary. The extent of their speed, however, had never really been clear. But at that moment, staring into the cold, unforgiving eyes of the fae elders and remembering nothing more than a blur and the unrelenting grips of her own dragging her back over the wall, she truly believed she'd yet to take a new breath since she'd seen the hindquarters of the centaur vanish into the forest.

Her lungs screamed as though it were the truth, but the cold, thick anger weighing down around her refused to let her draw in a single breath.

Shivering, Gwendolyn dared to tear her sights from the only elder to have spoken and seek a more forgiving response in the gaze of another. Then another. Then another. But each face held neither clue nor kindness for her; they all simply sat and stared, transfixed, as she shifted uncomfortably in the center of the small, dimly lit hut. There were no windows or lanterns, only a small, round port in the low, domed roof that allowed what remained of the late-afternoon sun to cast an accusatory beam into the center of the room, where Gwendolyn now stood. She was certain the only entrance was behind her—she couldn't clearly remember being brought in; she only knew that, when the chaos that had dragged her back into the city was over, she'd stood exactly where she stood now—but the small bit of reason that still murmured behind the boulder of guilt in her stomach told her not to look away from the five elders that sat behind the crescent-moon shaped desk before them. One of the elder fae rested their forearms along the length of wood before them, while others sat unusually straight with their cloaked torsos vanishing behind it. The last—the elder that was seated in the middle and the one who'd addressed her upon her arrival—had his hands steepled before his face, framing the young fae in front of him within a triangle formed between his pointer fingers and thumbs. Though he'd been the only one to break the silence with Gwendolyn's name, it was the only woman between the five, seated all the way to the right, to finally move forward.

"Do you know where you are?" she asked, leaning forward and folding her arms in front of her.

Gwendolyn felt her left ear twitch and she felt a cold tremor of condemnation creep up her back as she gave a slow nod. "I… um, I think—"

"Do you know *why* you are here?" the elder seated second to the left slammed his age-marked palm down on the desk, making both Gwendolyn and jump with alarm.

The same heavy, looming silence returned, and Gwendolyn opened her mouth to speak again only to find that it had gone dry. She coughed and whimpered, feeling her body tremble with a new sense of cold and dread.

She'd stepped outside the city walls. She, an apprentice—a *healing* apprentice!—who had no reason to even approach the boundaries, had crossed them. Not even the warriors in training were allowed to venture beyond that point. It was one of the oldest laws of their people: the wall existed as much as a message as it did as a barrier. Beyond that point dwelled savage and unholy beings, and the earliest fae, knowing that the dangers and impurities of the world, had erected the wall as a sign to future generations that they would not allow what lay beyond to tarnish their people any longer. And though it had been centuries since the evils of the elves or the destructive ways of the dwarves or the savagery of the centaurs had been allowed to plague their people, the fae recognized their ancestors efforts and they'd obeyed the law. The wall was not to be crossed. If something crossed over *into* the city, it was destroyed without pause and without mercy, and, likewise, if something crossed over *out* of the city, it was doing so as an invitation to others to do the same. For a fae to invite others over would be anarchy, but for a fae to invite something from the other side over...

It would mean the end of them all.

To cross the wall meant death.

And Gwendolyn had crossed the wall.

"I..." Gwendolyn forced herself to speak, beginning to see the circumstances she was in, "I didn't mean to!"

"You didn't mean to jump over the wall?" the elder seated second to the right asked, raising a bushy gray eyebrow.

"Or you didn't mean to get caught?" the middle elder added.

Gwendolyn shivered and shook her head, "No... I meant that, well, I didn't think that—"

"Then you *forgot* that it was forbidden?" the first to the right interjected.

"Absurd!" the elder seated beside him—his palm still resting against the desk's surface—spat, turning up a pointed nose at the young fae, "Even the simplest mind could not forget. The wall is too tall to simply *ignore* its meaning!"

"Perhaps we should let the girl speak," the female elder's voice was low and even, her eyes not shifting from Gwendolyn as she spoke.

The middle elder tapped his fingers against one another for a moment. "And what would you hope to hear? Perhaps an exception? Do you hold onto some hope that this one had a reason to cross that none other in all the years the walls have stood?"

"There is no such hope," the desk-slapper hissed, "because there is no such reason!"

The female elder finally turned her attention to the others, and a silent moment that seemed to carry an unheard passing of words lingered. Finally, the elder who'd slapped the table raised his hand and gestured to Gwendolyn with an open palm.

"Speak!" he demanded.

"I was playing," Gwendolyn felt the words come out of her mouth faster than she'd expected, and she found herself struggling to keep up with herself as she spoke. "I... with my fox! My mother... well, my mentor, Rosalind Clearwater"— she was careful to speak her mother's name clearly, hoping that it might motivate some mercy on the elders' behalf— "let me keep the fox after we healed it. So I was playing with Bren—the fox, you see, I named it Bren—and... and while we were playing I heard a sound, an awful sound! Like... it was like a baby crying or an animal shrieking! It was awful! And… and when I hear a sound like that—*whenever* I hear a sound like that—I get this horrible feeling in my stomach like I'm going to be sick and I have to help. I *have* to! So… so that's what I did! I followed the sound—"

"Over the wall," the center elder added in a cold tone.

Gwendolyn trembled again and nodded, "Y-yes, sir. I followed the sound over the wall. I swear I wasn't trying to break a rule, I just wasn't thinking about anything but the sound and trying to make it stop."

"And then what happened?" the female elder asked.

Gwendolyn's eyes went wet with a well of tears and she choked around the tightening knot in her throat. "I…" she gulped the knot down and tried to speak again with a little more success, "I spotted one of our warriors' traps in a clearing on the other side. You know the ones? The deer—"

"We are aware of what they're for, little one," the desk-slapper cut her off. "Now tell us what happened!"

Gwendolyn stifled a sob and looked down, unable to face the elders any longer. Outside the hut, she heard the faint voice of her mother calling to somebody to let her pass, but whoever was standing guard refused. A moment of inaudible squabble passed through the entrance, but it was quickly silenced by a third voice that said, loudly enough for everyone inside the hut to hear, that a sentencing with the elders was in session and not to be interrupted.

Then silence.

Gwendolyn's breath cut short. A sentencing? She'd been hopeful that she was at least being offered a hearing—a chance to plead her case and offer her end of the story—but it wasn't so. She was being foolish. She'd been startled in the wood and terrified to find herself before the elders, and the shock of it all had numbed her of her reason. But, with clarity returning to her, it was obvious what was happening. She'd been discovered outside the wall. The ones that had brought her in had *found* her there. There was no mystery to her actions or doubt to the truth. She'd even admitted to it from the start. There was nothing left to be said.

*To cross the wall meant death.*

Taking in a ragged-but-full breath, Gwendolyn did what she could to steady her nerves and finally looked back up at the five elders.

"Well? We're waiting!" the desk-slapper pressed.

A quick glance between the five didn't offer Gwendolyn any insight to their thoughts, but she'd learned enough in her studies to know what sympathy looked like. They held none for her. Gwendolyn's fate was decided the moment she'd been placed before them.

She was to die in the labyrinth.

Gavrael continued to think back on Alastair's words of wisdom and sighed, shaking his head. He had hoped that the grandfather centaur would help him see things more clearly, but he'd only burdened his mind with even more questions.

What answers could he possibly find in the labyrinth?

Why would such a wise centaur not only allow their kind to be demeaned, but actually *plan* for such a thing?

He sneered at the thought of what the fae must have thought of his kind. There were those who knew the truth, there had to be, if only a few, who kept the savage union going. But what of those that the elder fae lied to? Just what did they tell the others? Just what sort of snarling beasts did the fae masses take them for?

Even more upsetting: considering how his herd scrambled for the so-called honor of filling the faes' role of a labyrinth beast, were they *not* snarling beasts?

In some sick way, hadn't their union given some truth to the faes' lies?

And all that—all the humiliation and ugliness and cruelty—for nothing more than scraps and garbage!

When his kind did all the work to eradicate *their* mistakes!

Why should he feel any honor in participating in *that*?

How could Alastair even suggest it?

He spoke of volunteering for the faes' labyrinth as if there was pride in it! As if it was some kind of heroic act! As if—

The sound of uneven galloping and panicked gasping took him back from himself and he shifted his attention to Lysoks as she hurried towards him. The sight of his little sister's limp swept all thoughts from his mind as he turned to meet her, then he saw the dried tears coating her face. A swell of fury took him and he felt his muscles tense with readiness to rain death down on whoever had brought harm to his kin, but before he could demand a name Lysoks' young face was buried against him and her small arms struggled to wrap around him.

"She was only helping me, Brother!" her wails were muffled against his stomach. "She was only helping and they took her!"

Gavrael frowned, holding her tightly but struggling to free her mouth so he could better understand her words. "Slow down, Sister; speak steady. What happened? Who was helping you?"

"I… I was galloping near the fae wall," she stammered, already looking away.

"What have I told you about going too close to there?" Gavrael scolded, beginning to examine her for injuries and catching sight of a length of fabric knotted around her leg.

"I know!" she whimpered. "I know, and I'm sorry! I got too close, and… and I got caught in a fae trap!" She trembled, seeming to relive the pain of her ordeal through the memory, and she lifted the bandaged leg. "It was so painful,

Brother," she confessed, "I was certain I would meet my end by a fae's arrow out there!"

"It's alright now," he soothed her, running his hand over her head. "You said that somebody helped you get free? Who else would be out that far? This is why I tell you to stay away from the fae wall! They're horrible, violent, cruel creatures, Sister! They can't be—"

"No, Brother! It was a fae who helped me! A beautiful and kind fae!" she looked up, her eyes brightening. "And she didn't just free me from the trap, you see, she healed me; she used fae magic to heal me! Look! See?"

"A fae?" he shook his head and moved to examine the wound. Shifting the material, he saw that a length of blood-stained bark wrapped around her ankle. Though the amount of blood looked substantial, he couldn't see any evidence of a wound behind the bark. "It... it certainly *looks* like fae magic..." he admitted. "Are you sure it wasn't an elf that you confused for a fae?"

Lysoks shot him a look. "As certain as I am that you're not an ogre!" she stomped her opposite hoof, "I may be young, but I'm not stupid, Brother! Just look at the bandage! It was a part of her sleeve! See? It's fae!"

Gavrael stared down at the fabric and resigned to his sister's truth. When the centaur champions returned from the faes' labyrinth, the scraps that they brought occasionally included makeshift satchels filled with bits of stale bread. The fabric was a match.

Drawing in a deep breath, he nodded. "And you say they took her? You mean other fae? Back over the wall?"

She nodded, her lip trembling.

Even little Lysoks knew what that meant. With the exception of their warriors, the fae were forbidden to cross the wall. And none of their warriors would know a healing spell from a hoof in their face. The fae that had helped her had broken one of their most sacred rules to save his sister's life, and that meant only one thing for her:

She would be sentenced to die in the labyrinth at the hands of a volunteer centaur...

The fae were a coldhearted and brutal people. If they viewed one of their own as a traitor then they'd waste no tears in condemning them to die. And because of the wretched agreement between their people and his herd, any fae cast into the labyrinths was a target—a prize—for whatever centaur had elected themselves to occupy those tunnels. But if this fae was an exception to her kind—if she could be kind and compassionate where others were cruel and cold—then it was only fair that she find a different sort of centaur waiting for her in the death-maze.

"Have you told anybody else about this fae?" Gavrael asked.

Lysoks shook her head.

Gavrael nodded slowly. "Can you tell me anything about the fae?" he asked, "Other than the fact that she was beautiful?"

"She has hair that reminds me of those maple trees we used to sit under during the Autumn Equinox. Why? What are you thinking, Brother?"

"I cannot say yet," he smiled, pressing a kiss to her forehead. "Just promise that you will keep the fae a secret, alright?"

"If that is your wish," she nodded and smiled.

"Good. Now, go lie down and rest your leg. You need to get better."

# FOUR
## *~Nine Days Later~*

Gwendolyn Clearwater couldn't remember a time she'd felt so cold. With the exception of a torn section of fabric that she was certain had once been a part of a window curtain, there was nothing to fight the aggressive frigidness. The underground cells that neighbored the only entrance to the labyrinth at the north-eastern corner of the city sat below the vast shade of an apple orchard. The ground above the imprisoned vagrant faes' heads didn't know the heat that the treetops did, and so the many meters of damp soil and rock leading into the rooftops of the dank chambers offered no trace of warmth. In that, however, it was much like the treatment they received from their own people; friends and loved ones were told of the crimes and reminded of the dangers, and by the time they were informed of the transgression there was no sympathy left to reach the one they once held close. Not that it mattered, since the only visitors allowed in that place were the immediate family of the vagrant scheduled to die that day.

Gwendolyn's parents were due to arrive any second.

Shortly after her sentencing before the five elder fae, Gwendolyn had been dragged out of the hut and paraded in front of everyone on her way to the cells. Friends and neighbors all gawked and whispered as they recognized her through her mask of tears and shame. Though she hadn't wanted to look, the familiar sound of Bren's barking dragged her focus from the passing clumps of dirt at her feet to the panicked fox as it cleared the crowd and angrily yapped at her captors. Then, crying so loudly that her throat still ached from that day, Gwendolyn watched as a fae guard following behind them lifted her friend from the small of her back and wrung her neck. As the fox's limp body fell to the street, Gwendolyn caught sight of her mother's face amidst the crowd.

Gwendolyn had acted without the wisdom of self; without the clarity to see the before, the now, and the after. Her eyes had been clouded by raw sympathy, and she had followed it in the wrong direction.

Right over the wall.

Right into the role of a vagrant.

The lesson her mother had taught her only days earlier had been disregarded in a single act of brashness, and her reward from that lesson—the only friend she'd ever shown her and Hawkes' secret place—lay in a lifeless heap between her and Rosalind like a twisted symbol of that lesson.

She'd let her mother down and brought death to a creature that Rosalind Clearwater had offered new life to.

And now she was awaiting their final meeting…

Knowing this only added to the young vagrant fae's relentless chills. She knew, thanks to the malicious taunts of one of the guards, that her brother had refused the invitation to see her one last time. The shame, they'd explained, of knowing his own sister was willing to risk all of their lives to free a savage beast from a trap was too much for him to bear seeing her.

And while their words and the truth it carried hurt her terribly, what plagued Gwendolyn even more was the horror of what her parents would say. With this thought prattling about in her head, she paced as best she could within the confines of her cell. Even that luxury, however, was limited. With the width of the already narrow board that was embedded within the stone wall to serve as a bed occupying more than half of her available space and a waste bucket in the opposite corner and shaming her from even facing in that direction, Gwendolyn's only option was to teeter from one foot to the other as she peered through the small opening in the stone door. The opening, which was no bigger around than her wrist, offered the small cell the only shred of light that the already modestly lit hall on the other side had to offer. When the guards had come to offer the vagrants their single daily meal, the stone door would lift and flood the room with lantern light. While the vagrants struggled to cope with the blinding impact of their arrival, the guards would drop the trays on the beds—often spilling the meager contents in the process—and trade out the waste buckets with emptied (but rarely cleaned) replacements. Then, before the door was dropped back into place, several fists of straw would be tossed into the rooms. Gwendolyn heard one of the softer-spoken guards saying that this was to keep the cells warm, but one of the neighboring vagrants explained that, between the dampness of the cells and the tendency for the waste buckets to overflow, the straw was an easy way to control the growth of mold.

If there was any truth in that sentiment, Gwendolyn thought, it was failing… miserably.

Several days earlier, during the guards' visit, one of the vagrants hadn't been quick enough in stepping clear of his cell door, and as the stone slab was dropped back into place they were all startled by the pained shrieks as it crushed one of his legs. The sound of his agony, despite her ongoing starvation, had put Gwendolyn off her appetite, and her pleas with the retreating guards to let her heal the injured vagrant were left unheard…

Or simply unheeded.

"It's better this way," he'd assured her between clenched teeth. "It'll be faster for me once I'm in there with the beast."

The next day, once his cell was empty, she overheard one of the other vagrants muttering that, crippled or not, the centaurs in the labyrinth took pleasure in making a vagrant's death a slow one.

"Fae meat tastes better to them when their victim's still alive," he'd said.

Despite the other vagrants agreement, Gwendolyn was steadfast in her belief that she should have been allowed to heal him.

"But with his leg broken he never stood a chance!" she argued.

"There never was a chance."

"Even the fastest of us meets the same fate."

"But there's an exit! We all know there's a passage out of the maze! No matter the odds it's not fair to take that chance away!" Gwendolyn was persistent. "What if they could have made it out?"

"Nobody ever does," the solemn response was slow in being spoken aloud, but it was the response that that question always received. Hearing it was like an echo to any who'd heard the question preceding it.

It was the only answer.

But it was not the truth.

In the centuries that the labyrinth had existed beneath the fae city—in all the time that it had housed the murderous centaur and been fed a steady diet of vagrant faes—there had only ever been one who made it out of the tunnels. Only one who had evaded the beast and navigated the nearly infinite maze and stepped out of it unscathed.

*"A fate worse than death in the labyrinth awaits him,"* the elders said.

Life beyond the wall was a treacherous and violent one. It was why the wall existed. It was a truth that needed no lesson to be learned: the wall existed because everything on the other side of it was too dangerous to face. Their ancestors' had labored for who-knew-how-long to ensure a safe place for their children to thrive. And thrive they had. None questioned the horrors that existed beyond; they simply knew them to be truth. So, though a single vagrant had evaded the centaur and navigated the maze, the world that they'd emerged into was one that was certain to kill them.

*"A fate worse than death in the labyrinth…"*

The elders' words were a haunting memory. While everybody knew of the single vagrant who had escaped their fate, none could imagine just what sort of agonizing end they'd met out there. It was just too frightening a thought to ponder, especially since Gwendolyn didn't stand a chance of surviving the labyrinth alone. Her own mother had said more times than she could count that if it weren't for the long ears on her head and the sharp wit between them she'd never be able to find her way home from the woods. There was no chance of her knowing the right path to take in those tunnels; they could plant her in there without the centaur and rest easy that she'd starve to death before finding the exit. But those tunnels *and* a murderous beast…

Before her encounter with the little girl in the trap—the encounter that had condemned her to that cell awaiting her death in the labyrinth—Gwendolyn had never seen a centaur. She'd been offered descriptions and shown pictures in the past, usually when scary stories were being traded or when she overheard a warrior fae boasting of a conquest against one of the beasts during one of their outings. In all of those accounts, they were always massive—"taller than the proudest helitrad tree," she'd heard them say—and snarling like a rabid mongrel. Gwendolyn certainly hadn't seen anything like that in the deer trap on that day, but it *had* been only a child, and a female at that.

Though it was difficult for her to believe that such an innocent and fragile creature could be a part of a bloodthirsty species of behemoths, she couldn't argue with the screams of bloody murder that had echoed through the cells nearly every day since she'd been locked away.

Just what was waiting for her on the other side of that iron gate?

Gwendolyn shivered, though not from the cold.

Though iron was toxic to almost every species but one, her people had made a single exception to their ban on the awful substance, perhaps as some sort of cruel irony, and replaced the stone gate to the labyrinth with a slab of the cold, lifeless metal. None of the other vagrants seemed to be able to agree just where the fae had acquired such a massive piece of processed iron in the first place. Some said that it was a gift during a since broken truce with the dwarf minors of the northern mountains while others claimed it was stolen during a raid against the bumbling idiot humans, who appeared to be the only species immune to the toxic effects, while still others had a different story entirely. In the end, it didn't matter how the iron gate had come to be where it was. Like so many things it simply was, and so nobody bothered to question it. And since the only ones who had to suffer from prolonged exposure to the metal were vagrants waiting to die anyway, nobody bothered to care. For more than a week Gwendolyn had been struggling with her limited magic and lack of supplies to fight off the itching, burning spots that had begun to spread since her first day there, but it was, like everything else, a losing battle.

The rashes had grown, and after so many days condemned to darkness and offered little to eat and no way to bathe, she was certain she looked like every bit the monster her people were convinced she was.

As she heard the footsteps begin down the staircase to the cells and one of the guards announce that her parents had arrived, however, she had to wonder what breed of monster they were about to see...

"Oh my beautiful baby girl!" Rosalind Clearwater's voice was a divine song in Gwendolyn's ears.

The young vagrant was still accustoming herself to the bright and cheerful lighting of the visiting chamber that she'd been ushered into as her mother's arms wrapped around her. Breathing in her mother's scent and feeling the first traces of her familiar warmth begin to seep into her skin, Gwendolyn's resolve to stay strong in front of her parents shattered and she choked on the first of many sobs.

The guard that had retrieved her had been quick to strip her of the rags she'd been wearing and herd her into a cleansing hall at the top of the stairs. A series of hot, fragrant bursts washed away the week old layers of grime and stench, and as the too-quick bath drew to an end a gust of enchanted air passed over her. Though it had only taken a matter of seconds, Gwendolyn was surprised to see that her hair and skin looked every bit as vibrant as it had the day she'd been arrested.

*So much for facing them a monster*, she'd thought as the guard handed her the dress she'd been wearing the day of and ordered her to make herself presentable.

It took less than five minutes to go from the dark, dreary, death-reeking pit of the vagrant cells to the bright, beautiful, and flower-scented room where her parents were already waiting for her. And, in that time, they'd somehow been able to wash away every trace of the misery she'd experienced. Sobbing into her mother's shoulder, Gwendolyn was certain that neither of her parents would believe her if she even tried to convince them of the conditions she'd been facing.

"I'm sorry," she wailed, clutching the fabric of the back her mother's dress, trying to pull as much of the warmth and sweetness as she could into herself. "I'm so sorry, Mother, Father; so very, very sorry."

"What's past is past," her father reassured her, running a broad, powerful palm over the top of her head. Though his words, as they always did, carried the sturdiness and strength of his character, Gwendolyn heard a crack in his voice that only made her feel that much more guilty. Nothing had ever buckled the proud and noble Garret Clearwater, and the thought that she had done just that added to her shame. "You're still our little girl, songbird; you always will be."

"Let calmness be you, Gwendolyn," her mother kissed her cheek and slowly worked herself free of her daughter's embrace. "It will all be over soon."

Afraid that she might start crying again, Gwendolyn only nodded.

"Your brother was sorry that he couldn't be here," her father lied, "but he's beginning an early entrance exam for the warrior training program, and today was the last day to enter."

Again, Gwendolyn nodded.

A long silence followed, and the young vagrant fae watched as her parents, the strongest fae she had ever known, struggled to contain whatever they had locked away inside of them. It was an unspoken understanding that the final visitation for a vagrant was to be a solemn one, and Gwendolyn had already dashed much of that solemnity the moment her mother had held her. Finally, Garret Clearwater cleared his throat, capturing the attention of both his wife and daughter, before nodding back to a small table carved from the wood of a helitrad tree. There, atop the pale, intricately detailed furniture, was a basket almost too large for the table's surface with a bright red ribbon nested on top.

"Oh! Yes," Rosalind Clearwater turned to retrieve the basket and, as she did, the rear-facing door opened and a guard stepped inside.

Rosalind stopped as the dark-eyed fae in the traditional green uniform placed himself between her and the table and crossed his arms behind his back.

"Apologies, Missus Clearwater," the guard said in a tone that carried no sincerity, "but it's forbidden to offer a vagrant any sort of gifts."

In an instant of raw fury that Gwendolyn had never witnessed before, Rosalind Clearwater retaliated.

"You may be trained with a rapier tongue and an inflated ego, young earling," Gwendolyn's mother hissed, "but you have still one tongue and two ears as long as you are daft. So, since you're twice as equipped to heed my words than speak down to me, *boy*, I suggest you take notice of what I am about to say." She took a long, bold step towards the guard and, even without seeing her face, Gwendolyn knew that her eyes were burning with rage, "I am Rosalind Clearwater, wife to Garret Clearwater and mother to what would have been this city's greatest healer. And since she has done wrong and is sentenced to die I am burdened with continuing that title alone. So, bold little rapier-tongued idiot boy, unless you're prepared to convince the elders to execute *two* healers and cast the likes of you brutes into several decades of pain and death, I suggest you step aside and let me offer my final sentiments to my daughter."

The guard lingered for a moment, every bit as taken aback as the others in the room, before he looked to Gwendolyn's father for any sort of assistance with his wife.

Garret Clearwater offered only a shrug. "She's the best healer you'll ever know," he offered, "so if she tells me to break your arms you're going to have a hard time having it properly mended by another."

In an arrogant-but-predictable display, the guard scoffed and turned away to leave the room.

The moment the door closed behind him, Garret Clearwater let out a heavy sigh and shook his head. "By the gods' grand design that was intense!" he grumbled.

"Would have been even moreso had that guard not had sense enough to leave," Rosalind Clearwater said as she retrieved the basket and turned back to her daughter.

"Mother," Gwendolyn stared, awestruck, "that was... you could have gotten yourself killed!"

She only shrugged and held out the basket. "I suppose I could have. But let's just say I was taught a powerful lesson about acting on love without concern of consequence," she winked as Gwendolyn took the gift.

"Mother, I..." Gwendolyn couldn't find the words to go on.

"Enough chatter, songbird, now open your damn present! I was up all night finishing it," Rosalind pressed.

Nodding, Gwendolyn drew the top of the basket away and marveled at the crimson garment waiting within. The dress, made from the same material as the ribbon that had adorned the basket, was the most beautiful thing the young fae had ever seen.

"I... oh my," she stammered, unable to look away from the present, "I couldn't possibly..." Gwendolyn began to cry again, "Mother, I'm about to be killed! You can't expect me to wear this just to—"

"Hush now!" Rosalind went to work pulling the dress out of the basket and waving to her husband to look away. "It's customary for a healer to be presentable on their funeral pyre," in a few quick motions she had Gwendolyn naked and began to pull the dress over her head. "And while this might not be a traditional ceremony I'll not allow the finest healer I've ever known to break tradition."

Gwendolyn whimpered at how well the dress fit her and how beautiful she felt wearing it. "But I'm not even a true healer!" she protested.

Her mother's hand fell across her face with such an alarming speed that Gwendolyn couldn't bring herself to cry out. With the impact of the slap still hanging in the air, Rosalind jabbed her pointer finger in her daughter's face while, with the opposite hand, motioning to her husband to once again face away.

"You're about to die, Gwendolyn Clearwater, and when you do you'll be stripped of your name and title, so you have precious little time to claim your legacy before it's no longer yours and you have no wits left to claim a breath. Here and now, though, you are Gwendolyn Clearwater, the only fae brave enough to climb the wall and spare faithmist and sootheoil and the gifts of the god-tree on a creature in need. You *healed* that young centaur, songbird," Rosalind took her daughter by the shoulders and gave her a single shake as she had so many times to awaken her, "and you never once expressed a regret for it. You may have gone over that wall an apprentice, my daughter, but you came back over it a healer. And though you can't be offered the pyre of your kin, Gwendolyn Clearwater, I will not allow you to die in anything less. Now go face your destiny!"

Like strawberries and wheat...

Hawkes had told her that her hair was the color of strawberries and wheat.

It was like looking back at a dream now, as though everything before that moment had been the sweetest, most beautiful lie that could have been told to her. She wanted so badly to convince herself that it was the other way around;

that she was in a nightmare and looking back on a life she missed so terribly. Now, however, the mixture of agony stirring in her belly held no awe for her, and she knew that when it settled it could wear only one hue:

That of a vagrant.

One who died beneath a centaur's hoof...

She'd once been told that the only color anybody would remember her for was brown, but at that moment, standing in a beautiful crimson dress and reciting her mother's last words to her, Gwendolyn Clearwater finally felt like she could die with pride.

# FIVE

"… like the vagrant, herself, the iron doorway to her absolution is an affront to nature and to our kin," the fae priest's words were a painful attack to Gwendolyn Clearwater's pride laced with the insult of being delivered in what sounded like a song. Perhaps it was just how familiar the old fae was with delivering the final rites, but a part of it felt almost celebratory!

Unable to stomach any more of the passage, Gwendolyn focused on the only thing she had left to focus on: the gate.

Though her training had brought her in contact with iron shavings to help illustrate its toxic effects, she'd never seen anything like it. The gate, though dented and wearing spots of age that the guards called "rust," wore a surprisingly intricate pattern that traveled that latticework design. Gwendolyn hated comparing such an ugly thing to such a beautiful memory, but she found herself reminded of the carefully laid woven system that was baked into the top of her mother's apple pies. It was there that any sort of pleasant comparison ended, however. Until that day, the tallest thing that she'd ever known had been the stone wall surrounding the fae city, which could be seen from a distance even from the roof of her home.

Or, rather, what had once been her home…

The gate, however, rose so far into the darkness of the underground ceiling that she had to wonder just how far beneath the city they were. For such a massive gate to lift open would mean that even more space existed to keep the gate from lifting from the grounds of the apple orchard every time they cast another vagrant into the labyrinth. And for as tall as the awful gate was, it was that much wider! During her time in the cells, Gwendolyn had been offered a decent estimate of the space they occupied. Each cell was not much longer than the bed that occupied it, and only about twice as wide. With the cells occupying either side of the slightly wider hall, which offered safe passage up the steps on one side or the last march of the vagrant on the other that opened up into the vast gate room where Gwendolyn now stood, the small space that she'd come to know so well for a little over a week was no more than eight meters wide. With the cell doors raised, she was certain that only ten fae of her size would be able to stand side-by-side with their arms outstretched. By comparison, she was certain it would take over one-hundred fae doing the same to stretch the distance of the monstrous iron gate before her.

No wonder she and the other vagrants had been feeling its toxic impact from their cells.

As the priest's voice finally began to inflect an end to the last rites, something popped loudly above Gwendolyn's head and a sharp, metallic rattling began to echo against the other side of the gate. For a moment the sound chimed freely, sounding simple and loose against whatever source it issued from, but then there was another, much louder pop and the base of the gate trembled against the floor. The rattling slowed to almost a stop, and what had sounded free and loose suddenly groaned with a new strain. The mechanical groan continued and rose in effort until Gwendolyn was certain the entire room was about to collapse around itself, and then the gate began to stir. The left corner seemed the most eager to rise, and as a small, triangular opening formed between the lower-end of the gate the whirring mechanics of the door began to issue a new breed of whines. When the left corner could go no further without its cousin, the right began to slam again and again against the floor, seeming to protest its own purpose. Behind Gwendolyn, several guards murmured, and a third finally shouted to somebody out in the darkness to "switch the gears."

The gate's noisy activities stopped suddenly and the massive slab of iron slammed loudly to the ground, causing both Gwendolyn and the priest to jump. A short moment of silence passed, and after the din that had come before it felt almost more ominous than the mechanical roar. Then, following a third pop and another round of free, loose clatter, the iron gate snapped to attention under the renewed force and began a steady rise.

The first thing that Gwendolyn noticed was the smell. For so long the labyrinth below the fae city became known as the place where the vagrants' final steps would fall, and those steps were to be stained within its depths to kill them. And while so many rumors and songs told of the shameful march of those who trudged through the pits of death and muck, Gwendolyn had never dwelled much on the subject. Aside from it being simply too disgusting a thought to entertain, they were just words—albeit disgusting words—to what was nothing more than a scary story, a cautionary tale used to keep young faes from missing curfew or being rude to their elders. With the solid length of patterned iron no longer locking away its secrets, however, Gwendolyn was certain that they weren't just disgusting words.

It was a very real, very disgusting truth.

Both the priest and the guards pulled a mask that had hung around each of their necks up and over their faces, but even the priest wasn't fast enough to hide his gagging. By some bizarre blessing Gwendolyn kept her final serving of stale bread and chicken fat in her belly, and as she worked to keep her breathing steady she overheard the muffled voice of the priest as he renounced her name and title.

She was no longer Gwendolyn Clearwater…

The gate slowed and finally stopped when it was high enough for her to pass beneath it, and it was then that one of the guards stepped forward. Placing his right hand on the small of her back and beginning to apply pressure towards the long, dark hall on the other side, the guard reached with his left and plucked a torch from the nearest anchor point and set it within her own grip. As the solid length of wood met her palm and the bright, angry flame it held glimmered in her vision, she played with the idea of trying to fight her way free of this fate. Glancing behind her, though—seeing the guards standing wait at the tunnel that led back to the cells and mapping out the heavily-policed route that would finally take her right back into the walled-off fae city that already counted her among the dead—she could already see the futility in any sort of effort. Holding the torch out in front of her, she succumbed to the growing pressure at the small of her back and stepped into the labyrinth.

Gavrael had hoped to volunteer for the labyrinths for the few weeks following Lysoks' savior's arrest. With any luck, he'd have been able to intercept the condemned fae that had saved his sister and, using the map and supplies that the centaur volunteers were given for their services, get her away from the labyrinth and the dreadful faes that maintained it.

He had hoped for such a simple thing to be, but simplicity was more than the divine were prepared to offer.

After his continued refusal to accept the herd's request and volunteer, the herd had moved on with their search. The invitation had already been passed to Bowen, a headstrong centaur with aspirations of leadership. And, of course, he'd accepted. Though none in the herd were allowed to humor petty indulgences like rivalries within their ranks, it was a non-spoken understanding with all that Bowen and Gavrael were the top choices with the Alpha to assume the title when they came of age. Gavrael neither wanted nor strove to claim the role, but, though he didn't work towards it, it seemed his indirect refusals weren't pushing him out of the running, either. For every day that he went off on his own to clear his mind with a run or leveling patches of forest with his axe, Gavrael's body grew stronger and more equipped to fulfill the demand of leadership. Bowen, being one with the herd and acting as they did, was only as strong as the others; was only as fit as the others. It was only his desire that rivaled Gavrael's. Stepping out of the fae labyrinths a champion and a provider for the herd was his only chance of tipping the scales in his favor.

And with Bowen waiting in the hellish maze for the beautiful fae healer with the hair like maple trees in the Autumn Equinox, she had no chance of surviving.

With this in mind and a resolve as strong as his axe, Gavrael committed to what none in the herd had ever thought to do.

But wasn't that what made him a *vernunt*?

The vagrant formally called Gwendolyn Clearwater couldn't be certain if she'd been trudging for mere meters or miles. After the iron gate had slammed shut behind her, casting her into a blackness that was staved off only by the torch she'd been sent in with, she'd been faced with a straight tunnel that grew narrower with each step. This was a gradual process, though, and it hadn't been until she'd caught sight of the mold-laced stone of the walls on either side of her that she noticed that the passage was no longer as wide as it had been when she'd first entered. Then, with the passage only wide enough for her to stand in its center with both arms outstretched and tall enough to be unable to reach the ceiling without jumping, she came to the first intersection.

For a long time she stood there, staring as far as she could down the three tunnels.

Left. Right. Straight ahead.

*There's no way out,* she reminded herself. *You're already dead.*

She played with the idea of throwing the torch in the middle of the intersection and calling to the beast that was already lurking about. The other vagrants had said that the centaur was ushered away from the main entrance to allow for the condemned to at least enter the maze (though she was certain it was to ensure that a renegade centaur didn't breach the iron gate and gain entry into their city). While she couldn't be certain how far the centaur was from her at that moment, she was willing to wager that, should she call out loudly enough, it would hear. And then it would come.

"*It will all be over soon,*" her mother had said.

"Not nearly soon enough…" the vagrant fae grumbled.

Then, as if fate had finally heeded her anguish, she heard the centaur roar to her left.

The passage to the right suddenly looked better than it had before, and the vagrant fae's fleeting thoughts of self-sacrifice and her mother's promises of a swift end vanished like a plume of smoke on a windy day. She wanted to live. Birthdays and holidays had repeatedly aroused the question of desire, and on those occasions she swore a fondness of jewelry and dresses and pretty-smelling things, but she had never wanted anything more than she wanted the gift of life at that moment. So she ran. She ran as far as tunnel stretched, and then, only because her right foot was already planted as a fork in the path arrived, she chose the left.

Behind her, the sounds of the centaur offered torturous hints towards its progress in its pursuit. For a time the pounding of its hoofs seemed so close that she was certain its next step would fall upon her back, but a moment later another roar told her that it had yet to reach the prior turn. Mere seconds later, however, she was certain she could feel its breath on the back of her neck.

*This is madness!* she thought, choking on her own fear and fighting to keep from tumbling in a coughing fit. *Utter madness!*

Another intersection—only a straight-or-right option…

Hadn't she just escaped from the right? Would taking that turn bring her face-to-face with the beast? But a centaur's speed was greatest when it didn't need to stop to turn. Was she handing herself over by offering it a simple sprint? The torchlight wavered and something behind her echoed with an impact—was that a hoof or a loosened stone?—and the dancing shadows against the left wall urged her to turn right.

Her legs burned beneath her as she pushed herself to run faster than she ever had before.

Another intersection—straight or right—and she forfeited the turn out of fear that she'd be completing a circle back towards where she'd come. Straight. Straight. Finally a left!

Dead end…

The vagrant fae's heart leapt into her throat as she was forced to backtrack and continue straight once more. Then…

A footprint? A cluster of other prints, hoofs…

Were these hers?

Had she been here already? Or did these belong to one of the prior vagrants?

The vagrant fae's heart drummed in her ears and her breathing rasped as it lurched from her lungs in panicked gasps. She couldn't hear anything past the sounds of her own terror. Struggling to hold her breath, she finally coughed and flinched as the sound echoed through the halls like a ripple in a pond.

The centaur answered with another roar.

The echoes that had moments earlier seemed to point straight at the vagrant fae now offered no clue towards the beast's whereabouts. Every path seemed to carry the roar so clearly that it could just as easily be its source. Every turn could be the turn that carried her into its clutches.

*Madness! Utter madness!* she repeated to herself, whipping her head to-and-fro in an effort to catch sight of a shadow or some sign of where to turn. *Coming from everywhere... complete madness!*

Then a moment of clarity.

The madness wasn't in the maze, it was in her head. Fear was giving her pursuer an advantage! The fae guards might have supplied the centaur with a map and provisions, but they had no way of leading the beast to her. For that it had to rely on its senses, just as she had to rely on hers to evade it.

What if its roars weren't a declaration of impending victory?

What if the labyrinth's echoes were just as confounding for it as they were for her?

The vagrant formally called Gwendolyn Clearwater drew in a strangely confident breath as she cemented her certainty that she was going to die. But just because she was going to die didn't mean she had to make it easy for her killer, and she certainly wasn't going to give it or the faes ogling at her struggle from the viewing pools in the public square the satisfaction of seeing her like that.

"I'll show you madness!" she hissed between clenched teeth, tightening her grip the torch.

Garret Clearwater still wasn't sure why he'd decided to watch his daughter's death in the viewing pool. Rosalind's conviction to avoid the public square that day had been strong enough to keep her away from the neighboring markets, which bothered Garret little, since he was certain none of the Clearwaters would have an appetite for anything that night. And while Garret was certain that Gwendolyn had seen her brother's absence at her final visitations as one motivated by shame or hatred, he'd known better than to tell her the truth that Arden Clearwater hadn't been able to leave his bed since the day she'd been arrested. He hated himself for lying to Gwendolyn about him pursuing advanced training, but, seeing her the way she was, scared and ashamed and already so down on herself, he'd known that telling her the truth would only add to the guilt she carried.

Gwendolyn Clearwater had enough pain, of that her father was certain.

And so, though he, himself, couldn't fully place reason on the need, he shouldered his way through the crowd of gawkers so that he could watch the vagrant fae that he still loved as his daughter finally see an end to that pain.

The public square was, as it always was, bustling with any number of activities. Entertainers lined the streets with their array of musical instruments or various spectacles to lure viewers willing to part with their parcels or potions. Others sat on blankets alongside various goods awaiting trade. And then there were the beggars and the one-or-two pickpockets who were too impatient to simply plea with the others. But the real spectacle that drew the crowds to the square day-after-day—the reason that so many found profit in occupying that square in the first place—were the viewing pools. Whether the elders saw it as a means of deterring their people from vagrant activity or whether they truly meant for it to be gazed upon as some morbid form of public entertainment, the city was invited to the viewing pools to witness every vagrant's trip into the labyrinth. Though the magic involved confounded the simple working fae, Garret Clearwater understood this much: each of the four pools that stretched occupied the center of the public square now showed his daughter in her final moments.

Finally getting through, nodding his thanks to a fae who recognized him as the father of the condemned and demanded he be allowed to watch without obstruction, he cast a forlorn gaze into the rippling water. There, as though her struggles were taking place just below pool's surface, he could see his daughter frantically racing through the muck and darkness of the maze. He suppressed the urge to call to her and reach out in a lingering hope that he might spare her fate as he saw the massive centaur, it's mane of grayish-blond hair shimmering in the light of his prey's torch as it bared down upon her. A six-fingered hand reached out, ready to grab the vagrant fae's mass of strawberry-blonde hair, and narrowly missed its mark as she banked down another tunnel. Garret Clearwater let out a celebratory hiss that earned several grave stares from the other onlookers as he watched the centaur topple in its effort to follow, catching the side of the shoulder belonging to its outstretched arm against the adjacent tunnel and roaring in fury.

The vagrant fae didn't even seem to notice what she'd done. Instead, as the enchantment followed her—leaving the enraged and disoriented centaur to vanish in the view's background—she only seemed to grow more terrified. Several more frantic turns were taken, each one putting the vagrant that much further ahead. A sudden turn down what the onlookers could already see was a dead end, and a collective murmur began to spread around the public square as everybody prepared to watch the fae that had once been known as Gwendolyn Clearwater to meet her end. Garret watched with a growing lump in his stomach as she stopped and gazed about her in horrified bewilderment. Her body pitched with uneven breaths and he watched as she coughed and stiffened at the sound.

And then something strange happened.

The growing murmur of excitement—the collective recognition of the fae community that they were about to see the same sort of death they'd seen before in those same pools—turned to confused ramblings as the subject of their focus shrugged off her fear as though it were nothing but a leaf upon her shoulder. A new sort of fae occupied the pools then; a fae that only Garret Clearwater recognized.

He'd seen it in every defiant tantrum that Gwendolyn had ever thrown.

He'd seen it in his mother every time he'd tried to throw a tantrum as a young fae.

He'd seen it in his wife just earlier that day when a stubborn guard had stood in her way.

It was the unmistakable face of a Clearwater female who'd had enough.

Though Gwendolyn Clearwater had been stripped of her title and cast away, she was still every bit his daughter.

And she was about to prove it yet again.

*THUD*

*THUD THUD*

The vagrant didn't flinch at the noise as she brought the handle of the torch down on the corner of a section of jutting rock in the wall. Let the sound come. Let the echoes carry them through every chamber of the labyrinth. The first intersection had been a gift for the centaur. He'd *known* that any vagrant entering those tunnels would be forced to start at that point. She'd fooled herself into believing he'd tracked her there; she'd let fear convince her it had the power to determine her location.

She wouldn't make that mistake again!

*THUD THUD*

*THUD*

She paused to listen as another roar echoed through the halls, this one sounding more agitated than the others. Was her pursuer truly becoming frustrated, or had she simply been too deaf with fear to hear it before?

"That's right, beast!" she grumbled, bringing the torch down on the stone several more times. "I'm not afraid of you anymore! If I'm to die in this sewer, then it's going to be as a thorn in your side!"

*THUD THU-cccrrraaack!*

She smirked as her efforts finally paid off and a chunk of the rock fell from the others and fell into the muck. Without a pause to consider what she was reaching into, she retrieved it and started down the nearest hall.

"And I hope I give you a belly ache when it's done!"

Bowen's roars had grown closer together; his rage was taking over and confessing his secrets to any who knew how to read him. Gavrael knew how to read him. He knew that the vagrant had been released into the maze as they always were when the sun reached its highest point, he knew that fae agility would elude the impatient centaur's brutish approach to all problems, and he knew that no centaur roared over a successful kill. But he also knew that Bowen, though certain to crash and fall at least once or twice, would not fail. He knew that, if he was going to act, then that time was now.

But it was an act that would change everything.

Was he truly prepared to see his life irreversibly shifted at that very moment?

Another roar sounded like another call to action; an invitation to do what Gavrael knew in his heart was the right thing to do.

"I'm sorry, Lysoks," he whispered to himself, using his flint stone to light the torch he'd made for earlier and starting towards the single entrance to the fae labyrinth known to the herd, "but I won't be coming home…"

***

"DO YOU BELIEVE THIS TO BE A GAME, WHELP?"

The centaur had graduated from roars to words, and while the vagrant fae wanted to take some satisfaction from this she was too busy swallowing and re-swallowing the gut-wrenching terror. Like the other vagrant's broken leg, she knew that the fear would be what crippled her, but where the other vagrant's handicap had ruined any chance of survival she had a more realistic goal that she aimed to keep unhindered: her pride. If she allowed the fear to take her once again, she knew that the death that her people witnessed in the viewing pools would offer them some validation in condemning her. To force them to see a vagrant die with pride, however, would send them all to their beds with no satisfaction whatsoever. And though the centaur may be returning to his people with a prize for killing her, she had every intention of spoiling that victory.

*"Two rabbits with one snare!"* as her father would have said.

"I'LL WEAR YOUR EARS AROUND MY NECK WHEN THIS IS OVER, VAGRANT!" the centaur screamed after her as the sound of its gallops picked up behind her.

"SO LONG AS I WON'T HAVE TO HEAR YOUR WAILING ANY LONGER, BEAST!" she called back, keeping the rock clutched in her throwing hand as she lit her path with the torch in her left.

Another roar issued—closer behind than she was expecting—and the impact of the centaur's hooves resounded through her bare feet.

*Too close!* she panicked, realizing she'd miscalculated her pursuer's speed, and resorted to diving for the next turn.

Muck coated her as she crashed to the ground and rolled around the bend, narrowly keeping her legs as the centaur trampled the ground she'd been occupying only a moment earlier. Repulsion was a distant concern as the relief that she'd survived washed over her, and she hurried to wipe a glob of brown from her vision as she jumped to her feet and turned…

Directly into the centaur.

A square jaw adorned with a short, braided, gray-blond beard twisted into a smirk as a pair of dark eyes took her in. "Was it worth it, vagrant?" the centaur mocked, raising a bloodied arm to take her.

Calling upon her mother's wit and reminding herself what she was dying for, the vagrant forced herself to smirk back. "I hope they ask you the same of this moment, horse's ass!"

The vagrant fae thrust with all her might, driving the flame of her torch—her only source of guidance—straight into the centaur's chest, setting a thick patch of hair ablaze. A howl of pain issued, twisting about in her insides and ruining any sense of victory she might have felt, and she leapt back to avoid the centaur's flailing limbs as it worked to slap out the flames. In the chaos, the torch was knocked from her hand and cast into the muck, where the flame nearly died and cast the hall into near-total darkness.

"KILL YOU!" the centaur roared, clamoring towards her as it continued to bat at the flames with its palms.

Knowing she had no chance to outrun the beast, let alone navigate without her torch, the vagrant dropped to her hands and knees and darted between the clattering hooves, rolling free as one of its hind legs kicked out at her face. As the centaur struggled to turn his massive body in the narrow hall, the vagrant fae caught sight of a chance at stripping the beast of more than just his pride.

"I'll *let* you kill me, centaur," she announced, taking aim with her rock, "but I won't allow it to be a tale for any children!"

Calling upon her father's strength, she hurled the jagged rock with all her might and cast a prayer to the divine that her aim was true.

Another, much higher-pitched howl of pain followed as she watched her last weapon meet its mark, and, once again, her healer's empathy refused to let her celebrate the rupturing of more than just the centaur's pride.

It was the only time that Garret Clearwater had seen the entire public square go silent. Every set of eyes was locked on the closest viewing pool, each fae there trying to come to terms with what they'd just witnessed. Nobody for generations had ever seen a vagrant fight the centaur in the labyrinth, and while the boldness alone was something new and awe-inspiring, it was the soon-to-be late Gwendolyn Clearwater's final strike against the lumbering beast that had rendered the massive crowd speechless.

*Well,* Garret Clearwater though, fighting a persistent smirk, *she* is *her mother's daughter.*

He then began struggling with the decision of sharing this detail with Rosalind when he got home.

The snarling centaur's hind legs were still trembling by the time it had finished getting itself turned around to face the vagrant. In that time, he'd gotten the flames on his chest out—though he was missing most of the grayish-blond fur that had once been there, as well—and a series of angry-looking burns stretched across his torso, shoulders, palms, and neck. As the vagrant took in the sight by the dying torch's light, however, she doubted that any of those injuries were the one that plagued him the most. They certainly weren't what enraged him the most.

"And now I die…" she said to herself, humbly accepting the fate.

As she stared upon the still-shaky centaur and prepared for whatever murderous intent it had in store, she felt her ears perk and twitch in response to a soft thud in the hall behind her. She was prepared to pass it off as another rock falling from the section of wall she'd beaten with the torch, but a moment later another, more demanding and far closer impact sounded. And then another.

Finally, eager to catch sight of the source before the torchlight went out entirely, she turned…

Gavrael had never heard anything like it before.

Though he'd always been one of the loudest in their herd, Bowen was not one to carry on quite so much. And if the tone was to be any indicator, he was actually in pain.

*Has that fool gone and finally broken his leg with all his thrashing about?* he rolled his eyes to himself as he navigated the tunnels towards the sound. Though the echoes were a bit disorienting, he'd had plenty of practice tracking small animals through rocky chasms to know how to follow them to the source. Catching sight of the faint glimmers of another torch's light against the corner of the next turn, he realized he'd reached his mark.

"And now I die…" a soft, tired-sounding voice said with a sigh of resignation.

It was more than he would have expected. For so long, Gavrael and the other centaurs of his generation were told of the faes' labyrinths and the cowardice of the condemned that were cast therein. The mother and father centaurs would boast of their own time spent within those halls during their moments of glory, and the tales always seemed to grow more and more heated as they'd turn the sniveling masses their vagrants had become or the time it took to end them into a competition that could see no victor. As nights like those drew on, the stories would shift ever-so-slightly with each retelling: hours becoming minutes, whimpers becoming shrieks, and the pools of blood growing ever larger.

Never, in all those tales, had any ever mentioned a vagrant that fought back.

Nor had any mentioned a fae humbly accepting their fate.

This was, indeed, a rare creature, and at that moment Gavrael had not a single doubt that she and Lysoks' savior were one in the same.

*To kill such a creature in such a manner; in such a place...* Gavrael felt something push him around the corner, his seven fingers snaking around the handle of his axe.

He didn't want to kill Bowen, he didn't even want to draw his axe on him, but with his kind and in this place violence was the only language that would be heard. Spotting the vagrant from behind and, leering a short distance ahead of her, Bowen, looking like he'd just galloped out of battle, he finalized his decision.

"... *maple trees we used to sit under during the Autumn Equinox.*"

Lysoks' description could not have been more perfect.

And then she turned to face him...

In less than a minute the public square went from quiet enough to hear the mice raiding the grain sacks to a riot of urgency so deafening that Garret Clearwater couldn't tell which thoughts were his own. Many cheered at the elders' decision to add a second beast to the pits, declaring that they'd come ready at the next execution with a proper wager to bet on the centaur of their choosing. Others seemed outraged at such a blatant perversion of their tradition, stating that no execution needed two executioners. But it was the few who seemed to know better—the ones that everybody else were unable to hear over their own racket—whose outrage at the second centaur had a greater air of truth than all the others. Though he had no reason to believe one claim over another, Garret Clearwater believed their words over all the others.

It wasn't their certainty that swayed him, or their rank or their merit. He'd lost faith in his fellow fae the day a single one had thought to condemn his daughter, let alone each and every one of them. If it weren't for the fact that he'd be following her into the labyrinth, casting the rest of his family into further turmoil in the process, he'd have made his rage known a thousand times over. Until the day he died he would never take pride in his kin again, but his family shouldn't be made to suffer because of that. Nevertheless, his faith in the higher-ranking faes' words reflected neither on their certainty nor their rank nor their merit, for in his eyes they had none of each, but while everybody else shouted their certainties amongst themselves, it was Garret Clearwater who kept his gaze locked on the viewing pool, and the first centaur's face, though it wore recognition of the second, was hardly one of joy or even expectancy.

That second centaur was not meant to be there.

The squared jaws of the beasts wagged back-and-forth a few times, and, though any hope of recognizing a single word was swallowed in the chaos around them, the father of the condemned had a strange and unexplainable swell of hope.

And then the viewing pools went black.

She'd been prepared to die.

She'd understood what it was that was going to happen.

She'd made peace with all of it, but she was going to go out on her terms!

She'd put her all into making a final statement, and she still suffered the churning in her guts from bringing pain to another creature.

But she'd not expected a second centaur in the tunnels…

And, after everything she'd struggled to stay strong against, there was nothing left within her to cope with this new turn.

And this one was bigger.

*Much* bigger!

And he was armed…

The axe that the new centaur drew from its back was as long as she was tall, and the double-sided blade would easily reach from one of her shoulders to the next. In the dying light of the torch, the silhouette was more terrifying than anything she'd seen so far, and as the centaur gave the massive weapon a single spin in his palm as though it were nothing more than a piece of starter kindling, the vagrant fae's resolve crumbled with exhaustion and she dropped to her knees.

Behind her, the centaur—the *first* centaur—made an unexpected sound, one of confusion.

"You?" its lingering pain and anger turned the single word into something that sounded like so much less. It hadn't been expecting the newcomer, either; and it didn't sound happy about the company. "You've come to steal my glory? Are you here to take my kill?"

"Not in the way you believe, brother, but yes," the new centaur's voice sounded different. While the first spent his words in the same way he spent his roars—without pause and with no regard to the cost—the newcomer spoke as though he'd had the words saved away; as though he didn't wish to use them but recognized it as a necessary expense.

His words seemed to carry heavier than even his axe.

She heard the first centaur shift his weight behind her. The muck squelched under a few steps, and the hairs on the back of her neck rose in defense as she felt him looming over her. A single stomp of its hoof splattered more filth along her side and she flinched, whimpering as she felt the impact nearly clip her thigh upon its landing.

"You can't have her, *brother*," he growled, the last word coming out as another non-word sound. "Whatever honor you've come in here seeking you will leave without."

The newcomer rested his axe on his shoulder and nodded as the torchlight finally died. "There's some painful facts in what you claim, Bowen, and those will be my facts to bear, I'm afraid," the words felt even heavier in the new darkness. "But your burden will be every day that you do not understand the falsehoods that you speak."

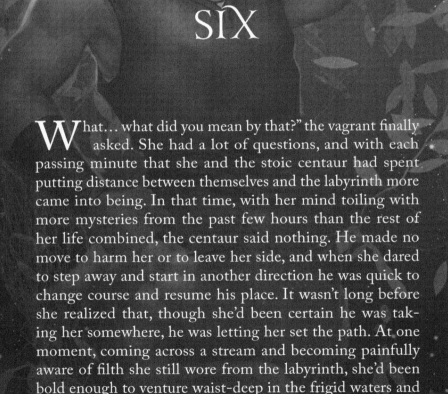

# SIX

"W hat… what did you mean by that?" the vagrant finally asked. She had a lot of questions, and with each passing minute that she and the stoic centaur had spent putting distance between themselves and the labyrinth more came into being. In that time, with her mind toiling with more mysteries from the past few hours than the rest of her life combined, the centaur said nothing. He made no move to harm her or to leave her side, and when she dared to step away and start in another direction he was quick to change course and resume his place. It wasn't long before she realized that, though she'd been certain he was taking her somewhere, he was letting her set the path. At one moment, coming across a stream and becoming painfully aware of filth she still wore from the labyrinth, she'd been bold enough to venture waist-deep in the frigid waters and use their current to rinse herself. In the short time she'd spent in the water, however—trying to ignore the centaur's persistent gaze from the shore—even more questions arose.

but every possible answer she sampled was too unnerving to risk being revealed to be the truth.

Was he waiting to kill her? She dared not press that.

Why had he not killed the centaur in the tunnels? She worried how he'd take such a brash inquiry.

What did he want with her? Too many horrific possibilities to even consider, let alone invite.

But there was the one question that, above all else, burned with a need stronger than any other: Why had he helped her? She'd been in that labyrinth to die at the hands of his kin; what reason could he have to stop that?

That question preceded every cycle of questions and was reborn anew dozens of times with different phrasings. Even in the short time she spent in further silence washing the filth from herself and her dress it returned to demand an answer at least a dozen times. And when she'd climbed free of the stream, ignoring the extra weight of the waterlogged dress, the centaur had been kind enough to step away to allow an easier passage to the shore.

Which, of course, only aroused more questions.

With so many questions demanding to be answered, it was only a matter of time before one of them grew impatient and asked itself. Even so, however, it came as a surprise to her—as well as to the centaur, who had seemed to grow accustomed to the silence—when, with the silence finally being broken, it should be *that* question that had broken free of her racing mind and leapt free of her pursed lips.

*"What did you mean by that?"*

As though none of the other questions mattered so much. The vagueness of it all only seemed to add to the vagrant fae's own confusion.

The centaur paused and looked at her.

"Pardon?"

The vagrant fae replayed the question in her head and finally decided it was as good a place as any to start. And, unlike all of the other questions, this one didn't seem to carry any possible threat with the answer. Clearing her throat and trying to hide the nauseating mixture of terror and confusion and uncertainty from her voice, she spoke again:

"In the maze, when that bea—when the other centaur was talking about honor, you said…" she frowned, shaking her head, "Well, I don't quite recall *how* you said it, but you admitted he was right about you not leaving with honor, but that he'd never understand…"

"—the falsehood that he spoke," he nodded, looking off into the distance. "Yes, I remember what I said."

The vagrant fae grumbled "I had a feeling that you might," before rubbing the back of her neck.

The centaur's wandering eyes shifted back towards her, and though he remained silent she sensed that he was pushing her to ask her question.

"So what did you mean by that?" she repeated.

The centaur shrugged and started walking again. Though she wasn't sure why, the vagrant fae moved to follow.

"There are different types of honor," the centaur said in his heavy tone. "The honor of my people—of my herd—was the particular code to which he was referring. It's the same honor that he believed he was earning by killing you," he sighed, and the vagrant fae realized it was the first time he'd shown any sign of emotion. "It's an honor that my herd's been hoping I'd earn, and one that I've refused for a very long time."

The vagrant fae nodded, understanding. "So the other centaur thought you were there to kill me?" she asked, thinking of the brief struggle she'd listened to between the two back in the labyrinth after the torchlight had left them in darkness. She'd been certain that the new centaur would mean to kill the first with his massive axe, but after a few sharp impacts and the crash of a heavy body crashing into the muck, she'd been led away by her unexpected companion with the ragged sounds of the other centaur growing distant in the darkness.

The centaur rolled his shoulders at the question and then nodded. "I'm sure he still thinks I mean to kill you."

She stiffened and stopped following. Though she'd been avoiding the topic, it had naturally come to that point. Sensing that she was no longer following him, the centaur stopped as well. The question she dreaded most hung between them, unspoken by known by both.

"But…" she drew in a deep breath as quietly as she could, keeping very still as he turned to face her. "But you're *not* going to kill me, are you?"

The centaur finished turning and locked his deep, dark eyes on hers. Though she'd just inhaled, she suddenly felt breathless and something in her chest burned with demand. Once again, she felt herself wondering if things were as tense as they appeared or if fear was just altering her perception.

"No," the centaur's single word put a thousand questions to rest.

"And…" she blushed, coming to her own conclusion, "Was that the honor that you meant? The one that he wouldn't understand?"

The centaur only nodded.

*"There's some painful facts in what you claim…"* he'd said back in the pits.

Painful facts…

"What did you have to give up to save me?" she asked, biting her lip as soon as the words were past.

The centaur tensed, and she couldn't help but mirror the act as she realized that the question pained him. Looking away, he clopped his front hoof several times before finally turning away and beginning to walk once again.

"Everything," he finally answered. "But such is the cost of my code of honor, I suppose."

The rest of the walk was in silence. Fortunately, it didn't take too long before they arrived at a clearing and a nearby hill. Though the silence stretched on as the two climbed to the surface, they seemed to agree that this is where they should rest. The vagrant fae, spotting a stump, moved to sit down and catch her breath as the centaur began to collect branches to start a fire.

The silence stretched on further, and the tension seemed to weigh heavy even on the centaur, who the vagrant fae was certain couldn't be bothered with such trifling affairs such as immense weight or even emotions.

"What's your name?" he paused in his task to look up at her.

The question was innocent enough, and, happy to have an end of the crippling silence, the vagrant fae forgot herself as she jumped at the chance to contribute to the collapse of the dreaded quiet.

"Gwendolyn Clearwate—" she paused at that. It was such an innocent question—one that had been asked so many times in the past that its answer was as casual a response as breathing—but the truth cut her response short. That wasn't her name anymore. The fae had stripped her of everything before setting her to the labyrinth, including her name. "It *was* Gwendolyn, but it's not anymore. Everything that I am is gone now…"

Scoffing at that, the centaur returned to gathering wood, and the vagrant fae caught sight of him shaking his head.

"And what is it, centaur, that you find humorous about all of this?" she demanded.

"You," he answered, not bothering to pause in his errand. "You and your kind, I mean. You think that you're not who you are because your people—what?—simply said so. Is it really so easy to rob a fae of themselves?"

The vagrant fae glared. "You're one to talk about robbing the fae of themselves! Your kind have been butchering ours for—"

"Allow me to clarify one very relevant fact to you, *Gwendolyn*:"—the way the centaur spoke her name, with defiance and purpose, gave the vagrant a strange sensation of rebelliousness—"my kind have killed yours only because of a deal made by *your* elders and one of the last centaur *vernunt* in my herd!"

The vagrant couldn't find words as she absorbed this information. She'd known that the horrors of the vagrant labyrinth were controlled by the fae elders, but it had always been implied that they were making use of a preexisting need for the centaurs to kill. Could it really have all been a lie?

She stiffened her jaw and offered a scoff of her own. "And how would you know? The killing's been going on for centuries!"

"I know"—the centaur still hadn't paused from his wood collecting, and his tone made it clear he would have rather been doing so in silence—"because the killing's been going on for *less* than a single century."

"And how would you know that?" she asked.

"Because the *vernunt* who made the very first deal was my guru," he said, finally stopping to glare over his shoulder at her, "and he won't be a century old for another few years."

She felt her cheeks go hot as embarrassment flooded them. Realizing she'd not only insulted her savior but also dredged up more pain, she withdrew under his glare and cast her gaze to the dirt.

"I… I'm sorry," she whimpered, feeling a swell of sympathy as she realized just how much her kind had wronged his. "I had no idea."

A long silence followed as his hooves gently impacted the earth with his approach. Finally, when he stood before her, he set a massive armload of firewood to the side of her makeshift seat and cleared his throat.

"I don't blame you for what you couldn't have known," he said. "But I do blame you for letting others take from you the one thing that none can take." He turned away and began to use his front hooves to dig out a fire pit. "I chose to go against my herd and save you despite the deal we'd made with your people. I accepted that I would not be welcomed back after I did, but they could never, nor *would* they ever," he added with a quick glance towards her, "try to tell me who I was or wasn't simply because I could no longer run with them."

The vagrant fae looked at him for a long time, realizing she'd already begun to see past the parts that divided them—the features that had labeled his kind as beasts to the fae—and started to see so much more. His size, what had been at first something that terrified and intimidated, she realized had quickly become a comfort the entire time they'd been walking. Though she was outside the fae city, unguarded by its walls, and immersed in a world that she'd been taught from birth was certain death, she hadn't felt a single twinge of fear for anything that they might encounter. But there was more there, she realized; something greater than just his capacity to frighten away potential dangers. The centaur's brown eyes held a wisdom that, before that day, she would've thought impossible for his kind, and when he spoke it was clear that his eyes didn't lie. Coupled with his mane of long, black hair, chiseled features, and, despite his vast bulk and brawn, formidable grace, she was finding it more and more difficult to see him as the monster her people had relentlessly painted his kind as.

*No*, she thought, calling upon his wisdom, *not my people. Not anymore.*

"You're right," she said, standing up and moving to collect a few nearby rocks to help him with the fire pit. Her words and the sound of her movement distracted the centaur from his task, and he moved to look at her as she began to lay the stones in a circle around the area he'd been working on.

"I'm right?" his words carried no hint of doubt, and the vagrant fae realized he wasn't questioning her words, but urging her to elaborate on them.

She nodded, finishing with the semi-circle of rocks and beginning to collect more to finish it. "The fae *can't* take who I am from me," she admitted. Still, she found herself plagued by the guilt of her crime and the punishment she'd been spared from. "But nevertheless," she sighed, looking down at a large, smooth rock and feeling a fresh pang of guilt for the one she'd thrown at the centaur in the labyrinth, "I think it's wrong to continue as 'Gwendolyn Clearwater' from this moment on."

The centaur drew his shoulders back and straightened the human-half of his body. Though she'd never seen a gesture like this before, it felt like he was showing pride in her at that moment.

"Then what shall I call you, fae?" he asked, clopping his foot gently. Somehow it felt like a sign of respect to her.

The vagrant fae blushed again, this time from anything but shame. "Gwen, I suppose."

"Very good. In that case, you may call me 'Gav,'" he smiled.

"Gav," Gwen spoke the name aloud and smiled at it, "Was that not your name before?"

Gav shook his head. "I was Gavrael when I ran with the herd," he explained, "but, as Gwendolyn Clearwater shall henceforth be Gwen outside of the fae city, so shall Gavrael be Gav without his herd." He smiled and offered an awkward bow, kneeling down on one of his front legs.

Gwen felt another blush at the gesture, which Gav was quick to rise from before continuing with the fire pit. With Gwen's circle of rocks in place, he retrieved a few of the pieces of starting kindle. For a moment, she could only watch his methodic actions, then, finally, feeling a renewed sense of purpose with her renewed sense of identity, she began to search the clearing for anything she might find useful to gather. As she circled the area, scanning the hilltop for anything she could recognize as useful, she could once again sense her traveling companion's gaze on her back and, at the sound of his approach, she turned to face him.

"Just what are you doing?" he asked once he'd gotten a better vantage point to watch.

Gwen's hand faltered at the confusion in his voice, still coming to terms with her growing sense of trust and admiration for him. Since the moment she'd met him he'd exuded wisdom, and, at the sound of skepticism in his otherwise certain voice, she found herself in a moment of doubt. Looking down at the small bundle she'd already collected, however, she assured herself that her actions were sound.

"If you must know, I'm gathering."

"I can see that you're gathering," he chuckled, folding his arms in front of his chest, "but I was hoping you might shed some light upon *what* it is that you're gathering and *why* you're gathering it. We need to make a fire and find food, and none of what you have there can burn, and, unless fae are *that* different from everyone else, I'm certain that none of it is edible, either."

"I can't make fire," Gwen confessed, plucking a few etherweeds from the ground, "and I haven't cooked since I tried to follow my grandmother's stew recipe."

"And what happened when you tried to cook your grandmother's stew, exactly?" Gav asked, taking another step closer.

"It was..." Gwen frowned at the memory, recalling it as a bad one but suddenly missing that time in a way she never thought she would. "I won't say any more than that it did not become stew."

Gav laughed at that and advanced again, watching Gwen as she continued. "So what are you collecting?" he asked again, "And why?"

Gwen sighed and turned, holding out the stretch of fabric from her dress that she'd formed into a makeshift basket. Inside were the simple-yet-necessary ingredients to the basic concoctions her mother had taught her.

Gav tilted his head in confusion. "This is just... just leaves and seeds and..." he sneered at some of the petrified mouse droppings that Gwen had collected. "Why would you need these?"

"Everything around you has magic in it," Gwen recited one of her mother's first lessons. "It's just about knowing how to draw it forth and what to mix it with to serve your needs."

Gwen watched as Gav studied the contents a moment longer and then shrugged before turning back to the fire pit and beginning to strike a flint stone against the head of his massive axe. Sighing, she turned her attention back to collecting more ingredients for her potions and elixirs, finding the chore somehow soothing for the first time in her life. Finally, after selecting a few more ingredients, she took her collection and made her way towards the fire, which she was surprised to see already built up into a sizable blaze. Gav, who was still tending to the flame, looked up at her approach, and she tried her best to ignore his gaze. Since they'd arrived he'd made a show of knowing exactly how to set up a campsite, and she'd done little more than construct a circle out of rocks and pick up bits of this-and-that from here-and-there; with her pride feeling a little bruised, she hoped to soon impress him as he'd been, even if unintentionally, impressing her. With every nerve tensing under the sensation of his gaze, she began to work, hoping that she wouldn't wind up turning her skin purple…

Again.

"Do you think that's going to make enough of whatever it is you're making?" Gav asked.

"Honestly?" Gwen sighed, making a few calculations in her mind as she continued, "I'd need a lot more supplies than what I can find here to have enough of anything worth carrying. Plus I don't exactly have any of the tools or supplies I usually have," she frowned, realizing that she'd already confessed that this was a fool's errand. "Still, it will be more than what we have"—nothing, she kept that to herself even though it was obvious—"and my mother always said it was better to practice and gain nothing than to do nothing and gain even less."

Gav smiled. "Your mother sounds very wise," he offered.

Gwen bit her lip and nodded, fighting the sudden urge to cry.

No doubt seeing the sadness in her face, Gav steered the conversation: "I know of a small village that's not too far from here," he nodded towards the meager supplies and shrugged, "I'm certain we could find anything else you might need there. Tools and supplies and…" he lingered on Gwen's gatherings once again, "and better ingredients."

Sadness was immediately replaced with fear, and Gwen looked up nervously. "Do you really think it's safe to visit villages?"

Gav looked at her, confused, "Of course! How else would we get what we needed?"

"But…" Gwen felt her face go hot with embarrassment from how casual he sounded about the matter. "But I'm a vagrant now! I won't be welcome anywhere! Nobody will take in a—"

"Whoa! Whoa there!" he held up both hands, and Gwen realized that he had seven fingers on each hand. Though it was an alarming feature, she realized that she didn't feel repulsed or afraid like she might have been mere hours earlier. "Listen," Gav pressed on, "I do not doubt that your people told you many things of life outside your walls, but I assure you that most of it, if not all of it, is a lie. Just as my kind are not thirsty for fae blood, very few outside of your kind even know what you being a vagrant would mean! And even less would care! If nothing else, the reaction you'll find upon your arrival just about anywhere will be awe and admiration at a fae that's left the walls. I'm sure word of that much would travel fast."

Gwen shivered at that. "Word would travel… Will they mean to kill me then?"

Gav laughed. "Kill you? Why by the thundering hooves of the sky galloper would they want to kill you? Just what sort of nonsense did your people tell you of the outside world?"

Gwen paused at that, feeling her cheeks redden in embarrassment once again. "Well, they…" she shrugged and toiled more over her gatherings, "It does not matter! It was all like you said: just nonsense. Villages are safe and villagers mean no harm. I see that now. I wouldn't have imagined a centaur would have much need of such luxuries."

"I wouldn't believe you've imagined much of centaurs before today," Gav chuckled.

"No," Gwen mumbled, seeing how true that was, "I suppose I haven't." She looked up then with a new interest and, more importantly, a new topic to draw away from her ignorance: "What about you? What's your story?"

Gav shrugged. "Not much story to tell. Anything before this wouldn't be very interesting at all."

"I can't believe that," Gwen countered, "You said you personally know the centaur that plotted the vagrant labyrinth. I'd say that's quite interesting."

Gav smiled and nodded. "Yes, I suppose Alastair is an interesting one."

"Is? He must be quite old now," Gwen found herself drawn from her own distraction.

"I suppose he is," Gav admitted. "One of the oldest of the grandfathers, I believe."

Gwen cocked her head. "How many grandfathers do you have?"

"Well, Alastair's not my grandfather." He paused for a moment, "Not that I know of, anyway. But in the herd we are all seen as family; all elders are our grandparents, all below them are our parents, and all below them are our siblings."

"That must get very confusing," Gwen said.

Gav shrugged again. "It makes things strangely personal and impersonal all at once, I'll admit. It's one of the last matters that Alastair and I discussed. As the only other *vernunt* in the herd, he was expected to talk sense into me for distancing myself. Because I behaved differently they were concerned, especially because I refused to volunteer for the labyrinth and they saw that I favored my sister over others."

"Your sister? You mean another centaur of your generation?"

"No," Gav shook his head, suddenly looking sad, "my blood-sister. She's always been smaller, so I made certain she had more than an equal portion at mealtimes."

"How could that be viewed as wrong?" Gwen finally set down her gatherings.

Yet another shrug and an even sadder face. "Because she was everyone's sister in the eyes of the herd, but you can't favor one over the others. That's not how it works for them."

"But for you…?"

Gav chuckled, but there was no humor in it. "I see things differently. It's the double-sided sword of being a *vernunt*: wisdom above the rest of the herd."

80

Gwen leaned forward, intrigued. "A *vernunt* is what then? A leader?"

"No alpha would allow that," Gav scoffed, "but they would certainly employ the wisdom of one in secret. A *vernunt* is…" he sighed, clearly struggling with the translation. "It is the centaur who would sooner run within his mind than with the herd. They're the thinkers, the ones who see things differently; when the herd needs a new perspective they turn to the *vernunt* for guidance. But seeing things differently comes at the expense of never fully being a part of their ways." His shoulders sagged, "I suppose that's why it was so easy for me to save you and accept a fate outside of the herd."

Gwen felt a lump of sadness grow in her throat as she witnessed his own sadness take hold of him. "I was ready to die, Gav," she admitted, "I don't wish to sound ungrateful for what you did, but why would you sacrifice so much to save me?"

Somehow the question seemed to alleviate some of his sadness, and she watched as he looked up to meet her gaze. "Because you were prepared to sacrifice so much to save my sister."

Gwen had some time to think on Gav's confession while he left to find them something to eat. Though it was true that hunger had been gnawing at her for some time and she could only imagine the same was true for him, she felt that his urgency to leave was just as much a convenience as it was a necessity. She had only known him a short time, but she could already see that the wise young centaur was used to keeping his thoughts to himself. She saw a conflicted sense of freedom in how he shared with her, but in sharing came the bitterness of exposure, something that she recognized from her father.

"Pride," her mother once said, "is a man's greatest strength and his worst weakness."

Gav's decision had exiled him from his loved ones much as hers had, but where Gwen had acted on impulse and, in a moment of instinct, lost sight of fae law, he had acted with a rigid understanding of what would happen.

All because he put his sister above the herd, just as Gwen had put his sister above herself.

*"...such is the cost of my code of honor..."*

Even with an empty belly that roared to be fed, she felt like she was going to be sick.

*I've ruined both our lives...* she thought, fighting to contain herself as she heard Gav's approach.

The sight of the centaur coming into view over the hillside with a decapitated deer slung over his back brought a flood of mixed emotions. The casualness of Gav's stride despite such a sizable weight was admirable and intimidating all at once, but seeing the dead animal awakened the healer's instincts within Gwen, and she felt a strange swirling of dread and sadness and rage that she was too afraid to express. As tormented as she was by the sight, the idea of casting a harsh tone on Gav, who'd already saved her life and was now returning with a meal fit for a banquet, not only seemed unfair, but outright foolish. After all, his axe was still stained with the deer's blood, and Gwen wasn't certain she was ready to test the limit of his gentle nature towards her.

"It didn't suffer," Gav grunted knowingly to her as he let the body slide off his back.

Taken aback by his words, she stared at the headless deer before looking back up at him. "How can you be sure?" she asked, not sure if she sounded sad or angry but regretting either instantly.

If Gav was offended by her tone, he didn't show it.

"Because you need a head to feel pain," he said flatly. "And by the time she could have realized she didn't have a head, she didn't have it to realize it," he smirked.

"You… you got close enough to kill it that fast?" Gwen gawked at the size of the body again.

Gav shook his head as he turned his massive axe to begin butchering his kill. "Didn't need to get close," he explained, cutting open the deer's belly and forcing Gwen to look away, "I just threw the axe."

This time Gwen gawked at his weapon. "You *threw* that giant thing?"

Gav paused long enough to look up at her and nod.

So much strength and power with that sort of speed and precision? No wonder his herd wanted him to volunteer for the labyrinth. He could've killed a month's worth of vagrants in a matter of hours!

Staring at the axe, she found herself wondering where he could've found something so massive.

"Where did you get that?"

Though she felt like she should have been used to questions that were eager to ask themselves after the afternoon she'd had, she still felt her cheeks burn as soon as the words were out.

He grinned up at her, not even trying to mask his pride. "I made it," he boasted as he pierced a sizable slab of deer meet on a length of starter kindling and held it over the fire.

"Really? I've never seen anything like it," she said. "How did you make it?"

Gav shrugged as he worked the meat over the fire. "While exploring a nearby beachfront, I found a large rock that had been smoothed down by many years of the ocean's current. I worked to sharpen and shape it into the blade, then I wedged it through the top of a large trunk I'd found in the forest. Once I secured the blade, I pulled the stump out of the ground, tore off its roots, and shaped it. One of our mothers had some extra hide to offer, so I used the leather for the handle and…" He glanced over and grinned, "Am I boring you yet?"

Gwen blushed as she realized what she'd interpreted as boasts had been nothing more than casual steps for him. "Not at all, actually," she admitted.

"Well, it may not be as tough or as sharp as the humans' iron, but it gets the job done and I've never had any trouble cutting down whatever needed cutting down," he smiled.

"I see," Gwen's mind began to wander as the first wafts of the promised meal did away with any lingering regrets she might of felt. Hunger was no longer gnawing at her, it was consuming her entirely. Suddenly one deer didn't seem like enough…

Gav gave her a knowing nod before motioning to the powders and elixirs that Gwen had finished while he'd been away.

"Looks like you were able to make quite a bit, eh?"

Still intoxicated by the aroma, she turned back to her work and bit her lip, reminded of a conundrum. "Yes, but… do you have anywhere I can possibly store these?"

Gav raised an eyebrow and made a note of illustrating his limited supplies, including a bladder strapped at his hip. "All I have is this, and that's used to hold drinking water. Centaurs aren't ones to carry excessively."

Gwen cast a skeptic eye at what remained of the large deer carcass. "Yes, I can see that," she teased.

Chuckling at that, Gav let his eyes wander around the camp before he caught sight of the red dress her mother had given her. "Why don't you use some of that? There's plenty of extra fabric to make a few satchels from. They'll be simple and probably not last long, but it should be enough to hold what you have there until we can get some proper supplies. Besides, that's an awful lot of train to be carrying about, and I saw how heavy it got in the stream earlier." He gave her another smirk, "Better to not carry excessively, after all."

Gwen's eyes went wide at the suggestion. "How dare you! This was a gift!"

Gav shrugged. "An impractical gift."

"It was from my mother!" Gwen pressed, glaring at him. "She gave it to me so that I could look beautiful in the next world."

"So you're going to stumble around the forests in a full formal gown that your mother was prepared to see you die in?" Gav shook his head, poking at the meet and smiling at its progress. "If she could be here now and see that you were no longer about to die, would she let you cut away some of the unnecessary bits so that you had something to hold your supplies, or would she demand that you look ridiculous and impractical until you either regained your wits and found something else to wear or got yourself killed because you couldn't move in that thing?" He looked away and shrugged, "Because the way you described her earlier led me to believe she was wiser than that."

Gwen paused at that and pouted, looking down at the dress for a long, appreciative moment before she finally pulled at the hem and began to tear away a sizable length of fabric, exposing the bottom-half of her legs in the process.

"That smells incredible, by the way," she grumbled, not ready to admit that he'd been right.

Gav smiled all the same, nodding. "I know."

# SEVEN

Gwen's eyes shot open as the sound of pained shrieks flooded her ears. She bit her lip as the nauseating response to the sound of agony crashed into her like a punch in the stomach, and before she realized she'd moved she was on her feet and scrambling to the edge of the hilltop to catch sight of the source. She saw nothing, but the sounds intensified. Instinct pulled at her, demanding that she track down whoever was suffering and make it right, but, though she couldn't deny her own stubbornness, she wasn't about to make the same mistake a second time. She couldn't just rush into the situation. While her decisions before had risked death because of the laws of her people, out here a wrong step could be death due to sheer foolishness. And while Gav seemed insistent that this world wasn't nearly as dangerous as she'd been led to believe, she wasn't prepared to test those claims without the proper precautions. As another pained shriek filled the air, she rushed to the best precaution she'd ever known:

"Gav! Gav, come on!" she pulled the slumbering centaur's shoulders. "Somebody's hurt! I need to see if I can help them!"

Stirring out of sleep and looking up at her, Gav wet his chapped lips. "Wha…?" Another pained cry issued then and his eyes opened the rest of the way, though he didn't wear the same concern as her. Waiting for the screams to die down, he looked back to Gwen. "Last night you were afraid that everything out here existed to kill you, and now you're ready to leap straight into the unknown?"

"Please!" The pain in Gwen's stomach was becoming too much to bear, and any modesty she might have been driven by took its place behind urgency. "I can't stand around and do nothing, but I can't go out there alone… Please!"

Gav studied her for a moment that felt longer than she was sure it was. "You trust me that much?"

"You've saved my life once already. That makes you a safer option than any other," she answered.

Though she felt that her frantic choice in words might have been offensive, Gav didn't seem upset by them. Instead, he nodded and, acting with the urgency that she felt, lifted himself up and retrieved his axe.

Seeing the weapon, Gwen's face paled. "Do you really think we'll need that?" she asked.

Gav shrugged. "Something's hurting whoever's down there," he pointed out, "would you want to get there and discover whatever was causing their pain would be better cured with this axe than one of your potions?"

Gwen paused. She hadn't considered the possibility that something might have to be killed to save whoever was in pain. Her lessons had always been on the sick and injured. There'd never been a need to intervene in an attack or place herself in harm's way while she was healing. She thought she'd been clever in waking Gav to protect her from anything dangerous that might be lurking between their hilltop and the source of the cries, but she suddenly realized the source might come with its own dangers.

Another scream, this one more frantic, and with it came more pain and a stronger pull. Gwen shuddered as she was forced to admit, despite everything she'd been taught, that Gav's axe may very well be a solution.

Though she'd die a thousand times over before she ever called it a "cure."

With no more than that brief look between them and a single nod, the two bolted down the hill and towards the direction of the sound. Gav needed no more motivation than her own speed, and soon after the centaur began to gallop he was beside her and matching her pace. As the slope of the hill faded and fed into the first few trees of the forest, Gwen found herself stealing glances at her companion, amazed at the speeds he could achieve regardless of his size.

Gav was amazed that such a petite creature, looking like she was built of twigs and moonlight, could summon the strength to move as fast as she was. This, however, came as no real surprise to him. Gwen had continued to amaze and confound him since before he'd even laid eyes upon her. First with the selflessness she'd shown to Lysoks, then the bravery and fortitude in the labyrinth, and time and time again since then. While others seemed nervous to walk beside him, she'd done so—fresh from the hell of the death-maze—and even had mind enough to seek the cleansing waters of the stream when they'd presented themselves. She'd spoken clearly and with honesty and sincerity where so many others stammered or tried to work their deceit. And he'd watched her turn weeds and waste into magic; *real* magic. Now, despite any lingering fears of his kind she might still harbor, she'd once again put herself second to ensure safe passage to selflessly save another.

And she could run!

His sister hadn't been untrue when she'd spoken of this fae's beauty, and as he pumped his hooves to keep pace with her he felt like he was still asleep, like his wonderful meal and the lingering sight of a pale-white feather carried on a brisk wind was creating some wonderful dream. But the magic of the moment was made even more so as he came to grips with the truth that this was no mere dream. There was actually a creature, a fae at that, who was this caring and committed to what she knew in her heart was the right thing!

He didn't just admire her compulsion to help others, he envied it. While he'd dwelled on his code and concerned himself with its place in others' lives, she acted with confidence and without a shred of remorse. Even when her actions earned her a death penalty of the most terrible breed, she stood true to herself and even refused to go silently. He'd seen her remorse at the pain she'd inflicted on Bowen, but at that moment it was about more than fighting back—she knew she wouldn't win against the centaur in that pit; she'd actually expected to lose—but she wasn't about to let the fear of death and the humiliation that her people wanted from her show. She was the strongest fighter he'd ever met, and she was committed to never hurt another.

She truly was a dream come to life.

The closer they got to the source of the sound, the more palpable the suffering became. It was as if the pain had become an invisible mist that was growing thicker and more putrid with every step they took. And that only made the drive to continue that much stronger. Ahead of them was a cluster of bushes and ivy-strangled trees that created a large, wall-like barrier. For an instant, Gwen felt a tug of panic as she wondered how they'd get around such a barrier. Then, still in mid-gallop, Gav took one swing with his axe. It was as if the foliage never existed, and the two jumped a small patch of bramble that remained amidst a pile of its severed cousins.

Almost instantly Gwen doubled over, feeling a flood of sickness rush through her as the stink of blood, the burning itch of the iron, and the pained screams collided at such close range and all at once. There, on the other side, they found the source: a very terrified, very pregnant elf caught in an iron trap. Though she'd never encountered the humans or actually seen any of their cursed ironwork, she recognized what it was the instant she saw it. She looked over at Gav, noticing his own repulsion at the sting of the trap's iron hanging in the air.

But the elf...

Gwen bit her lip, remembering everything her kind had said about the elves—what they called the 'dark long-ears'—and her nausea doubled as her fear made her linger. While the faes' ears were long and beautiful and reached back from their heads with pride, elf ears were stunted and pointy abominations. And the magic that the elves implemented was said to be of the most wicked sort, practically consorts to demons. Or at least that was what they'd been told. Except that this elf didn't look dark or dangerous or ugly. The female she saw, though her ears were shorter and pointed upward and her skin was the color of snow, was beautiful. She watched the poor woman crying and writhing in pain, and Gwen once again found herself questioning everything her kind had told her.

Gwen finally stepped forward as Gav looked on but maintained his distance. Seeing her approach, the elf began to pull against the trap to keep her distance. A bitter memory seized Gwen as she remembered the way Gav's sister had done the same in the fae trap she'd been caught in, and she fought the instinct to look back to see if he'd made the connection, as well. The subject was clearly still a painful one—*it might never* not *be*, she thought—and she couldn't bear to see if he was suffering from the sight. Still, in a strange way she was thankful that the incidents were so similar…

It meant she knew exactly how to handle it.

Though her supplies were limited and probably not nearly as powerful as she was used to working with, she moved to retrieve the spells she'd concocted the night before. Opening the first makeshift pouch and silently marveling at how well the fabric of the dress worked for the purpose, she poured a small portion of the faithmist powder into her hand. Though it wasn't as vibrant as the batches she'd made with her mother and the texture seemed a bit off, she could feel that magic within it was stable and she gently blew it from her palm and in the direction of the elf. The air shimmered with the enchantment as it swirled about the air and, as it reached its target, Gwen marveled as the elf's frantic and pained whimpers started to settle; her body beginning to relax as the fear and pain in her eyes dulled to a calm-yet-curious stare.

*"Faithmist for stillness,"* Gwen heard her mother's voice in her head as she marveled at the effects of the first spell she'd created on her own. Confident that they'd be able to approach the elf without risking her safety or their own, she finally glanced back at Gav and nodded.

"Come on. I'll need help with the trap while she's still calm."

"How do we open it without hurting ourselves?" Gav asked, frowning. "Anybody who isn't a human will feel its burn just by touching it."

Gwen bit her lip and nodded, "I know, and it's already tasted blood; it'll burn hotter now…"

Gav raised an eyebrow. "I don't think it works that way…"

Another wave of embarrassment—was anything the fae elders said true?

"Have you ever encountered the humans' iron?" she shot back, narrowing her eyes at the hideous trap.

"Well… no," Gav admitted, "but I still don't think it—"

"So there's a chance it's true then?"

Gav sighed and shrugged, finally offering her a nod. "I suppose I can't prove otherwise, though that doesn't mean I'm eager to find out."

"Nor I…" Gwen nodded. Then, spotting his weapon, she perked up. "What about your axe?" she asked. "You could pry it open!"

"I'm not sure it'd be strong enough against the likes of human iron. I've never tried such a thing," Gav frowned.

"We have to try! We have no other choice," Gwen motioned again for him to join her. "The spell won't last for much longer."

Resigning to her urging, Gav stepped forward and began to work the stone blade of his weapon between the iron teeth of the trap. Gwen watched, shaking like an Autumn leaf, as he strained to work around the elf's leg without hurting her even more. When the axe was finally worked into place, he planted his hooves and began to push the opposite side of the blade, beginning to pry the trap open. Slowly, still struggling to keep from causing further injury, the trap began to open, and as the last few teeth slipped free of the elf's flesh he nodded to Gwen to pull her free. Wasting no more time with the concerns of her peoples' tall tales, Gwen gingerly moved the elf's leg from the trap and pulled her away before Gav allowed it to snap shut. As he began to marvel at his weapon with a renewed appreciation, Gwen went to work. Pulling one of the other pouches open, she let her training guide her hand as she began to mend the wound. With the hazy expression instilled by the faithmist beginning to fade, the elf's senses began to return and Gwen watched as her face once again started to twist in pain. Just as Gwen braced herself for another gut-wrenching shriek of agony, she watched her patient's body tense with effort and she pursed her lips, swallowing the first traces of her scream. Instead, only a stifled, shrill whimper bled out as she shook her head against the pain.

"It's okay to scream," Gwen offered a reassuring smile. "It won't hurt much longer, but it's not worth hurting yourself more trying to hold it in."

The female's withdrawn efforts continued as she refused to even make eye contact or offer a response to Gwen's words. She frowned, looking over at Gav as he moved towards them. While she felt a pang of offense at the elf's refusal to acknowledge her, his gentle smile towards her showed an understanding that eluded Gwen. Still working to reverse the effects of the iron as she treated the wound, she gave the centaur a questioning look, hoping he might be able to explain.

Though he hadn't looked away from the elf, Gav seemed to sense Gwen's confusion.

"She won't speak a word; she can't," he explained. "Nor can she gesture or look upon another or do anything to communicate with anybody."

"What?" Gwen glanced back, still working to reverse the burns from the iron. "Why?"

Gav motioned to the elf's belly. "She's pregnant," he said, as though that was all the answer Gwen needed.

"I... I don't understand," she confessed.

Gav sighed before stepping forward to join her at her side. "When an elf is with child, they're bound to a vow of silence for the duration of their pregnancy. Only the father of their child can hear their voice in that time, and only so that he can provide what she needs."

Scowling, Gwen shook her head. "What an absurd practice!"

The elf tensed at Gwen's words, but otherwise offered no sign of offense at what she'd said. The display made her instantly regret her words.

"The elves view pregnancy as a sacred time," Gav went on, his voice more stern after Gwen's outburst, "one where the to-be mother turns her focus inward to her unborn. Is that really any more absurd than your people casting out one of their own for saving the life of another creature?" he countered, kneeling down over the elf to help brush away some dirt that been caked around the wound. "Remember, Gwen, that just because it's not your way does not mean it is the wrong way," he chided, then paused to look down, seeming lost in a sudden thought. Then, shaking his head, he motioned to the severity of her injuries. "That she even screamed after being caught in the trap says much about how badly she was suffering." Looking up at the elf, he placed his right palm over his chest and bowed his head. "You've dishonored none on this day, noble sister. We hold true to this."

Though her face showed no change, the elf's body relaxed upon hearing this.

Nodding slowly, Gwen continued to work her magic and repeated Gav' words: "We hold true to this."

Though she was certain she wasn't supposed to, Gwen caught a flicker of warmth in her patient's eyes as she glanced up to gauge her response to the treatment. Seeing how much the tradition meant to the elf, she pretended to not notice and returned to her work.

Finally, Gwen finished mending the burns and treating the wounds, and began to wrap the leg in some of the extra fabric from her dress.

She sighed, shaking her head at the wrappings. "I wish I had some helitrad bark to heal the wounds." She paused and shook her head, "Though without my own *speradikt* it would only do so much…"

"A *speradikt*?" Gav asked.

"It's… I suppose it's like a song… or a spell. It's hard to explain," she frowned, realizing how Gav must have felt the other night trying to explain what a *vernunt* was. "It's a healer's greatest tool. Every *sparadikt* is different—no two healers share the same—and the magic it conjures is unmatched by any other form of treatment." Gwen sighed, feeling suddenly ashamed. "Unfortunately, I was declared a vagrant before I had a chance to finish my training. I... I have no *sparadikt*," she confessed.

Before she could go on with any apology, however, Gav laid a hand on her shoulder and offered a reassuring squeeze. "It's alright," he spoke gently, "You didn't need a *sparadikt* to save my sister"—he nodded towards the elf's leg, which, though riddled with burns and the ugliness of the toxins running through her veins moments earlier, now wore the healthy, snow-colored hue of the rest of the elf's body—"and you didn't need it to help her. Even if you couldn't *fully* heal either of them, you can't deny that you *have* saved their lives. The time you earned them will be more than enough to heal the wounds on their own."

Gwen blushed at that, not sure what to make of the sensation she felt. She looked up at him and realized that, with his warmth and reassurance, she'd felt better about her efforts than she had in over a week.

"Thank you."

With their work done, Gav offered to help the elf to her feet, making sure she could stand before letting go. As the elf began to test how much weight her wrapped leg could handle, Gwen stepped forward, ready to catch her if she started to falter.

"We could help you home if you'd like," Gwen said.

Gav nodded, "You can ride on my back to keep from risking—"

Before the two were even done offering her an escort, the elf threw an arm around each one of them in a sudden and awkward embrace. Then, before the two even had a moment to blink, it was over. Stunned by the gesture, Gwen was speechless as they watched the elf run off, showing only the slightest signs of a limp after everything she had been through.

Gav whistled as she vanished into the forest. "They really are as graceful as everyone says."

"Shouldn't we help her?" Gwen looked up at him, "Her leg is still... she could hurt herself again!"

"No," Gav answered, still staring in the direction she'd vanished into. "Elves are light on their feet, and I'm certain she doesn't have a long journey—not in her condition. That she was out this way in the first place proves that her village must not be far off." He looked back at Gwen, "Besides, arriving at her village with the two of us might have made things difficult."

Gwen looked back. "She wasn't supposed to embrace us like that, was she?"

Gav shook his head, "No, but we won't dishonor her for it. You did her a great service today in saving both her and her baby, something that your people clearly don't approve of. Everyone knows of the strict and unfair policies of the fae, so I'm sure that she was willing to break this rule to honor your willingness to break one of yours." Turning away then, he started back the way they'd come, pausing long enough to bring his axe down on the iron trap and beaming as he watched it burst into several pieces. "And now I know it can do that," he mused.

Gwen followed after, keeping her eyes to the ground to avoid stepping on any of the iron pieces. "But they're not *my* rules anymore, Gav. I'm a vagrant, remember?"

Looking over his shoulder at her, Gav smiled. "How does it feel to find such freedom in exile?"

Gwen tried to fight a rising giggle and lost. "It's really not the sort of thing one is supposed to find happiness in."

"Is that another one of rules that's no longer yours, *vagrant*?" Gav teased.

Though he used the title of her shame, Gwen was surprised to find that she felt none upon hearing it.

Freedom.

Gav called her situation "freedom," and, while she wasn't sure she was ready to accept such a powerful word for her situation just yet, she couldn't bring herself to reject it, either.

"I suppose you make a good point," she responded.

Gav nodded, slinging his axe over his back and chuckling. "It's the only sort of point I like to make."

Gwen lost another fight, this time with a bout of deep, rolling laughter.

# EIGHT

Ever since she was a little fae, Gwendolyn Clearwater found joy in healing the sick and injured. Whether it was something as simple as a pat on the back and a reassuring smile to mend a broken heart or something as crucial as helping her mother save the life of a fae who'd suffered a shark bite during a fishing expedition, she found peace in ending the suffering of others. It motivated her. It elated her. More than anything, though, it defined her. Just as the suffering of others resonated within her like a sickness, so did their relief fill her with euphoria. With every person she helped, Gwendolyn Clearwater felt a piece of herself thrive because of it. But then, because of the instincts she'd relied on her entire life, she'd been stripped of her name and, she was certain, stripped of her life.

Gav had told her on that first night that her people couldn't take who she was from her. They could take her name and cast her away to die, but he hadn't let her go on believing that she'd been robbed of anything more than her name. Doubt lingered with her on that first night, as doubt always lingers when one has heard something life-changing for the first time, but with the rising sun of that next morning a dawn of truth followed:

Gwendolyn Clearwater might have allowed her people to take her name, but Gwen didn't need their walls or their rules to be a healer.

In the few weeks following her encounter with the pregnant elf, Gwen and Gav paved a directionless path on a journey that had no destination. The two journeyed forth, stopping at villages as they came upon them and trading spells and rations alike for new supplies. As Gwen's confidence grew so did the quality of her potions and elixirs, and fae healing magic, as it turned out, fetched a handsome price in just about every village they came across. The faes' reclusive nature and refusal to share their supplies with others gave Gwen the benefit of being the only active market, and, coupled with Gav's strength, willingness to work odd jobs, and expertise as a hunter for large game, they were never without a means to acquire whatever they needed. New villages meant new supplies, which allowed for higher-quality magic. And while the new clothes and supplies were pleasant, and while their growing fame offered them hospitality and comforts from each village they paused in, it was, as it always had been, the healing that drove Gwen and Gav, who had stayed true to his word to travel by her side and keep her safe.

Though he never could have predicted that the beautiful fae with a hair like maple tree leaves during the Autumn Equinox who he'd saved from the fae labyrinth would lead him on such a fantastic path.

Despite the praise and comforts of the village, each day that they awoke in a village was short lived for any luxuries. After any final jobs were offered, the duo would acquire their last-minute needs from the market and head out in any direction except the one they'd arrived in. Then, with ear and axe poised for anything, they'd continue onward until the familiar sound of suffering beckoned them.

So it was, though she'd found joy in healing the sick and injured ever since she was a little fae, that Gwen found something even greater than the life as a healer she'd come to know within the fae wall, that of life outside the wall and offering her services to *any* who needed it. Whether it was something as simple as a splint fashioned out of a twig to mend the broken wing of a small bird or something as crucial as a troll prince who'd had an unfortunate run-in with a pack of wolves, she found an even greater peace in seeking out and ending the suffering of others.

It motivated her more than ever before.

It offered a new level of elation for her.

But, more than anything, she felt herself become redefined by her new life.

And, as an unexpected result of their efforts, the two discovered that every new village they entered had not only already heard of them and their cause, but anticipated and even celebrated their arrival. Where Gwen had once feared the response she'd earn in a new place with unknown faces, she now found that she had allies she'd never thought to gain. They met dwarves and elves and enchanters and all other breeds of creatures that offered gems or jewelry or empowered garments in exchange for a rescued loved one. And the bards—oh, the bards! There were dozens-upon-dozens of excited travelers who had written songs and stories about them. By the second week of their travels, Gwen and Gav could not go a single day, whether camped out in the forests or enjoying the comforts of a village, where they didn't encounter an unknown face who knew them well.

And they only continued to add to their stories.

And word of their activities only continued to spread.

The morning was painfully similar to that first morning:

Gwen's eyes shot open as the sound of pained shrieks flooded her ears. She bit her lip as the nauseating response to the sound of agony crashed into her like a punch in the stomach, and before she realized she'd moved she was on her feet and scrambling to the edge of the campsite to catch sight of the source. As was usually the case, the visibility in the forest was limited, and she was not surprised (though no less disappointed) when she saw no sign of the source. The sounds intensified, and instinct pulled at her, demanding that she track down whoever was suffering and make it right. Gav had learned to recognize the sound, as well, and he needed neither to be awoken nor spurred like he had on the first morning.

In that regard, Gwen was glad that this morning wasn't the exact same; while that day had been a success for them, it was as much a product of luck as it was skill. But they'd learned since then. They'd grown in confidence and skill and they had enough supplies to tend to a small army.

Snatching up her leather pack, Gwen swung the bag that held her potions and elixirs and other necessities over her back and secured it over her shoulders. Though it was filled with all manner of things, an enchantment allowed her to carry what should have been an immense weight as though it were nothing. This and the lightweight-yet-durable elven fibers that her new clothes and boots were woven from allowed her to run with a swiftness and freedom that no fae had ever known. She'd been sad to part with the tattered remains that her mother's dress had been reduced to by the fourth day of their travels, but, between the newer, more practical clothes and the new leather satchels and blown-glass vials that now held her magic, she could find no reason outside of sentimental value to mourn its loss.

No longer bound by fear and its tethering effects to Gav, she started ahead without her centaur companion—sharing the briefest nod with him before leaving the campsite—and started towards the sound.

Gav returned the nod to Gwen as he fastened the new saddle to his back. Though Gwen was still more likely to run beside him than let him carry her, there had been a few times already that the need had arose, and, between the awkwardness and aches that followed, both agreed that the saddle was a sound investment. It was, however, a tolling annoyance to work the straps. The first few times Gwen had stayed and tried to help, but the sight of the fae's face twisting in agony as she held herself back from her need to help others soon compelled Gav to let her go on ahead while he handled that detail. The first time she'd been hesitant, still afraid of the potential dangers that came from being too far away from his side, but on the single occurrence that a mangy mountain cat had tried to attack her she'd seen firsthand just how precise and quick he was at a distance with his axe. And while there was a moment of sadness for the fallen animal, Gav could see that the fae was beginning to come to grips with the necessary cruelties that came with life outside of the fae city.

With his saddle secured and his axe strapped to his back, Gav retrieved the shield that had been bestowed upon them by the head of a village they'd visited several days earlier. The shield, long and wide enough to cover the full of his back when strapped over his axe, also proved useful as a makeshift cot for Gwen to sleep upon during their nights away from a soft bed. Gav had no need for such luxuries, however, though he never turned down a layer of fresh straw to soften his sleep if it was offered, but the leather gloves and vest he'd been gifted had proven not only useful in gripping his axe and protecting his torso from low-hanging branches when he was running, but also quite comfortable. That somebody had gone to the trouble of fabricating a pair of seven-fingered gloves from the finest leather he'd ever touched was also no simple gesture, and, recognizing this, Gwen had offered to double the pouches of faithmist in return.

She truly was a dream come to life.

With all of his supplies finally secured, Gav took off in a full gallop after the celebrated fae healer. New clothes and enchantments might have granted her a bit of extra vigor in her running speed, but Gav's legs had grown stronger in their travels. Like her, he found a new sense of freedom from his exile, and, without the need to return to a herd, he had no reason to limit the distance he could travel in a day. Added to that, the moments when Gwen's own two legs paled in comparison to his four and she'd had to rely on him to continue on had offered even more strength training. He could now go an entire day—dawn to dusk and beyond—without the need to pause or rest. At that moment, however, he valued speed over stamina, and, having gained this, as well, it was not long before he'd caught up to Gwen.

Gav, in defiance of his size, possessed the strange gift of stealth along with his speed. Despite this, though she might have missed it if she hadn't known how to listen for it, Gwen was still able to hear his approach, and as he started to flank her on her left side she sacrificed a moment of her own agility to raise her right arm above her head. They'd already practiced the maneuver several times, but, while confidence in her companion's abilities never waned, she was startled nonetheless when the rock-solid grip of his leather-clad right hand took her by the wrist and lifted her off her feet in mid-sprint. The moment she left the ground, she parted her feet and caught the edges of the shield strapped to Gav's back as he plopped her into the saddle.

"You made sure to secure the cinch strap this time?" Gwen asked him, keeping her eyes and ears open for the source of the screams.

Even over the din of Gav's thundering hooves, she could hear him sigh.

"I forgot that one time, and you can thank the mountain cat for the interruption," he said. "And it's not like it was any more comfortable for me!"

"Not much use in thanking the mountain cat..." Gwen sighed.

"Should I still be sorry?" Gav groaned. "It *was* going to—"

"Do you hear that?" Gwen's ears perked and she felt the pain in her stomach intensify.

Gav slowed his gallop enough to train his smaller ears towards the source, but still shook his head. "I hear nothing more than before, why?"

"Th-the screams..." Gwen could barely stand to say the words around the twisting in her guts. "There's more than one!"

Gav, needing no further instruction, doubled his speed.

The sting of iron was a familiar one. Since she'd first felt the unnatural burning itch of the metal's hellish aura, Gwen had known of nothing that could match it. No magic, not even of the destructive variety, could replicate that sensation. It was as persistent and unforgiving as the most severe sunburn, but with the relentless, screaming pain of a fresh burn. And the itch that followed: a driving urge to scratch that was instantly punished should any dare to try. And it only got worse with continued exposure. Yes, the sting of iron was a familiar and unmatched one, but hardly one that anybody could grow used to.

So it wasn't a surprise for either Gwen or Gav when they could feel the iron before they could see it, and with all those they'd helped who'd found themselves on the opposite end of its effects it was of little shock that they'd feel it again. And while the sheer volume of its instant, toxifying impact should have been what concerned them the most, they shared a simultaneous shiver as they mutually came to the same conclusion:

There was something very different—and very, very wrong—with this particular iron.

Leaping out from between two helitrad trees and into the open air of a dirt road paved through the middle of the forest, the two were startled to find a full caravan of ogres that was under attack. Gwen counted at least three raided carriages, but several piles of splintered wood and torn cushions from the interiors proved that there had originally been several more. Most of the horses were already dead, their carcasses scattered about the scene and wearing a bizarre combination of burns and deep lacerations that, strangely enough, already appeared to have succumb to several days' worth of rot.

Gwen's eyes widened at the sight as her mind raced for an explanation for how a raid that was happening before their very eyes could leave wounds that looked days old.

"Gav…" she whispered, seeing the iron-clad human soldiers cutting down everything in their path. Carriage, horse, and ogre alike.

"I see them," Gav's voice was a carnal growl as he helped her off of his back with one hand and, with the other, retrieved the shield that covered his axe. When her feet were back on the ground, his free hand returned to his back and retrieved his weapon. "Do you think you're ready for this?"

Gwen could barely hear her centaur companion's words; dumbfounded, she watched in horror at the massacre taking place before her. The week before, when they'd come across the troll prince, Gav had needed to chase off a few of the bolder wolves who hadn't been scared off by their arrival, but that moment had paled in comparison to the threat they now faced. These were humans. Where wolves had nobility and sense and a simple and natural drive for food and shelter, humans did not. They'd been clumsy, destruction-worshipping beasts; building small empires in the mud and then killing themselves to earn the privilege of destroying them. The only thing that seemed to motivate them was the promise of finding something new and beautiful to extinguish and the competition they held between themselves to see who could wear the most blood by the time it was over. They were horrid creatures, but nothing worth their concern. That was the simple legacy of their kind. That's what Gwen had been taught. And though Gwen's misconceptions of all creatures outside the fae city had been proven again and again to be lies, the horrors she'd learned of the humans were not only confirmed by others, they'd been amplified. The only news of the humans she'd learned from the fae was their savagery, but they were said to be too simpleminded to organize themselves into anything threatening; nothing more than hairless apes who occasionally wielded simple and crude iron instruments. With each village they'd visited, however, the news of the humans' uprising during the past few years turned from a scary tale to a horrifying revelation: they'd finally organized, and they were aiming their destructive nature outward.

The humans that Gwen saw were hardly the hairless apes wielding crude iron weapons she'd been told of. They carried themselves not as beasts, but as a terrible creature of strength and power that knew what it possessed and aimed to prove it again and again. Their armor, though dented from past battles, was expertly shaped. And their weapons...

"Their iron is enchanted..." the words pained her to speak aloud.

It shouldn't have been possible!

Magic was supposed to be beyond the humans' grasp. That they'd collected themselves from the mud pits and squalor and found a way to rise to such power in only a few short years was already beyond belief, but to have somehow found the ability to imbue their perfected ironwork with dark magic…

"GWEN!" Gav stepped in front of her and thrust his axe outward as one of the human soldiers came down at them with his sword.

The enchanted metal—its full length glowing sickly blue and radiating a stronger wave of the familiar burning itch—impacted loudly against the stone blade, and the two watched in bewilderment as the wood of its handle began to darken and rot from the contact. Seeing that the enchantment would eat through his weapon in a matter of seconds, Gav reared back on his hind legs and drove both of his free hooves into the breastplate of the human's armor, roaring as the contact with the iron scalded him.

The human crashed noisily to the ground with a pair of fresh indents in his chest, his pained grunts and metallic clattering drawing the attention of his comrades.

As Gav worked to right himself, trying to remain upright despite the iron burns on his front hooves, he moved to pull Gwen away from the scene, preparing to retreat.

"No!" Gwen pulled free, still staring at the few ogres who'd yet to be cut down in the humans' raid. "We…" she felt her breath catch in her throat as she struggled to admit what was right against every urge to flee from it. "We have to help them!"

Like the centaurs, the ogres were a race that had earned their fair share of misconceptions due to their size and appearance. With sickly-looking green flesh, disproportioned features, and large, sloping heads, they were often seen as being either brutes or fools or a dangerous combination of both. And while Gwen's experience with their race, like many others, was still brief, she'd come to realize that, though the protruding teeth, massive muscles, and strange habit to adorn themselves in animal bones were intimidating in their own right, they were actually quite gentle. Trying to convince others that they were a harmless race might have been a difficult task on any other day, but with the number of dead ogres outnumbering that of the humans a nauseating seven-to-none it was obvious that none in the caravan had the means or the know-how to defend themselves.

"Gwen, there's no way we can—NO!" Gav was once again forced to fight as three more humans advanced on them.

Gav already knew that there was no changing Gwen's mind when she set it on a goal. Though he couldn't fully understand why, he knew that she had some sort of negative response to the suffering of others—some pain or immense anguish that showed in her face each time—that compelled her to commit to their plights until she'd seen them through it. It was an admirable (albeit at times unbearable) quality that she possessed.

And, at that moment, Gav was certain it was going to get them both killed.

Knowing there was no way he'd be able to protect Gwen against three armored humans without directly endangering her or leaving himself exposed, he resigned to her need to stay and pushed for the only available option.

Lifting the feather-light fae by the enchanted leather pack strapped to her back, he summoned what he hoped to be equal parts of strength and precision and hurled her into the air. Ogre and human alike all froze in a moment of shock and awe as a fae seemed to gain the power of flight and passed over their heads, only to arc soon after and crash down on the partially-caved in roof of one of the ogres' carriages. A heavy sigh of relief washed past Gav's suddenly parched lips as Gwen's natural agility landed her on her feet—awkward and crouched, but on her feet all the same—with only the same shock and awe that everyone else seemed to share stunting her movements.

"You... YOU THREW ME!" she shouted at him.

"BETTER THAN THE ALTERNATIVE!" he shouted back, not feeling that he needed to mention that the "alternative" was both of them dying.

Whether or not that point was obvious to Gwen, she didn't offer any further argument.

Already over the spectacle of the flying fae, the three humans continued their assault on Gav then. Knowing that he would be seen as the most prominent threat given the idiot-ogres' apparent inability to defend themselves, he aimed to draw the humans' attention as best he could while Gwen did what it was she did best. The plan was a sound one, and at its surface it was even a potentially simple one.

And then Gav felt one of their enchanted blades sink into the muscle of his left-front leg...

Their time together those past few weeks had earned Gav more of Gwen's respect than most that she'd met in her life. With the exception of her parents and a few of the more honorable fae that she'd met, however, it hadn't been a very long list to begin with. In a strange way Gwen resented this fact, as she would have preferred to have a more impressive collection of names to catalogue to herself while placing the wise and powerful centaur at the top of it. However, whether or not Gav had achieved his standing against four or four-hundred, Gwen was sure she could go the rest of her life adding names to that list and have his place on it remain unchanged.

In a short time she'd come to trust him with her life, and whether it be in matters of the mind or in muscle, she believed him to be practically unmatched.

So when the hulking centaur lifted her off her feet and sent her hurdling through the air over the heads of armored humans wielding enchanted iron swords, she had no choice but to believe it was the smartest and best executed option he'd been able to muster. But with her right knee still screaming from the hard landing on the carriage and the haunting vision of being skewered on a glowing blue blade still throbbing in her mind, a part of her—the part that found the ability to speak before any other part—was not happy with the decision.

Still, it had gotten her closer to the surviving ogres.

Jumping down from the carriage and starting towards an ogre mother and the young child she clutched to her bosom, Gwen hoped above hope that she'd at least heard one bard's song of their travels.

At that moment, she didn't feel that stillness from faith-mist was a good idea.

It didn't take long to come to a conclusion, however.

"You… you are Gwen, yes? Gwen and Gav, yes?" the ogre mother's frantic voice sounded like smooth stones rolling over dried leaves.

Relieved, Gwen nodded. "Yes, yes we are. Are you hurt? Is your child—NO!"

The ogre mother's eyes went wide with pain then. Still focusing on her child, she opened her arms and allowed the startled young ogre to crash to the ground as one of the glowing blades pierced through her chest, passing through the spot her child's cradled head had been but a second earlier. Horrified, Gwen watched as the ogre's rolling eyes worked to focus on the enchanted length of iron that a human soldier behind her kept embedded within her. With the sword's entry through her back coming in low, the tip of the blade pointed upward, seeming to stare back up at her, and the exit wound began to darken as the enchantment started to rot the wound from the source. Blackness filled the ogre's veins and crept like worms up the sides of her neck and across her shoulders, and, despite her distance, Gwen could feel the toxic burn of the iron as it seemed to amplify itself with the ogre's death. Finally, as the dying ogre's knees began to fold beneath it and the sword noticeably dipped under her weight, the human soldier withdrew the blade and let his newest kill fall on top of her screaming child.

Though it pained her to disregard the lost life so quickly, Gwen felt her attention drawn to the young ogre as he cried out under the weight pinning him down, and as the soldier moved to kill him she felt her legs carry her before she even knew what she intended. Diving for the child, Gwen flinched at the sound of the sword cutting through the air— even the air seemed to grow sick and putrid around the enchanted iron—and cried out as the back of her left ear burned with the weapon's pass. Scooping up the child and rolling free of the attack, she moved her hand to check how badly she'd been cut and discovered that, despite the continued burning, the attack hadn't even made contact with her.

*What breed of magic could birth such an awful weapon*, she thought, cradling the child in much the same way his mother had.

Though the young ogre was probably only a year-or-so old, he was already large enough to stand above a fae of five years, and the new weight brought a number of concerns as the human soldier turned to face her. While Gav had condemned himself to the bulk of the human soldiers, Gwen knew better than to think she stood a chance against even one of them, especially when she had no weapon and doubted she'd be able to use one if she did. Taking a step back from the advancing human, she cried out as the back of her heel caught between the splintered spokes of a wheel that had been cut from its carriage. Falling back, she felt her back crash into the carriage the wheel had belonged to and, still struggling to remain upright, she cried out as the impact forced it to teeter against the missing support and fall against her, sending her and the child toppling to the ground. The human soldier laughed—a cold, hollow sound behind the lowered iron visor of his helmet—and he started a calm pace towards them, letting the tip of his sword grind against the edge of the dirt road as he walked. A short distance away, where the grass met the paved dirt, Gwen noticed the lush greenness begin to wilt and brown from the enchanted weapon as it passed nearly a meter away.

"I can't wait to wear your ears like a necklace, fae!" the human chimed.

Gwen shivered in repulsion. "Why is that always the first place you monsters go?" she muttered, more to herself than the soldier, who she didn't expect to answer.

"It's the only part of you ugly things worth sporting as a trophy," the unwanted reply came.

Shivering, Gwen struggled to crawl away from the approaching threat with the ogre child still in her arms. Again she knocked into the teetering carriage, and the shifting weight forced the strained door to pop open and spill the body of a murdered ogre male down the steps. The new weight drew a groan from the unbalanced carriage, and Gwen whimpered as she heard it begin to teeter further in her direction, threatening to roll on top of her and the child. Rolling away as the final wheel shattered under the growing weight, the fae tried to get free of the collapsing mass of wood.

*Too slow! Too slow!* she realized, already seeing that she'd never get free with the child in her arms. Still, the option to abandon him didn't flicker in her mind for a moment, and she huddled over him in the hopes that she might shield him from her fate.

Something impacted noisily overhead, and then again, softer this time, a short distance beside her.

Looking up, she saw that the tipping carriage had fallen against a few helitrad trees running along the side of the road.

The young ogre's screams rattled in her burning ears.

"Let calmness be you," she whispered, running a gentle caress along its back. "Let calmness…" she trailed off as the soldier stepped in front of her.

"Pity," he groaned, looking up at the wedged carriage, "I would've liked to see you get crushed after all that jumping around."

Gwen thought she heard a soft murmur—barely even a whisper, but something greater than a breeze—call out to her. Though the human and his awful weapon loomed over her, the call tugged to her with a more impending need, and she cast her gaze down at a fallen helitrad branch that lay on the ground beside her.

*The second impact…*

Though it was hardly as straight as one of the whittled helitrad walking sticks the length of sacred wood seemed oddly straight and sturdy compared the trees' normally gnarled and thin branches. This, along with its mother-tree stopping the falling carriage from crushing them, felt like more than just a mere coincidence to the fae. Moving to retrieve the branch, the human lunged with his sword and Gwen cried out as she frantically thrust her only means of defense towards him, already crying without fully under-standing why.

Gav's injuries felt like death without offering the soothing benefits. Prying the blade of his axe from the twisted iron and softer contents of the last soldier's stomach, he felt the full weight of his injuries. He could barely stand, and only one of his legs had been cut. His left arm hung at his side like a dead fish, numbed from the shoulder-down due to nothing more than a simple scratch—barely enough to even break the skin—that was already blackened and reeking of bad meat. Even the areas of his body that hadn't met even a simple graze from the wretched weapons, which now lay scattered beside their downed owners, burned from being too close to them.

For the first time since he'd started traveling with Gwen, he found himself in need of her expertise.

"Gwen…" the simple process of speaking felt impossible as he struggled to take in and hold a breath. Still, he struggled to call out as he pushed his shaky legs to carry him forward. "Gwen?"

The larger of the three pieces that remained of their shield cracked under his hoof, and Gav frowned down at the sight of it. He remembered the blow that had destroyed it, a simple overhead lunge from the smallest of the three soldiers, and despite the lack of actual muscle driving the attack it had been enough to instantly rot the wood of the framework and shatter through the five-layers of reinforcement that divided him from the enchanted iron. Though he hated to admit it, that shield would have been strong enough to stay off a direct blow of his axe from his own hand, but a pathetic rage-ape with less power than a newborn colt had shattered through it like it was nothing more than a clay plate.

"Hiding behind… your enchantments… and iron," he heaved angrily down at the nearest human, not caring that it was the same who'd destroyed the shield. "Cowards!"

He heard Gwen let out a sharp cry then, and the sound of her sobbing followed. Disregarding his injuries, Gav summoned the strength to close the distance, and found her under a carriage that had fallen against several tall, papery-barked trees. At the opening, he could see the only other human soldier kneeling, seeming to gaze in at her, but as her sobs grew louder and more frantic he saw that he wasn't responding; wasn't even moving. Still only able to use one arm, he struggled to move the carriage out of his path, tipping it in the opposite direction and flinching as it crumpled loudly on itself as it hit the ground, and caught sight of Gwen.

In one arm she clutched a dead baby ogre—a single wound in its chest wearing the same ugly hue as the injuries he'd sustained from the enchanted iron—and, in the other hand, she clutched one end of a tree branch.

The other end was still buried in the exposed throat of the kneeling soldier.

"I… I didn't mean to, Gav!" Gwen proclaimed between sobs, her hand, blistering from the fallen sword not far from her, shaking around the branch as though she wanted to let go of it but couldn't. "I didn't mean to!"

# NINE

Gav's first attempts to get her up and away from the dead human's sword, which still glowed toxic without its owner wielding it, proved futile. With her too far in shock to notice her body slowly dying from the nearby weapon, Gav had been forced to grab the sword's grip and throw it back towards the dead soldiers and the other swords. The awful scorch of the iron had burned even through the bound wood surrounding it and the leather of his glove. In the short time the sword had been in his hand, the enchantment had scorched through the leather of his glove and seared his palm.

Then he'd gone to work with Gwen, ignoring his own pain to try and coax the traumatized fae back to him. Over and over he told her she'd done the right thing; that she'd acted out of self-defense in the hopes of protecting herself and the young ogre. Still she stared off, repeating those same words.

"I didn't mean to."

Finally, frantic and exhausted, Gav dropped to his knees and wrapped his arms around her, repeating, just as desperate as her own repetition, that he knew she hadn't meant to.

"I know, Gwen," he whispered back to her, "I know you didn't mean to."

Over and over and over...

Hours passed, and it wasn't until the sun hung in the middle of the sky that he was able to coax the dead ogre child from Gwen's grip and finally get her to her feet. Despite the shock she still felt at having taken a life, she refused to let the branch she'd brandished against her attacker leave her hand. Understanding her need to keep the weapon close to her even if she did not, Gav made no further attempt to take it from her.

"It served you well," he told her, helping her away from the carnage-laced scene. "It will stay with you as long as you need."

"Ser-served me... well?" Gwen blinked, looking down at the branch. "Called... called to me. Gift... from Mother-Tree."

Though he didn't understand, Gav wasn't about to argue or even question what she meant by that. Whether she was still in shock or trying to explain something that was beyond his reasoning meant little; at that moment it meant something to her, and that was all that mattered.

"It's a beautiful gift," he forced a smile and, once again ignoring his injuries, he helped her onto his back and into the saddle. "Come on. We're going back to camp. There's nothing more we can do here."

Gav felt the fae's small hands move to grip the shield as she usually did, but, finding it missing, whimpered.

"Wh-where... it was here. Right here..." she sounded as if she might start crying again.

Nodding, Gav sighed. "I know. They destroyed it," he started a slow and agonizing trudge back towards their campsite. "I don't know how, but their weapons smashed through it with nothing but a single swing."

A long silence passed then, and when Gwen spoke again it was with a clarity that was almost more painful than her prior ramblings.

"What were those weapons, Gav?" she asked. "How could anybody create something so terrible?"

For the first time in Gav's life, he found himself unable to offer any answer.

Renewed guilt racked Gwen's brain after Gav had left to catch their dinner for that night.

It had taken the rest of that day's sunlight and almost all of her supplies to mend their injuries, and even then they still wore a number of aches and pains that would not soon fade. She was certain that Gav would be limping for the next few days if they were lucky. If they weren't, however…

Gwen had never seen a weapon like the swords that the humans had wielded. The effects were unlike any injury she'd ever seen or heard of; there was no way of telling how an injury like that would heal, of *if* it would heal.

The thought sent a fresh tremor of fear through her. Healing was what she knew. She repeated its mantra to herself:

Healing motivated her.

Healing elated her.

But, more than anything, healing defined her.

So what would become of everything she swore by if there was a weapon from which none who even encountered it could be healed? She'd already had purpose ripped from her, only to begin to build it again. She hadn't finished coming to grips with her new purpose in life, but already it was being challenged again, this time by something she had no reference for. Though the aftermath of that day's events was still a haze in her mind, she knew that she would not have gotten through it without Gav. While the numerous injuries that they both wore from the humans' awful enchanted iron swords spoke a great deal of how much they'd fought through, the story the cuts and burns told were still only whispers from what she could remember.

She'd killed a man.

In a single instant, though she'd never meant any harm, a life had been ended by her hand. She wondered, though, if she'd hoped that waving the branch at the human would keep him at bay long enough for Gav to save them, but that only meant she was willing to let the blood be on his hands rather than her own. All possible scenarios led back to the same result. And when she thought of the terrified child who had died in her arms, she realized—though she hated to admit it—that Gav hadn't been wrong. While she still refused to call his axe or the branch she still clung to a "cure" by any stretch of the imagination, she was sickened by two truths:

One—those humans had to die to ensure her and Gav's survival.

Two—after seeing what they'd done to the ogres' caravan, she wasn't the least bit upset that they had died.

The first truth unsettled her because it proved that, no matter how sick it made her, being a healer in this world would mean accepting that sometimes death was a solution. The second truth, however, hurt her more than anything else, because it meant that she was already to accept that first truth only after a few weeks in this world.

Whether or not they could heal from the effects of those strange new weapons, she'd suffered another blow to her character with that revelation that she wasn't certain she could recover from. Had she already become so corrupted in so short a time? Would she awake the next morning with a revised mantra:

Killing to heal motivated her.

Killing to heal elated her.

But, more than anything, killing to heal defined her.

How many more weeks would it take before healing got crossed out entirely? Would she wake up to find her entire life driven by death in the same way the humans drove themselves?

Could a fae really fall to such a low?

Guilt and fear of this variety had kept her awake every night since the first she'd spent with Gav on that hilltop. Somehow, when he was around and awake, she felt free of the burden of those thoughts, but in the moments when he was away or after he'd fallen asleep were so much different. She was able to cope with the journey to self-discovery knowing that Gav was beside her with every step. He was an anchored point of wisdom and strength that offered her room to explore without delving too far into the unknown. Somewhere beyond the light he cast, however, she sensed anger and sadness within herself that she wasn't ready to face. However, that day's tragedy was without a doubt the single worst moment she'd ever suffered through, including everything she'd experienced in the fae cells and the labyrinth. Because, no matter how many times she told Gav or herself that she hadn't meant to put that branch through the soldier's throat, she couldn't be so certain. And if that was true, then it was only a matter of time before she'd be the monster in Gav's eyes.

That, more than any other thought for some reason, terrified Gwen most of all.

The sound of clopping hooves was like torchlight in the labyrinth of her mind, chasing away the darkness and the monsters that lived there. Clarity returned as Gav stepped into the light of the fire, and she felt herself smile without telling herself to at his approach. Seeing her, he smiled back, and Gwen found herself wondering if it was as natural for him as it was for her.

Stopping on the other side of the fire, he plucked the several rabbits that he had bound with a length of twine over his shoulder. Then, after setting aside his axe, he moved to retrieve the clay cooking pot they'd been traveling with from his own pack, which held the supplies they reserved for their campsites.

"The rabbits are too small to use your axe," she speculated, "so how do you catch them?"

"Very carefully," Gav smirked as he began to prepare a stew. Dropping a few vegetables they'd picked up at a grocer the day before, he looked up and smiled again. "You're looking better. Happier, at least."

She bit her lip. "I... I was struggling with some guilt while you were gone," she admitted.

"Oh?" Gav frowned and paused to look up, "You're welcome to join me on a hunt if you'd ever rather not be alone. I only go without you because I worry about how you'd take... well, the whole hunting process."

"I think I could handle it, actually," she said, feeling a warmth spark in her cheeks as she prepared a confession. "Provided you were there with me, at least."

Gav smiled at that and nodded before returning to the vegetables. With them in the pot, he began to butcher the rabbits.

She watched as Gav finished the preparations and then set it over the fire, and she caught herself using the light to appreciate his illuminated features, something she found herself doing more and more often. As he stoked the fire, she watched as several freed embers were caught in a passing breeze wind and swirled around him like glowing specters. For a moment, she enjoyed the view, taking in the moment of both relaxation and admiration.

"Are you cold?"

His words caught her off guard and she suddenly found herself wondering what she'd been thinking about.

"N-no, the fire's helping a lot. Thank you, though," she smiled, following his movement as he circled the fire and knelt down next to her.

With his legs tucked under him and his upper body at level with hers, it was too easy to forget what he was. Though she'd been losing track of their differences more and more lately.

"How are you holding up?" he asked then. "I know it's been a rough day, and I feel like you've been keeping something bottled up."

Something in his concerned voice resounded within her, and she began to feel safer about the idea of sharing her thoughts with him. Though she didn't fully understand them herself, she suddenly realized that the thought of opening up to him didn't spark the same sense of dread it had before.

"Gwen?" Gav laid a hand on her shoulder, trying to stir her from her obviously wandering thoughts, "Are you alright?"

"I'm…" she gazed down at his hand, feeling reassured by the warmth emanating from it. "Y-yes, I'm fine," she stammered.

He must have misinterpreted her response as one of discomfort, because he was quick to remove his hand.

Gav wasn't sure what to make of Gwen's behavior. Prolonged gazes followed by seemingly forced periods of halted eye contact; extended moments of silence where she seemed lost within her own mind; and all the blushing! If it hadn't been for her skills as a healer, he might have believed she was growing ill and didn't know it. But he'd seen her identify an encroaching illness in passersby at the villages they'd visited with nothing but a single glance to go by. Surely such a precise eye for preventing and curing ailments would allow her to know if she, herself, was getting sick. Though the absurdity of the thought was blaring, it felt like the only rational thought.

Because the only other explanation was that she had started to look at him in the same way he looked at her, but that, given their differences, was an even greater absurdity. While he was hardly a novice when it came to females—having dodged more than just a few obvious advancements from the ones in his herd—he had been unable to get a handle on Gwen. She was bold where others were afraid. She was silent where others would be loud. She was considerate where others would act on their own desires. Gav relied on patterns when it came to his interactions, but Gwen followed none of the patterns he'd come to recognize. It was awkward for him to come to the conclusion that a part of him had loved her before they'd first met; the concept of such a female enticing his thoughts in ways that none of the centaurs in his herd could. And when he'd first set eyes on her, true to his sister's word, he'd been unable to see her in the same light as the rest of her species. Everything since then had only made it that much more impossible for him to deny his own thoughts, but he'd sworn an oath of protection and scaring her off with absurd proclamations of love would leave him without a herd and without a purpose.

Absurdities. Every thought he pursued ended in the absurd.

He'd never felt so stupid!

It was only when Gwen gave him that smile—that confident and knowing look that made his thoughts feel validated—that the absurdities seemed a little less absurd.

And though it felt like the most absurd plan, he was prepared to take his absurd thoughts and even more absurd feelings to the grave. To hope for anything else was…

Gav stifled the desire to groan at himself out loud.

*By the might of the Sky Galloper, let calmness be you, Gav!*

Still, as brief as it had been, the feel of her shoulder beneath his fingertips was—

*LET CALMNESS BE YOU!*

Gav shifted on his knees, favoring his right side to take the weight off his injury. As he started to lean away from Gwen, she felt a strange chill and adjusted herself to be nearer to him once again.

She thought she caught sight of him smiling at that.

"You know, you've done surprisingly well all things considered," he said.

She felt her right ear twitch, and she saw his smile widen. "Oh?" she pouted, "And what does that mean?"

"I just meant that I'm impressed. No matter what's happened, you have been able to handle the situations thrown at you. Not many can react so fluidly in the face of chaos, but you just keep rising to challenges that others would buckle at the thought of." He smiled and looked back at her, "For someone who hadn't a clue of the outside world, you've adapted better than I'd have ever expected."

Gwen's cheeks burned hotter than she'd ever remembered. "Th-that's mostly thanks to you though," she looked down, "I was only pretending in the tunnels, and every second I've spent out here has been thanks to you saving me in the first place, Gav. I never could've made it this far on my own."

Gav scoffed and shook his head. "That's nonsense! For starters, pretending to be brave in the face of danger is what bravery is all about, and even if you were only pretending I'd never seen Bowen as injured as he was when I arrived."

Gwen blushed. "He was a lot more injured after you were done with him," she chuckled. A moment passed before she realized that she'd found humor in the pain of another creature, and the guilt and panic returned.

124

"It was nothing he won't recover from, I promise you," Gav said, seeming to read her mind. "I've only been here to help. I wasn't the one who pushed you to help the elf, I wasn't the one who knew what to get from the villages and how to help any of the others we've found along the way," he smiled. "That was all you."

The fires of Gwen's guilt roared as hot as the blush in her cheeks at Gav's praise, and she was certain if she didn't confess her burden it would burn her from the inside-out.

"I think I…" she choked on the words at first and gulped a fresh lungful of air before trying again. "Do you feel that I ruined both our lives?"

She blinked for a moment, startled by the words that had spilled from her own mouth. While it hadn't been the confession she'd meant to utter, it somehow didn't feel like the wrong one.

Gav's face lost its smile and, with it, the warmth and friendly glow to his cheeks that had grown since vanished. For the first time since their first night on the hilltop, he seemed driven by nothing more than strength and wisdom; absolute sincerity.

"How could you ask me that?" he sounded genuinely insulted, but before Gwen could offer an apology he'd continued: "I… I felt trapped with the herd. My being a *vernunt* was like a wall that never let me truly be a part of them. I'd stare at sky while the others galloped in the fields. I'd question morality while others questioned which females would make the best mates. And while everyone expected me to fill some predetermined role that I couldn't bring myself to understand, I found myself feeling guilty for not being like them. I tried to pretend it was them—questioning Alastair on their savagery so that I didn't have to accept how wrong I felt for not fitting in—but I knew the truth all along: I didn't belong there with them."

He sighed and shook his head. "Do I feel that you ruined both our lives?" he repeated, seeming even more disgusted by them then. "Is that what you believe, Gwen? Truly? In your heart of hearts? Because I chose to make my life better the day I raced into that labyrinth to save the beautiful fae with the hair like leaves in the Autumn Equinox who had disregarded the savagery of her people by saving my sister, and I've never felt more alive than I have since that day. And you!" he laughed and looked up at the starry night sky, "There are so many under this very sky who owe their continued lives to you. People you've never met see you in the distance and remember songs about your kindness written by poets we might never meet!" Looking back at her, Gwen felt a sudden wave of cold as she saw that he looked angry at her, "Ruined lives? Gwen, everything about who you are is dedicated to making lives better; mine and yours included!" He shook his head, and the smile began to creep back into place. "You weren't exiled by the fae, you freed yourself from the walls that were holding you back," then, with his familiar warm smile back in place, he reached out and touched her cheek.

Gwen couldn't contain herself as she leaned into the warmth of his palm, letting herself fully enjoy the sensation. So many nights had been plagued by doubt and fear and the certainty that she was falling victim to corruption when the wisest person she had ever met saw so much more clearly who she was. While she was worried about finding herself, he'd seen her as she'd always wanted to be seen. This beautiful centaur had taken a future she'd looked upon with dread and turned it into a future without a fear of tainted mantras or dark thoughts. He'd helped her see the horrors of the single worst moment she'd ever suffered through earlier that day for what they were:

Another challenge they'd survived together.

He'd taken weeks of doubt and secrets and in a single instant given her the promise of the first peaceful night she'd see in nearly a month! Her eyes found his and she allowed herself to believe that there was something more between them.

"Not so absurd after all…" he spoke so quietly that Gwen could barely hear, but something in his words told her that he'd felt the same way.

How many nights had they wasted doubting themselves?

With the intoxicating aroma of Gav's stew rolling along a gentle gust of wind, he moved his hand to stir the pot. Even with his touch lifted, she still felt the warmth as though it never left. She couldn't help the attraction she had for Gav and she wasn't going to try any longer to stop herself from feeling it. Especially now that she knew he felt it, too.

# TEN

G wen sighed, walking beside Gav as they set out for the
last village they'd visited. Though it was a long journey
to backtrack, they agreed it was a necessary one, neither
knowing when they might come across another village nor
certain that it would be as large as the last. While the size
of a village had never swayed them prior to that moment,
they sought to find out as much as they could about the
humans.

The night before, after falling asleep nestled between the
groove of Gav's two backs, Gwen's dreams had been filled
with his speech as it cycled over the vision of her helitrad
branch passing through the human soldier's neck. Though
she couldn't bring herself to feel any pride at the life she'd
taken, her dream had warped and expanded until the ogre
child in her arms was every creature she'd ever saved or met
in their travels and the soldier had become a vast army. As
the vision of an end to all life at the hands of a human force
armed with their enchanted iron, she once again felt the

helitrad branch meet her grip and a voice asking if she'd still react as she had before.

*Could you kill him to heal the world?* it demanded. *Would you kill him to save them all?*

She'd awoken at that moment, wondering if the voice had been Gav's or her own.

Still trying to answer the question to herself, she'd told Gav of the dream and said that, while she couldn't bear the thought of being the hand of death again, she knew that they had to be stopped.

That was when the decision to return to the last village and its vast population was made, and their awkward, bitter-sweet journey began. It was, though without much need for words, a walk that found either of them finding whatever excuse they could to touch the other. It started innocently with a series of casual nudges, but as they grew more comfortable with the contact it grew upon itself until Gav settled his arm around Gwen's shoulders. Then, feeling at peace with this, she closed the already short distance and leaned against his leather-clad chest as they pressed on.

The village was quick to welcome them back, celebrating their return as a reflection of the greatness they'd worked to build. Neither of the two had the heart to say otherwise, and so they were forced to play the parts of the returning heroes for several hours as admirers returned to shake their hands a second time or recite a story with a slightly altered arrangement. More gifts and praise were offered, and with every attempt to refuse the former they were bathed in more of the latter and then given even more gifts for their humility. Several of the villagers—women and elders, it seemed—saw something new between them and offered, along with any intended gifts or praise, a knowing smile and a coy smirk. Though she wasn't sure why, Gwen received those small gestures with the greatest sense of pride, because it was the only thing in which she felt any pride to begin with. Though it was certainly earning her an ample following, she didn't want to heal for the glory. It was to her as natural as the swimming fish or the flying bird, and surely neither of them did what they did for pride. Her and Gav's newfound feelings, however, was something she wanted to shout from rooftops. Those few who recognized it for what it was to let on that it show gave her the gift of renewing it again and again for her, and that she carried more happily than another clay pot or an enchanted brooch or a new dagger in exchange for what she happily did for free.

Realizing that they were taking time from helping by accepting tokens for other times they'd helped, Gwen finally found a way to steer the excitement towards something more productive. Though trying to break free from the crowd to conduct their interviews had proven several times to be futile, it seemed that the crowd eagerly hushed and calmed at the promise of some retelling of one of their encounters. Noticing this, she and Gav began to tell the villagers of their encounter the day before, sparing the more gruesome details while being sure to let them know that there were gruesome details to be left out. As the crowd followed their story, reliving every horrible instant, the whispers began. The whispers became murmurs, which turned into statements, and before long they had the villagers sharing facts they'd never considered to be useful.

"I heard that the humans that used to roam about the North-Western region took the great Northern mountains."

"The mountains? Oh, yes! They were seen there, but many more than just the few from the north-west. They said there were thousands! As if every one of them decided to flock off!"

"Thousands? In the North? No, no! Not with those mountains! Nothing but dwarves brave enough to travel those! No, the humans wouldn't risk heading north. They all went east!"

"East leads to the sea, and only elven ships stand a chance against the Eastern Tide."

Yes! Yes! Did you not hear about the fleet of ships they stole? There was a small navy of elves in the pub only a few years ago grousing about the loss."

"Really? I heard it was west? And weren't the ships those of the fae?"

"No chance! The fae keep their ships walled off, just ask Gwen!"

"Yes, I heard west."

"I heard say they robbed a gremlin town of all its machines. With those they could travel by any sorts of means. By land, by sea, even by air!"

"Mad! Yer mad! The gremlins have no such machines, and not nothing but the birds can travel by air! Yer mad, I say!"

"Travel all that way by foot then?"

"Aye, but not wit'out stirring up a bit o' trouble as they did. Pillaged ev'ry home if mem'ry serves."

"No, you fool! The pillaging was the goblins' doing! My brother-in-law said he saw a bunch of the wretched beasts shadowing the humans as they headed north!"

"Had an elf leading them, I hear."

"Why by the sacred gems would any want to lead or shadow the humans? The humans bring death to everything in their path, and the only thing that follows those critters is even more death! Any who choose to try stand with 'em—leading or following—is sure to find exactly that: death!"

Before long the facts, if they could be called that, turned to theories and then arguments, none of which served the needs that the two were after. The only thing that anybody seemed to be sure of was that just prior to the human's sudden uprising there was some sort of convergence that drove them to travel. Without a direction or a means or a reason, however, Gwen and Gav had no place to start. And with no place to start, they had no way of stopping another massacre like the one of the ogres' caravan from taking place.

Discouraged, the two finally slipped free from the crowd as the villagers' passions shifted from idol praise to idle banter. Certain they'd spent the bulk of the day traveling all the way back for nothing but a few new trinkets and some freshly swelled egos, Gwen felt the looming demand of her dream begin to gnaw at her again.

*Could you kill him to heal the world?*
*Would you kill him to save them all?*

The questions boiled in her mind and it wasn't until Gav gripped her shoulder to still her that she saw a short, stout, and very old man standing to the side of the road beside a cart covered with all manner of tools. Studying the contents more closely, she spotted several devices that she recognized only as mining gear, but the rest of it was a mystery to her. The man stared back at her as she returned from her thoughts, his round face furrowing occasionally around a nose that seemed too big for the rest of him. Realizing she'd almost walked straight into the cart she began to apologize, wondering to herself if the cart was meant to sell the old man's wares or if it was simply a means of transporting his own supplies. As she apologized, his eyes—which seemed hidden under the rolls of his sinking forehead and a pair of wide, wire-rimmed spectacles that by some miracle hung from his too-low, pointy ears—raised along with a pair of bushy brows.

"Are ye the fae an' centaur all them idjits keep babbling about?" his voice reminded Gwen of a crow's call. "I say, I've heard jus' about enough of their hero worship! No work ethic! No responsibility! Tell you what—wouldn't need no saving from nobody if they learned to do what's right! Don't know rights from lefts any longer, I keep saying…"

As the old man's rambling rolled on, Gwen leaned close to Gav.

"What is he?" she whispered.

"A dwarf," Gav frowned at his own answer. "Though I've never seen one quite so… uh, matured, and it's unusual for them to stand out in open spaces. Typically they prefer small places—caves and tunnels and the like. It's why they usually take jobs as prison guards or miners; puts them in their element while giving them an outlet for their aggressions."

"Miners…?" Gwen bit her lip, looking back at the contents of the old dwarf's cart.

"See? That's what I'm talkin' about right there! Whisperin' an' plottin' while an old man is standin' right in front of ya an' talkin' some sense! Ya got somethin' ta say, long-ears, ya say it to me!"

"I'm… I'm sorry," Gwen made a show of bowing as she apologized. The dwarf, seeming pleased with this, puffed out his broad chest as she straightened. "I meant no insult, I'm just very new to… well, all of this, actually."

"Yes, yes," the dwarf waved away the explanation with a small, pudgy hand, "I've heard all about you. Fae girl left that box of a city and out seein' the world for the first time with a hoof-man." He nodded to Gav and smirked, "Can't imagine there's too many pairs like you two gallivantin' around!"

He laughed at his own joke, and Gwen, hoping to keep him in high spirits, laughed as well.

Gav stared down at him.

As the laughter subsided into a few dry, labored coughs from the old dwarf, Gwen cleared her throat and spoke carefully.

"Maybe you can help us," Gwen paused, trying to figure out the best way to ask. "As I'm sure you've heard, we've been traveling for some time now, trying to help as many as we can. But the other day we were attacked—nearly killed, in fact!—by some human soldiers with—"

"Humans, huh?" the dwarf grumbled, shaking his head. "Ugly things, those humans; like bald dogs, I always said!"

another laugh, "Jus' like bald dogs! Got a taste for iron, though, those ones; those bald dogs just love their iron. But they turn the ore ugly, you see, real ugly. Iron's not bad when it's in the ground, not bad at all, but when those ugly, bald dogs get their grimy mitts on the stuff… well well well, that's when things get real ugly. Ol' mine used to be teemin' with the ore—not hurtin' nobody no way—but then they got into the mountain. Not on it, mind ya, but *in* it! One day that whole place is teemin' with iron ore, an' the next there's all sorts of a wicked racket going on down there—never heard nothing like it nowhere!—an' then the next day it was all gone; no iron ore left! Nothin' but gems an' diamonds."

Gwen shook her head and asked, "How could the humans possibly get into the mountain and mine *that* much iron so quickly?"

"D'ya think we meant t'ask 'em that all polite-like, long-ears? Them ugly, bald dogs made an entire mountain's belly roar and ya think any o' us dared to wonders *how*? Are ye daft? We was happy to *not* know, we was! An' after it all went real nice an' quiet there was nothin' but gems an' diamonds left! We all thought the bald dogs had done us a favor—takin' all the ore and leavin' all the pretties like they'd done—but then we started seein' the Winter Sun startin' to rise, an' that damn dawn—like somethin' outta the worst kinda darkness, I tell ya—done woke up one fury of a dragon. An' let me tell ya, long-ears, that dragon might'a been a big, scary beastie, but she like us—jus' like us, y'hear?—an' she flew as far from that Winter Sun as her wings could carry her." The old dwarf sighed and shook his head, pausing to mop a glistening spot from his forehead. "Turns out her ol' wings could only carry her as far as the mine—our mine—and we had to choose 'tween the pretties the bald dogs left in the mountain and savin' our own skins from the damned dragon the ugly, bald dogs chased away with that Winter Sun! Like I always said, those humans are ugly; uglier on the inside, though. Bald dogs on the outside, but somethin' far, far uglier underneath."

"A dragon?" Gav frowned, shaking his head, "In the mountains? You mean the Northern Mountain range?"

"Ain't ya been listenin', clip-clop? Them mines was *ours* b'fore the humans came in under it and took all 'er ore! Then their Winter Sun—"

"What is the Winter Sun?" Gwen blurted, frowning and immediately apologizing for interrupting before the old dwarf could begin ranting again.

"Ain't no soul nowhere knows what the Winter Sun is. Kept thinkin' it was a second sunrise—blue as ice; s'why they call it 'Winter Sun,' I suppose, heard a few of the bald dogs call it that while we was hidin' in the mines. But the damn thing ain't like no sun nobody ever saw! It never rises, y'see; jus' hangs there on the horizon in the north! But whatever it is, it was enough to scare a dragon our way, an' when a dragon comes yer way, ya run! I ran—packed up my ol' minin' cart"—he gave the cart a few slaps for emphasis then—"and hobbled down off that ore-stripped mountain. Let the dragon have it, I say; lay 'er eggs and make a nest of it, if that's what makes her happy. That's what I say, least; long as she ain't down here. Not much else place to run to, these days." He raised a bushy brow at Gwen then and chuckled, "Maybe those fae granddaddies of yours had the right idea, huh?"

"Yes," Gwen looked down, trying to make sense of the stream of cawing thoughts they'd just listened to. "Perhaps they did…"

"Thank you for sharing your story," Gav nodded to the dwarf before taking Gwen's hand and hurrying off with her.

After he'd put some distance between them and the old dwarf, he glanced back at her and took in a deep breath.

Gwen blushed, seeing a glimmer of something that she nervously recognized as fear.

"Gav…" she laid a hand on his chest. "Did anything he said make any sense to you?"

"More than I'd have liked, actually," he admitted. "Listen, I know you're serious about this, Gwen, but this sounds like something we don't stand a chance of standing against. If we head into those mountains in search of answers, we need to be prepared for the terrible possibility that there *are* answers to be found up there. I don't know what in that tale was the exaggerations of an old man and what was the Sky Gallopers sincerest truth, but whatever the Winter Sun is sounds a lot like the swords those soldiers attacked us with, and that makes at least that detail a strong possibility." Gav shivered and Gwen felt a chill at the sight of such a strong, wise creature succumbing to the effects of fear. "An entire sunrise's worth of that enchanted iron, can you imagine?" he shivered again.

*Could you kill him to heal the world?*
*Would you kill him to save them all?*

"Unfortunately I can," Gwen whimpered, burying her face into Gav's chest. "But if the humans have that sort of weapon, I have to try to stop them."

She felt Gav nod against her.

"Then I guess I have to try to stop them, too," he said, wrapping his arms around her.

# ELEVEN

Though centuries of mining and nomadic travel had created a path into and through the Northern mountain range, it was by no means an easy journey. What many had taken to simply calling 'The Mountain' was, in fact, a system of three larger mountains—the tallest of which jutted out from between the other two—and two smaller ones that framed the mass on either side. Gav had heard a legend that the natural barrier between their long, narrow continent and the treacherous, northernmost region had once actually been a single, far larger mountain. According the legend, it had been the setting of a battle between two dragons thousands of years earlier, and it was during this battle that the bulk of the mountain was shattered and it crumbled into what it had since become. Gav wasn't one for putting faith in legends that he couldn't also put evidence towards, but as he and Gwen started towards the valley that fed into the "entrance" of the mountain's safest path, the sight of the vast peaks nearly felt like evidence enough.

"You're sure that you want to do this?" he asked again.

Gwen nodded, staring up at the mountain range, as well. "As long as you're with me, I know I can do it," her voice, though a whisper, was still as strong as ever.

Gav nodded back, though he found himself wondering how it was that she could attribute her bravery as somehow being his doing.

She truly was a dream come to life.

Gwen shivered as they started down between the tight corridor of rock that, according to a troll they'd passed nearby, would open up into a valley. There, the troll had explained, they'd find a path—marked by many years of miners' carts coming and going—that led up the side of the mountain. While this wasn't necessarily the fastest route, he'd said, it was certainly the safest.

"So what's the fastest route?" Gav had asked, seeming more curious than interested in other options.

The troll laughed at the question and disregarded it with a shrug. "Why, flying it, of course!"

Once again Gwen let her eyes drift higher and higher...

And higher.

*If only...* Gwen thought.

Gav offered early on to let her ride on his back as they traversed the terrain, but the thought seemed unfair. The past few weeks had been spent with Gwen seeing him as more and more of an equal, and now that they'd revealed their feelings for one another the idea of treating him like an animal in any way repulsed her. Were he any other sort of creature, she realized, her feelings would remain, and then she'd still be forced to walk beside him. Even then, his morality had compelled him to urge her to stay to his left so that she would be as far from the cliff-side as possible. The gesture, though touching, was also refused as Gwen pointed out that, her lightweight fae body and natural agility not-withstanding, if there should be any weak spots in the edge of the path his size would be certain to drag him over the edge in a landslide. Clearly displeased with this but unable to argue against it, Gav had begrudgingly taken his place on the inside of the path.

"So what do you think we're going to find?" Gwen asked, shivering as a cold mountain wind passed.

Gav shook his head. "I'm not sure," he admitted. "There doesn't seem to be much sign of anything living up here—human or dragon or otherwise—so I suppose the most we can hope for is some sign of the humans' empire on the other side of this range."

Gwen bit her lip nervously, "And the Winter Sun?"

"If such a thing truly exists," Gav said, keeping his eyes straight on the path, "I'd never go so far as to say I'd hope to see it."

Though Gwen didn't say it, she couldn't help but to agree with him. They walked on then without a word, and she enjoyed how comfortable, even in silence, being with Gav could be. Even in such dreadful conditions. Unable to keep from smiling at this thought, she leaned her head against his chest and let his warmth chase away the bitterness of the mountain chill. Their hands met then, and she marveled at how his seven fingers perfectly enveloped her five; his thumb following the curve of her wrist and gently rubbing the back of her hand. Feeling calm and content despite the possible danger they were walking towards, she smiled and cast her gaze out at the scenery overlooking the mountain. From their vantage point, the roaming forests and occasional villages—many of which they'd visited—looked so beautiful; so peaceful. Seeing it like that, Gwen felt her commitment to do everything she could to protect it renew itself.

She was so engrossed in the scenery and the thoughts it inspired that she didn't even realize it when they'd finally reached the top.

"What is that?" Gav whispered, his hand slipping free of hers as he stepped away.

Frowning, Gwen turned to follow his gaze. Before she could see whatever it was he saw she was suddenly aware of how unnaturally warm it felt up there. The entire time they'd been walking she'd been huddling for warmth as icy winds kicked up every few seconds, but it was as if the wind and the cold it carried had suddenly decided to stop the moment they reached the top. And though she was willing to believe that the shape of the mountain had been funneling the gusts around them, what she couldn't explain was the warmth that seemed to welcome them. It was like there was some strange source of energy heating the entire mountain's surface. This, however, didn't concern her enough to distract her from whatever Gav had seen.

All she saw at first was rocks and a jutting mountain wall along the eastern side of the peak that tapered off in an angry-looking point. To her left, nearer to the south-side of the mountain and overlooking the entrance of path far below, was a cluster of rocks that seemed to have been stacked into some sort of crude pyramid. Those, she realized, were a different color than the rest of the rocks along the peak, and as she looked closer she realized that it appeared that that entire portion of the mountain range had been somehow stained; a strange blackness that was somehow integrated into that area seeming to have long since settled into the rock. Not far from that, Gwen spotted a twisted and blackened length of iron with a crude hilt jutting from one end.

*What in the world...*

Gav, kneeling over the discoloration, dragged a finger across the area, seeing it come back clean.

"It's not soot," he said, sniffing at his finger and cringing, "but it does reek of sulfur."

"What could have done that?" Gwen asked as she started towards him.

"I'm not sure," he said, turning and looking down at the misshapen hunk of iron. Raising an eyebrow at it, he moved a leg to kick at it.

"Gav, don't!" Gwen warned.

"Don't worry," he said, letting his foot tap it for show. "It's iron alright, but it's... dead." As if he hadn't made the point enough, he brought his hoof down on it and Gwen stared in amazement as it shattered and split into two pieces. "See? Nothing more than a cold shell."

Gwen nodded slowly.    "Iron's not bad when it's in the ground," she repeated to herself, then, to Gav: "Do you think that's the iron the old dwarf was talking about?"

Gav shook his head, poking at the hilt on one of the piece's end. "Not likely. This thing might be *like* the ore the old coot was going on about, but it was forged at least once."

Nodding again, Gwen turned away and examined the rest of their surroundings. From where they stood—not far from where the path from the south-side led—she could barely see to the opposite end, which overlooked the northern territory. The humans' territory, if the old dwarf's story was accurate. The vast space, what Gwen imagined was once a bustling site for the dwarf miners, now felt all the more lonely with just how little there was. Just stained rocks, mountain range, and...

"Is that... an egg?" her eyes widened as the setting sun cast its light at a new angle and illuminated what she'd previously thought to be a large rock.

Gav turned at that, clearly as stunned by the possibility as she was.

"It... it certainly *looks* like one..." he answered, and she could hear the disbelief in his own voice. "But that's not..."

141

His doubt wasn't his alone. While the giant, white orb was certainly smoother than any other rock they'd seen on that mountain. And it appeared to have scales.

And... hair?

Gwen and Gav cautiously approached the bizarre object, taking in the scale-like pattern running along its length and the mass of long, silver-white strands that hung over one side. As they drew closer, Gwen felt the warmth intensify and she realized that the source of the strange energy she'd been feeling was coming from inside of it.

Arriving at it only a few paces ahead of Gav, she reached out with a shaky hand. Behind her, she could hear Gav plant his hooves and the familiar sound of him drawing his axe from his back. Knowing that he was ready for whatever might happen, Gwen felt her nerves calm and the shakiness in her hand subsided. Then, still moving slowly, she rested her hand along the smooth surface. Though it had appeared to have a series of scales from a distance, she saw, or rather felt, that it was completely smooth, and the pattern they'd seen was actually *under* the surface. Moving her hand up the side of it, she felt the heat shift in response.

"There's definitely life inside of it," she whispered.

Gav clapped his hoof against the mountaintop. "That's what I'm afraid of."

Gwen's hand moved upward, marveling at how every touch seemed to echo a new wave of energy. As she reached the hair-like strands hanging from the top, she felt another pulsing wave of heat—hotter this time—and she wondered if the strands were somehow keeping the egg incubated.

"I don't understand how it could have survived up here like this all on its own," she said, rolling the strands between her fingers before giving them a gentle tug.

Another wave of heat emanated, and Gwen cried out as it felt like she'd been burned. Starting to yank her hand away, the egg shifted and a pale-white arm shot forward and grabbed hold of her wrist.

"That... hurt!" a gravelly voice emanated from the egg.

"GWEN!" Gav started to lunge forward.

"I wouldn't do that!" the voice warned and the grip on Gwen's wrist tightened, causing her to cry out and stilling Gav in mid-lunge.

Awestruck, Gwen watched as the smooth surface of the egg shifted—rolling like a stretching muscle—and revealed what she'd originally thought to be an eggshell to be flesh. The strands rolled back as the gentle curvature straightened into a back and the base of a neck and... a head? A pair of bright-orange eyes with a pair of diamond-shaped pupils took her in, a secondary set of lids blinking over their unforgiving gaze before the more familiar set of eyelids dropped. When they'd opened again, the pupils were narrow, angry slits that looked past Gwen and burned towards Gav.

"Is the egg hatching?" Gav asked, sounding frantic.

Gwen gawked, marveling at the sight. "I... I'm not sure."

The pale man flexed as he finished uncurling his body from the egg-like orb they'd discovered him as. Joints groaned within him and he grimaced with a few of the noisier pops before he used his free hand to sweep the length of white hair out of his face.

Gwen whimpered at the ferocious gaze that danced between her and Gav. Again and again she felt the roll of heat, as if every move he made radiated with some inner fire.

"Let... her... go!" Gav growled, stomping his hoof. Though she couldn't see him, Gwen was certain he was making a show of his axe for emphasis.

The pale-white hand released Gwen then, though she had a hard time believing it was because of Gav's threat, and she hurried back to join the snarling centaur at his side.

The man, despite his small, lean form and long, skinny limbs, seemed unafraid of Gav's display, and even made a note of taking a long, threatening step towards them.

"Who are you?" he demanded, his voice a scalding-hot hiss that carried the threat of becoming an explosive roar. "What are you doing here?"

"We could ask the same of you, egg-head!" Gav seethed, holding his massive axe forward in a single, outstretched hand.

The pale man chuckled, and Gwen noticed his right shoulder twitch several times. As he finished he let out a long exhale, and a small plume of pale smoke rolled past his lips. "By the stars! A centaur with a creative flare in my presence! I feel so... *privileged*!" a wave of nearly unbearable heat coursed across the mountaintop then, forcing both Gwen and Gav to take a step away from him. "However, privileged or not, you seem to forget yourselves. I'll admit that I'm not one for interactive excursions, and, as you can see, I'm hardly the sort to entertain company. However, despite my *limited*"—another wave of heat and another forced step back—"prowess for social graces, even I know it's rude to storm into another person's home and make demands and..." he took another moment to assess Gav's full frame before letting out a soft chuckle, "*incredibly* idle threats."

"Show you an idle threat," Gav growled, stepping forward then only to have another blast of heat force him back again.

The man cocked his head. "I thought the creative ones were supposed to be armed with a brain to back it up." He frowned then, seeming to be suddenly saddened, and turned away. "I'm not interested in company, so if you could both—"

"The humans!" Gwen blurted out, afraid that they might be cast away from the only clue they had. "We... we want to stop them! We've heard that they have a new weapon—an awful weapon—and we want to stop whatever they have planned before it's too late!"

Gav sighed and nodded, making a show of returning his axe to his back, though Gwen could see he was still ready to attack at a moment's notice. "We aren't here to harm you, dragon. We didn't even expect to find anybody still living up here. We just wanted to get a glimpse of the northern region and see if we couldn't get a glimpse of whatever it is the humans have built up there."

The man glared at Gav, his eyes flaring up like stoked embers before he shook his head—an action that looked more like somebody shaking out a fire than rejecting a thought.

"It's already too late," he answered, crouching down and beginning to curl back into to his egg-like shape.

"We can't allow ourselves to accept that!" Gwen stepped forward, feeling Gav's tension rising behind her as she once again approached the strange man. "I watched only a few humans butcher an entire caravan of ogres—men, women, and children! All of them!—with nothing more than these awful, glowing swords! That was four humans! *Four*! And we heard that there's so many more with something even more awful on the other side of this mountain," she pointed off towards the north with a shaking hand. "To accept that it's too late is to accept a life waiting for them to destroy everything; to kill everyone."

The egg-man uncurled again and, still crouching, looked up at her. "Everything is destroyed," he said with a smirk, "and everything dies... in time. Do you mean to stand in the way of the only certainty to ever exist?"

"I'm a healer!" Gwen spat, "Everything I believe in centers around avoiding death and pushing for more time!"

"Then you're the worst sort of fool:" the man spat back, "the sort that wastes her life denying that it has to eventually end!"

Gav let out a loud, angry sigh. "Just because death and destruction are a certainty doesn't mean that a person can't have the choice to fight it! Even you were quick to stay my axe when it was aimed for you, dragon; if you believe what you say then accept your own inevitable fate and let me take your head!"

The man started to laugh at that, but, after another rigorous head shake, looked upon Gav with an angry scowl. "I am no dragon, centaur, and my fate—inevitable though it may be—is far worse than a simple death."

Gwen frowned at that. "What could be worse than death…?" she wondered aloud.

"Not a dragon?" Gav narrowed his eyes, "But you emerged from the egg? Was it not a dragon's?"

"It *is* a dragon's egg," he corrected, "and I didn't emerge from it, I *am* it!"

"What does that mean?" Gwen frowned.

"I am a dragon's egg. My flesh is the proverbial shell, and the dragon's spawn grows within me, waiting to get strong enough to finally…" he sighed and shook his head.

"To finally hatch," Gav finished for him, shaking his head. "Your life is nothing more than a walking, talking incubator to a monster? So one day you'll just tear open and let a death-bringer into the world?"

Gwen's eyes widened. *A fate worse than death…*

The dragon egg looked as though he were about to go into a rage, but after a long, tense moment he forced out a slow breath and glanced at Gwen. "A healer, you say?" he nodded towards Gav, "Is the sort of bedside manner your patients get to look forward to? Telling them the horrible news they already know just to make sure their insides hurt as bad as their outsides?"

"What's this talk of 'hurting,'" Gav demanded, "aren't you supposed to be thrilled about your role?"

146

"Do you truly believe the egg awaits the chick's arrival with excitement, centaur?" the man asked, rising out of his crouched position to meet his full height. "Do you think that I'll continue some sort of life after the beast has clawed its way from my guts? I am not the dragon; the dragon is not me! I am a placeholder for something terrible; a reliquary for death incarnate! I am the envelope containing a dreadful message; the container for extinction! Nobody remembers the container! Nobody mourns its loss!" The heat across the mountaintop intensified as and began to advance on Gav. "Do you understand, centaur? Does this sound like a thrilling role to you? The so-called life of an egg cursed with self-awareness?"

Though he stood menacingly before Gav, neither made a move to attack or distance themselves from the other.

"The offer still remains," Gav spoke in a low, calm tone, "if you would like me to take your head off."

"If I believed that the thing inside of me wouldn't set your body ablaze before you had the chance to drop your axe," the egg replied in the same fashion, "I might actually let you try."

"Please…" Gwen stepped between the two, "I don't like this tension." She looked at the pale-skinned man and nodded, "We didn't mean any harm or offense. We just didn't understand." Then, turning to Gav, she laid a hand on his chest, "I know you mean well, but I truly believe that he fears his fate. Be kind."

Looking into her eyes, Gav noticeably relaxed and nodded, taking a step back and offering a bow of his head. "My apologies."

The pale man, upon hearing that, also relaxed and crouched down again.

"What is your name?" Gwen asked, not wanting to call him "egg" any longer.

He looked up at her then, seeming confused by the question.

"My name?" he asked.

Gwen nodded, "Yes, your name. What is it?"

He looked down. "Nobody names eggs."

Gwen crouched down beside him, "They do when the egg walks and talks and has feelings."

He frowned at that and looked at Gav. "You seem to have a mind for this sort of conundrum, centaur? What do you think of this?"

Gav smirked and shrugged, "I think that the fae has an awful habit of making painfully obvious points that aren't always what you want to hear to easily wallow in misery."

He frowned. "You speak from your own experience?"

"I do," Gav nodded. "She's ruined many of my own miserable thoughts. I've found it's easier to just accept it."

"I see…" he looked back at Gwen, who was already smiling from Gav's words. Sighing at her beaming face, he rolled his fire-bright eyes. "Merciful darkness… fine! Call me… call me Blay. If you must!"

Gwen smiled wider and stood, nodding. "Nice to make your acquaintance, Blay. I'm Gwen, and this handsome brute is Gav."

Blay only nodded at the painfully belated and awkward greeting.

"So is this your home? How did you get up here anyway? An old dwarf miner said that a dragon chased them from this mountain years ago, but nobody's seen much else since."

Blay nodded. "It's been several years since I first found myself up here."

"Several years?" Gwen's eyes widened, "How could you survive up here on your own for that long?"

"And without hatching?" Gav added. Both Gwen and Blay gave him a look and he shrugged an apology.

148

"It's *because* I've stayed up here that I've yet to hatch," Blay explained. "The dragon inside me craves death and destruction to grow stronger. I can't imagine dragon mothers are good caregivers—cold and scaly and destructive to just about anything they touch—so I suppose laying eggs that care for themselves is the next best thing. If there's danger nearby, the egg will move itself. If conditions aren't perfect, it will seek better ones. But while the birds' eggs might rely on time and heat to hatch, dragons are more demanding. Not a day goes by that I don't feel the urge to leap from this mountain and torch the entire countryside, and for every corpse I leave upon the ground and every acre I turn to ash I know the dragon will grow stronger. I've taken some liberties—walking the streets of the nearest village to enjoy some real food and drink or listen to the scholars argue over their tea—but if I stay too long the urge to destroy it all grows too strong. So I always return to this place so that I might prolong the life I know."

"You purposefully withhold power from the dragon inside you so that you can go on living?" Gav smirked, nodding. "I have to admit, that is impressive. It can't be easy to control those sorts of impulses."

"You have no idea..." Blay nodded solemnly. "More often than not, when the urge gets too strong, I look off to that side of the mountain, though," he motioned off to the north. "You say that you're up here to see if you can't stop the humans, and believe me when I say I've dreamt of the day when I might free all of my rage upon them. I hate them, I truly do, but more than that I feel a deep terror for that place—a terror that's held me at bay and reaches deeper than my bones."

"Can an egg have bones?" Gav asked, offering another apology when Gwen shot him a look.

Surprisingly enough, though, Blay laughed at his comment.

"Why do you hate the humans, Blay?" Gwen asked.

"Honestly? I don't know," Blay answered. "I've never met one, and I've certainly never gone to *that* side of the mountain. I've just felt nothing but hate and fear for the ones that live with that ugly blue glow."

Blay, though passive about it, agreed to let the two stay until after nightfall to see the "ugly blue glow." Though neither said a word, both Gwen and Gav exchanged a knowing glance at the mention of what they were certain was the "Winter Sun" the old dwarf had spoken of. After that, while the three waited for sunset so that the glow would be visible from the peak, they spoke more of the humans and their strange rise to power. Gwen was sure that everyone felt that it was needless parroting of hearsay and rumors, but it offered a sense of comfort to have somebody to talk to—most of all for Blay, she was sure—and none of them seemed to mind that. It was clear, however, that Gav still didn't trust him, though, and it was hard to blame him for being cautious. Like him, she could feel that he was lonely, and she knew all too well that pain like that had the potential to turn into something dangerous if left to fester on its own. The reasons for his forced isolation seemed rational, but only on the surface. An egg that did not want to hatch *would* resist the process that led to its hatching, but this was no ordinary egg. Though his beautiful pale skin and his strange sleeping habit certainly gave him the appearance of one, it was impossible to look at Blay—listen to him talk and watch him move—and not instantly see him as something else. Like the fae and the few elves she'd met, he was extremely beautiful, though he more closely resembled a carved statue because of his whiteness. Not even the elves could match that hue with their own pale skin. Granted, he looked enough like any other creature to be able to pass unnoticed through their villages during his excursions out of the mountain, but that could reflect more on the villagers' lack of perception than it could Blay's ability to blend in with a crowd. At least he knew to dress the part, sporting a pair of black elven leggings, which Gav explained were traditionally worn under armor to prevent chafing, and a pair of dwarf mining boots. Upon closer examination, Gwen realized that the boots didn't even belong to the same pair, however. Though he kept his back and torso exposed, allowing him to crouch into his egg form, it was not uncommon for others to dress in the same fashion during the warmer seasons.

So while he could certainly *look* the part and, thanks to his fascination with listening to intellectuals, *speak* the part, he'd still chosen to isolate himself...

Gwen frowned at the thought, trying to decide if it was better for an egg with such a dangerous cargo to keep itself from hatching but risk its own control or throw caution to the wind and coexist in a world it was compelled to burn to the ground.

*Can you truly keep a dragon's egg from hatching?* she kept asking herself.

Like Gav, she couldn't deny that she wasn't sure what to make of him, either. She believed in looking for the best in others, and, though she didn't feel anything inherently evil from him, nothing like she had with the human soldiers, at least, she could sense something else lurking beneath the fear and loneliness. It showed in the way he moved; something he seemed to be working to bury just as fast as it presented itself. Seeing this, she realized that a part of her, the part she'd always recognized as herself, wanted to help him, but another part, a part she was growing more acquainted with, wasn't certain he could be helped...

Or even that he truly wanted help.

"There it is," Blay announced as the sun was nearly completely swallowed by the horizon.

Everybody turned to face north, following his direction.

There, just as they'd been told, was the blue glow. There was no denying that it was the same enchanted iron that they'd seen the swords forged from the prior day, but this was different. *Very* different. The swords' power had been immense on their own, and while Gwen couldn't imagine anybody not looking at any sort of sword as an instrument of death, the enchanted blue iron took it to a morbid new level. Those swords could kill without even making contact; blistering the skin and forcing it to rot even on the living. Even the trees and plants and grass—even the air itself!—grew sick around those swords. But they were still only swords—a meter-or-so of sharpened iron!

The old dwarf had called it the Winter Sun, and they could see why now. The entire northern sky was lit up like a new sun was peeking over the horizon; the same sickly blue glow shining for miles!

"The Winter Sun..." Gav muttered to himself, shaking his head. "Those monsters actually have *that* much of that enchanted iron?"

"Couple of swords made of that stuff turned an entire ogre caravan into a rotting trash heap, you say?" Blah raised an eyebrow. "Just imagine what rolling that thing down this mountain would do to every village on the other side."

Gav shook his head. "They'd never be able to move that much."

Blay shrugged, "Then *half* of it! Or less, even! Just load up their cannons with big chunks of that thing and start firing towards the south—*BAM BAM BAM!*—and there'd be nothing left."

Gwen felt her stomach sink.

Seeing her expression, Blay nodded and crouched down again. "See what I meant? It's already too late. They've got that thing, and they sure didn't build it to a pretty light in the night sky. So sooner or later they're going to do with it whatever it's meant to do. And then..." he didn't bother to finish, only shook his head again and started to curl up.

Gav growled. "They can't use it if they're all dead!"

Though the solution was sound—impossible, but sound—Gwen's natural aversion to death demanded an alternative. But even she couldn't think of one.

*Could you kill him to heal the world?*

*Would you kill him to save them all?*

"I don't think a philosophical centaur and a fae healer are necessarily equipped to take on the entire human army," Blay speculated, raising his head to look back at them, "So what do you *actually* intend to do about this? Since neither of you seems ready to walk away from this anytime soon."

"We can't let the humans continue on as they are," Gwen sighed. "That magic is unnatural. Everything that's alive starts to decay if they even get too close to it. That thing"—she nodded towards the Winter Sun—"isn't just a danger to us, it's an apocalypse threatening to rise and destroy *everything*!"

"They aren't as weak and stupid as they used to be, Gwen. They've built cities out there," he nodded to the scattered patches of light that littered the northern territory leading towards the ominous blue glow. "They're organized, they're growing, and now they have magic."

"I'll say they have magic!" Blay stared at all the city lights, "I've seen my fair share of firelight from up here, and *those* are not lanterns. That means that each and every city down there has magic powering their homes."

Gwen sneered at the sight. Even as a child she'd been taught that magic was a sacred gift, and there, before her, were dozens of human cities squandering it like some sort of toy. They took one of the most powerful energies on the planet and used it to murder and torture and comfort themselves.

This was *dark* magic.

153

"Gwen? Are you alright?" Gav asked.

"Yeah. I'm fine," she could tell her voice gave away her anger. "It's just not right."

"No, I know. It's not right," Gav said, taking hold of her hand and guiding her back to him, putting an arm around her and easing some of her rage. Looking over at Blay, he let his tone take a stern hold of his words: "And we're not just going to do nothing."

Gwen leaned back against him, searching out the warmth of his chest and clenched her eyes shut, calming herself. After a moment she and turned, noticing Blay looking back at them.

"I know that there's no chance of surviving this, but we have to at least *try* to stop them. That magic… it's dangerous. Very dangerous!" she said, "But sometimes when you're facing death you've got to admit that it's better to die fighting it than just letting it take you."

Gav smirked at that and looked down to meet her eyes. "And sometimes, when you're willing to fight in the face of death, things wind up working out in your favor."

Gwen blushed and smiled.

Blay cleared his throat. "Yes, well, I'm sure all that's remarkably relevant to something personal between you two, but I'm just getting a stomach ache listening to it. Still, you two have managed to intrigue me, and while I'm not one to get romantic over talk of suicide, if it's answers about that magic that you're looking for than might I suggest aiming your fighter's spirit towards one of those smaller cities and simply taking them?"

Gav raised an eyebrow at that. "Are you volunteering to help us?"

Blay shrugged again. "I'm volunteering to tag along if it means ruining a few thousand human lives, sure."

# TWELVE

"This was a mistake!" Blay screamed, scrambling to his feet and bolting after Gav and Gwen as they made their way through the howling streets of the human city. Locking his right arm around his chest and hooking his fingers over his left shoulder, he almost hid the entire length of the gash that reached across his upper body. *Almost.* Turning a bend to keep on the other two's trail, he slammed into the wall of a building and cursed in an unknown tongue. "This was a very big mistake!"

"We're not out of it yet!" Gav growled, using the handle of his axe to knock a human soldier back through the door he tried to jump them through before using the blade on the neighboring wall.

Blay watched with no small bit of astonishment as the ridiculously large weapon actually gouged through the side of the building and, as the centaur's momentum kept him galloping forward, progressively tore along the entire length. When the job was finished, there was a crooked, gaping maw in the side of—judging from the smell pouring through—a bakery. Though Gwen, who still held the lead, continued onward, Gav stopped and turned.

"Bravo, clip-clop!" Blay rolled his eyes as he admired the uselessness of the act and caught up before patting Gav on the back, "There will be no rolls with the soldiers' dinner after they've killed us!"

"Move," Gav hadn't taken his eyes off the length of street they'd just covered, the rising clamor of the approaching soldiers echoing around the bend. Still trying to follow the centaur's motives, Blay saw his intense and danger-filled gaze shift to him. "Watch after Gwen!"

Blay shook his head. "Watch after Gwen? Just what in the bloody blazes do you intend to—"

"GO!" Gav roared, gripping his axe and preparing to swing it again as a dozen guards spilled into the street after them.

Blay, more intrigued by what the centaur had planned than intimidated by his roar, hurried past him and after the direction Gwen had run off to. When he was satisfied that he'd put enough distance between them to spy on the plan—hoping it was more than attempting a single-handed stand against the small army with what amounted to a tree and a big rock—he turned. He watched as Gav took several more chopping swings into the already mangled wall of the bakery, the furious acts and the roars that chimed with every swing slowing, but not stopping, the human soldiers as they neared him.

Blay was almost embarrassed for him.

"Oh, Gav, just what was that supposed to—"

The bakery actually groaned from the blows, and the soldiers finally stopped. Then everyone, with the exception of Gav, turned to face the building as more of the beams whined under the broken weight they were expected to support. The door swung open, and an old man in a stained apron scuttled out to see what was destroying his shop. Old, tired eyes found new energy as their owner discovered himself planted between a dozen perplexed soldiers and one very angry looking centaur. Choosing the side he feared less, the old man actually ran past the soldiers.

"Who knew those old bones had it in them," Blay mused to himself.

Gav snarled and spun the axe in his hands, bringing the flat of the broad blade to the side of the building. Several of the guards, already seeing his intent, began to back away. Letting out another bellow, he drew back his weapon and threw the full force of himself—strength and weight combined—into driving the broad side of his axe into the destroyed wall. The sound was thunder being born within the bakery. In a cloud a dust and splinters and flour, the tortured wall blew out and collapsed, forcing the full weight of the building to drag itself down into the street. As the process began, Gav spun on his hooves and began to gallop back towards Blay, who could only stare on as the bakery buried several soldiers and forced the rest behind the makeshift barricade.

"I don't believe it," Blay blinked, "you did it! You actually destroyed all their rolls."

"I bought us time, smart-mouth!" Gav growled, galloping past him. "And I told you to watch Gwen."

Blay groaned and turned to follow. "Funny thing about *watching* somebody, clip-clop," he called after him, "you've actually gotta be able to SEE them first!" With a little effort and more than a lot of pained groaning at the throbbing in his chest, Blay was able to catch up to the centaur. "So tell me, big guy, do you *see* her?"

Blay's answer came as Gav stopped and began to look around the length of the street. The human city, they'd first noticed upon entering, was built on what appeared to be an obsession with rectangles. Rectangular buildings neighbored other rectangular buildings in rectangular pairs that occupied rectangular lengths with perfectly rectangular streets—ironically paved with triangular tiles—that intersected in perfect…

Squares.

*Well we* did *overhear them calling them 'blocks,' I suppose,* Blay thought, following Gav's wandering gaze about the stone-and-iron mess of perfect angles.

"I don't see her…" Gav muttered, shaking his head.

"That's the point of hiding," Gwen's voice sounded from above and two pairs of eyes shifted upward, catching sight of her reddish blonde hair and pointy ears poking up over the rooftop.

Gav's full body noticeably relaxed then and he smiled up at her. Holding out his arms, Gav nodded to her and Blay watched as she rolled off the roof and allowed herself to fall into his reach. Blay could only stare for a moment.

"Takes a lot of trust to throw yourself off a building at someone," he speculated.

Gav glared. "I caught her, didn't I?"

"I'm not saying you didn't catch her. After that little stunt back there with the bakery I'm still trying to figure out what you *can't* do," he nodded towards Gwen as Gav set her on her feet, "but to trust someone so much that they'd just drop out of the sky in an instant—no doubt or second thoughts—says a lot about a person."

Gwen frowned at that, "Are you saying a day might come when Gav *won't* catch me?"

"Not at all, beautiful," Blay couldn't help but cast a cautionary look over his shoulder to make sure the soldiers hadn't found a way over the barrier. Satisfied, he turned back. "I'm just saying that a day might come when you'll have to catch yourself."

Gav shook his head at him, "Well that day's *not* toda—OOMPH!"

Two guards emerged from the doorway nearest the Gav and jumped either side of him, letting their iron armor do most of the work as they struggled to hold onto the thrashing centaur. The smell of burning hair and flesh wafted up as the iron made its mark, and one of the soldiers reached for the sheath at his side, letting a sliver of sickly blue glow free as he started to draw his sword.

"No!" Gwen cried out, lunging at the two only to cry out as she was kicked back with an iron boot.

"HEY!" Blay growled at them, stepping forward and sacrificing his hold on his bloodied chest to slam both his palms down on the guards' iron faceplates. Grimacing at the itch that rose instantly in both hands, he shot Gav a look and sneered. "You'd better appreciate this, clip-clop!"

Though the helmets of the humans' armor stifled much of the guttural grunts they called words, Blay was happy to find that they could still scream just fine.

And scream they did.

"See how you like getting burned!" Blay hissed as he watched the cold hue of the iron helmets turn bright-red around his palms.

The contents of the metal sizzled as the screams intensified within them, and the pair's grip on Gav lifted as the two tried to retreat from Blay's hold. He didn't allow it. Held tight on either side of the centaur, the human soldiers' cries began to cut out as their bodies slumped, held upright by Blay's hold and whatever belting system kept their helmets tethered to their heads.

The screams had stopped but Blay still held firm, feeling a chuckle rising in his throat as he did.

"Blay?"

It felt right. *Too* right. The glow of the helmets started to pass to the breastplates, and the irritating metal began to warp around the heat.

"Blay!"

159

*More!* the all-too familiar voice called out to him, pushing him to cook the two man-shaped pieces of iron until nothing remained. *Burn them! Burn them all to the—*

"NO!" Blay jumped back, trying to distance himself from the voice but seeing only a very startled centaur in front of him.

"Gav...?" he blinked.

Two bodies inside warped iron armor crashed to the ground on either side of him, but Gav didn't look away from Blay as they did. Realizing what he'd done, Blay glanced over at Gwen, who stared back at him in horror.

"They..." Blay paused to shake the thoughts of fire out of his head. "They were going to kill you."

Gav had known that the dragon's egg had fire in him somewhere. The fact that he was a dragon's egg notwithstanding, the sheer volume of heat he'd let off on the mountain the day before was proof enough of that. He'd said that he didn't like to use the fire because it acted as an incubator for the dragon inside of him; the dragon he was fighting so hard to keep inside him. He'd spoken of instinct and control, and after the show he'd just put on—literally cooking a pair of humans inside their own armor with nothing more than a touch—Gav was beginning to see what he meant. A moment of conflict arose as he realized that they were now traveling with a far more powerful ally than they ever could have guessed; Blay, as it turned out, could be a powerful weapon. But he was a weapon that would eventually burst open and free something much more dangerous.

At that moment, Gav came to grips with the fact that they were standing beside something that might, at any moment, become a towering, fire-breathing beast that would sooner eat them than help them...

But it might also be the thing that could help them save the world.

Blay hadn't just killed the soldiers, he'd *enjoyed* it.

The look on his face as he'd done it, even after the two were gone, hadn't been relief that they couldn't hurt Gav anymore or even happiness that they'd survived the surprise attack. It had been pleasure. The wildness in his eyes had burned brighter than any fire that Gwen had ever seen, and the heat he'd exuded had been nearly enough to burn them with the soldiers. Even Gav had a fresh sheen of sweat coating his face and arms, and it wasn't from trying to evade the humans.

Blay had, with glee and without pause, burned those humans alive…

But he'd saved them in the process.

Gwen stared at him, locked once again in her turmoil. Everything she'd just witnessed along with everything she'd been raised to believe screamed that Blay was evil and that she and Gav needed to run and put as much distance between them and this new world of homicidal dragon's eggs and glowing swords from Winter Suns so far behind them that they might never have to face the truth of either again. But everything she'd learned outside of the fae city's walls told her otherwise. That sort of brutality might have meant at least one of those ogres at the caravan attack might have survived; maybe even the child that had died in her arms. If Blay had been with them on that day, then what might have been different? She'd just watched two soldiers, no different than the ones before, drop to the ground in a matter of seconds from nothing more than a touch of Blay's hands. The caravan massacre had been manned by only four!

If Blay had been there, they could've stopped it; they could've saved them all!

161

Dragging her gaze from Blay, she looked down at the smoldering pair on the ground. He'd saved Gav just then. Gleeful murder or not, the centaur she loved still stood—shaken and burned, but standing all the same—because of what he'd done.

Could she truly condemn him for that?

But to praise him for it…

The pain in her stomach intensified as she struggled with the dilemma of it all. Causing pain and murdering shouldn't be justifiable, her entire life she'd believed that to be so, but in her time trying to pursue her ambition of healing any who needed it she'd been forced to see just how easy it was to justify not only spilling blood, but actually enjoying it.

She wanted to hate Blay for that; for his ability to smile and even laugh at it. She *wanted* to hate him for it…

But at that moment she could only love him for saving Gav and giving her hope that they stood a chance.

# THIRTEEN

*B*etter to see it than to be it!"
    The words swirled like the campfire smoke and
wafted away before resurfacing again and again and again
in Gwen's mind. As she gazed into the flames, she was
reminded that much more of Blay's eyes. Over the past few
days and over the course of several more raids on the smaller
human cities, she'd discovered a strange attachment to Blay.
Granted it wasn't nearly the warmth or affection she felt for
Gav—she couldn't bring herself to say she loved Blay, after
all—but he seemed to represent something that neither she
nor Gav did: exactly what this world needed. Before, when
it had just been her and Gav, everything had been about
healing, and though Gav had helped shown that sometimes
fighting was necessary to protect and allow one to be healed,
the world didn't seem satisfied with such a simple approach.
The world that allowed the Winter Sun needed somebody
who outright thrived on mass destruction, and after the
laughable episode that was their first attempt at a city raid,

the three had decided that luck wouldn't always be on their side.

Gav creating a barrier and Blay killing the two soldiers had been the only impressive thing to come of that first attempt. They hadn't been in the city more than a minute before a wailing alarm echoed through the streets, and the hindsight view of dozens of soldiers tailing the three of them as they bumbled and crashed about the city would almost be funny if it weren't so embarrassing. Or dangerous. After coming to grips with Blay's abilities, the three of them were forced to continue through the city, eager for not only the answers they'd gone there seeking but any available exit. However, like the fae, it turned out the humans were quite fond of walls, and while the massive gate that they'd first entered through had offered an illusion of convenience, they soon found it was the only way in or out. With more and more guards converging on them, they'd barricaded themselves inside a large building of strangely smooth stone—what Blay explained was a mud-like substance that hardened into the material, though he wasn't sure what the humans called it—and, though they couldn't see the source, iron. Lots and lots of iron. At first Gav and Gwen had been eager to find a light source to see escape the blinding darkness that enveloped them, but Blay was quick to assure them that light was the last thing they wanted.

"Light is fire, and we're surrounded by something that's begging for fire," he said.

"How can you know that?" Gav demanded.

"Because the dragon in me is begging for me to grant the demand."

Neither Gwen nor Gav needed to hear more. After what they'd seen the dragon egg do, they were certain he knew

what he was talking about, and they knew they didn't want
to tempt him, either.

As accepting of their situation as he was, however, Gav
was not happy about being in the darkness, or such a tight
space. Restless, he kicked up a nearby stack of crates and, as
they crashed down on the ground between him and Blay, the
three watched a portion of the floor fall away and a bright
blue glow spilled into the room. Though they welcomed
the ability to finally see, they also instantly recognized the
source of light for what it was, and, all around them, Blay
recognized what he'd sensed before.

"These are explosives," he informed them. "A lot of
explosives!"

"What would they need those for?" Gwen asked, whimpering as she realized they were surrounded by the stuff.

"Mining, warfare, sending loud, colorful bursts into the
air," Blay shrugged and gave a morbid chuckle. "This is a race
that finds some sort of weird pleasure in seeing everything
explode, even the air!"

"Must feel like cousins to you then," Gav grumbled,
stepping away from the blue glow. "Care to explain that."

That detail, however, Gwen had already figured out:

"It's an artery," she'd explained, staring down at it. "The
humans are using the Winter Sun as some sort of power
source as well as a weapon, so they must use arteries like
these to carry energy to every city."

"So that death-spreading enchanted iron is snaked
underground from the source?" Gav sneered, staring down
at it.

Gwen nodded solemnly, not liking the idea, either.

"Then let's send the murderous monkeys a message!"
Blay growled, his orange eyes burning bright enough to cast
their own light in the dim room.

"What sort of message?" Gav's voice mirrored the same
skepticism that Gwen felt at that.

Blay was already trembling with excitement. "This place is filled with explosives—teeming with the stuff! And we're dead-center in this city and squatting over some artery as you call it that goes back to the Winter Sun. So I say we find a way out of this box and give them the explosion they all secretly crave!"

"You mean the explosion you secretly crave!" Gav snapped. "And how do you expect to get us far enough away to not get us all killed in the process?"

"Oh, sorry," Blay sneered back at him, "does my plan not work for you? What would you like to do then? You've already taken out a bakery, so maybe there's a nice shoemaker whose workshop you'd like to trample on with your hooves!"

"STOP!" Gwen shouted, holding out her arms between the two. "Can't you see that the enchanted iron is doing this? It's getting to more than just our skin; it's actually darkening our thoughts!"

The three dwelled on that for a moment, realizing that the more time they spent in there the more they'd be affected by it.

"Okay…" Gav sighed, "Revised plan."

"Oh I can't wait to hear this!" Blay groaned.

Gav glared, "It's still your plan, smart-mouth!"

Blay smirked. "Then I already love it!"

Nodding, Gav looked back at Gwen, "We run. Straight through the humans. They'll be out there by now, probably forming some sort of barricade to keep us trapped. They'll have the place surrounded, but they'll be thinned out to do it, so—"

Blay laughed, "So we ram our way through them and blow the place to hell as we do!"

Gwen frowned, looking down.

Seeing this, Gav set a hand on her shoulder, nodding. "I know. It's going to be tough to see that much death happen all at once, but—"

"Better to see it than to be it!" Blay cut him off, looking straight into Gwen's eyes, "Now is not the time for a healer's heart; now's the time for the dragon's fury, got it?"

Gav frowned, obviously not liking the brashness of Blay's words, but also not disagreeing with them.

With both Gwen and Blay taking a place on Gav's back, the centaur had leveled his axe in front of him and galloped straight through the door and few guards standing directly in front of it. As the other guards that had been stationed around the building tried to reconvene and start after them, Blay's fire had sparked the explosives.

They'd miscalculated the amount of the explosives.

They'd managed to run half the necessary distance.

They'd barely made it out of that city alive.

With the force of the explosion taking everyone, including Gav, off their feet and hurdling them through the rapidly incinerated streets, Gwen was certain that they were about to die. Somehow, though, Gav had managed to catch her out of the air and hug her to his chest as his body crashed to the ground, taking the full force of the impact while Blay, who was actually laughing, collapsed in a heap slightly further off.

"We did it," he marveled. "We actually did it!"

"We were lucky!" Gav groaned, dragging himself to his feet and making sure Gwen was alright before glaring back at Blay. "And sooner or later luck alone won't be enough!"

Since then, after what Gav had called "the most successful failure I've ever seen," they'd destroyed three more human cities. The tactic, though more rehearsed and better planned since the first, remained the same: find the Winter Sun artery—which, as luck would have it, was always anchored in their munitions building—in the center of the city and blow it up. Though some storage buildings had less explosives than other, Blay seemed more and more up to the task of ensuring the blast remained approximately the same size.

And that concerned Gav more than anything else.

He could see that they were *literally* waking a sleeping dragon, but with the ends still justifying the means. With every city Blay was getting that much more drunk with the use of his powers; that much closer to hatching. And, with every city they'd taken out, he'd gotten *that* much more crazy from it. He always eventually came down from his laughing spells, but each time it seemed a little bit harder for him to come around.

It was almost enough to make Gav want to call it all off, but there was no denying that it was working. The Winter Sun was actually growing dimmer with each city they destroyed. For every artery they severed, the heart seemed to grow weaker.

How could they possibly stop with that sort of progress showing?

"I'm going to get some more firewood," Gav announced, deciding he wanted to be alone with his thoughts. Securing his axe on his back, he looked at Blay and asked, "Can you stay here with Gwen?"

Blay shrugged. "Where else would I go?"

Gav offered Gwen a warm smile before turning and leaving.

Gwen felt her cheeks heat up at Gav's smile—just the same as they always did—and she found herself smiling back even though he was already gone. Since meeting and starting their travels with Blay, the two of them hadn't had a chance to further explore the feelings they'd finally admitted the night before first heading up into the mountain, but the glances they were able to steal at moments like that only proved that nothing had changed between them. It certainly hadn't changed anything for her. Though she couldn't deny that Blay intrigued her, it felt no different than the intrigue she'd felt with her brother when he'd shown off the latest fae combat technique he'd learned from spying on the warrior camps. He was undeniably attractive, and his views were definitely helping Gwen develop her own shifting senses of right and wrong, but that was where the relationship ended.

At least that's where it ended for her.

Several times she'd caught Blay watching her with the same coy smirk and devious intent that she remembered the fae boys back at her old home staring at her with. It was the same look she'd been waiting to see from Gav before she realized he didn't think like other males. Blay, however, despite his social awkwardness and a level of sarcastic pessimism that bordered on the suicidal but flared into a homicidal fury, was still somehow exactly like other males. Even with his isolation, his instincts remained anchored, and though the glances that she caught him stealing were flattering, she wasn't sure how long he'd remain satisfied with glances alone.

She caught another such glance as Gav disappeared into the darkness in search of firewood, and as she turned to face him his eyes quickly darted back towards the fire. A long moment passed in silence as she tried to decide if it would be worth it to confront him outright with her thoughts, but then she caught sight of his face as he stared into the flames. An entranced, blank expression was beginning to grow; the flames reflecting in his eyes until she was certain that his eyes were made of fire.

"Blay," Gwen frowned, "are you okay?"

"I can't," he whispered.

Gwen bit her lip. "Can't what?" she asked, nervous about what he might answer with.

"Because they're my friends."

Gwen shivered as she realized he wasn't talking to her at that moment.

"Blay," she called out again, louder this time.

His shoulders tensed and his gaze darted away from the flames and he nodded. "Yeah, I was just… off in my own little world, I suppose."

"It must be hard. Fighting your instincts, I mean," she said, hoping to reinforce his focus on keeping the dragon at bay.

"I… I try not to think about it much, honestly," he said as he looked down, beginning to run his finger through the dirt as he chewed on his lower lip. "It's scary knowing that I'm only here to be a vessel for the dragon. I mean, it can't be me in there, can it? It's not like I'm going to split open and what emerges will still be me; I can't be two minds… can I?" he shivered and sighed, burying his face in his hands. "It feels so right to… to do all those things that it wants me to. I'm finally getting to turn the fire inside me on the humans; finally feeling like I'm doing something right… but it's just speeding up what I've worked for so long to hold back. But I guess I couldn't have held it back forever. There's no way to stop it from coming…" He looked up at her and said, "I just have to accept that I'm doomed to die."

"You can't let yourself think that way," Gwen said, shaking her head. "You have to believe that there's always hope."

Blay shook his head. "There's no healing the bits of shell once the egg has hatched, Gwen. Its job is to break open. That's it. And for the egg that knows it's an egg, its job is to die."

Gwen looked down at that, unable to argue what she knew was right. She'd been raised to be a healer, but she'd lost count of how many eggs she and her mother had cracked on numerous breakfasts or times baking. They'd even laughed at the few eggs that had rolled free of the counter and shattered on the floor.

*The egg's job is to break,* she thought to herself.

That was all there was to it.

170

"I guess that means you just have to enjoy the time you have," she finally said. "Just like the rest of us."

Blay stared at her for a long moment, seeming comforted by her words. Then, in a quick motion, he moved from the log he'd been sitting on to the one that Gwen sat upon, moving closer.

Gwen could only blush and ask herself what he had planned.

"The way that you…" he sighed, looking down for a moment and finally taking her hand in his own. "The way that you look at Gav… is that—" he cut himself off and shook his head. "Is your mind made up? About him, I mean? Does he… is he the one for you?"

Gwen blushed at the forwardness of his question and looked down at his hand on hers. It was warm, bordering hot even, much like it felt when her hand was in Gav's. On those occasions, however, when Gav held her, it felt natural; it felt right. The heat from Blay's hand felt artificial, like her body's response was no different than the response she felt beside the fire or a warm bowl of stew. It wasn't love.

"I… I'm sorry, Blay, but he is the one," she admitted, carefully working her hand free of his. "I care for you a great deal. More than I've cared for many of my own kind, I might add, which surprises me a great deal considering how long I'd known them and how short a time we've known each other." She finally got her hand free and shook her head again, "But I don't feel that way for you. That part of me belongs to Gav now."

"R-right… Sorry about that," Blay frowned, moving back to his original seat and looking back into the flames of their campfire.

Gwen watched as the flames seemed to grow under his gaze, and a chill worked its way under her skin despite the new wave of heat.

"Do you... do you like fire that much?" she asked, eager to change the subject.

"Honestly?" Blay looked up at her again.

She nodded, "I'd prefer it."

Blay looked back at the fire. "Honestly," he muttered, "I hate it." He frowned and wiped his face. "It's enchanting to me. It entices me. It's hard to explain, but it motivates me; it's elating." He smiled and shook his head, muttering something about "the scholars and the poets" before he said, "I guess you could say it defines me, but it's because of all that that I hate it. I hate it because I can't stop loving it. I hate it because it brings out this side of me that I despise. A side that I can't understand that keeps proving itself to me." Another head shake and a louder sigh, "I'm sure none of that makes any sense to you, though."

"N-no, not really," Gwen lied, not liking how similar Blay was proving to be to her. She suddenly missed Gav terribly.

Eager for a distraction, she picked up a twig that had snapped off from a piece of firewood and began to draw in the dirt. Digging for the deepest, most innocent subject she could hope to draw, she began to trace the outline to form a fox's body as she started to draw Bren. Though she'd never been a great artist, she'd loved to doodle with charcoal when the urge called to her, and before long she was happy with the rudimentary figure in front of her.

"What's that?" Blay asked.

"It's a fox," Gwen said. "Back in the fae city, I had a pet fox. My mother helped me heal it, and it stayed with me after that." She sighed and shook her head, "But she was killed the day I was arrested. She tried to bite the guards who were taking me away, so they..." Gwen couldn't finish the sentence and she trembled. "I guess she just represents the most innocent person I've known since all this began. And even against the fae guards she fought to keep me safe.

I guess that's what I'm doing now, huh: trying to protect an already condemned world from an unfair sentencing?" She sighed and shrugged, "Either way, I miss her."

"I think the poets and scholars that drink tea in the village I visit would love to hear you speak," Blay smirked. Then, as an afterthought, he said, "Your people just killed a fox because of what you did?"

Gwenn nodded.

"Don't take this the wrong way, but your kind seem kind of twisted," Blay scoffed.

"I agree," Gwen muttered. "More and more I'm seeing just how twisted they really were. They taught me—taught all of us—to fear anything outside the wall. Every creature out there was painted to be an ugly mockery of their true selves to keep us afraid of them. But my time with Gav has taught me so much and has opened my eyes to all of their lies and deceptions."

As if he'd heard his name then, Gav came into view with an armload of new firewood and, draped across his back, a large boar.

Catching sight of the wild pig on his back, Blay smirked and rubbed his hands together. "Guess we feast tonight!" he said with a laugh.

Gav smiled and nodded, setting the firewood and the boar aside before removing his axe. As he started back towards the fire to warm his hands, he smiled at Gwen again—earning another smile in response—and then caught sight of her drawing.

"Oh, Gwen..." Gav whispered, kneeling down and draping his arms around her. "Are you thinking about Bren again?"

Gwen tried to hold her tears as she looked down at her drawing. The memories of the short time they'd had—of playing in the forests and the soft warmth of her fur against her when she slept—crashed over her all at once, and she felt Blay rest a hand on her knee as Gav tightened his hold around her and she realized she'd been crying.

After another moment of their comforting contact, Gwen felt the pain subside and she nodded her thanks to them.

"I'll get to work on that boar," Blay jumped to his feet and began to raid Gav's camp gear for a knife. "Nothing chases away tears faster than the sizzle of bacon!"

Gwen watched as Blay went about preparing their dinner before she looked back at Gav as he settled in beside her. His gaze burned into hers and made her feel safe and certain again, and, reaching forward, he ran his thumb under her right eye to sweep away a lingering tear.

"It'll be alright," he smiled reassuringly.

She smiled and blushed, nodding. "I know it will be," She leaned against him.

"So those fae sound like grade-A jerks," Blay cut in. "I mean, not quite as bad as the humans—alright, nowhere near as bad as the humans—but still jerks. All this 'vagrant' business?" he made a sound and shook his head, "What sort of people can just throw their own into a maze with a slobbering, crazed monster?" he paused then and looked at Gav, "No offense, clip-clop!"

"None taken," Gav rolled his eyes, "and have I mentioned how much I hate being called 'clip-clop'?"

"Can't remember," Blay admitted, continuing: "But still, this whole vagrant mess has me curious. Are you the only vagrant to actually survive?"

Gwen frowned and looked down. "I… technically I didn't survive the labyrinth," she admitted, looking at Gav. "I was saved. I wouldn't have made it out without him."

"That's not what I asked," Blay pointed out.

"I'm actually curious about that, as well," Gav said. "I can't say that I ever agreed with the process, but it always struck me as certain death for any fae that was sent down there. My kind might not be the slobbering, crazed monsters"—he shot Blay a look as he repeated his words—"that yours makes us out to be, but there's a reason the fae elders came to us in the first place: we're reliable when it comes to tracking and hunting. Volunteers in there had rations and a map—more than they ever offered the vagrants—but there was still that wide-open exit offered to any who could survive long enough to find it. None of the volunteers would have admitted to letting a vagrant elude them, but that's not to say that none ever did."

Gwen looked up at Gav, realizing that the two of them weren't about to drop the subject. "It's... it's not really my place to say," she mumbled.

"What a load of hoofmeat!" Blay countered, "You can tell us, Gwen."

Gwen took a deep breath at the painful memory the topic brought and nodded slowly. "Alright... there *was* one other vagrant who at least survived to make it out," she looked up at Gav, "and he made it out without help."

Gav rolled his eyes.

"He..." Gwen sighed, "He was actually a childhood friend of mine. Hawkes; his name was Hawkes Stormbreak," she felt her cheeks go hot at the mention of his name. "We were... we were actually really close. Our parents always used to talk about how we were going to be married someday."

Gav shifted at that and frowned. "Then he was sentenced at a young age, too?" he asked, not sounding terribly upset about the fact.

Gwen gave him a knowing nudge and adjusted herself against him to remind him where her heart lay before she nodded. "It's not common for a child to be deemed a vagrant—mostly because fae children are so closely watched and mentored that they rarely get the chance to break the rules—but Hawkes was a lot like me, I guess. He found a lot of ways to get out on his own, and he did what he felt was right."

"And what did he do that got him thrown in the maze?" Blay asked.

Gwen sighed, thinking back on those days. "He... uh, he—" she laughed as it dawned upon her then, "He did the same thing I did: he jumped the wall to help a non-fae on the other side."

Gav raised an eyebrow at that. "He was a healer, too?"

"No..." Gwen frowned, "He was training to be a mage, like his father. He heard somebody in distress on the other side of the wall and, when he went to explore it, found an old woman on the run." She shook her head, "I didn't get to hear much of the story," she admitted, "Hawkes tried to explain while he was being arrested, but everything after that was what we were told by the elders and the guards." She glanced back at Gav and pursed her lips, "You already know how trustworthy they are..."

Gav nodded slowly.

Blay, entranced by the story, had stopped working and only stood over the partially gutted boar. "So what happened? What'd he do?"

Gwen shrugged, "Nobody's sure. The story told was that he was tricked by a wicked old crone and gave her a defensive spell to protect herself."

"That's it?" Blay frowned, "That doesn't sound like much."

Gav shrugged. "Until you consider that they labeled Gwen a vagrant for saving my sister's life."

Blay scowled. "Oh... right."

"The spell Hawkes gave her wasn't created properly," Gwen explained. "Normally, it should have been nothing but a masking spell, for keeping pursuers or predators from picking up on your trail. But in the wrong hands... well, magic is a lot like the words on a page, they can be rewritten to mean something different if it's not done right. The crone apparently worked her own magic into the spell—made it work for her against our kind—and the next time a fae hunting expedition set out past the wall she masked herself from them and…" Gwen looked down. "Jumping the wall is bad enough on its own, they say it risks inviting something else back over, but when Hawkes did it it caused the deaths of five fae who'd never even seen their attacker waiting for them. Only one of the hunters survived the attack to tell the elders what had happened."

"And the crone?" Gav asked.

Gwen shrugged. "She made off with all the hunters' supplies. Originally Hawkes' sentence was a lighter one because of his age, but after the deaths and the losses… it's because of him that the laws regarding fae children and crossing the wall were changed in the first place. If it hadn't been for him, I probably would have only faced public lashings or some other minor sentence."

"Just like I said earlier, your kind are twisted," Blay scoffed.

"Not my kind anymore," she corrected.

"So, what happened to Hawkes? How did he escape the labyrinth?" Gav frowned.

"Well, I wasn't allowed to watch him from the viewing pools. My parents knew what he'd meant to me and they figured it was better I not watch him die. But everyone else seemed to see, and they talked… a lot. Apparently he'd found a way to sneak a spell he'd made in his cell into the labyrinth; some sort of reflective powder or something. The story I heard from the fae that had watched his escape said that the instant he was in the maze he'd thrown the powder into the air and a bright light had filled the tunnels that led the way out."

"I'd call that cheating," Blay sighed.

"I'd call it smart," Gav shrugged.

"Whatever you call it," Gwen rolled her eyes, "Hawkes got out. Without the mystery of which direction to take he was able to outrun the centaur and he made it out." She shrugged again, "Before that, no one had ever escaped the labyrinth, even the warriors that had been deemed vagrants weren't able to do it. That a child had managed it had everyone in an uproar, but the elders had pronounced him dead shortly."

"He died?" Blay sounded disappointed by that. "That's anticlimactic. How'd he die?"

Gwen shrugged again. "The other side of the walls are a dangerous place to be. I might be alive to tell the story, but I've seen enough to know that at least that much of what the elders told us was true. A child would have had no way of surviving out here."

"Well… *they* could be wrong," Gav added. "I mean, you got out and you aren't dead."

Gwen paused and looked up at that, "I had help from you, Gav. He didn't have anybody to help him."

Blay shrugged, "By that logic he shouldn't have been able to make it out in the first place. Far be it for me to question the authenticity of your lying, scheming, terrible fae elders, but it's possible to survive out here. Hell, a family of passersby feeling sorry for a lost kid and suddenly he's in the care of others."

Gav nodded slowly. "Ogres will adopt lost children of any species. They're family instinct is strong enough to look past differences better than most."

"Exactly!" Blay nodded, finally returning to the boar with a loud chop that made Gwen jump. "It's not just possible, Gwen, it's probable. And if there's another fae vagrant running around that knows magic, we might have another person to join this war we're waging with the humans."

Gwen fell silent. If there was a possibility that Hawkes had survived more than just the labyrinth, he might actually be out there somewhere. The thought scared her as much as it excited her. Hawkes, even as a young child, had been so impressionable and passionate about the fae way. He'd held their people and their laws in such high esteem that, to then be on the outside—away from the life he knew and loved and stripped of the title that had come with it—truly would have been a fate worse than death. Even if he could have survived the horrors that Gwen had witnessed in her time outside the walls, what would seeing those sorts of things have done to him?

Though she wasn't sure why, Blay's words from the other day popped into her mind at that instant:

*Better to see it than to be it...*

# FOURTEEN

P resident Stormbreak," the general burst through twin doors of his commanding officer's private chambers and assaulted his sensitive ears with the sharp slap of his boots against the hardwood floor. "I've received urgent news that demands your immediate attention!"

It took all of Hawkes' already limited control towards General Thougher to not kill him on the spot. While he wanted to consider himself a patient fae, the general's brashness and lack of tact for all things ranging from actual military strategy to something as simple as etiquette was growing tiresome.

But what did he really expect from a human being?

He only had himself to blame if they hadn't learned proper manners yet.

"What is it, General?" Hawkes sighed, turning in mid-step away from his bedchambers and facing the yapping nuisance. "I don't suppose it can wait until morning?"

"Sorry, sir, but no," Thougher's voice carried several tones, none of them sincere or apologetic. Hawkes was somewhat pleased, however, to detect a hint of fear trembling through each syllable.

Hawkes rolled an open palm to urge his unwanted company to speak.

General Thougher snapped back to his normally rigid stature as he began to speak. "It's those three creatures, sir! There was another attack by them earlier today; another city has fallen!"

Hawkes' back tensed and he realized with no small amount of rage that he was going to have a lousy night's sleep. "And I doubt there's any further news, right? Three assailants but only one identified: a centaur. Am I correct, General?"

"Well…" the human shifted uneasily.

Hawkes began to turn away, ready to disregard him with a command of increased soldiers with more Winter Rays at the remaining city gates when the human spoke again:

"Actually, sir, reports have identified one of the other assailants. Th-that's why I decided it demanded your immediate attention and couldn't wait until morning!"

"Oh?" Hawkes wasn't sure if he should be outraged that the creature was making assumptions that interrupted his sleep or impressed that he possessed the capacity. "Well, by all means then, General, impress me!"

And then the impossible happened:

General Thougher actually uttered something interesting.

"Though the third assailant's race still can't be identified—but rest assured we have our best working on it—the other is a fae, sir; a female fae."

Hawkes stared at him for a long moment. "You're certain of this? It wasn't just an elf that some oaf mistook for—"

"No, sir, we checked the reports from several survivors who got a good look at her. They all match: slightly golden skin like yours, not pale-silver like an elf's. And the ears were long and drawn back, not short and pointing up. Sir, please give me some credit."

Hawkes normally would have laughed at such a request, but at that moment he was too consumed in his spiraling curiosity. Another fae? Had the wall finally fallen? Was there some sort of uprising that had led to others of his kind freeing themselves from the city? Or, by some chance…

His eyes widened.

*A fae who traveled with a centaur?*

Could it be another vagrant? One who'd convinced their would-be executioner to lead them out of the labyrinth?

"Are there any other details pertaining to this fae?" he demanded.

"Sir?"

"Details! You say there were multiple survivors to see her, correct? Could none offer an age? A hair color? Anything?"

General Thougher shrugged and said, "Young, sir. The reports say she's young—a-also like you, I suppose—and… uh, reddish hair?"

It was as if the entire world had stopped turning solely to grant Hawkes his single greatest wish…

"Like strawberries and wheat?" he was distantly aware of himself pressing the general further for that detail.

"I… uh, I suppose so, sir."

He'd told her that her hair was the color of strawberries and wheat.

It was like looking back at a dream now, as though everything before that moment had been one tolling trial of his patience and ability after another. He wanted so desperately to believe that the strain he'd put on himself to turn the brutish savages that the humans had been when he'd first found them wallowing in the mud and bludgeoning one another with bones and crude iron clubs would not be for nothing. He dreamed that one day his efforts would be

182

recognized and he'd be offered some sign from the divine. This news felt like the news he'd been waiting for; the news he'd dreamed of. Only in his dreams did he ever get to see Gwendolyn Clearwater again and, with the divine's blessing, finally make her his queen. He recalled seeing her, all those years ago, and remembered how beautiful she'd been even then. Her green eyes and perfect smile illuminating his world with such brilliance as that hair—*the only hair like it*, he thought—trailed after her in spirals of radiant colors. That dream had all but been lost to him after all this time. His hope that the dream might come true and she'd be there grew stale and, eventually, stagnant. And while the visions of her in his memories were always breathtaking, he'd been forced to live in the here-and-now. It had become, in many ways, the ironic truth of the faes' punishment. Casting him away as their kind's youngest vagrant was, in many ways, a gift—they'd already given him everything he'd ever need, so freedom to build his legacy was the natural next step—but in losing his one true love to the other side of that wall the fae had genuinely robbed him of the one thing he needed to be truly happy. The mixture of irony and excitement stirred in his belly as new possibilities dawned for him:

That of a ruler who could finally oversee the taking of the entire planet with the only person he'd ever wanted by his side!

He'd once been said that her hair was the color of strawberries and wheat, and in a single instant a human idiot had confirmed his dreams by identifying her most distinguishing feature, leading him to turn away from his bedchambers and cast his case out at the magnificent glow of his most spectacular creation:

The Winter Sun.

He couldn't wait to show it to her!

"Bring me the fae," he instructed. "She's not to be harmed; not a single hair plucked and not a single mar upon her flesh. Do I make myself absolutely clear in that regard, General Thougher?"

"N-no, sir... I-I mean yes, sir! Perfectly clear; no confusion, sir!"

Hawkes leveled his gaze on the human and, before he could react, closed the distance between them and loomed before him. Though the general was sizably taller than him, the fae president of the human empire was not incapable of making his power known without the need for physical stature. General Thougher did not miss the point.

"Allow me to clarify further, General," he seethed, "should I spot, detect, suspect, or be in any way informed of any harm that you or your subordinates allowed to come to the fae during her capture or while bringing her to me, I will personally see to it that you die at my feet."

"S-sir. Y-yes, sir!" the general's stammers offered Hawkes some faith that his message was properly received. "A-and what of the others?"

"Other what?"

General Thougher frowned and stammered again, "Th-the centaur, sir, a-and the third assailant. Do you wish to have them brought to you, as well?"

"What? No! What would I want with that filth?" he waved off the question, turning away. "I don't care what you do with them, but don't waste unnecessary manpower—and certainly don't try to use any non-existing brainpower—in trying to place some sentence without my say-so. The fae is clearly the brains behind the trio, so once she's out of their grip they'll no-doubt return to their caves or swamps or wherever it is they come from."

"Sir..." General Thougher bowed, "Yes, sir."

Gwen woke up from the lingering phantoms of a dream, not sure if it had been a good one or a bad one. In it, she thought she remembered seeing Hawkes as a young boy staring at the Winter Sun, whispering something to her, but she couldn't remember what. He'd seemed calm, happy even, which felt oddly reassuring in the blue glow of the Winter Sun, but as she reflected on the dream she wondered if she was simply viewing an old memory through the ominous lighting of her new focus. The more she thought about it, the more ridiculous it all seemed.

Something in the distance caught her attention—not quite a sound or a movement, but enough of the two to draw her attention. Still grumbling at the dream, she pulled herself from the crevice between Gav's human back and horse body and walked past the meter-tall egg that Blay resembled while he slept. Both shifted slightly as she passed, but neither awoke.

The forests of the northern region were denser in between the regions surrounding the human cities that had been all-but stripped of any plant life. The only exception to this, they'd found, was along a wide, seemingly invisible path that led straight from each city back to the capital city, where the Winter Sun was housed. While it had been too dark on the first night in the mountain when they'd taken in the sight of area to notice the naked paths that reached from each city back to the capital, it wasn't hard to miss in the daylight. Then, it was easy to see the vast stretch of dead land littered with the skeletal forms of what they'd realized after some deliberation had once been trees. They now looked like twisted and deformed branches jutting from the pale, lifeless soil; they were their own tombstones. This was the effect of the Winter Sun's arteries: the paths they followed underground could be seen above it in the death-roads they created. In many ways, they were a sign of what was to come.

The forest that remained, however, thriving between the mountain and the first few human cities and then existing in patches to the east and west, was lush. It stood as a comparison to what had been before the humans' empire had risen. And it was there that the three set up their camp each night. Blay had explained that he'd never seen humans willingly venture that far without good cause, and if there was a cause to motivate them that far they were more likely to venture on foot past the mountain to the non-human colonies where the richer supplies and potential prey were.

It was, in some small way, at least, comforting to know that the mountain still served as a barrier from a full invasion.

A breeze passed through the camp as Gwen shuffled through it, shifting some of the foliage and sparking up several of the dying embers from the fire pit. The gentle whistle and faint rustling was the only sound even her sensitive fae ears could detect. She frowned at that, certain that she'd heard something and humoring the thought that some sort of animal—maybe even a fox!—was having a game at her expense. Stepping further towards the original source, she let herself venture past a few of the trees, hoping that being outside the border of their campsite might entice whatever critter was out there to present itself. None did.

"Damn…" she muttered, staring out into the night bathed forest.

The wind died down a bit, no longer offering any sort of whistle but still rustling the leaves in the trees a bit. With the forest growing slightly quieter, Gwen was able to make out a footstep drawing nearer from camp, though she couldn't tell if it was one of Gav's hoofs or Blay's boots. Still staring out, she called out "I'm here" in a whisper to tell whoever it was where she was, not wanting to panic them to her absence.

"Just thought I heard a noise, that's all," she offered when no response came.

The next footstep paused, seeming to wait for her, and she wondered if whoever it was thought she was relieving herself behind the trees and trying to offer some privacy.

"Hello?" she called out, trying to offer some invitation to approach without becoming awkward.

Still no answer, though she could still sense somebody lingering just beyond the trees. Turning to try and get a look, she was met with only darkness, and she found herself cursing the dead firelight for no real reason. Whoever was there moved, and she could hear a shift of weight on the soft earth.

But it still offered no clue towards who it was.

"Hello?" she called again.

Still no answer.

Sighing and starting back towards the camp, she began to chide the darkness, "Do you realize it's quite unnerving when you don't answer like tha—" she stopped, both in speech and in step, as she rounded the last tree and saw that nobody was there. "H-hello?" she said, more out of desperation than curiosity.

Looking down at the spot she'd heard the footsteps at, Gwen spotted several spots of disturbed earth, though there was no way to discern between foot or hoof with how many times both Gav and Blay had walked in that very spot earlier that day. Still, this area of disturbed earth was fresh...

"Where...?" she looked around for a moment and then looked back at the clearing, where both Gav and Blay are still sleeping. "But... who—"

The wind had nearly died down completely, but she felt her ears perk as she caught the sound of a rustling branch above her. Before she could look up, however, she felt the itching burn of iron and the dimly-lit campsite went dark as something was pulled over her head.

Startled, she called out to the others, but just trying to speak seemed to draw all the breath from her lungs; whatever had been pulled over her head was already beginning to suffocate her.

In the distance, she heard the muffled sounds of Gav and Blay, but they, too, sounded like they were dealing with similar circumstances. Their clearing was suddenly a muffled trio of futile cries and stifled futility. And the sounds seemed to be growing distant! It took a moment of trying to get her bearings before Gwen realized she was being dragged back away from the camp. Again and again she tried to call out, but it only sped up her suffocation.

The sounds grow more desperate and even more distant, but she was still able to hear Gav demanding her return as well as an inhuman roar that she somehow recognized as Blay.

"They've got them covered," a voice directly behind her spoke, grunting against her efforts. "They won't be able to for long, though, so stop wasting everyone's time! Let them do their job and start doing yours… NOW!"

"But he said…" the two hands pulling her suddenly became one and the other voice went silent.

"I know what he said; I *know*!" the second hand returned, this time with greater determination. The fingers dug into Gwen's shoulder, forcing her to stop squirming against them. "But"—the grip tightened more—"I am not dealing with this beast thrashing about for the entire trip. I'm not! So just do your—"

The sounds of her struggling comrades and the voices turned muggy as something pinched her right hip, and Gwen felt a rush of heat spread across her entire body. As the heat intensified, a dizzying blackness ushered her into its embrace. With the last traces of sound, looming in the distance like a setting sun, she recognized the strange whirring of one of the humans' vehicles. For a moment she fought to call out to the Gav and Blay and warn them, but the dizzying blackness' hold on her proved too intoxicating and a deep sleep took her.

"—job!"

# FIFTEEN

"… told you…" a voice growled on the horizon of Gwen's consciousness, just on the other side of the dizzying blackness that held her so tightly. "… said you could do anything… *not* to… to be *un*injured! Was I at all unclear about…"

Who…?

Seemed so familiar…

"… fought back, sir," another voice said, coming in clearer than before. "There was no way we could've made… be a little dizzy, but she *is* otherwise—GAH!"

The sudden cry of the second speaker scared the dizzying blackness away and startled Gwen out of her strange sleep. Though her eyes were finally open, she found her vision still wavering; her eyes uncertain of anything they saw. Ahead of her, however, she could vaguely make out the hazy form of a blond male leaning in close to another with long, brown hair. At first she was certain the two were locked in some sort of prolonged embrace, but, as she continued to watch

189

and her vision continued to clear, she could see a thin trail of blood as it began to roll from the brown-haired man's mouth.

Seeing this, the blond man's body relaxed as the other's only seemed to grow even more tense. Then, slowly—so slowly that Gwen wasn't sure at first if he'd moved at all—the blond man stepped away. Something in the movement and how the he carried himself seemed different than the others; something almost familiar. The brown-haired man, Gwen could see now, was human. It was strange to see them clothed and standing upright with the same pride and dignity of a fae or an elf, but the characteristics were unmistakable, and, in contrast to the blond's movements, it was easy to recognize the clumsiness that she'd heard so much about.

The other, however…

As the blond man continued to put distance between them, Gwen caught sight of the dagger in his hand—the dagger buried in the human's chest.

"I understand, General Thougher, that our relationship these past few years has been a shaky one. I understand that you don't like me, that you don't like my kind, and I'd like to take this moment, if you'd do me the honor of being silent for once, to tell you that I've never liked you, either. In fact, I'd go so far as to say I hate you. I hate you, General; I hate you, and, quite frankly, I hate your kind. I hate how you operate, I hate how you quarrel, and I hate that, despite all your nonsense about being an advanced race, you couldn't handle one… simple… task." He drew in a deep breath and slowly, carefully—as though turning the key in an old, rusty lock—twisted the blade. His inhale continued as the brown-haired man's dying gasp escaped, and it grew ragged until he couldn't inhale any further. "Thank you for your cooperation, General," he said, his voice almost a whisper as the blade shrieked against one of the dead man's ribs. With the dagger finally free, the blond pushed the dead man away, letting him fall to the floor, "But your services are no longer necessary."

*That voice,* Gwen lingered, *why was it so familiar?*

The sound of the body hitting the floor was like a jolt to Gwen, and the last of her sleepiness vanished as she realized what she'd just witnessed and a panicked whimper jumped from her lungs.

The blond man, hearing this, turned to face her, and, with her vision rapidly beginning to clear, she caught sight of the sharp features she'd been missing. His sharp, proud jaw. His long, thin nose. His penetrating blue—no, Gwen saw then, thin though it was, a bright-red ring that circled the blue like a shore of blood bordering an otherwise clear lake.

And his ears...

Fae ears!

"No..." she whispered to herself, trying to convince herself against what she already knew. "It's not possible."

"Oh, but it is, Gwendolyn—or do you prefer 'Gwen' now?" the matured, war-worn face of Hawkes smiled back. "It's *more* than possible. It's the *truth*." He stepped towards her, arms outstretched, "It's me."

Gwen trembled, her eyes darting to the dead body on the floor before returning to him. He was still holding the knife! Something flipped in her stomach and she lurched forward as her empty stomach tried to purge itself.

"Oh my! That's, well... they said that you'd gotten sick several times on your way here." Hawkes bit his lip and offered her a sympathetic smile, "A reaction to the drugs, I'm afraid." He shook his head, glaring back at the dead body and muttering to it.

"Dr-drugs?" Gwen shook her head, "I don't... I don't understand."

"Drugs," Hawkes repeated, setting the dagger down on a nearby desk. "Like spells. Well, in a way, at least. The humans' version of spells, I suppose. They're not very good with magic—totally ignorant of it, in fact—but they *are* rather good at figuring out how to make things work without it. For example…" he turned to a small, golden orb on the desk and opened the top-half to expose a small container. From it, he plucked two small, berry-looking objects and held them out to her. She stared back at the strange, smooth things, realizing they were not berries at all. "Pills," Hawkes said the word in the same flat tone he'd said "drugs" before, as though it was answer enough on its own. "You swallow them. Just don't chew! They're… well, they don't taste good if you do. Anyway, pills are a type of drug. Those particular pills will help your stomach and dizziness. I have to take them often myself, living in this place and all."

Gwen allowed him to drop the pills into her hand, but she couldn't bring herself to look away from him. "This place?"

He nodded, moving to the other side of the desk and sitting down. "Yes, the human city. Well, *the* human city; the first one. They have been spreading quite quickly, haven't they? Interesting creatures. They couldn't get a brick to lay even on the ground if you had a dozen of them working together, but I—even as a child!—was able to teach them. Now look at them! Still buffoons, I'll admit, but just look at how like us they are!" He spread his arms as a smile spread across his face. "Walls, Gwendolyn! Walls within walls within walls! And, surrounding it all, more walls! Walls of wood and stone and…"

Gwen shivered and rubbed her arms, recognizing a growing burning itch that whispered across her skin.

"Iron…" she finished for him.

Hawkes frowned and nodded. "Yes, iron. It's a troublesome material, but useful." He motioned to the pills in her hand again, "Another reason for the pills, you see. Now swallow them. The iron around us will only continue to harm you until you do."

Whimpering, Gwen dropped the pills into her mouth and wrestled against her body's urge to spit them out the moment they touched her tongue. It was like when she'd been a girl and licked the back of a burning gecko on a dare from her friends. It was bitter and sour and wrong. But even the gecko had tasted of nature. These were...

"Awful, I know," Hawkes nodded, steepling his fingers and resting his lower lip against the tips of his thumbs.

He stared expectantly as Gwen continued to struggle with his pills. Her throat went dry as she pushed to gulp them down, and what little moisture remained on her tongue clung to the pills and made the awful taste spread. She whimpered and flailed her hands.

Hawkes looked up, frowning at her reaction before suddenly nodding and moving a hand beneath his desk and pulling out a glass decanter with two curling ends that resembled a bull's horns. The base, deep and thick, sloshed with a deep red liquid. Tilting this, he let the contents roll into one of the horn-looking spouts and run like a narrow stream into a small glass he produced from behind the desk in time to keep it from staining his desk.

"I'd forgotten how hard that first swallow can be," he offered along with the glass. Gwen hurried to take the drink and gulped the contents, letting relief wash over her as the pills were washed down her parched throat. Gasping from the ordeal once the act was done, she looked up at Hawkes.

The fae male must have confused her relief for something else, because he immediately nodded and held up the liquor with pride. "My private reserve," he explained, pouring himself a glass. "I used to keep the decanter on my desk—it was a gift from the glassblowers, you see—but that one"—he nodded towards the dead body—"had a nasty habit of helping himself whenever he found himself in my office, which was too often if you ask me." He took a long sip from his glass, yet the contents of the glass barely diminished as he did.

Though she hated to offer any sort of credit to the awful pills, Gwen felt her body's reaction to the iron around them begin to fade. Feeling more comfortable with breathing in the air, she sucked in a hard breath and tried to regain a sliver of composure.

"You live here then? With the humans?" she asked.

Hawkes frowned and set down the liquor. The liquid sloshed within the base of the glass and, like it, his head bobbed back-and-forth. Before Gwen could decide if he was nodding or not, he spoke:

"And where else would I live, Gwendolyn? You're like me now, yes? A vagrant? According to our kind, there is no place for us!"

"But…"

Gwen's mind raced. For so long she believed her childhood friend to be dead. Though cases like hers, with a vagrant fae being so young, were incredibly rare, Hawkes had been an exception. Just like she had been an exception. Her parents hadn't let her watch Hawkes' progress through the labyrinth, knowing her heart was broken enough without watching the centaur rip him to pieces or for him to get turned around in the maze and slowly starve. But he hadn't been ripped to pieces. And he hadn't starved to death in the maze. He'd been condemned to what the elders at that time had called "the worst of the labyrinth's fates." The news of his escape was a shock to everyone. Never before had one escaped the complex network and the beast occupying it, and for a child to succeed where others, warriors even, had failed was something noone could have expected. Death in the labyrinth, however, was expected—it was known; understood—and what waited beyond them was not. That world was where centaurs roamed in great numbers, where elves practiced their dark magic, where deviants and rogues and murderers waited. The world out there was the nightmare that had driven the earliest fae to build their wall in the first place. Hawkes surviving the labyrinth was a great surprise to everyone, of this there was no question, but, like the elders had said, what awaited a young fae beyond those walls was a slow and certain death. And that's what Gwen had grown up knowing: Hawkes was dead. No matter the cause, no matter the time. It was, no doubt, exactly what her people were saying of her at that very moment. How foolish they'd all been. How foolish she'd been. Hawkes' crime had been sharing the gift of their people. For it, he'd been condemned to die, and, refusing even that, he'd come all this way.

And *this* was how he'd used his gifts…

Even as a child he'd said that he, like his father, would grow up to be a mage. Unsure of what this meant, Gwendolyn sought the wisdom of her mother, who explained that the mages practiced the opposite fields of magic that the healers did. Rosalind had said that, though the magic they used *was* meant to hurt and even kill, it was necessary to keep their people protected. If it weren't for the spells that the mage's created, the evil forces that would do harm to the fae warriors during their outings would rival their simple hunting tools and kill them. Then, without the warriors and the game they returned with, the fae city would be doomed to starve. And though her mother's explanation hadn't redeemed the mages in young Gwendolyn's eyes, and though it stood against everything she believed in, her friend's dreams didn't bother her. What she felt for Hawkes was stronger than her hatred for what the mages represented.

Looking at what had come of it, however, Gwen couldn't believe she'd ever seen promise in such magic.

"But why?" she finally asked. "Why come all this way? Why help the humans? Why let them become this powerful? And why would you allow them to keep the Winter Sun?"

Every hint of Hawkes' happiness faded then, and he leaned forward on his desk. "Our people cast us out, Gwendolyn. They condemned their own children to die. I'm sure they told you the same stories they told me, yes? That escape was impossible? That, should the gods new and old be kind enough to lead us out of those tunnels and out of the clutches of their beast, it would be an act of damnation. Was I to hope for sympathy where I was told there was none? Keep in mind I didn't have a savior, Gwendolyn; my centaur came down upon me with a spear, not compassion." He shook his head, "So before you judge me, old friend, I'd like you to ask yourself where you'd turn to if it wasn't for your centaur savior? Where? Would you take your hope to the elves? Would you trust your safety to the dwarves? Would you cast yourself to the taverns and their patrons to do with you as they wished? Or would you push yourself to march so far that all of the dangers you'd been warned of were a mountain and a dragon away? I sought the one people who I knew were too weak to hurt me, because they were too busy hurting themselves. And what I found in the humans was aggression, yes, but an aggression that was misplaced. They yearned to grow and expand and change the world. By joining them, leading them, I get to have a place in that new world; I get to decide how it's reshaped!" He smiled, "That's why I had you brought here as soon as I heard just who the new mystery vagrant was. You see, while I might not agree with our peoples' ways, I *do* believe in something I was taught during my studies: everything happens for a reason." He smiled, "It could've been anybody, I suppose, it's not like most of the to-be healers don't share your compassion, though I can see why it would've been you over any of them. But it *was* you, Gwendolyn, and through some miracle of fate you were given every opportunity to escape and find your way here. I believe this was our destiny! You and me: the Vagrants who will help rebuild the world as king and queen."

Gwen's eyes widened and she felt the urge to choke rise again. "Qu-queen? Me? Y-you and me? I... I don't—"

"You must have known how I felt?" Hawkes interrupted, "We might have been young, but you must have felt it, too? I've always loved you, Gwendolyn, and that you're sitting here now, at the peak of our work, cannot be some simple coincidence!"

"Hawkes," shock and fear were ensnaring Gwen and her heart was pounding so hard she could barely hear her own voice, "you can't possibly think that this is right. The humans... they care nothing of balance or nature or compassion. Before you they were bashing each other's heads in with rocks. They couldn't even care for their own kind! And you want *them* to take over? You think that any world shaped by them is going to be a better one? Hawkes, I understand that you're upset, angry even—I know because I feel the same way!—but this is not the way! You can stop it now! Leave this place and stop letting them use you!" She shook her head, "But we can't allow them to have the Winter Sun! I don't know how they got it, but—"

"They didn't get it, Gwendolyn, I created it for them," Hawkes' voice was so calm and proud that the information seemed wrong because of it. Gwen stared, stammering, unable to form a response to her old friend's confession. "Oh stop it, Gwen!" Hawkes rolled his eyes. "You didn't think they could've figured out something like that on their own, do you? They needed a way to make the job easier. A tree's roots are strong, and by enchanting iron with dark fae magic I discovered the perfect tool to weaken the roots and soften the ground."

197

Gwen glared at him, "Is that why you forged swords from it instead of shovels? Admit it! You helped them make a weapon!"

"What you call a weapon I call a symbol. Our hunters carried swords to go on a hunt. I should know, I was being trained how to enchant the blades," he smirked, "it's what gave me the idea, actually."

"Those swords were carved from bone! And the enchantments were to minimize the suffering of the game our hunters brought in!"

Hawkes cackled. "You believe that? Gwendolyn, have you ever gone on a hunt? Ever even seen one?" He shook his head, "No, of course not. Couldn't stomach it, I'm sure." He scoffed and shook his head, "Our hunters went out for deer and boars and fowl! None of which require a sword to take down!" He glared at her then, "Would you like to guess how many arrowheads they had us enchanting?" When Gwen didn't answer he nodded, "That's right! NONE!" he roared, slamming his fist down on the desk. "The swords were a symbol, and one that got a quick and immediate response: give a fae hunter reason to draw his sword on you, and you wouldn't live long enough to know you'd been cut!" He folded his arms in front of his chest, "So why give humans swords instead of shovels? Because, like the trees, some peoples' roots hold too deep, and it's better to loosen their grip with a solid message than to wave a glowing shovel!" Standing abruptly, Hawkes circled the table and stood over her with a swiftness and fury that reminded her all over again that he was a fae. "I'm offering you a chance to grow with me, Gwendolyn, and while I'm prepared to offer credit and merit to that clattering beast that saved your life, I'm hopeful that there's enough fae wit left in your head to know when you're being offered a golden opportunity! I want you to stand by me in this new world, but I will not allow you to stand between me and my progress. Now what will it be?"

Gwen, unable to answer, can't stop shivering. Despite this, she was still able to shake her head.

Hawkes shook his head, seeming disgusted with her suddenly. "The way you talk about the humans, it's just like the way our people talked about everything." He tilted his head, "What have you learned of their claims since your *assisted* escape? From what I've heard of your activities you've been indulging in a great many revelations in regards to just how wrong our people were. And yet, despite that—despite seeing the centaurs in a new light; the elves and the dwarves and the deviants, all of them—you *still* think you know the humans. Now, *were* they a violent and uncoordinated lot? Yes, absolutely! And without me they probably would still be! But you don't stop to consider the bigger picture. I gave them direction and magic, and with it they built a city that's *uncomfortably* similar to our own! And, unlike you with your four-legged savior, I was alone in my travels, and I chose to use that time to *think*! I thought about the humans as the selfish, self-destructive, violent lot that our people preached them to be, and then I thought about *our* people: a race *selfish* enough to wall themselves in and *violent* enough to wave enchanted weapons around to keep others away; a race *self-destructive* enough to cast away their own children as criminals!" He sneered and leaned over her, "Now you consider all those similarities, Gwendolyn Clearwater, and then consider this: of the two—the fae and the humans—which ones *lied* to us and condemned us to die? Who's truly more savage in the grand design: the race that has it all and kills for nothing, or the one that has nothing and kills in the hopes for everything?"

"You're..." Gwen sobbed, "You're asking me to help you kill the planet..." she looked down, remembering how easily

Hawkes had killed the man on the floor. "And that's some-thing I just can't do."

"Alright then…" Hawkes inhaled and shook his head before leaning over to kiss her forehead. As he drew away from the chilling act, he paused—his lips so close that his breath tickled her left ear—and whispered "If you won't listen to reason…"

# SIXTEEN

In the blink of an eye Hawkes paralyzed her body, binding her in place before slowly guiding her to the floor as sweetly as though he were laying her to rest. Her face, however, was hers to control. Screams came uninhibited, and control of her eyes, whether wide open or clenched shut, meant nothing against the pain. It was a pain unlike anything Gwen had experienced; one that she'd neither felt nor seen painted on the agonized faces of any she'd ever healed. Her mind was a jumble of fragmented thoughts and partial memories, as though somebody had snuck into her head and broken everything into tiny pieces and scattered them about. Hopes for peace stirred together with a trip to the beach with her mother which coincided with a botched stew recipe that reminded her of that time a fox whose name she couldn't remember was killed in front of her. Nothing made sense…

But, then again, it hadn't been making much more sense hours earlier.

Or had it been seconds?

Gwen cried out again, her throat feeling like a tortured length of fabric that could tear at any moment. Hawkes shifted and the pain subsided enough to feel his navigating fingers move across her head to target a new point. She tried to focus on the sensation to keep a hold on reality, but the fingers became giant spiders' legs dancing across her hair. Then they bit her. Again and again and again; venom-laced fangs buried deep into her scalp, drawing a renewed string of shrieks as she struggled within her own, unmoving body.

"I don't want for you to think this brings me a sliver of pleasure, Gwendolyn," Hawkes spoke so softly into her ear, and she wondered how he could be so calmly separated from the torment he was inflicting. His calmness only insulted her further as he said, "But it took great pain for me to see the path, and I'm beginning to think that centaur of yours may have spared you a bit too much pain for your own good."

The storm of pain died down long enough for Gwen to suck in a fresh lungful of air, cringing as her windpipe throbbed against the demand. "Puh... p-ple-ase," she stammered, sections of the simple word slipping out as rogue whimpers, "Th-thi-is... n-not you..."

"It's not?" Hawkes pulled his fingers away, and the spiders vanished; the segmented thoughts and partial memories rebuilding as every nerve on her body that was, moments ago, positive of the pain suddenly felt nothing.

Gwen blinked at the sudden calmness. Only the pain in her throat and the ache around her tear-filled eyes remained. Slowly, she felt control of her body begin to return and she marveled at how the simple act of wiggling her big toe brought her such tremendous relief. She managed to say "what...?" with nary a trace of difficulty before Hawkes planted himself over her, straddling her waist with either foot—his heels pinching her sides—and crouched down to bring his face closer to hers.

"I've loved you since the day we met, Gwendolyn Clearwater," he announced, though the confession felt more like an accusation, "and since that time there's hardly been a day that goes by without you in my thoughts or a night that passes without you in my dreams." He shook his head and reached out with his left hand to trace the knuckle of his left hand across her cheek, following the path of tears. "And now the divine have granted you to me—a symbol of their approval for all my hard work—and you…" he drew his hand away slowly before bringing it down with cringing force across her cheek once again. The sound of the slap echoed throughout the room as the ache did the same in her jaw. "You sully my moment with arrogance and defiance!" he hissed past clenched teeth.

Gwen trembled more under the weight of his glare than the force of his attack, though her cheek still burned from the slap.

Hawkes sneered, seeming insulted by her shivers. "You torture me for years—memories of you haunting me and prayers for you escaping my lips every day since I was cast an entire world's distance from you—and when you finally see the empire I built on sweat and blood and an entire ocean of tears you refuse accept the role I've built *specifically* for you?" He moved to slap her again and, but, as she howled in protest and cringed, he suddenly stayed his hand in mid-swing.

Shaking his head, he dropped his raised hand to his side. "You say this is not me? You think that I've been changed, my beloved?" he asked, finally rising to his feet and stepping back. "I say you've been spoiled. You haven't had to fight a day in your life. You were pampered in a world where everything could be healed with a spell and a smile. And then, when reality caught up with you and actually meant to punish you, the bringer of your death—the centaur who was

203

supposed to kill you!—had a change of heart and whisked you away from our peoples' walls and allowed you to start your own personal campaign of *nonsense!*"

He sauntered away from her, stepping beside his desk and retrieving one of pills from the golden orb. After making a show of gulping it loudly, he turned back to her, already shaking his head once again. "I love you, Gwendolyn Clearwater, and I am a fae who was cast away from his people and away from you. I have suffered. I have struggled. I have, on my own, had to still my dagger as it hovered over my heart on more occasions than you've ever even faced down the receiving end of any weapon." He scoffed, "You are a fetus kept safe in a womb of your own sheltered world, and you think you can tell me who I am or who I am *not* simply because I've played with the cards I was dealt while you were coddled every step of the way?" He moved to crouch behind her to begin his torture all over again, his head still shaking back-and-forth, "Take your first life on your own, Gwendolyn Clearwater, and maybe then you can talk to me about who I am."

Gwen shivered under the weight of Hawkes' speech and the growing fear that his torture was about to begin anew. "Y-you're wrong," she fought to keep her voice steady, hoping to hide how scared she really was. "You're wrong"—she repeated, more satisfied with the tone this time—"about many things."

"Oh?" Hawkes', still crouched, withdrew his outstretched hands and rested his elbows on his knees, "Do explain."

"For starters, the centaur who saved me wasn't the one meant to kill me. He came in to save me from one of his own because in my world of spells and smiles"—she smirked—"people have a way of repaying kindness."

"I see," he chuckled. "Is that all then?"

"No…" she fought to keep from trembling, "There's two more things."

Hawkes motioned with his hand for her to go on.

"I... I *have* killed!" she cringed at her own confession, unable to take pride in it the same way Hawkes did. "It was one of *your* human soldiers armed with one of *your* cursed iron swords, out on what I can only assume was one of *your* orders. And after all the suffering I saw that *you* were responsible for, and meeting your own criteria to say so I can say with every bit of certainty that you are not the Hawkes Stormbreak I once knew and loved."

He seemed taken aback by her proclamation, and she caught sight of a glimmer of something that she wanted to believe was regret. Any shred of emotion, however, was washed away by a stony rigidness that washed over him a moment later.

"How very enlightening," his voice was every bit as rigid and cold as his posture. "And the second thing?"

"Right," Gwen nodded and locked onto his gaze, narrowing her eyes at him. "I wasn't sent by your divine as a gift for your work. And while you may see our work so far as nonsense, it's only because you still consider the fae *your* people, and they have an ugly way of walling themselves off from the truth. But I promise you, Hawkes, those walls will come down."

"What a beautiful sentiment," Hawkes chided, rolling his eyes and reaching out once more to begin his torture, "but I'm afraid you won't remember any of it after I'm done with you."

Gwen drew in another breath, bracing herself for what she was about to do, clenching her fists against her own body's refusal to act upon her plan. She had to act. She *had* to!

"Did I mention the centaur and I are lovers?" she let the words flow with as much ice and malice as she could conjure.

After all of Hawkes' efforts to keep his composure during Gwen's corrections, she knew that detail would be the one to break him. Still hunched and reaching out, his balance was compromised, and with the shock of her words seeping into him she saw him falter. It was a minor shift, but it was all the shift she needed to act.

Calling upon her fae reflexes and every bit of bravery that had carried her that far, Gwen folded her body as tightly as she could until her knees were pressed to her chest and the pads of her bare feet were pressed against Hawkes chest. Her old friend's face twisted as he saw her intention, but before he could act she'd already begun to follow through with the motions. Kicking outward, she sent Hawkes tumbling back as she rolled to her feet.

"Well that was certainly unexpected and... uncharacteristic of you," Hawkes groaned, coughing from Gwen's assault on his sternum, as he struggled to stand. "So tell me, Gwendolyn, after your little display of aggression what was to come next? Just what did you have planned to escape this kingdom of concrete and iron and manned by thousands of soldiers? I'd gladly draw you a map to the front gate just to see you try to bunny-kick your way through their iron-clad forces!"

Jumping away, the phantom agony propelling her to keep her distance from the dark mage her childhood friend had become, Gwen tried to decide what to do next. Admittedly, she'd made no plan beyond that one simple act, and even that had almost been too much for her to follow through with. The simple command of "FIGHT" was still more than she could follow, and, even then—staring at the fae clutching his chest and shuddering from each breath—she felt a part of herself tugging at her to help him while another part struggled with the growing nausea at being the source of his pain. Willpower and fear alone kept her standing her ground.

Concrete and iron and thousands of guards...

Just what did she have planned...?

Hawkes, as though he could read her thoughts, smirked and straightened himself.

"Thought so," he chortled. "Then this was nothing more than a violent outburst?" he asked, cracking his knuckles. "Fine, then allow me offer my rebuttal."

Then, reaching into his jacket, Hawkes retrieved a small wooden box with a powerful containment spell carved into its surface. Even with the distance between them, Gwen could see the power radiating off of it, and she found herself curious what sort of trinket her old friend could have waiting in the container to warrant such powerful magic. Opening the box, he slipped the fingers of first his right hand and then his left; fitting a pair of iron knuckles across each. His face twisted as the skin surrounding the toxic metal began to discolor from the contact, but he made no move to remove them. Then, letting out a long, pained sigh, he slipped out of his thick jacket and let it pool around his feet on the floor.

"All of my generals have a set of these, as well," he flexed his hands to illustrate the weapons, but Gwen could only see the growing signs of iron poisoning spreading across his palms. Scowling at her concerned face, he lowered his hands and motioned for the dead human a short distance away. "You're more than welcome to retrieve the late General Thougher's if you'd like to try to even the odds, but I'm willing to wager you won't."

"You're insane…" Gwen whispered, not meaning the words as an insult but a terrible revelation.

Hawkes' ears twitched and he scowled. Meant or not, he'd taken Gwen's words as an insult.

"Then you have only your empathy to blame for what's coming!"

Lunging at her, Hawkes led with a punch aimed for Gwen's chest. Seeing the toxic metal driven by an even more poisonous madness, she jumped blindly away from both.

Landing with her lower back against the edge of Hawkes' desk, she grimaced both at the sharp pain as well as the realization that she could back away no further. This realization, however, came a few seconds too late for her to properly act, and Hawkes and his iron knuckles finally connected the attack with her left shoulder.

Fire consumed Gwen as different degrees of pain converged all at once.

"Only yourself to blame!" Hawkes' voice seethed with the same fury as the sizzling iron pressing to her shoulder.

"H-how could you…?" she struggled against the pain to speak, looking up at him. "Y-you're… d-don't you see that you're hurting yourself?"

Hawkes scoffed and, pulling away with the one fist, drove the other into Gwen's side, forcing her to kneel.

"Hurting myself?" he laughed. "Gwendolyn Clearwater, you're the only person I know who could wake up in the middle of a war and actually worry about the winning side." He reached over her to retrieve three more of the pills and swallowed them one by one, making a note of hanging his free hand in Gwen's face so she could watch the toxic effects of the iron around the weapon begin to fade. "Be sure to speak up when you begin to understand just how dire the circumstances are for you. Allow me to illustrate the full scope of the situation: I have the numbers, the magic, and a real plan, where you are few, untrained, and acting on impulse while relying on dumb luck. I have a unionized race rising in strength with each passing day and possessing an unmatched power aimed at reshaping a planet that will soon be reclaimed by uncoordinated herds of grunting idiots." He flexed his fingers within the iron knuckles and shrugged, "It won't be long before the full bulk of my forces have the means to get past that mountain with all of our superior weaponry and supplies, and when that happens there won't be a single race, not even our own with their walls, with the means to stop what's coming. We will come, and we will come with the rising of the Winter Sun to fulfill our goals. And not to get overly boastful, my fellow vagrant, but I have the cure to the only arguable weakness that I share with those nature-loving simpletons."

Gwen looked over her shoulder at the golden orb that held the iron-defying pills as she pushed herself to stand. Not seeing her as a threat, Hawkes stepped back to allow it.

"You've... you've surrounded yourself in poison. So much that you've let everything good about you rot away..." Gwen heaved, hugging her arms around her waist to hold back some of the pain.

"Weren't you listening?" Hawkes laughed, "I have the cure to your so-called poison!"

"Take it from a healer, Hawkes Stormbreak," she gritted her teeth as she took a single step towards him, "there's a difference between being cured and being numbed. But you'll learn that the hard way..."

Then, ignoring the fire in her shoulder and in her side, Gwen vaulted over the desk, scooping up the golden orb and cradling it to her chest as she did the one thing she knew she could do better than Hawkes:

She ran.

Landing on the other side of the desk, Gwen had precious few seconds to decide which direction in the windowless room would lead her out. The door off to her left felt peaceful and calm to her—in some strange way it felt almost like her home back at the fae city—while the door to her right was practically saturated in the stink of iron and death and danger.

Coming to grips with her circumstances, she committed to the unthinkable...

In a few short weeks Gwen had become so painfully accustomed to iron that she could practically smell it. In every instance, she knew that no matter what direction the stink of iron was in, she wanted to point herself away from it. It was this instinct that kept her several steps ahead of the human soldiers during the raids on their city, and it was this instinct that kept her from running face first into danger. Every fiber of her being screamed their familiar warnings to her as she forced herself to ignore this instinct. Hawkes had gone to great lengths to protect his chambers from the metal that was laced throughout the entire capital, which meant that, in order to distance herself from Hawkes, she had to follow whatever traces of the stuff she could find.

Still clutching Hawkes' 'cure' to iron, she sprinted to the right, ignoring the enraged calls of her childhood friend as she did. Finding out too late that the door opened inward, Gwen crashed into the surface, startled to find it was carved from helitrad wood, and cried out at the renewed pain throbbing in her shoulder. Not needing to look to know Hawkes was already starting after her, she fumbled with the handle—crying out as she discovered it was iron—and finally stumbled out into a long, cold hallway.

"YOU'LL DIE OUT THERE, GWENDOLYN! MARK MY WORDS, YOU WILL DIE OUT THERE!"

*Better to die out there than live in there with you,* she thought to herself as she picked a direction—seeing no worse fate in a wrong turn at that moment than being dragged back into Hawkes' madness—and sprinted for her life.

"GWENDOLYN!" Hawkes' voice grew distant but evermore desperate. "GWEEEENDOOOOLYYYYYYYYYY...!"

Turning a bend, Gwen finally put the horrible call far enough behind her to lose it under the clamor of her footsteps slapping against the ground. Ahead of her, she saw another doorway with a sign over it wearing a strange set of markings that she'd never seen before. Not caring what they meant, she pushed through and cried out as the floor vanished beneath her and she collapsed down a flight of stairs. Body still screaming from the pain—both the new aches of her fall as well as the old—she worked to get her feet under her and turned her fall into a clumsy run down the remaining steps and onto a platform and, beyond that, down another set of steps. More platforms and even more steps followed, and Gwen happily descended each one. Eventually she'd reach the bottom, and the bottom would mean ground, and ground would mean she was one step closer to getting out of that awful place. After growing used to the pattern of platform-to-stairway, however, Gwen found herself nearly running straight into the concrete wall and stopped in time to keep herself from injuring herself that much more.

"Hate this place…" she grumbled, fumbling and cursing with another iron handle.

She was still hissing in pain as she stepped through and found herself staring at nearly a half-dozen humans standing between her and the exit. Turning at the sound of the door, the five unarmed men blinked at what Gwen was certain was an unusual sight for them. A flash of panic urged her to go back before the still-young and forced instinct of sprinting towards danger suggested a reasonable alternative.

Heeding this, she once again ran straight into the face of danger, and watched as the five scrambled around one another, some seeming to look for a weapon while others simply trying to avoid what they believed to be an impending attack. In the chaos of their movement, Gwen saw an opening and slipped through it before starting straight for the row of windows that rested on either side of the door heading out into the humans' capital city. Through the windows, however, Gwen could already see a small army of soldiers starting towards the building.

Hawkes had already called in his troops…

Tightening her hold on the golden orb she'd stolen from the other vagrant fae's desk, she veered off her intended course. The first of the soldiers were already starting through the door as she leapt for the furthest of the windows to the left. With half of the soldiers already inside the building and the others already starting away from the door to try to intercept her, Gwen used her stolen prize to smash through the window. Bracing herself for more pain before she'd even landed, she begrudgingly let her body tumble through the shards of broken glass and crashed down on the other side, trying to distance herself as much as she could from the shards as she rolled to her feet.

Try as she might, however, her right foot still fell upon a shard.

Crying out, Gwen felt the speed she'd been relying on fade into a haze of searing pain that racked her entire body with each step. The call of the soldiers behind her spurred her onward, however, and she forced herself to push on. A voice in the back of her mind, one that now chose to sound like Hawkes, itemized all the reasons she was doomed to fail in her attempts to escape. She was no longer able to boast speed over any of them. She was already leaving a bloody trail to alert any humans *not* already following her of her location. She was unarmed and unable to commit a single act of violence without making herself sick. She was a single fae in the largest of the human cities; she was grossly outnumbered and slowly being poisoned by the iron that existed just about anywhere she could hope to turn. Rounding the building and feeling the first wave of dark energy from the Winter Sun, however, Gwen came to realize that she'd barely begun to scrape the surface of her futility...

She'd heard of the gremlins and their machines before. The fae elders spoke of roaring "death traps" powered by coal and built of crudely shaped wood and stone that allowed the tiny creatures to travel more efficiently and tear apart forest and fae as they did. During her time away from the fae, however, Gwen had learned that the gremlins, like all other non-human creatures, meant no harm to nature or any other creature and, in fact, relied on their unique ability to build strange machines as a means of bartering with others. Dwarf miners were able to work faster with digging machines while ogres found a faster means of brewing the ale that many villages celebrated almost all occasions with. It seemed for just about every task, there was a machine that the gremlins could construct to make the job easier.

Just about every task...

Gwen recalled the few villagers who'd mentioned the rumors of humans robbing the gremlins of their machines, but in the chaos of everyone else's shouts they'd been swallowed into the mass of assumed absurdities.

The old dwarf had talked about the humans making a roar *inside* the mountain, and how when it was all over they'd mined every trace of iron ore. Even then Gwen had a hard time believing such a thing was possible, but as she rounded the building and felt the first wave from the Winter Sun burn her skin, she caught sight of a new breed of machines—built of iron and powered by a familiar blue glow—as they roared about the massive clearing ahead of her.

Smaller machines piloted by several humans cleared a massive distance in a short period of time to deliver supplies from one side of the Winter Sun to the other while much larger machines piloted by many humans worked diligently around the massive space. And though none of the machines seemed built specifically to kill, it didn't take much imagination to see how even the smallest of them could easily crush an entire army on foot.

A fresh wave of dread washed over Gwen as she heard the first explosion in the distance, followed soon after by a familiar voice shouting her name.

*Megan J. Parker & Nathan Squiers*

The collective pain in her body suddenly seemed so overwhelming that she wondered how she'd made it so far, but, by some strange miracle, Gwen remained upright as she turned towards the source.

"Gav…"

Just saying his name brought her relief.

# SEVENTEEN

G av and Blay had arrived in time to stir up enough may-
hem to slip away while the humans were distracted, and
though she was, for the time being, safe and rejoined with
her comrades, her body was still trembling. Even several
hours after escaping the human capital and with the bulk
of her injuries healed, she couldn't stop shaking. Both Gav
and Blay insisted that they, too, could still feel the burning
itch of the Winter Sun after only a few minutes of exposure,
but Gwen knew there was more to what plagued her than
the enchanted iron.

"I've spent countless hours staring off at the humans'
capital and dreaming of setting fire to the entire place,"
Blay's voice was either incredibly controlled enthusiasm or
poorly concealed disappointment; it was heavy and slow
and trembling. "But that was my first time ever setting foot
inside of it."

Gav seemed to share Gwen's uncertainty of their
friend's emotional state from his words, and the centaur

raised an eyebrow as he finished setting up their new fire pit.

"So what do you think about your first step into the humans' capital?" he asked, pressing for some clarity.

Blay shrugged and stared at the stack of firewood in the pit for a moment before it burst into flames, forcing Gav to jump back at the sudden blaze.

"I think I understand why my hatred for them is outweighed by my fear of them," he sighed, shaking his head. "And that only makes me hate them more."

Gwen chewed her lip and glanced over at her friend. She'd watched Blay slip into a dark place during previous raids and use his powers in shocking and often terrifying ways, but she had never seen Blay lose himself as badly as he had this time. In the past it had always seemed excessive, but they'd survived because of those actions. This time hadn't seem, at first, much different, but the sight of Blay lingering behind as Gav took advantage of the confusion to carry Gwen towards the front gate had served as an ominous hint that it wasn't going to end the same. They were already beyond the walls before they saw Blay following after, but a myriad of explosions and the sounds of screams coupled with several-dozen plumes of smoke rising from within the city echoed a tale of fiery carnage too gruesome to fathom. The city was still standing, however—Gwen doubted that even the dragon within Blay had enough fire to burn it all down—and though she was thankful for the rescue, she couldn't help but feel that the suffering she'd endured from Hawkes was as upsetting to Blay as that fact. At that moment, Gwen realized that the threat of what was waiting inside of their friend might be closer than they'd anticipated.

And everybody seemed to realize it...

A long, quiet moment hung over the three; an awkward silence impregnated with the potential to become far more uncomfortable.

"So…" Gwen cleared her throat and inched closer to the fire to make a show of enjoying its warmth, "H-how did you find me?"

"We didn't find you," Blay answered too quickly with a wide smirk, his eyes already glued to the fire. Without looking away, he nodded towards Gav and added, "The big guy never lost sight of the machine that carried you into the city. Even forced me to ride on his back because I was moving too slowly for his liking." He looked up at Gwen then, his smirk remaining, "Thank you for that awkwardness, by the way." His eyes returned to the fire and he sighed, "We tailed the damn thing for a few hours. It was too fast to keep in our sights, but it was noisy and smelled like an ogre's trousers, so it was easy enough to track."

"I was inside one of those machines?" she asked.

"One of the smaller, faster ones," Gav nodded, settling in beside her. "It was like a carriage that needed no horses to pull it…"

"Still don't know how that works," Blay scoffed, but the humor didn't seem to reach his eyes.

Gav sighed and shrugged. "Either way… When we saw it pass the last of the northernmost cities we knew it was heading for the capital, so we broke away from the road it was on to make better time through the forest. We reached the capital in time to see the machine take you inside We were still in the process of planning a way inside when we overheard a bunch of soldiers going on about the president's prisoner getting loose."

"They were too busy clamoring around to find you they didn't even see us sneak in…" Blay's voice sounded suddenly distant, as though it was every bit as consumed by the flames as his eyes.

Gav frowned at their friend, but said nothing about it as he focused all his attention on Gwen.

"Can you tell us what happened to you while you were in there, Gwen?" he asked, beginning to gently rub her back.

She nodded slowly, collecting herself and stealing one last glance at Blay before turning away, as well. " It was…" she stifled a shiver, "It's been Hawkes all along. You were right, he did survive out here after escaping the labyrinth. He said he found the humans shortly after his escape and… and I guess he was able to scare them into following his command."

Gav frowned at that. "You're saying a young fae organized the humans and allowed for this uprising in only a few short years?"

Gwen nodded, frowning at it as well. "I can't explain it more than that. Maybe they were already close to their own advancement and saw Hawkes as a means of making it quicker, or maybe he had help… I don't know. I just don't know! But he's their president now, and he's the one that created the Winter Sun! He… he said I was some sort of divine gift for all his hard work, and when I refused him he…" she started trembling again.

"It's alright," Gav moved his hand from rubbing her back to hold her close, "he can't hurt you anymore."

"No, you're wrong," Gwen said, already beginning to tear up. "Hawkes said that they've found a way to get past the mountain, and that it won't be long until they arrive to destroy everything and rebuild it how they want. He kept saying he would be the king of that new world, and that he wanted me…" she shivered again, "He wanted me to be his queen."

Gav sneered at that, but said nothing more.

"So what happens now?" Gwen finally asked.

"Well, that much is clear," Gav sighed. "Obviously we can't let Hawkes continue. He'll be weakened without those things," he nodded towards the golden orb with Hawkes' pills in it, "but it's clear that we aren't strong enough to fight this on our own."

"Then we don't," she said. "We can go back to the other side of the mountain. This new information should be enough to motivate others to join us. After what you and me and Blay have seen, I'm…" Gwen paused at that, wondering if that was truly the case. Most of the villagers they had come across in their journey weren't interested in fighting, and most seemed more inclined to run and hide rather than risk a conflict. After all the lies the faes had fed her about the savagery of other races, she'd been surprised to find that, for the most part, even the most intimidating beings would sooner take to their homes than risk any sort of danger. The acts of violence that scattered about the region were from rogues who thrived on unsuspecting travelers and surprise attacks, and even they were quick to flee at any sign of a threat. For this they'd need warriors that weren't afraid to stand up for a cause and fight for what was right.

But the last warriors she'd seen were in the fae city, and she knew they would never offer help to outsiders.

Let alone outsiders led by a vagrant.

"I can see your worry, Gwen," Gav smirked. "Fear not, while the creatures we've met aren't ones for fighting in most situations, this situation is dire enough for them to begin fighting."

"I hope you're right, Gav," Gwen whispered, glancing over at Blay, who was already curled up in his egg-like form and asleep by the fire.

Though she was still unsettled by his behavior earlier, something about the sight offered her some peace of mind for the time being. Feeling a sense of privacy with Gav, she looked back up at him and pressed further against him, relishing in the feeling of warmth and security his powerful body exuded.

"Do you think Blay's going to be okay?" she asked. "Earlier today he…" she bit her lip. "He seems to be losing control more frequently, and the destruction…"

Gav nodded, following her gaze and sighing. "I can't say I'm happy about his methods, but there's something calculated happening in that egg-shaped thing. We might not always be able to see it, and we might not always agree with what he does, but I'd be a liar if I said we weren't alive today because of him. More times than I'd care to admit it's been him and his fire that's saved the day over me and my axe. And though his story might not have made it sound like it, he was just as hell-bent on getting in there to save you as I was. And it's not like I didn't leave my own fair share of bodies," he shrugged, "it's just easier to tally up a higher number when you're not taking them out one-by-one."

"But what about the dragon?" she asked, "Aren't you nervous that he's getting closer to hatching?"

"The thought's crossed my mind," he admitted, "but until that day comes there's bigger things to worry about."

Gwen scowled, "You're not usually the type to throw caution to the wind."

Gav nodded at that, "And normally you'd be right, but in this case throwing caution to the wind means keeping the strongest weapon we've got right now close by while we face down a human-made doomsday. The idea of him suddenly tearing open and becoming a fire-spewing monster is definitely a risk, but we're facing far more impending risks each day to quarantine ourselves from him."

"The lesser of two evils, huh?" Gwen sighed.

Gav shrugged and smiled down at her, "I like to follow in your footsteps and keep a positive outlook on things, so until we know for certain I'd like to believe the dragon inside him won't represent any sort of evil."

Gwen chuckled at that, "You want to believe a dragon will be good just because you're keeping a positive outlook on things?"

Gav laughed, "I said it was *your* way, not the *smart* way."

Though she couldn't help but laugh along with him, Gwen still moved to drive one of her tiny fists into his arm. "You're mean!" she accused, though her lingering giggles gave away how strongly believed those words. When their laughter had passed, she felt a moment of serenity pass as she reflected on her place in the centaur's arms.

"I was so scared I was going to die back there," she confessed. "That I wouldn't ever get to see you again…"

"It sounds like you were really brave," Gav whispered, continuing to hold her. "I know it doesn't take back what happened to you in there, but I'm really proud of you for standing up to that fae all on your own."

She nodded and rested against his chest and leaned her head against him. "I told him we were lovers," she confessed.

Gav tensed as he looked back down at her. "Oh?" was all he could seem to reply with.

Gwen blushed at his reaction and nodded. "I knew telling him that at the time would distract him so that I could get away, but just saying it…" she blushed and smiled, "It felt right. I think it actually gave me the strength to attack him."

Gav's eyes widened, "You attacked him?"

Gwen raised an eyebrow at him, "I think you're missing the point."

Gav mirrored her gesture. "Oh?" he said again, though this one carried more confidence, "And what's the point?"

"A-about what I said… about us," Gwen stammered, feeling her cheeks burn under his stare.

"Then are we *not* lovers?" he pressed, "Are you saying you lied to him?"

"Wha—no! No, I… I meant it! I…" she trailed off as she saw him smirking humorously at her. Sighing, she looked away, embarrassed. "I suppose I wanted to make sure I wasn't lying," she admitted, "I meant it, but… well, it takes two to make that decision."

Gav smirked and nodded, "And I thought we already had made it." Shrugging again, he traced the knuckle of his hand over her cheek, "I guess that's why I thought you were talking about *attacking* him! That seems like new news to me, at least."

She blushed and leaned against his touch. Though Hawkes had done the same thing earlier that day, the act felt so much more right with Gav's hand caressing her face. At that moment, any shred of doubt she might have had was washed away.

Giggling, she nodded, "He seemed surprised by it, as well. He even called it 'uncharacteristic' of me."

"It seems we're in agreement about something, then," Gav smirked. "Though it's worth noting that I'm feeling pride where I can't imagine he feels the same. You going to be some kind of warrior now?"

Gwen blushed again and shook her head. "I didn't *like* attacking him, Gav! I'm… I'm still a healer," she looked down, suddenly feeling guilty. "I just… I had to—"

"Hey," he hooked a finger under her chin and guided her gaze back up to him. "I'm just glad to have you back. Warrior or healer, you'll always be Gwen to me."

He wrapped both of his arms around her, hugging her tighter against his body. Gwen allowed herself to be swept up in his embrace, taking comfort in their closeness.

As the two gazed at one another, Gav moved his hands slowly to cup her face and she lifted her chin towards his own. Understanding the growing need in the other, they closed the distance between them, and Gwen moaned, accepting his kiss and instantly returning it with her own, working to match his passion. Like everything Gav did, his kiss was deep and meaningful and stronger than she ever could have imagined, and though her eyes had closed to appreciate the moment a part of her felt a glow that rivaled even the Winter Sun rising between them. Even after the momentary eternity passed and their lips parted, she almost thought she could see the shimmer hold between them.

The two held one another's gaze for a long moment after that, as though their souls had yet to finish their own kiss, and the serenity only seemed to grow between them. Then, so slowly they barely seemed to move at all, the two settled in beside the dying fire to sleep.

"My sister was right about your hair," Gav smiled, lifting a red maple leaf from the ground and holding it up beside her. "It is the color of a maple tree leaves on an autumn's turn."

She looked at the leaf and smiled at that, "I like that better than Hawkes' comparison."

"What did he say?" Gav raised an eyebrow, already beginning to position himself for her to lie against.

She accepted his offer and moved to lie against his body, already finding herself growing tired from just the contact. She yawned loudly as she snuggled deeper into his fur, enjoying the feel of his warm horse body against hers.

"He said… strawberries in a wheat field, 'cept I always hated strawberries," she mumbled, beginning to fall asleep.

"I see," Gav chuckled.

"Sleep well, Gav," she murmured.

"You too, Gwen," Gav whispered back. "Sweet dreams."

# EIGHTEEN

The trip through the northern forests and back over the mountain to get back to the village took several days, and with each day that passed Gwen's skepticism grew. The nights belonged to her and Gav after Blay fell asleep, and, staring into her lover's eyes and enjoying his kisses, she could scarcely conjure a full sentence let alone a negative thought. But sleep eventually took them, and the new day would await her awakening with a renewed reminder of every doubt that plagued her the day before.

She cared too deeply for all the souls she'd come to meet, and the idea that they would allow their fear to pave the way to their deaths ate away at her. And yet, though she wanted nothing more than to believe that the threat of the humans' plans to destroy everything would be enough to spur a fight for survival, she'd seen the kindness and gentleness inside of them. Like hers; too much like hers. This thought, more than any other, tortured her, because she knew that if the tables were turned and it was her being called upon to fight she'd be unable to. She'd want to survive, of course—every bit as she wanted to survive now—but she'd be no more willing to become a soldier in those circumstances than she was now. She still couldn't stomach the idea of raising a fist against another, but she was now committed to a three-day journey to push others to do it for her?

*An all new low*, she thought to herself as she trudged beside Blay and Gav. *A war-mongering hypocrite...*

How could she expect others to take up a fight when she could barely stomach the guilt of the few she'd brought pain to?

How could she push the killing of human soldiers when the face of the single human she'd accidentally killed stared menacingly at her in her dreams?

*Could you kill him to heal the world?*
*Would you kill him to save them all?*

She hid behind the comfort that, in a group of three, she was the only one not willing to kill to do what needed to be done. There was, however, no guarantee that for every three souls they called upon, two would rise, and it was even less likely that, of those that did accept the call, they'd be half as driven as Gav or half as powerful as Blay.

Knowing who they were asking, Gwen was certain they'd be every bit the coward she was...

"You've got this," Gav whispered, nodding her forward into the crowded pub.

Gwen fought the urge to bite her lip, knowing that even if Gav didn't see it somebody else was bound to. Stepping forward, she pulled a chair from a vacant table and stepped up in the middle of the room.

"Uhh... p-pardon? Excuse me? I... I have something to..." she trailed off, looking around; nobody had so much as batted an eyelash in her direction.

Gwen sighed and sucked in a deep breath. She realized that if she didn't exude her own confidence, she wouldn't stand a chance at rallying any confidence in the others. Though she was still teeming with doubt and guilt, she swallowed it back and decided it was better to pretend than to doom them all without trying.

"EXCUSE ME! CAN I HAVE EVERYBODY'S ATTENTION?"

The entire pub quieted into a hushed murmur as every pair of eyes turned their attentions on Gwen, though none seemed more surprised than her at that moment. Slowly, a wave of recognition passed, and it wasn't long before the patrons began cheering and waving to the celebrity fae healer. Seeing their excitement at her return, she began to wonder if her standing with them might provide some sway on their decision. With a cautious optimism rising in her, she urged the crowd to settle so that she could speak.

"WE'RE IN DANGER!" she announced, pressing onward and keeping her eyes moving around the room. "ALL OF US—YOU, YOUR FAMILIES, YOUR FRIENDS; EVERYONE!—AND WE NEED YOUR HELP! THE HUMANS ARE COMING"—a series of stifled gasps rippled through the crowd and Gwen caught sight of several patrons immediately looking away—"A-AND THEY MEAN…" Gwen paused to swallow a knot that was forming in her throat. "THEY MEAN TO DESTROY EVERYONE AND EVERYTHING! ANOTHER FAE NAMED HAWKES HAS BEEN LEADING THEM, AND THEY ALREADY HAVE A MASSIVE WEAPON BUILT OF ENCHANTED IRON CAPABLE OF…" she saw more eyes drift away and more murmurs pass. "THEY WANT… THEY WANT THE WORLD, AND… a-and they need… to be stopped…"

"So what are we supposed to do about it?" someone finally called out.

226

"If he's already led them this far, how are we supposed to stop them? Mixing magic *and* iron, there's no way to fight that!" another added.

"N-no! We can! If we just band together, I know we can fight against the humans!" Gwen bit her lip. "Please, listen…"

"If what she says is true, we should spend whatever time we have left with our families!"

"It's hopeless…"

"… saw what the humans could do *without* enchanted iron and fae leadership!"

"COWARDS!" Blay roared, silencing the entire room in an instant, and pushed through the group to stand beside Gwen. "Cowards:" he repeated, this time so quietly that the patrons had to strain to hear him, "each and every last one of you!"

"We're cowards because we refuse to join a suicide mission?" one of the patrons called out. "You heard the fae! They mean to kill us all and they've got a weapon that can do just that!"

Blay turned towards the speaker and took a step towards them. "Yes, they do. They have the weapon and the intent, and standing against that is almost certain death, isn't it?"

"Exactly! So what right do you have to call us cowards for refusing to die at the hands of the humans and some super-weapon?"

Blay paused before the speaker, a well-aged elf male with long, graying hair who was sitting behind the bar.

"Do you know what I am?" he asked the elf.

The elf scrunched his nose, trying to figure out the answer to that question. When no answer came to him, however, he shrugged. "Just a fool tagging along with that pretty, naïve fae, I suppose."

"I'm a dragon's egg," he boasted matter-of-factly, pausing long enough for everyone in the room to do with that information what they would. "And if you want to see what a doomed and futile life is, I suggest you stare long and hard at possibly one of nature's cruelest jokes."

More nervous murmurs passed around the pub.

Gwen frowned, looking around, and moved to pull Blay back. "Maybe we shouldn't—"

Blay pulled away and held up a hand to silence her.

Not sure what he had planned but seeing that he at least had the crowd, Gwen didn't fight it any further.

Blay took another step towards the elf. "Why don't you tell me what it's like to see the futility in fighting? Me? I've been fighting the thing inside me for *years*! It is my fate— my purpose—to carry the dragon until it's strong enough to finally rip free of my body! I exist to 'hatch' and die! There's no stopping it; I either carry the beast to full strength or I fail to protect it and kill us both! See, a good life for an egg is lasting long enough for the creature inside of them to violently rip itself free; that's what I have to look forward to if I'm successful!" he looked around the room, continuing his speech: "However, if you're successful, then you not only get to see a full life and enjoy your families, you maybe even a shred of self-respect at not simply rolling over and accepting death like a bunch of roaches waiting under a giant boot." Finally, after making a full revolution, he came to face the elf again. "But, please," he muttered, the disgust in his voice oozing like venom, "tell me all about why you shouldn't even bother *trying* to fight."

The murmurs passing around the room began to grow stronger; more boastful.

Blay narrowed his eyes at the elf. "Well?"

The elf shifted uncomfortably, looking around as other patrons began to change their expressions from pride to shame.

"It just… it sounds too dangerous," he admitted.

"Ah, yes. *Fear.* Now *that's* an emotion we can all agree with, right?" he glanced around the room, but everybody had once again fallen into silence. "RIGHT?" he roared.

The room exploded into agreements.

Smirking, Blay looked back at the elf, nodding. "Well, there you go. You're afraid, so it's okay to condemn everyone to a shameful, painful death. Tell me, elf, you got a family? Your parents still with us? Any siblings? Maybe a wife? Ooh! Maybe you've even got a little one or two scampering around, huh? What of it, fearful one; you got any that carry your coward genes?" he stepped closer and leaned in, "Because I can offer to tell them on your behalf that you were too busy answering to your fear when you could've been answering the call to *try* to save their lives."

"How dare you—" the elf lunged from his seat to strike Blay, only to have his fist caught at the wrist.

A wave of heat flooded the pub, forcing everyone to shift uncomfortably as several panicked whimpers passed at the growing tension.

"I'll show you how I dare, elf," Blay snarled, holding up his free hand and birthing a small flame in the center of his palm. The spectacle earned a panicked response from the crowd, who moved back at the sight.

"Blay! Don't!" Gwen called out, "This isn't how—"

Gav rested a hand on hers and nodded up to her.

"There's something calculated happening in that egg-shaped thing," he whispered to her, reminding her of their prior discussion.

Slowly, Gwen nodded. "'We might not always be able to see it, and we might not always agree with what he does...'" she repeated to prove she understood.

Carefully, Gav helped her down from the chair and the two stepped away to let Blay do whatever it was he planned to do.

By the time they looked back on their friend, the ball of fire was large enough to fill his hand; several traces of flame spilling over the edges of his palm or slip between his fingers as a liquid that burned up before it reached the floors.

"What do you say, family-elf? Would you rather die here at the hands of a dragon egg?" he shrugged, "Not as exciting as standing proudly on a battlefield for the sake of the planet, I'll admit," he leaned in close, cocking his head and grinning widely, "but it'll fit the coward's dream, won't it?"

Slowly, Blay began to move his fire-filled hand towards the elf, who struggled against his grip to back away. Blay neither released him nor stopped the approach."

"Somebody get the general! Tell him his cousin's in danger," Gwen overheard one of the patrons behind her calling out.

If Blay heard them, he didn't let on.

"Well?" he pushed, beginning to chuckle. "What'll it be?"

"Mad!" the elf cried, struggling, "You're mad!"

"Oh no no no!" Blay's chuckle turned to laughter, "If I was mad you'd be terrified!"

With his laughter filling the pub, Blay moved to finally crash the fire in his palm into the elf. At the last moment, however, the would-be victim cried out and began to land punch after punch on his attacker's face with his free hand. Though Blay's face slowly succumbed to each blow—bruising and bloodying each time the elf's fist landed—he didn't move to protect himself or stop the attacks. As the elf continued to fight, however, the fire vanished from the dragon egg's hand and he let go of the elf's wrist. Free to work with both hands, the elf continued his attack, finally knocking Blay to the ground and kneeling down to continue the assault.

230

"NO!" Gwen cried, hurrying forward with Gav to stop the assault, planting herself between her friend and the enraged, heaving elf.

Though he was nearly unrecognizable from the bruising and his right eye was swollen shut, Blay still chuckled and looked up at the elf.

"And *that*, my friend," Blay's voice was choked through a bruised windpipe, "is what it feels like to forget fear and fight an unwinnable battle."

"Come on, egg-head," Gav muttered, helping him to his feet and starting to escort him to a table in the corner of the pub, "you're going to get yolk all over their floor."

"WHAT IN GAIA'S GREEN HELL IS GOING ON IN HERE?"

The breath seemed to get sucked from every patron's lungs as a new voice called out from the entrance.

Shaking from the impact of the voice, Gwen glanced back.

*Where was this guy when we needed the crowd?* she thought.

The sound of heavy boots slapping the wooden planks of the floor in the otherwise dead-silent pub made everyone there jump with each impact.

"I... I was just—h-he said that... I didn't want..." the male elf was already beginning to stammer when the crowd parted and another elf with short, dark hair and a hardened gaze the color of pine trees in winter stood across from him, standing no taller than the first but somehow seeming to loom over everybody.

"Save it!" the new elf cut off the first's ramblings and started looking around. "Where's the other guy?"

All at once the pub exploded into scattered explanations, all of which boiled down to the single outcome: he'd been beaten to the ground and then led off by the centaur that traveled with Gwen.

"Alright. ALRIGHT! Everybody just calm down!" he demanded, giving the other elf a stern look before turning to face Gwen and smirking. "It truly is you."

"I… I'm sorry, I don't mean to be rude," Gwen looked at him, trying to remember his face, "but have we met before?"

"No, not personally, at least," he shook his head and smiled. "But you and your centaur friend saved my wife and unborn child a short time ago. She told me of your courageous act, and even said that, though you didn't understand our ways, you were respectful of them. If not for you two, my family would be dead before we'd ever really had a chance to be together."

Gwen blushed and offered a small bow. "It… it was nothing, sir, it's just—"

"Let me stop you right now and say that there'd be no greater insult you could extend to me right now than to say that saving my wife and child was 'nothing.' I know it's habitual for those who do good to shy away from praise and offer that same, lame response, but it's utter hoofmeat. Granted, you don't know who I am, so you've yet to harness the full scope of just how much of a 'something' your courage truly was, but you're about to find out very, very quickly."

At that moment the elf dropped to his knee and set his right fist across his chest to rest over his heart as Gav had the day they'd helped his wife.

While the pub had been active with the hushed murmurs of its patrons, the sight of the new elf dropping to his knee send a flurry of gasps and calls about the room before several others managed to hush them. As the room once again fell into a loaded silence, the elf spoke:

"Fae healer Gwen, for your courage and selflessness in saving my wife, Leanna Diren, and unborn child, I, General Fynn Diren, offer my services and, with them, the services of the entire elf military fleet."

A pained chuckle issued then, and the entire room shifted their focus to Blay, who was still being treated by Gav at the corner table.

"See?" the dragon egg called out, "Had it planned the whole time!"

# NINETEEN

"You have our gratitude," Gav said as General Diren led the three of them outside the pub.

After his declaration of service to their cause, many of the other patrons began to volunteer their services, as well. Though Gwen still hadn't come to grips with what had happened—certain that at any moment she'd wake up on the mountain and realize they'd yet to make it to the village—she went through the motions all the same.

"I just can't thank you enough," she said.

"Nonsense! Like I already told you: it's the least I can do for what you did for my family," he bowed... again. "Plus, and I don't mean to downplay my oath to you in saying this, but a threat to the entire world is sort of something that we'd be inclined to fight against anyway. Truth is, we've had our suspicions, but nobody's heard whisper or whereabout from the humans in years. We've found the aftermath, sure—entire groups slaughtered by some unholy means; just like that ogre caravan you described—but we

234

couldn't be sure who was doing it or how. Now that we've got a target and a breed of motivation I don't think any previous generation could boast, I'm happy to say that my team will back you. And if the excitement back there"—he motioned back towards the pub—"is any indicator, your numbers will only continue growing, especially when word begins to travel, and travel it will!" He smirked and pulled a pipe from a pocket inside his jacket and filled the bowl with a sweet-smelling mixture from a small leather satchel. Lighting the mixture with nothing more than a tap on the pipe's bowl, he sucked in a lungful of the aromatic blend before blowing it out of his nostrils in twin streams. "I won't lie to you, Gwen—not out here where nobody can hear us, at least—but it sounds like this Hawkes-fae has us in a bad way. If this weapon of his is as dangerous as you say, then I'm confessing now that my most optimistic expectations are total and utter failure."

"Wow," Blay groaned, still nursing his swollen eye with a small block of ice wrapped in a towel that the bartender had offered after the pub had settled. "I'd hate to ask what your most pessimistic expectations are."

Fynn glanced back at Blay and shook his head. "I'm not going to say that my cousin didn't have what was coming to him back there, and I won't say that I'm not impressed by your little speech. And I'm definitely not about to pretend to understand any of this 'dragon egg'-nonsense you were going on about—last time I checked an egg waited to become breakfast, not pick fights. Either way, I want to like you—I really do—but try any of that sass on me and, egg or not, I'll split you in half and eat your insides for breakfast."

Blay raised an eyebrow at that and smirked. "Careful, General, my insides bite back."

Fynn smirked and shook his head, "You're lucky you make me laugh, egg-man, it gets you off the hook."

Gwen frowned and shook her head, "I'm sorry, but how are we supposed to go on with this if you don't believe that we can survive long enough to stop the humans?"

"Because it's not about what I believe," Fynn answered, looking back at her, "it's about what you believe. As of this moment, Gwen, we're following you."

While Gav and Blay went with Fynn to discuss their strategy, Gwen sought the local mage. She'd started to explain the pills she'd stolen from Hawkes to the elf general, only getting far enough to say that they, despite all appearances, were not berries and that they somehow healed and protected non-human races from iron poisoning. When it was clear that a mage would have an easier time with her explanation and, moreover, doing something of any importance with them, she and Gav parted ways with a kiss—the first they'd shared in front of anybody else—and she began asking around for directions. It was some time before she got a clear answer, most of the villagers not even knowing what a mage was let alone if they had one, but she was finally pointed in the direction of a small shop that had been built into the trunk of a massive tree that grew on the outskirts of the village.

Sure enough, as she started away from the bustle of the village market and started towards the forest, she caught sight of a towering cypress tree with a set of steps carved into the trunk that led to a doorway. Marveling at the sight for a moment, Gwen noted the unmistakable traces of magic lingering in the air and, hugging the golden orb tightly to her chest, she descended the steps and knocked on the door.

"Come in, we're open," a voice called back.

Taking a deep breath, Gwen took the knob and let herself in.

"Greetings!" a chipper, middle-aged elf with long, braided hair the color of the tree bark and a thick pair of glasses waved from behind a counter at the far end of the circular room.

Gwen looked around, stunned at how big the shop was despite every hint offered from the sheer size of the tree on the outside. Even the ceiling looked high enough to comfortably fit an ogre despite the entrance being far too small to accommodate such a client!

"How...?" Gwen couldn't keep from staring.

"How was all this made?" the elf finished the question as though it was the first thing anybody who visited asked. Grinning, she shook her head and shrugged, "The same way all great marvels are made, dearest Gwen: with time, dedication, and just the right amount of magic."

Gwen blushed and took a cautious step towards the elf. "How do you know my name?" she asked.

"Oh, sweetie, I might live in a tree some ways from the hubbub of the rest of the village, but I could have set up shop under a rock and still heard all about you and your handsome centaur."

"The gossip includes the detail that he's handsome?" Gwen raised an eyebrow.

The elf smirked, "No, but I've had my suspicions about you two, and you just confirmed them. Congratulations!" she winked.

Gwen blushed again and closed the rest of the distance, feeling at ease with the shopkeeper. As she got closer, she saw that the elf's thick glasses had several different lenses attached, some smaller than others and a few even containing different colored lenses.

"So what can I help you with today?" she asked.

Gwen bit her lip and presented the golden orb. "I was captured by the human empire a few days ago," she explained, "and I discovered that an old childhood friend has been helping them. He's there, living with them, and helping to create weapons of enchanted iron meant to kill and reshape the entire planet."

"Oh dear…" the elf frowned, looking down at the golden orb, confused.

Gwen turned the orb to face the elf and flipped the lid, showing the stockpile within it. "They're called 'pills,' and they seem to help prevent iron from poisoning non-human races and even heal the burns and rashes caused by iron. He forced me to swallow two of them after I arrived in his chambers, and they *did* cure my own iron sickness. I even watched them heal burns from iron while he was still in contact with it. I was hoping that the mage might be able to figure out how they work."

"Oh, well, that's me. That is to say that I'm the mage… and the clerk… and the shopkeeper. Actually I'm everything around here; it's my shop," she chuckled, holding out her hand, "I'm Diana."

Gwen blushed, taking her hand and offering a slight bow. "I'm sorry, I just thought… I mean, when you said 'we're open' I just figured—"

"It's fine. I can see where that might be misleading, but I've just gotten used to hearing that wherever I go that I guess I just took to saying the same." Diana frowned, looking down at the pills again, shaking her head, "I don't mean to pry none, but why would you want to replicate such a thing? Don't take that the wrong way, a job's a job, after all, but it strikes me that the best way to avoid being poisoned by iron is to avoid iron. You don't actually plan on going back there, do you?"

Gwen bit her lip and shrugged, "There's not much choice, I'm afraid. The humans and their fae leader are planning to attack soon, and they'll be bringing the enchanted iron to destroy anyone and anything they find when they do."

"Oh my…" Diana looked down at the pills again and began to fidget with one of her braids. "I hope that you don't mean to face that sort of attack on your own."

Gwen shook her head. "We were afraid of that, actually, but we recently met with General Fynn Diren, and he's already offered his and his army's assistance."

Diana nodded, smiling. "That's right!" she exclaimed, "You're the one that saved his wife, aren't you?"

Gwen blushed again and nodded slowly, "I guess word *does* travel fast around here."

"No such thing as secrets," Diana chirped, poking at the pills with her index finger, "especially when you and your handsome centaur are involved."

"Have you… have you ever seen Gav before?" Gwen frowned.

"Is Gav the centaur's name?" Diana asked, looking up.

Gwen nodded.

Diana shook her head and looked back down at the pills. "No, haven't seen him. Wrote a few stories about you two, though, but you're not old enough to read them yet."

Gwen stared a moment, not sure what to say to that.

The elf mage either didn't notice her staring or didn't mind it as she pulled one of the pills and flipped one of the larger lenses over her left eye—the magnified effect almost making Gwen laugh out loud—to get a closer look at it.

Even from a distance, however, Gwen could already see what had the mage perplexed:

"No magic," both stated at once before looking up at the other.

Diana smirked, flipping the lens away. "I see you know your magic," she chimed.

Gwen smirked, "I see that I should have visited you sooner."

239

Diana shrugged. "We all make mistakes," she sang, flipping another of the lenses into place and squinting down at the powder for a moment before mumbling "Oh I see…"

"What is that?" Gwen asked.

"Well, while there may not be any actual magic in these pill-things, it looks like whatever does make it work must be on the inside." She set it down and pulled out a small, pointed piece of polished wood. "You see," she gently poked the pill with the tip of the wood, "this is just a skin, like the rind on a piece of fruit. So whatever's inside must be either a liquid or…" she poked harder and cut off her own spoken thought as the pill ruptured and a reddish powder spilled out. "… or a powder," she finished, quickly flipping another lens into place.

Gwen watched a moment longer before clearing her throat. "So do you think you can replicate it for the battle? Maybe help protect us against the humans' iron?"

"Oh, darling, I'll forgive that question because we've never met," Diana looked up then and Gwen lost the battle with her stifled laughter as the pair of eyes that gazed at her showed in different sizes and hues. Diana shared in the laughter as she moved the lenses back into place and smirked, shrugging, "Sorry, I forget about those sometimes. Anyway," she nodded down at the pills, "I may have never seen this sort of thing before, but give me a bit of time and I'll not only replicate it, I'll *improve* it!"

Gwen blushed, "I… I see." She bit her lip then, "I don't have very much to offer, I'm afraid."

Diana scoffed and waved away the concern. "Listen good, sweetie, you save this world—you know, keep me alive and in business—and let me keep writing stories about you and your handsome centaur, and we'll call it an even trade, kay?"

"Oh," Gwen blushed, suddenly beginning to wonder just what sort of stories the elf mage was writing. Nevertheless…

"Alright, I guess that works," she finally nodded.

"Excellent! Come back in a few days and I'll have something for you," the mage finally said. "Tell General Fynn to pay me a visit then, too, so I can see about arming his troops and any other soldiers you're able to rally in the meantime. And tell your centaur I said hello."

"Sure," Gwen chuckled nervously as she turned to leave, reminding herself to never leave Gav alone with the elf mage.

# TWENTY

"Step lively, boys!" General Diren called back to the small band of elves, "Or are you ready to admit that a couple of teenagers have more stamina than you?" He paused then and glanced ahead at the three, shrugging an apology and saying, "No offense."

Gav shrugged back, "None taken."

"Technically I'm not even a teenager yet," Blay offered with a coy smirk. "By that standard I suppose a child has more stamina than your army."

"Technically this isn't an army, it's a squadron," Diren replied, rolling his eyes. "And given that you're a child who can burn an entire human city to ashes in a matter of minutes, I'll take that as a compliment."

Gwen frowned, letting the conversation go on around her as they reached the top of the mountain. Behind her, the strange "stain" and the twisted remains of what she and Gav believed to be an old sword. Ahead…

242

Gav laid a hand on her shoulder and offered a reassuring smile before they started towards the opposite side of the mountaintop. Blay stayed behind with Diren and the three elven soldiers that he'd brought along for their mission. As Gwen and Gav walked, the chatter behind them faded to a low hum that, with the constant whistle of the air current over the mountain and the otherwise eerie quiet, became easily lost and forgotten even for the fae's keen hearing. It was almost as if they were alone up there. The idea, she realized, should have been a comforting one, perhaps even romantic should the mood take the proper turn, but the ghost of their intent haunted Gwen's mind too savagely to allow for such peaceful thoughts.

The elf general was every bit the military genius the gossip made him out to be. This, however, proved not so much to be an ease on Gwen's war-torn nerves as much as an entirely new degree of strain. He'd listened with an unshaking intrigue as she, Gav, and Blay described their various encounters; he'd taken notes and asked questions, pressing further for details that the three hadn't even realized they remembered. Rough maps were drawn, theories were proposed and rejected, and through it all Gwen realized that what General Fynn Diren had said was painfully more true than she would have guessed:

She *was* leading them.

What she'd hoped would be a passing of the torch—the chance to relieve herself of the burdens she'd unknowingly taken on—was actually a promotion in the eyes of everyone else. The hopeful consultant was, in fact, the involuntary general. Coupled with Diren's experience and dedication to the "art of war" (as he called it) drove the process forward where Gwen's leadership might have ground it to a halt, but it was her recounts that shaped and motivated each step the elf general took. Before long, Gwen and the others were being summoned to join Diren and three deadly-silent and fatally-serious elf soldiers for a "tactical invasion" on one of the humans' military bases.

So back over the mountain they went. Gwen, Gav, and Blay no more armed or equipped than they'd ever been with four elf soldiers in tow wearing enough weaponry to weigh twice what they would have without it. Blay's taunts at their inability to climb the mountain seemed to disregard the added weight that the three of them were spared, but Gwen was too preoccupied with her newfound role to point out to her friend that none of them were carrying any weaponry with them. But that wasn't entirely true, either. Gav was never without his axe, so much that it became easy for her to forget that it wasn't an extension of the powerful centaur, and Blay... well, Blay was his own weapon. Furthermore, though she refused to think of it as a weapon, Gwen had taken to carrying a helitrad "walking stick" at Gav's request. While her lover's intent was certainly no mystery, Gwen had already sworn to herself that the only thing that branch would ever pierce was loose earth. Nevertheless, it seemed to make Gav happy to see that she had something that could, in theory, be used to protect herself.

"We only have to help them get inside," Gav reminded her once they reached the other side of the mountain.

The sun had already begun to set, and enough of its comforting yellow rays had hidden behind the horizon to let the first phantom wisps of the Winter Sun's glow shine ahead of them. Though there were plenty of other places to look, including the military base they were targeting nearer to the base of the mountain, they both stared at it; out towards the capital. Towards Hawkes.

*Could you kill him to heal the world?*
*Would you kill him to save them all?*

Gwen shivered as the voice from the recurring dream rang in her head with a clarity that had her wondering if she was having the dream all over again. Gav's hand found hers again, however, and the warmth and serenity shattered through the mystery and found her back in reality. Looking up at him, she couldn't help but smile.

He'd never fully understand just how much he kept her grounded.

She'd never fully understand just how much her bravery kept him going.

Gav couldn't remember a time when he hadn't been able to see right through Gwen's forced smiles and phony upbeat inflections. There was plenty of sincerity in the beautiful fae girl, he had no doubt of that, but she was so driven by the wellbeing of others that he was certain she'd smile through the flames of her own pyre to keep a child from crying at her screams. He knew when she was afraid. He could tell; could feel it like a throb in the back of his head.

She was a healer through and through, but at her own expense. He'd finally gotten her to carry the staff that he'd whittled for her, but only after calling it a "walking stick" and only after enduring a vow that that's all it ever would be.

Stubborn. Every bit as stubborn as one of his own kind.

Or maybe they weren't so different.

So it didn't surprise him that she smiled then. He knew there was untold horrors playing out in her mind—all breeds of doubt and fear and visions of failure and condemnation—and still she offered him a smile so that maybe, just maybe, he wouldn't have to worry quite so much.

She was, by far, the bravest soul he'd ever met, and it was in the glow of that bravery that he'd found a wellspring for himself to push onward.

He nodded back, returning the smile and hoping it would offer her some genuine comfort.

"We'll go as far as the gate," he offered again. "Get the soldiers inside, and then stay back until they're finished. Nothing to worry about."

"Somebody tell me again why we didn't just stay at the damn gate!" Blay called out as he ducked under a human soldier's Winter Ray—hissing in pain as the glowing blue sword burned his back without even touching him—before slamming his fire-filled palms against the iron breastplate of his attacker's armor.

The human howled as their suit of armor became an oven around him, and Gav pulled Gwen away from the scene so she wouldn't be forced to watch. Dropping her onto his back, he galloped through the streets, cursing Diren again and again in his head as he swiped his axe into a barricade of three humans who fell into six parts. He heard Gwen cry out from his back and had to suppress the urge to trample one of the parts out of sheer frustration.

The elf general's plan to invade at night had been focused on the principle of stealth. They were to get in, get the information they needed, and get out; "they," in every written and spoken plan, being General Diren and his small group of elven soldiers.

*They* were the experts!

*They* were the soldiers!

*They* were the masters of stealth!

But somewhere between leading them down the northern side of the mountain and showing them to the front gate of the military base *they* became *them*, and before Gav or Blay could say anything to intervene the elf general did the smart-yet-sinister thing to ensure his needs:

He asked Gwen to join them.

There was no way for either of them to step in without undermining Gwen's say and risking a loss of morale from the other soldiers—soldiers who would be sharing the story with their comrades upon their return—and there was no way that Gwen could refuse a direct request.

*Somebody tell me again why we didn't just stay at the damn gate!*

Gav shook his head. It was almost enough to make him laugh.

*Almost!*

"BLAY," Gav called out over the chaos that the military base had exploded into shortly after their arrival, "FIND THE GENERAL AND FIGURE OUT WHAT'S TAKING THEM SO LONG!"

"OH, RIGHT! SURE! LET ME JUST POLITELY ASK THESE HAIRLESS APES TO STOP TRYING TO KILL ME SO I CAN—"

"BLAY!" Gav stomped his hoof, though he was certain Blay wouldn't be able to hear it.

Though no response came, Gav could tell that the silence was a sign of Blay's compliance and not one of his death.

"What about—GAH!"

Gwen's cry alerted Gav to the human behind him quickly enough to turn to face him, though not quickly enough to give him a chance to deflect the Winter Ray coming at them.

*thwi-thwip—TWA-TWANG*

With the helmet in place there was no face to gauge the human's reason for his sudden halt in mid-step, but Gav didn't have to wait long for an answer. The soldier teetered, lazily working his feet like a newborn in an effort to keep himself upright. His shoulders sagged as he turned his head, trying to look over his shoulder without compromising his momentary footing. The Winter Ray slipped from his grip and clattered to the ground; Gav quickly using the blade of his axe to knock the enchanted iron away from him and Gwen.

It was Gwen who broke the tense silence first, "Wh-what…?"

*thwip—TWANG!*

The soldier pitched forward then, slamming face-first into the ground at Gav's hooves and exposing the three arrows embedded through his armor—two in the center of his back and a third in the back of his helmet. Gav stared a moment longer, though he was certain Gwen was already looking away, before cautiously stepping away from the body and looking up. The cover of night had, as General Diren had planned, offered for a very limited degree of visibility, and much of the lighting in the streets had been put out by one means or the other during the course of their battle. It was nearly impossible to see anything with any real certainty that it wasn't a shadow cast from somewhere else, but the moonlight and the ambient lighting from neighboring streets that hadn't seen quite so much activity offered enough illumination. Though the street was, save for the bodies of other human soldiers, totally vacant, the soft whisper of a strained rope drew his gaze upward and he caught sight of one of the elven soldiers perched atop a drying line that hung between two of buildings. The rope, though only as wide as a newborn's pinky, swayed slightly as the elf stood from his crouch as casually as he would on the street and slipped his longbow back over his head. The silence carried a moment longer before the clatter of another soldier's approach sounded at the opposite end of the street, and the elf spun around—seeming to disregard gravity and the narrowness of his perch with every move he made—and had his bow back in hand and two arrows drawn in the line.

The silence lingered as Gav held his breath, seeing the glow of a Winter Ray bathe the street in blue a moment before the soldier wielding it came around the bend.

"NO! DON'T!" Gwen cried out, cutting through the silence.

248

*thwi-thwip—TWA-TWANG*

The soldier jumped at the sudden shout, but before his feet had a chance to meet the ground once again he had two arrows protruding from the left breast of his armor.

A choked and startled gasp echoed through the lifeless streets, and though the elf already had a third arrow drawn and waiting to drop the soldier he knowingly held the attack.

The body fell, and as it did so did a feigned whimper from Gwen.

"It wasn't supposed to be like this," she whispered.

Gav nodded, scowling. "I know it wasn't," he said, already turning away from the corpse-choked street and heading out to find General Diren. "It wasn't supposed to be like this at all."

The centaur stormed into the armory like a demon born of rage, and the teary-eyed fae on his back was a picture of contrast and irony the likes of which Blay was certain only a poet could appreciate. Gav's hind legs were barely through the door before his axe was raised and pointed at Fynn, but Blay could see from the way he held the weapon that it was an accusation and not a threat.

"It was *not* supposed to be like this!" he snarled, capturing the attention of the general and two of his soldiers.

Where the third was Blay had no—

A gentle impact sounded a short distance behind him and, sure enough, Blay saw the third crouched atop a stack of crates.

"Not eerie or anything," Blay muttered to himself, stepping away from the too-serious newcomer and moving to Gav's flank to help Gwen down from his back.

Fynn, despite the axe that was larger than his entire body hanging in the air between him and the centaur, was calm as he turned to face his accuser.

"No," he said flatly, "it wasn't. But our simple in-and-out became something more when the humans were alerted to our presence. What would you have had me do rather than defend ourselves?"

Gav's heavy breathing didn't calm, but his axe slowly began to lower.

Fynn sighed and nodded, holding up his hands then as he conceded to the point. "I'm not happy that it came to this, either, but from the wreckage we've found something better than we could have expected."

Gav scowled at that and Blay, already knowing what was coming, began to escort Gwen away.

"Come," he spoke loudly enough for Gav to hear him but quietly enough to not attract too much attention, "you're not going to like what's coming."

Gav glanced over his shoulder as Blay hurried Gwen out of the room, but he wasn't quick enough to keep her from spotting what he was leading her away from. Recognizing the shock in her wide eyes, he traced their path back to the source. There, behind General Diren, tied to a chair, was a human soldier. Judging from his uniform, Gav figured he was a higher-ranking official, and from the way Diren and the other elves had boxed themselves around him it was clear that he was the "something better" Diren had mentioned. Seeing the centaur and no-doubt recognizing him from their prior raids, the human, who'd already been gagged with a length of balled fabric to prevent any unwanted outbursts, struggled in the chair and let out several grunts.

"So we're taking prisoners now?" Gav scowled.

Diren shrugged, turning back to the human. "Seemed a waste to kill him with the others. We found him in here signaling for reinforcements."

"Signaling?" Gav raised an eyebrow.

Nodding, Diren motioned towards a north-facing window over their heads with a mirrored fixture angled over an extinguished lantern.

"He was beaming flashes of light back to the capital with that thing," he explained. "Can't imagine it will be too long before somebody shows up as a response, but I figured we could get the information we need out of him before they arrive."

Gav grimaced, "I'm guessing I don't want to know what you mean by 'get the information out of him,' do I?"

General Fynn Diren didn't look back from their prisoner as he said, "The dragon egg had the right idea."

It wasn't long after Blay had escorted Gwen out of the building that Gav followed after, not carrying the same rage he'd entered with but definitely not happy.

"Gav," Gwen looked up at him when he was close enough for her hushed voice to reach, "what are they doing with that man?"

Gav sighed, ignoring the question as he nodded his thanks to Blay before settling in beside her.

"Gav...?"

His body tensed as he drew in a long, slow breath before blowing it out loudly. Then, already shaking his head at whatever he was thinking, he wiped his face with his palm and looked at her.

"We need to begin accepting that what needs to happen from this point forward is going to be painfully outside of what we're comfortable with," he finally said, looking between both Blay and her. He shook his head again and rubbed his eyes with the pointer finger and thumb of his right hand, suddenly looking tired. "That human in there is..." he shrugged, "I'm guessing a captain or a general for this base. They found him signaling the capital with reflected light, and with the path leading from here to there totally barren thanks to the artery leading back to the Winter Sun, I don't have any doubt that they received the message."

"Then there's more humans coming?" Blay asked, not sounding entirely upset about that idea.

Gav nodded, "Better to assume so and not be startled when they arrive."

"Then we should go!" Gwen said, already shaking. "This entire thing has gone so horribly wrong already, if there's soldiers from the capital coming then…" her words trailed off as a sob stuck in her throat and she clutched the helitrad stick to her chest.

Gav nodded and reached out to rub her back, "I know, and General Diren seems eager to leave, too, but they want to see what the human knows first."

Blay scoffed and folded his arms across his chest. "So we're just going to wait here and wait that capital reinforcements don't arrive before those elves get done torturing a bound human for information?" he asked. "Don't get me wrong, I'm all for a bit of fun, but that's a bit grim even for my liking."

"And you think I like it?" Gav snarled, glaring at him. "But if it means the difference between getting to enjoy old age with…" he paused to look at Gwen and sighed, "If it means stopping whatever they have planned—stopping all that death and destruction at the hands of the humans—then I'll torture a hundred of them myself!"

Gwen whimpered at that and reached for him, "Gav…"

He looked at her, his wise eyes filled with worry. "Gwen," his tone was unnaturally desperate, "I'm not asking you to change who you are—I would *never* ask that—but, dammit, you have to start accepting that it's going to be either us or them. A few days ago that was you!" he pointed back at the building. "They took you and tortured you just the same."

Gwen shivered and nodded, "They did, yes…" she admitted, "But that's why I know that it's wrong to do it now."

Gav shook his head, "No, Gwen! No! It's different! He's a part of their military! He's a savage killer! You can't just change a savage killer's mind with kindness!"

Gwen frowned at that and stood, pulling free of his grip. "As far as anybody who sees me with you is concerned," she spoke slowly and deliberately, "that's *exactly* what I can do."

"General," it took every bit of control Gwen could muster to keep her pace steady and her tone level as she reentered the armory. "I'd like a moment with him."

Four sets of elven eyes turned towards her, though it was the general who turned away from the human. Though his expression was one of intrigue, he didn't wear any of the skepticism that Gwen had prepared herself for.

"Oh?" he stepped aside and looked back at the terrified-looking human.

Gwen guessed that, though he certainly wasn't looking better than he had before, the remaining gag and no new wounds was a sign that they'd yet to begin. Looking at the human for a long moment, she considered everything that Gav had said. She didn't want to prove him wrong—in many ways that she wasn't ready to admit aloud she already knew that he was right—but she had to, if for nobody but herself, prove that her ways could still make some difference.

She had to!

Looking up at the general, she nodded. "Please."

Surprisingly enough, General Diren smiled at this and nodded back. "As you command," he said with a bow, which the other elves more hesitantly mirrored, before stepping away and offering an opening for her.

The faint sound of hooves resonating behind her alerted her to Gav's entrance, but rather than turning to face him she opted to let him watch as she reclaimed her forced assertiveness. Setting her walking stick down, she drew in a deep breath and closed the distance between her and the human with several long strides.

"You know who I am, don't you?" she asked before motioning back to Gav and Blay, who stood just behind him. "You've heard of the three of us, right?"

The human refused to even look up at her, let alone acknowledge the others or her question.

She heard Gav take a step towards her. "Gwen, you don't have to—"

She crouched down so that she could look up at the human, forcing him to make eye contact while bringing herself at his level. The speed of her movement drew a flinch out of the prisoner, who must have anticipated an attack. When nothing more happened, however, she saw a flicker of hope pass before his eyes.

Smiling at this, she repeated the question:

"You know who we are, don't you?"

The human paused a moment longer, but finally nodded.

Gwen nodded in return, frowning then. "You've heard stories, right? From others like you? Others who were at the other cities?"

Another nod.

"And I'm sure they had a lot to say, didn't they? About how dangerous we are; about how we're monstrous killers?"

The human narrowed his eyes at her and nodded again.

Gwen bit her lip and returned the nod. "There were deaths, I won't lie. We were up against many soldiers with very dangerous weapons, but I'm sure you already know all about what the Winter Rays do to us…" she trailed off as she caught sight of the human's sheathed sword a short distance away. Looking back at General Diren, she asked, "Is that one of them?"

"It is," he answered. "The sheathes seem to contain everything, though. I was able to take that from him and set it there without any trouble."

Gwen nodded and sighed, reaching out and lifting the weapon. Despite the general's assurances, she was nevertheless startled to find that the sheathe protected her entirely. She remembered plenty of times when she'd been further from an unsheathed Ray that still burned her, but she could hold this as easily as she did her walking stick. Examining it, she saw that the outermost layer was carved from wood that she was certain had an enchantment to bind the poisonous effects within.

"Have you witnessed firsthand what these weapons can do?" she asked, looking back up at the human.

He let out a muffled chuckle through the gag, but offered no other answer.

"I'm certain you haven't," she whispered, looking back down at the sheathed Ray. "It's… it's ugly. Now I've heard plenty of other races say that the humans are all ugly—'uglier on the inside,' I've even heard—but…" she shook her head, "But I have a hard time believing that. You see, despite what you might have heard about us, we're not killers. He's actually a poet," she pointed back to Blay, who seemed surprised to be brought into her speech, "and him"—she smiled at Blay, earning one in return—"that big, scary-looking centaur with the giant axe… he's actually the most brilliant thinker you'll probably ever meet. If you're lucky enough to have him break his silence around you…" she smiled and shook her head, "It feels like you're learning something new with each word. And me," Gwen blushed and shrugged, "I'm a healer. Death, pain, all that stuff makes me physically ill—I've actually felt every death that we've been accused of, and I've felt that guilt every day since." She sighed, feeling the sadness welling up within her and choosing not to hide it. When she looked back up at the human, she was certain he could see tears in her eyes. "But when we're facing something as dangerous as one of these..." she pulled the hilt of the Ray and jumped slightly as a sliver of the blue glow breached from around the sheathe, flooding the room in its poisonous effects and instantly beginning to burn the skin around her arms.

"Gwen, no!" Gav started forward, but she stayed him with one hand.

Holding up her arm to the human's face so that he could see the burns begin to worsen and spread, Gwen struggled to maintain. "When something this ugly threatens you and the ones you love..." she let out a gasp and finally slammed the Ray back into its sheathe, banishing the toxicity of the weapon, "... then you find yourself committing ugly acts. I saw..." she drew in a deep breath and fought to hold the humans gaze, "I saw Hawkes... murder General Thougher... before my very eyes." She whimpered and moved back, "*that's* the sort of ugliness you serve."

Staggering to her feet, Gwen held out the Winter Ray for General Diren to take away from her, unable to even stomach holding it any longer. When her hands were free, she looked down at the blisters and dark patches of dead-looking skin that the short exposure had dealt. Her forearms looked like death, and the human was unable to hide his own disgust at the effect.

"I offered his sacrifice to you so that you can understand why we do what we have to do," she said to the human as she began to feel her body fall. In an instant Gav was there to hold her upright, though she never broke eye contact with the human. "My friends won't be happy about what I've done to myself with your weapon, so, please—so that you don't have to suffer and I don't have to feel any more guilt—tell them what you know so we can stop this ugliness from spreading."

"That was... it was just so... so..."

Gav shook his head, wrapping another layer of bandages around Gwen's arms. He'd already used far more of her healing elixirs than the was needed, but Gwen hadn't even tried to stop him. He'd been quick to carry her back out. Though the burns were already beginning to look better, he couldn't shake the panic and, because of that, he kept wrapping her arms. After the third layer of bandages had been taped off along her forearms, Gwen stayed him with both her hands pressed against his chest, her smile finally showing with sincerity.

"Gwen," he tried to speak again, finding the words easier to speak this time, "that was really, *really*—"

Gwen sighed and nodded, "I know it was stupid."

Blay, stepping out from the armory in time to hear her, scoffed and shook his head. "Yea! Really, *really* stupid!"

Gav glared at both of them and shook his head. "No," he smiled again, "It was brave. That was the bravest thing I've ever seen anybody do."

Gwen blushed at that. "R-really?"

Gav nodded, kissing her with the full force of his pride and astonishment.

"H-hey! Ow!" Gwen giggled at the onslaught.

Blay rolled his eyes and turned away, "I still say it was stupid. Though if you were really hoping to get that human talking, I suppose it's worth applauding the effort. He hasn't shut up since you left."

General Diren was not by nature a doubtful elf. He was certainly not a foolish or gullible elf, either, but he had built a great deal of his military career around taking somebody for their word. For the most part, it was his willingness to accept even the most fantastic story at face value that allowed him to avoid many potentially deadly situations. However, if somebody were to come to him and tell him that a fae teenager had put her life on the line and subjected herself to the worse iron burns they had ever seen instead of lifting a finger to a human soldier, he'd have called them mad. Moreover, if they boasted such a tale and added that the soldier not only complied to share his intel but did so with tears in his eyes, Diren probably would've imprisoned them on grounds of insanity to keep his other soldiers safe from them.

But he'd witnessed just that, and as he frantically worked to note every detail the human general fed them he caught himself marveling at Gwen's display.

Though General Diren was not by nature a doubtful elf, the teenage fae had taken his doubts at her ability to use her non-violent nature to get a human talking and flung them into the gutters. And, seeing the results she'd earned from it, General Diren found his doubts regarding the outcome of this war beginning to unravel, as well.

"WE HAVE INCOMING!" one of the elf soldiers shouted from the roof of the armory, and the three looked up at the source of the call.

"One of their machines?" Gav thought out loud. "One of those faster ones?"

"No…" Gwen frowned, hearing whatever it was the elf was seeing. Still looking upward, she found herself looking past the rooftop and into the sky. "Something else."

Before long the roar of the machine was loud enough for the others to hear, and Gav was quick to pull Gwen to his back and start away from the armory at a full gallop with Blay sprinting not far behind as the source of the noise began to kick up a violent wind around the building.

"WHAT IS THAT THING?" Gav demanded over the roar of the approaching machine.

"YOU WANT ME TO GO BACK AND ASK?" Blay asked.

Gav glared back at him, "IS EVERYTHING A JOKE TO YOU?"

"IT'S A DEFENSE MECHANISM!" Blay admitted.

Gwen shook her head, "WILL YOU TWO SHUT UP AND FOCUS ON NOT GETTING US KILLED?"

"OH!" Blay scoffed, "*NOT* GETTING KILLED? I THOUGHT—"

Gav roared and yanked the axe from his back and spun around, facing the roar emanating from the darkness above the armory. "I HAVE HAD ENOUGH!"

Clutching the axe handle in both hands, Gav used the bulk of his body to hurl his weapon towards the source.

The three watched with bated breaths as the weapon spiraled out of sight, and for a moment the sound of the roaring machine was the only thing interrupting the otherwise perfect stillness.

Then the sky seemed to fall…

"WE HAVE INCOMING!"

The human went silent and looked upward too soon to be reacting to anything other than awareness, and something tightened in General Diren's stomach as he saw there was no sign of any reinforcements coming on land through the north-facing window.

Grabbing the human by the shoulders and forcing his attention away from the growing roar descending on them, he asked what he could already hear was the truth:

"Tell me you bastards don't have anything that can fly…"

The human's silence and the growing roar overhead was more than enough answer.

Turning to the other soldiers, he nodded to the roof.

"See if you can't hold whatever's up there back long enough for me to finish with him!" he commanded.

"Sir," one of the soldiers spoke up, already shaking his head, "we were lucky that our arrows could even pierce their armor, and a few of the further targets were only getting dented until we got closer." He glanced up towards the ceiling, "We'll do what we can, General, but we can't make any promises."

"Then I guess it's a good thing I didn't order you to give me promises," he knew what he said was true, but he didn't have to tell him that. "I ordered you to give me more time!"

The elf's body went rigid and he slammed his right fist over his heart. "Yes, sir!"

Then, like a feather in a sudden gust, he was out of General Diren's sight and with the others on the roof. Before any of them could have done anything effective, however, the sky seemed to crash down around the armory.

"WHAT IN GAIA'S GREEN HELL IS GOING ON OUT THERE?" General Diren demanded as the already deafening roar of whatever reinforcements the human capital had sent let out a sharp, mechanical belch followed by a hard enough impact to shake the entire base. When none of his soldiers responded, he turned his demand on the human, who looked just as startled by the racket as he was. "I take it whatever's supposed to show up isn't supposed to sound like that?"

The human only shook his head.

The general shook his head. "Damn…"

The night came alive with a fresh series of explosions, and for the first time since they'd started their raids Gwen realized that it wasn't Blay's doing.

"I can't believe it," Blay stared out towards the growing flames. "You actually hit it!"

"Your damn right I did," Gav growled, lifting Gwen off his back and setting her down beside Blay in one fluid motion before starting towards the explosions.

"Gav, where are you going?" Gwen started after him only to have Blay knowingly hold her back.

"To get my axe back," he called back before lowering his voice, hoping—but knowing better—that Gwen wouldn't hear him add "and find something else to bury it in again."

"Gwen. Gwen! Stop! You've done your part," Gav could hear Blay saying behind him. "Now let him do his!"

He knew that his lover was upset, and that everything that happened was only upsetting her that much more. And that made Gav angry. Reminding himself to thank Blay for holding her back once they were out of there, he galloped back towards the armory, spotting the three elf soldiers as they began to nimbly jump from the roof and start towards the grounded flying machine.

"Did you do that?" one of the elves asked, seeing him approaching.

Gav only nodded.

"Remind me not to pick a fight with you," the elf shook his head.

Gav spotted his axe jutting out of a wall of dented iron and started towards it. "I don't think you'll need reminding after tonight," he offered, ignoring the minor burning in his arms as he yanked his weapon free—knowing that Gwen had suffered so much more already—and shook off a few lingering scraps of the metal. "You spot any survivors yet?"

"A few," the elf nodded towards to motionless, dark heaps a short distance away. "But there's at least one more that's unaccounted for."

Gav let out a heavy sigh and looked back, "How can you be...?"

He spotted the bloody footprints before he'd even finished.

Gwen was almost disgusted with how easily she accepted the violence Gav had set out to commit. *Almost.* As much as it saddened her to admit that her peaceful efforts wouldn't always be a solution, she could take some comfort in knowing that, in instances like the one with the human, peace could still find a way. But, like Gav had said, some things just needed to be accepted.

"I still can't believe he actually took that thing right out of the sky," Blay shook his head, staring out towards the giant mass that had crashed to the ground.

Though the machine had taken a great deal of damage, Gwen could almost see how such a twisted mess could be able to fly. Several wing-like protrusions jutted upward in the distance—their silhouettes hanging just outside the glow of the fires—and the pair that been attached to the other side, the side that the machine had landed on, lay in several pieces scattered across the ground. The iron body was longer, reminding her of a bird's, and a set of rudders like the ones she'd seen on the fae fishing boats hung from a length of tortured rope at the back. From the top, which faced them and allowed a clear view, was a device that looked like a windmill, and, though the machine looked otherwise dead, it still lazily turned and reminded Gwen of the final gasps of a dying soldier.

"Yea," she agreed, realizing that, whether or not she agreed with the act, the results were no less impressive. "It's sort of like watching a single fisherman bring down an entire whale."

"Yes," a cold, furious, and labored voice chimed from behind them. "We're all quite impressed with your centaur lover, aren't we?"

Gwen spun to face the source, already recognizing the voice.

"Hawkes?"

Though it had only been a few days without his pills, the fae standing before them was already falling victim to the effects of the iron he'd surrounded himself in. Remembering her time in the fae cells, Gwen recalled the other vagrants' reaction to the iron gate guarding the entrance to that labyrinth; how their skin had drawn tight against their frames and turned blistered and red with the slowly spreading burns. That had been a single iron gate at a distance, however; Hawkes' new home was, as he'd said, built on iron and concrete. No matter how guarded his chambers might have been, any step he took away from them was a poisoned one, and without his pills or any healing magic he was doomed to let the effects linger and grow. Though it probably had less to do with the iron poisoning and more to do with the crash he'd survived, she noticed that his leg was bleeding and leaving a trail of blood behind him.

"Enjoying your handiwork, Gwendolyn?" he hissed between clenched teeth, his gums already beginning to draw back inside his mouth and make him look almost skeletal with each leering syllable.

"Oh my… Hawkes, why? Couldn't you just have more pills made?" Gwen gaped at the mess he'd become.

"If everything were that simple to come by, my dear," Hawkes hobbled towards her, "then you'd all already be dead and the world would already be mine."

"Yeesh!" Blay took a step back, more out of disgust than fear, and looked back at Gwen. "Do all fae males look like that? No wonder you're with Ga—AAH!"

A small iron dagger found itself between Blay's ribs as Hawkes subjected his body to even more exposure. Though a pair of leather gloves hid whatever monstrosity his hands had become, Gwen knew that the material wasn't enough to protect him.

*What sort of madness could push a fae to torture himself like that?* she asked herself

Hurrying to Blay's side, she worked to heal him. Again and again she tried to pull it free, each time the burning being too intense to maintain her grip. And the preexisting burns to her wrist only worsened it. She watched Blay writhe and groan as the iron worked on his body, poisoning him both inside and out. His suffering and her inability to help him made her panic, which made the process all the more impossible. It made her desperate.

It made her angry.

And Hawkes stared, chuckling at the futile display. He made no move to attack her while her back was turned; took no steps to even stop her from helping Blay. He simply crossed his arms and watched, chuckling under his breath. He was watching her as though she were a fool.

And she did nothing but continue her frantic struggle with the dagger, burning her palms again and again and again. When all she really wanted to do was turn around and strike Hawkes.

*What sort of madness could push a fae to torture herself like this?* she thought, stopping her frantic attempts.

"Gwendolyn Clearwater," Hawkes sang, "how morbidly predict—OOMPH!"

For the first time in Gwen's life, she saw harm befall another creature and she liked what she saw. She swung her helitrad stick again, catching the iron-poisoned fae vagrant in the shoulder and knocking him off his feet. Something in Hawkes' body broke with the impact of his fall—one of the brittle bones in his right arm giving way as he tried to stop his fall—and it was the sweetest sound Gwen could remember. The next few strikes were aimed for the arm, Gwen suddenly wanting nothing more than to hear that sound again.

"Take it out of him!" she heard herself screaming at him over and over. "Take it out so I can put it in you!"

The staff stopped being a walking stick as its length was stained in blood, and Gwen slowed as she realized that she might actually beat her childhood friend to death before he'd obliged her demand and removed the dagger from Blay's side.

Slamming the staff on the street, she glared down at Hawkes. "Take it out *now*," she demanded, "or I'll show you uncharacteristic!"

Gwen watched with a twisted sense of satisfaction as the beaten, iron-poisoned fae crawled to Blay and, struggling with his own injuries, yanked the dagger out of his side. She was so engrossed in her own twisted revelation, that she didn't hear the roar growing in the distance behind her.

"Dammit! Boys, we got another iron bird inbound," General Diren called out, rushing to join Gav and the others.

The elf general paused to admire the five bodies that were scattered about—three wearing the arrows of his soldiers embedded within their armor while the other two were less recognizable courtesy of Gav's axe—before giving the four an approving nod.

"I wish I could say that was a job well done, but the work isn't over yet!" he nodded back towards the sound of a second flying machine before motioning back towards the gate.

"We're not going to fight them?" Gav asked, breathing heavily.

The general shook his head. "Truthfully, centaur, I wasn't expecting to survive *this* encounter, and while I'm aching to know exactly what happened out here, I'd rather have that discussion over a pint and a pretzel! Now let's go!"

The general and his soldiers were in mid-sprint before Gav could even think to respond. Galloping after, he slung his axe over his back and turned to the general.

"What about the human?" he asked.

"Consider him dead," he said evenly, patting the sheathed Winter Ray at his hip, "but we now have one of their weapons to show the others *and* we know everything he knows."

Gav broke eye contact with the general long enough to start looking for Gwen and Blay. "And what's that?" he asked.

"Not as much as I'd like, but enough to work with," General Diren admitted. "Now where's your—sweet green Gaia…"

As they came around the bend and started down the street where Gav had left Gwen and Blay, they spotted the two… and an unexpected third.

The shadowed silhouette of another fae offered little mystery to Gav, who guessed his identity with nothing more than the sight of his ears.

"Gwen!" Gav galloped ahead of the lingering elves and started to reach for his axe, ready to strike the humans' president dead on the spot.

Gwen turned at the sound of his voice, and as she moved her shadow shifted off of Hawkes and let the light of the flames behind them give Gav a good look at him.

Words escaped Gav as he caught sight of the fresh blood on Gwen's walking stick and the numerous injuries that the fae at her feet had suffered. Catching sight of Blay on the ground and clutching a wound at his ribs, he painted a few vague predictions in his mind.

"Well that's… unexpected," General Diren muttered.

"Gwen," Gav stepped slowly towards her, reaching for her staff after securing his axe to his back. "It's time to go."

Looking suddenly confused, Gwen shivered, letting him take the staff from her, and then looked back at Hawkes. "But," she murmured, sounding tired, "he has to die."

"Darling, death is not far for him from the looks of him," General Diren offered before glancing over his shoulder at the flying machine, which seemed to be having trouble setting down around the mess of its predecessor. "And the same can be said of us if we don't get out of here *now*."

"Sir, should we take the fae? Use him to motivate some kind of surrender?" one of the elf soldiers asked.

"No," General Diren shook his head, "if he means enough to them alive to motivate a surrender, then they'll follow us. And with that broken mess weighing us down we won't make it far. He'll either die where he's lying or he'll wish he had when we come back for him with greater numbers."

Before starting forward, the three elves pulled Blay to his feet and helped support his weight. Behind them, the sound of the flying machine making a noisy landing alerted the two that it wouldn't be enough to try to negotiate with Gwen, and, with a nod from General Diren, Gav scooped her off her feet and started towards the gate and the safety of the darkness beyond it.

"NO!" Gwen shrieked, staring over Gav's shoulder at Hawkes. "HE HAS TO DIE! HE HAS TO DIE!"

"While I appreciate this change of heart, darling," General Diren offered, looking up at her, "I don't think you'd be thanking us tomorrow morning if we let you carry through with that."

Holding her tight to his chest and galloping away from the military base, Gav remained silent, letting Gwen scream a little while longer before she passed out from exhaustion in his arms.

# TWENTY-ONE

Gwen's sleep was flooded with the images of Hawkes' iron poisoned body breaking again and again under her blows as the pure, pale-white wood of her helitrad staff suddenly showed only red. Then, certain that she'd be made a murderer all over again, the staff's purity returned and Hawkes stood before her as he had that day in the capital, ready to torture her.

She nearly killed him over a hundred times in her dreams, each time waking up and watching the night bathed forest pass her by. Then, content in the safety and warmth of Gav's embrace, she'd fall asleep again to begin the cycle anew...

*The first strike—one of self-defense—turning him into the near-dead vision that had laughed at her.*

*And that same voice...*

*"Could you kill him to heal the world?" it demanded. "Would you kill him to save them all?"*

She was so far into this madness, and it was only just the beginning!

268

There'd be so more death.

So much more chaos.

So much more pain.

What was she going to do?

"HE HAS TO DIE!" her own voice sounded so alien in her head; so wrong coming from her. But what was wrong, she realized, wasn't the words...

It was the frailty of the one speaking the words.

"I don't think you'd be thanking us tomorrow morning if we let you..."

The dream cycle started anew with General Diren's words echoing around her as the savagery of her beating grew more intense, and each impact sparked the voice's questions anew...

"Could you kill him to heal the world? Would you kill him to save them all?"

Every blow felt like a hundred souls healed at once.

"Could you kill him to heal the world? Would you kill him to save them all?"

Every broken bone was a thousand slings fitted.

"Could you kill him to heal the world? Would you kill him to save them all?"

Every drop of Hawkes' blood was ten-thousand bandaged wounds.

"Could you kill him to heal the world? Would you kill him to save them all?"

Until all that was left was his life...

"Could you..."

"No..." Gwen heard her voice call out, but the source wasn't from her lips. Turning, she saw the old mirror her mother had kept in her room; the mirror she'd always checked herself in since she was a little girl. There, inside the glass where her reflection should have been, she saw a smaller, frailer image of herself in a long, red dress...

It was a reflection of her before she'd entered the labyrinth!

*Again the voice called out: "Could you kill him to heal the world? Would you kill him to save them all?"*

*Again her voice called out "NO," but the words were still not her own. Gwendolyn Clearwater stared back at her, demanding that she say the word with her.*

*But she couldn't...*

*"You don't understand," she tried to say to the reflection; to herself.*

*"NO!" the fae in the red dress cried out, the reflection growing harder to recognize until it was no longer Gwendolyn Clearwater staring back at her.*

*"Hawkes?"*

*"You think that I've been changed, my beloved?" his words echoed in her head.*

*Gwen shuddered, feeling overwhelmed by her past-self and Hawkes trading places in the mirror. She felt cold and alone and—*

Something jostled her awake and she found herself back in Gav's arms, seeing the night sky from the top of the northern mountain and... and...

*... and she was staring back into the mirror; back at Hawkes and the ghostly echoes of her past-self just beyond the glass barrier.*

*But the warmth of Gav's embrace had somehow followed her back into the dream—Gav had somehow followed her back into the dream—and she felt his hand on her shoulder.*

*"...sometimes, when you're willing to fight in the face of death, things wind up working out in your favor," his wisdom, Gwen drew in a breath and felt revitalized by it, knew no limits...*

*Not even in dreams.*

*Hawkes called to her from the mirror again—"You think that I've been changed, my beloved?"—and Gwen found herself finally ready to answer him.*

"No," she stared past him and caught sight of Gwendolyn Clearwater, still wearing the impractical red dress and soundlessly shouting "NO" at everything. "You haven't changed in the least. You learned nothing, and you've gained nothing. And, worse than anything else, you've taken no responsibility. You haven't changed at all, Hawkes Stormbreak, but I have."

The reflection of Gwendolyn Clearwater stopped shouting then, and the familiar rattle of the faes' iron gate rumbled all around them, shattering the glass and allowing the impractical Gwendolyn Clearwater to step through and join Gwen.

Then there was nothing standing between her and Hawkes.

Just her with her helitrad branch in hand—a gift from Mother-Tree—and the monster who'd created the Winter Sun.

"It's a beautiful gift," Gav's voice echoed again, but he was nowhere to be seen.

Gwen tightened her grip on the staff, refusing to let Gav's absence rob her of the strength he'd motivated in her.

It was her strength, after all.

And he'd hear all about it later.

Finally the voice called out to her again—"Could you kill him to heal the world? Would you kill him to save them all?"—and she finally recognized it as her voice; her true voice.

Raising the staff to Hawkes, she nodded:

"Yes!" she answered, feeling empowered by her own admission. "Yes I can!"

"Yes you can… what?" Blay's voice stirred Gwen out of her sleep.

It had been a while since she'd woken up in a bed, but she recognized the decorations as those from the inn back in the village. An open window allowed a wave of familiar smells and sounds, and a strange sense of home that she never thought she'd experience again washed over her.

Sitting up, a small hand towel fell from her forehead and she blushed and hurried to cover herself as she realized she was naked under the covers.

Blay was already turned away and covering his face before he could have seen anything.

"Didn't see anything," he promised her. "See? Back turned and eyes covered? Can't... see... *anything*!"

"How did I get here?" she asked, covering up.

Blay made a motion several times that he was about to turn before Gwen outright told him it was alright, and only then did he relax enough to answer.

"You were feverish," he explained. "The mage, Diana, said that it was probably another effect of the Winter Ray you exposed yourself to." He shook his head, "Brave or not, I still say that was stupid. Anyway, she and Gav brought you up here and did... well, whatever was done. Including the towels and nakedness and anything else that was done. I had nothing to do with it! I was downstairs in the pub sharing a pint with Fynn and his cousin."

Gwen raised an eyebrow at him, "You seem awful nervous."

"Well, yea!" Blay shrugged, "I was put on watch here against my and Gav's will. But he'd already been watching over you for nearly twenty-two hours, so everyone told him he needed to get some rest and made me take over."

*Twenty-two hours!* Gwen blushed and shook her head at that before looking back at Blay.

"None of that explains why you should be so nervous?" she chuckled.

"Because Gav said if I saw you naked he'd cut my head off," Gav shrugged, "and I don't think he meant—"

"I understand, Blay. Thank you for being so kind and respecting my privacy."

Blay nodded and leaned forward, "So how do you feel? Do you... uh, remember anything about last night? More specifically the parts last night where you… umm, saved my life? And perhaps the details behind how you did that?"

Gwen chuckled and nodded, looking back at him. "Yea, Blay, I remember everything," she admitted, feeling even more liberated by the confession.

"You do?" Blay cocked his head, "Because everyone was pretty certain that you'd, well, lost yourself for a bit. Gav was worried that if you remembered any of it you'd make yourself sick over it, and, well, you say you remember everything… but you don't look too sick about it?"

Gwen shrugged and looked out the window. "I guess some things fell into place while I was out. Gav…" she smiled and looked back at her friend, "he helped… in a way."

"He helped? In a fever-induced dream? Your centaur lover—after using an axe to kill a giant, bird-like machine— helped you come to grips with a violent outburst against a childhood friend who created a giant chunk of glowing death-iron meant to destroy and reshape the planet? And he did all of this while carrying you over a mountain and back to this village in a single night?"

Gwen paused to look at him, wondering if it was worth it to try and offer any corrections. Finally, she shrugged and gave him another nod, "Yea, pretty much."

"And there it is," Blay stood up, "things have officially gotten insane enough around here to confuse a walking, talking egg. I'm going to go get your super-powered centaur now. You're free to get dressed, or not. I don't know. He'll be coming through the door, so look however you want, I suppose."

Gwen looked up as Gav stepped through the door. Though it hadn't felt like much time had passed since Blay had left to get him, it had already started to grow dark and she wondered how long she had spent sitting on her own. They were silent for a long moment, seeming to share a concern of what could be said after everything that had happened. Without saying a word, Gav moved closer to her, kneeling and then settling down on the floor beside the bed where she was sitting. After Blay had left, she'd gotten dressed to avoid any more awkwardness than what might already be coming—a decision she saw was for the better—but a part of her still felt exposed after what he'd witnessed from her the night before. Though the silence lingered a moment longer, he finally reached out and took her hand in his own, weaving her five small fingers perfectly between his seven calloused own.

"I'm sorry, Gwen," Gav sighed and she could feel the pain in his voice. "I hate that you had to go through with that."

Gwen saw the pain in his expression, realizing that he must have blamed himself in some way for what had happened, and moved her free hand to his cheek. "It's alright, Gav... really," she blushed at her admission to him and the feel of his face against her palm and she moved closer to him. "I... I think I had some kind of revelation last night. I remember waking up a few times in your arms and... and it gave me the strength I needed to answer some questions that have been welling in me for some time." She nodded and offered a reassuring smile; a *real* smile, "I've accepted what has to be done and I'm prepared to do it."

"Still..." Gav looked up at her and sighed, "I hate that you have to accept something like that. It's like you said: it's ugly. The world took your beautiful will and twisted it."

Gwen looked down and shrugged, "So long as you still find me beautiful, I think I can live with being a little twisted." She bit her lip and looked back up, suddenly worried that what he'd seen had changed his mind about them. "You... you *do* still find me beautiful, don't you?"

Gav looked up at that as though he'd just been injured. "Gwen... yes! Yes, of course I do! You think..." he shook his head, "You think I didn't want to let you kill that monster last night? I was..." he shook his head, "We were—the general and Blay and me, I mean—just afraid that if we stuck around then we'd either not survive the night or you'd wake up regretting what you'd done."

Gwen nodded and sighed. "I don't think who I was last night could have handled knowing I'd killed him," she admitted. "Knowing I didn't was actually what helped me decide I was ready to do it the right way."

Gav laughed at that, "There's a right way to kill somebody then?"

Gwen gave him a hard look, and he quickly stopped laughing.

"There's a right and wrong way to do anything," Gwen said. "At my core I am still a healer, and last night I would've become a murderer—no different than him. The soldier I killed at the ogre caravan was..." she sighed, nodding, "I'd known exactly what I was doing. I wasn't ready to admit that to myself—not like I am now—but I did it to protect the child. I was just too slow then." She took a deep breath, "But if it means saving the world and everyone in it, I won't hesitate when the time comes."

Gav stares at her for a long moment, smiling, and then chuckled, shaking his head. "I just can't believe how perfect you are sometimes. You're like a dream come to life."

Gwen blushed at that and looked at him. "You and your words," she giggled. "They helped me in my dreams, the ones that helped me come to this conclusion."

"Yea, Blay mentioned something about that, but I just figured he wasn't delivering the message right." He frowned then and gave Gwen a serious look, "He didn't see—"

"No," Gwen laughed and shook her head. "He didn't see anything. Though..." she arched an eyebrow at him, "I *am* a little curious about what you saw last night."

Gav actually blushed at that and looked down.

"Gav?" she pressed, leaning towards him.

Still blushing, he looked up at her. "I wasn't sure you'd want me to see anything, so I let the mage handle that detail. I just carried you up here and then waited at the door."

Gwen giggled at him and he frowned, looking stung by it.

"The so-called savage beast," she teased, "and he's more of a gentleman than most nobles."

Gav's blush grew brighter. "Saving you from the labyrinth was the best thing to happen to me," he told her.

She studied him for any trace of regret, but found none. "Even if it got you exiled from your herd?"

Gav shrugged, "Do you regret being banished from the fae now that you see them for what they are?"

"I..." Gwen stopped herself and thought for a long moment before shaking her head, "No. No, I don't regret it at all, actually. Despite everything that's happened... I'm actually glad I got banished."

"Feels good finding such freedom in exile, doesn't it?" Gav asked her, taking her back to the night that they'd saved General Diren's wife.

Gwen blushed at both the truth in his words and the moment of nostalgia it brought up.

Gav nodded, "And that's exactly how I feel. Gwen," he leaned towards her, "before you, I just lived life in a daze, questioning everything but never *really* seeking answers. I didn't feel like a part of anything, quite the opposite, actually. I just went day-by-day and dreamed of stumbling across my fate, some sort of destiny, but I never knew where to begin." He smiled then, "But then my little sister comes to me speaking of a beautiful fae with hair the color of a maple leaf on an Autumn's day and how this one fae—so different from any of the ones we'd heard of—actually risked her own life to save hers. Your act changed everything for me, and I wouldn't ever want to go back. Because of you, I am finally sure of my fate. My fate is and was always *you*; it's been my destiny to be here, now, with you, doing what we're about to do. Because I'm certain now more than ever that we're the only ones who *could* do what we're about to do!"

Gwen gaped at his confession and looked up into his eyes. His touch, his scent, everything about him felt so right. When she was with Gav, everything was right. She realized what she was feeling for him and finally understood it.

"Gav, I... I love you," the words felt so right on her lips that she wanted to spend the rest of her life saying them.

Gav smirked, lifting her chin to face his. "I love you too, Gwen."

With only the moonlight spilling through the open window of the village inn, Gwen found a new level of serenity staring into the silvery glow of her centaur, and she finally leaned in to press her lips to his with the full force of her reborn passion. Gav lingered, taken aback for a moment—but only a moment—before finally pulling her against him and returning the kiss. Gwen could feel the passion behind her centaur's kiss as he fought to match her own. Their hands trembled around one another, aching to move—to explore this new plateau of passion that had formed between them—but she felt him holding back. At that moment, though, she didn't want him to.

He'd been a gentleman long enough.

As she slid away from Gav's embrace for a moment, she stood before him and slipped out of her top before casting it aside. Gav's expression grew hooded from the sight and Gwen invited him further with her eyes as she returned to his embrace.

Exactly where she always belonged.

# TWENTY-TWO

The next morning, while Blay and Gav went to meet with Fynn to discuss their revised tactics, Gwen decided it a good time to meet with the mage. She knew that it was probably too soon to expect any results with her work in recreating Hawkes' pills, but anticipation was beginning to weigh heavier with her renewed sense of purpose. Stepping through the door carved into the side of a massive tree and welcoming the familiar energy of a place of magic, she spotted Diana behind her counter and hunched over a pile of weapons. As Gwen approached, she saw that almost every bit of the counter space was covered in arrows, daggers, and other weapons as well as some of the leather sections that she recognized as the elves armor.

"Ah! So you're finally awake," the mage grinned at her, pausing for a moment to squint through her lopsided lenses before suddenly beaming knowingly.

Gwen blushed and dodged the stare and cleared her throat. "I… I take it you've been waiting to tell me about the pills then?"

"I certainly have, missy! But, even better yet, I've been able to do even more with the Winter Ray that General Diren brought me last night!" the mage pushed some of the weaponry aside to clear a small space in front of her before ducking behind the counter. "Using both the pills and tracing the magic in that despicable blade, I was able to infuse these weapons with a special blend of magic to not will not only hold up against the humans' ugly blue iron, but actually be able to weaken it!

Gwen stared at the weapons littered across the counter. "You're saying that these can actually remove the enchantment from the Winter Rays?"

"Well, not *entirely*," the mage confessed, still rummaging about behind the counter, "but it'll take enough of the sting out of it to give you all a fighting chance. It'll still sting, though, make no mistake about that! Which brings me to… my… next—where in the blazes did I… Oh! There it is!" she exclaimed, pulling a large pouch forth and setting it on the clearing on the counter. Pulling at the drawstring, she opened it for Gwen and revealed a bundle of small vials filled with an elixir that shimmered with a similar hue to the powdered contents of Hawkes' pills. "After breaking down the components in the humans' pill-things, I was able to replicate the effects and, as promised, improve upon them. While the weapons I'm working on for everyone *will* nullify the enchantment on the humans' iron, *this* will take much of that sting out of any iron they come at you with. Now I don't want to make you cocky with these, a sword is still a sword even if it can't burn or poison you, but it will all, at the very least, ensure an evenly matched playing field… well, in regards to the supplies, at least."

279

Gwen frowned at that last part. "What do you mean?" she asked.

"Only that, darling," Diana shrugged. "The tools the humans will have won't be any more deadly than your own, but no enchantment or protection can counter greater numbers or superior training. All I did was ensure that the victory won't belong to the weapons or armor."

Gwen frowned and nodded, looking down at everything spread out on the counter.

"I guess we can't ask for much more than that," she admitted. "The rest will rely on General Diren and his army."

"And you," Diana added. Then, smirking, she also added "and your handsome centaur."

Gwen groaned.

"Sorry, sweetie," Diana chuckled, "but it's too much fun to stop."

Nodding, Gwen struggled to shift the topic. "So will there be enough of these weapons and protection spells for everyone?" she asked. "I don't mean to sound rude—this is all very impressive—but there isn't very much here and—"

The mage began to cackle. "Gwen, darling," she gasped between stifled laughter, "Diren could show up to my door *tomorrow* with the notice of war and I'd be able to supply him three times over with enough left to retire on! I've got a bunch of my apprentices out in the woods behind us assembling the kits for the soldiers as we speak. Everyone on that battlefield will have the enchantment to protect their weapons—a little pinch of powder for whatever you want to hit the humans with; hell, throw a pinch in their faces, I'd like to know what it does—and a vial of the protection elixir." She clapped her hands together, "Sprinkle, gulp, go! That simple!"

"Wow! You certainly did do a lot in this time," Gwen nodded. "Thank you so much!"

"Ha! You don't have to thank me, sweetie, you just have to win," the elf mage laughed.

"That's certainly the plan," Gwen chuckled nervously.

"Go off with you, now," the mage chuckled. "I'm sure Diren and the others will be excited to hear the news."

"Good to see you up and about. Heard you found yourself in those crazy dreams you were having," General Diren grinned at Gwen as she entered the pub and joined them at the corner booth they were seated in. "So, how did it go? That ol' mage impress you yet?"

Gwen nodded, smiling at that, "She really did." She looked between the general and Gav and Blay and chuckled, "But I'm guessing you all already know all about what she's done?"

"Well, you *were* asleep for a long time," Blay shrugged. "Can't expect the world to stand still while you get nearly a full day's worth of beauty sleep, now can you?"

Gwen laughed. "No, I suppose not," she found her eyes drifting to Blay's side, trying to catch any sign of the prior night's injury. When nothing presented itself on the surface of the clean bandages, she asked, "How are you feeling?"

Blay chuckled at the question and nodded towards Gav. "I'll be alright, though I'll say this much: I prefer your new boyfriend over your old one."

The table shared a laugh at that before slipping into a moment of silence as the three sipped from their pints. Seeing this and suddenly realizing she was thirsty, Gwen signaled the server to bring her one, as well.

"So I was meaning to ask..." Gwen started, already expecting the worst, "... what happened to that human soldier? The general or captain, I mean. Blay said that he was telling you what he knew, so..."

Both Gav and Blay's faces were already solemn, and Gwen realized that they must have already known.

"Actually…" the general leaned forward and motioned for the others to do the same—they quickly did—"What I'm about to tell you *cannot* leave this table, do you understand? We're not a bloodthirsty army by any stretch of the imagination, but in times of war there's a certain expectation of what's supposed to happen and not following those expectations can compromise a soldier's reliability or, in my case, a general's reputation…" he took a long drink and sighed, wiping his upper lip. "And without a reputation, a general can't lead an army as efficiently as he needs. So can I rely on you three to keep your mouths shut?"

They all nodded, awestruck at what the elf could be hiding.

General Diren sighed and emptied his glass before speaking. "I let the human go," he finally confessed, shaking his head at his own actions. "I… I'd never seen anything like it: a prisoner just… just opening up like that," his voice, even after all that time, sounded disbelieving as he looked straight at Gwen. "And after everything you said to him—all that peace-loving stuff about ugliness and whatnot—I just couldn't do what I knew I should do; what I normally would do. Most of the time the amount of torture it takes to get that much information leaves a prisoner more dead than alive, and with barely a scratch to show for his capture it just… it just felt wrong."

Gav stared at him, smirking. "You said to consider him dead," he whispered.

The general nodded and shot him a glare, "And as far as you're concerned—as far as anybody here or anywhere for that matter is concerned—he *is* dead. *That's* my reputation on the line, centaur! If my soldiers knew I'd cut that human loose and told him to not let his face be seen until well-after this mess has blown over, I'd probably be hung for siding with the enemy."

Gwen smiled, suddenly seeing the elf general in a new light.

"Thank you," she whispered to him.

"For what?" he asked, motioning to the server with his empty glass as Gwen's drink was delivered to the table. "It's like I already told you: consider him dead."

The atmosphere over the four felt lighter than it had for any of them in a long time. General Diren was looking ahead at a battle that would set his place in the stars for generations to come. Blay, despite years of fighting to stay alive, had actually discovered what it meant to truly live. Gav had finally found a balance between his strength and his nobility, and he was no longer tormented by endless questions about who he was or where he belonged. And Gwen finally felt more at peace with herself and her place in the world than she had even within the faes' walls. As the two lovers' eyes met they saw the same moment of peacefulness in where their lives had taken them, and they knew that, while each had found something that had been missing from their lives, it was—

"Blech!" Blay faked a retch and shielded his eyes from the two, "Why don't you two take that eyeballing out to the stables or something?"

He and Fynn laughed while the two shared a blush before glaring back at Blay.

"Way to kill the mood!" Gwen groaned.

"Perhaps you and the general should consider exploring your own feelings," Gav jabbed.

General Diren shivered.

Blay stared back at Gav, blinking in disbelief. "Did you…?" he looked at Gwen, "Did he…?" he let out a celebratory holler and slapped the table, making most in the pub jump and grow quiet. "By the gods golden graces, Gav just made a joke! This is truly a magical day! Server! A fresh pint for my four-legged friend!"

Some of the patrons, those who knew Gwen and Gav better than others, joined in the laughter while others, still bitter about being startled, grumbled under their breaths over their spilled drinks or racing hearts. Eventually, however, the air settled and conversations moved on, dragging away from the moment.

"So what happens next?" Gwen asked before taking a sip from her glass, wincing at the taste and gulping it down like a satchel of pebbles and then deciding it wasn't so bad and taking another cringe-inducing sip. With the second gulp settling in her stomach and her tongue already demanding a third, she followed with "Do we just wait on the humans now? Or do you have some plan to seek them out now?"

General Diren shrugged, "We hadn't decided that, to be perfectly honest. We've had plenty of talks about strategy and mulled over what the human told us, but we didn't want to move ahead with any specific plans without you."

Gwen frowned, "Without me?"

Gav nodded. "We weren't sure when you would wake up from your fever," he said, "or how you'd feel about everything once you did. We figured it was better to wait on you—hear out any ideas you might have—and move forward with a strategy from there."

Blushing, Gwen looked down at the table. Suddenly a sip didn't feel like enough, and, after gulping down more than half of the contents of her glass, she reevaluated the situation. "Well…" she thought for a moment, "what did the human have to say?"

"He said a lot about very little, I'm afraid," General Diren said. "He certainly believed he knew a great deal, and I'm sure that Hawkes is keeping the number of generals who know all the details in the single-digits, so I can't say in the long run that I'm surprised we don't have the particulars on their next move. However," he folded his arms across the table, "he admitted that the mountains were their greatest hurdle at this point. You see, the humans know how frail they are against the other races without their armor and weapons—specifically the enchanted iron and most specifically the Winter Sun—but their armor is too heavy to just lead an entire army over the mountain. They'd lose numbers to exhaustion alone, and by the time they got across they'd be too bushwhacked to survive an attack even with their armor and iron. He admitted that they've been sending small groups of their soldiers out to test out how their equipment and training held up against the real thing," he nodded towards Gwen and Gav, "I have a feeling that's what you walked into with that attack on the ogre caravan; probably seeing how well the Winter Rays worked on a group of that size. He said that, more recently, Hawkes focus had been *not* with the enchanted iron—I guess they've been sitting on that thing for a while and it's been all-but perfected by now—but with those machines. He said that they'd started small, starting with those quick little things you described that seat two humans at a time. When their engineers were comfortable building those, they moved up to larger machines, and then even larger still."

Gwen nodded slowly, thinking. "So those flying machines that we saw at the military base were their newest machines then?" she asked.

General Diren shook his head, "No, that's the weird thing. One of the last things the human told me after those things arrived was that they *weren't* new at all. He told me they were the newest that he'd seen built, but I guess those ones are over two years old."

"Two years...?" Gwen shook her head, "They were building those things *that* fast!"

"Exactly!" the general nodded, "They were pumping out those things day after day for almost a year-and-a-half, perfecting and growing each time. According to the human they could build a hundred of them between sun-up and sun-down. Then, one day a few years back, there were no new machines. The engineers were all still busy—still working just as hard as before—but nothing was showing for all that work. And the weirdest part is this: as time passed, a lot of those stockpiled machines—the ones that weren't used as often or the ones that didn't work as well as others—just started vanishing back into factories the engineers were working on."

Gwen's mind raced, trying to make sense of that. "But... why?"

Gav cleared his throat and waited for the general to allow him to answer for them. "We believe the bulk of those machines weren't supposed to serve any purpose other than advancing on the technology. They built in bulk not because they needed them, but because they were perfecting their process and the rate that they could build. It doesn't make sense that *that* sort of productivity would just suddenly stop..."

"Which is why we don't think it did stop," Blay cut in.

The general and Gav both gave him a look, but when neither said anything he continued:

"And if they didn't stop, then the fact that they weren't putting out a bunch of new machines must mean that they weren't finishing new machines. And if a lot of those bulk machines started vanishing, then it's probably because—"

"They needed all that iron for something else..." Gwen's eyes widened.

The three nodded.

"By the gods," Gwen shivered. "So you think that they've been building something ever since; something big enough and powerful enough to get all those soldiers and weapons and the Winter Sun over the mountain?"

The general gave a solemn smile and a single, slow nod.

Neither Gav nor Blay said anything else, but it was clear that was the theory they were working on.

And while Gwen was desperate to think of any other possibility, it kept coming back to that theory. It really was the only possible scenario that fit.

*If everything were that simple to come by... then you'd all already be dead and the world would already be mine.*

"Okay..." Gwen took a deep breath, "Well, the fact that they haven't gotten past the mountain *yet* is a good sign that whatever they're working on isn't ready yet, right?"

"Sure," Blay rubbed the back of his neck, "but all this increased activity means that they're getting close!"

Gwen nodded. "Right. Then we have to act quickly. If we can stop all this before whatever they're building is finished then—"

"It is already finished!" a voice bellowed from nearby, once again silencing the entire pub and turning all attention to a cloaked figure who sat only a few tables down from the four.

The figure stood then, not seeming swayed by the attention, and before he was completely out of her chair Gwen recognized the sheathe of a Winter Ray strapped at his side.

"Oh no..." she gasped.

Gav made a move to attack, but stood his ground as General Diren held out a hand.

"No," the elf whispered, "if he frees that sword in here then it'll be carnage before the blade even finds a target."

"Well said, General," the figure chuckled as he pulled his hood back, revealing a young human face.

A series of gasps and disgusted noises circled the pub, and several patrons started to stand and advance on him.

"STAY IN YOUR SEATS!" General Diren's voice was the unnerving pitch that Gwen had first heard; the tone that none could ignore and even fewer could disobey.

Everyone sat.

Everyone but the human, who bowed his head in a mockery of thanks. "Much obliged, though I'd expect nothing less than hospitality from the one who freed a prisoner of war before the war even began!" he laughed and shook his head. "No matter, I finished your job for you," he said, patting his sword's hilt. "He's Morrison, by the way; *Captain* Morrison…" he shrugged and snatched Gwen's glass from the table, gulping the contents and hurling the glass against the nearest wall. "He *was* Captain Morrison. No need to thank, though."

"So your kind are back to killing your own?" General Diren's voice, like his face, offered no trace of remorse or fear; offered no trace of anything. "Maybe I should be thanking you. Seems your peoples' bad habits might save me a lot of work."

A small round of laughter circled the pub and the human glared over his shoulder, clutching his sword and preparing to draw. Raising a single hand, General Diren silenced the pub once again and he patted the table's surface three times to return the human's attention to them.

"You're awful jumpy," the elf general speculated. "You wouldn't happen to be on your own, would you?"

"I've got all I need to clear this entire village of your lot should I care to," the human sneered. "All the same, a warrior in a wolf pit would be a fool to not be cautious."

"That's cute," Blay's eyes sparked and the pub grew warmer in an instant, "because from where I'm sitting *you're* the lone wolf in a den of sheep who's made the grave error of mistaking several lions' manes for wool." Slowly turning his palm upward on the table, Blay let a small ball of fire spark to life in his hand and he grinned wider, "Would you like to see my teeth, boy?"

"You listen and you listen good, *egg*," General Diren's voice was a sharp winter wind cutting between his clenched teeth. "You put out that fire before I finish this sentence or

288

I swear"—Blay extinguished the flame within a clenched fist—"it will be the last sentence you ever hear."

"My my, General," the human smiled, "I'm beginning to lose count of how many times you've saved my life already."

"State your business and keep your hands away from that hilt and I might consider continuing that service long enough for you to see yourself back over the mountain."

Gwen saw a remarkable amount of control in the elf's eyes as he fought to keep his calm.

The human nodded and looked around the bar, seeming to consider what other options he had. While he made a show of his examination of his surroundings, Gwen caught sight of the general slipping something from his lap to Gav's palm and showing the centaur three fingers before the human's gaze returned to them. "Fair enough," he pulled up the chair he'd been sitting in and sat across from them. "Since you all seem so eager to die, our leader"—he paused long enough to give Gwen a knowing grin—"has generously offered to take our new toy on an early test-run." He grinned at the confused looks that earned, offering a shrug, "You're right in assuming it's not ready to land outside this door, say, *tomorrow*—something of its size demands far too much power, and, last I checked, it's only at half capacity—but we're pleased to announce that, if you'd like to join us on the mountain before tomorrow's dawn, we're more than ready to offer a demonstration. *Especially* if that demonstration will see an end to this foolish little uprising; believe it or not, this really isn't about any of you filthy creatures… it's about progress. You all just insist on standing in the way of it."

"Damn right we do," Blay spat, the fire in his eyes burning brighter.

General Diren held up a hand to silence Blay, brandishing only one finger in his otherwise closed fist.

Gwen lingered on the sight, finding it strange.

Gav, also seeing it, narrowed his eyes and offered a nod so slight that Gwen almost missed it.

*Three fingers*, she recalled seeing the general's signal to her lover and began to wonder what he had hidden in his hand.

The human, however, only seemed satisfied that the gesture had silenced Blay.

"Well...?" he smirked at General Diren.

The elf sighed and scratched at his temple with two fingers. "Dawn you say?" he played with the words and finally set his hand back on the table as a balled fist. "Fine," he nodded, "tomorrow at dawn we will be at the top of the mountain. Then his madness can end."

"Lovely," the human stood and moved to return his chair to the table. "Now if you'd be so kind as to tell these savages to let me pass, I'd like to..."

Gwen caught the flash of three fingers rise from the general's closed fist and Gav became a blur of movement.

With the human's back turned and her lover's hooves not yet striking the floor, he unknowingly continued to address the general about his safe passage out of the village. The impact of Gav's first hoof alerted him to the movement and he began to turn. By the second impact the human's hand was moving for his sword's hilt. Blay grunted and Gwen saw a spark of flame catch at the sleeve of the human's shirt, forcing his sword-hand to stagger and offer Gav the extra fraction of a second he needed to bury the wooden fork that General Diren had slipped him into the human's throat. With his free hand, Gav secured the Winter Ray within its sheathe and snarled, giving the weapon a sharp twist and waiting for the human's gurgles to silence.

"No need to deliver the message." General Diren didn't bother to watch as he finished his pint. "I'm certain your president already knew we'd accept."

# TWENTY-THREE

After the pub had settled and the human's body had been dragged away, General Diren requested a moment with Gwen and Gav in his office. His "office," as it turned out, was the quietest corner of the elf army's sparring quarters. Watching the rows of elven soldiers train against one another, Gwen found herself wondering how she'd fair in a spar with any of them. Before she could dwell on the subject any further, however, the general had returned from briefing several soldiers on what had happened with the human. Behind him, two elves approached the group and, before long, they had all left.

"Where are they going?" Gwen asked.

The general shrugged as though it was a foolish question. "We're going into battle at dawn," he reminded her. "They're going to get ready."

Gav frowned at his tone, but didn't try to argue. "What's this all about?" he demanded.

"It's about your friend," General Diren's voice lowered even though there was nobody around to hear him, "the egg."

"He has a name," Gwen said flatly. "It's Blay."

General Diren turned his cold gaze on her. "Fine," he conceded. "It's about Blay."

"What about him?" Gav asked, matching the general's tone.

The elf glanced between them and sighed, picking up on the tension and holding up his hands. "Look, I know that he's your friend, and, over a pint and a few good jokes, I'd consider myself his friend, too…"

"But…" Gav pressed.

The general nodded, "*But* he's got me nervous about how he's going to hold up in a battle."

Gwen frowned at that. "He's been in plenty of battles," she said, "and he's been one of the strongest weapons we've—"

"Let me stop you right there," the general held up a hand, ignoring the disgruntled sigh from Gav. "Neither of you have seen a *real* battle. You've held up well in a skirmishes and, yes, I'd even go so far as to say that in the fight at the military base you all held your own quite admirably, yourself included, Gwen." He shook his head again, "But do not confuse a few dozen soldiers set on security detail for an army, and don't allow yourselves to go another second thinking any of that was *real* battle. And therein lies the source of my concern. The egg—*Blay*," he corrected himself before either Gwen or Gav could have the chance, "has only become more and more volatile with those smaller, much more contained circumstances. Now I can't say with any certainty that there's an ounce of truth to this 'egg' business—I'm sure you've already noticed he doesn't exactly walk and talk like other eggs, mostly because other eggs *don't* walk *or* talk—but if even a single word of all that is truth, then there's a monster in that boy that we're not going to want to add to tomorrow's circus."

"You've seen what he can do," Gav said flatly. "Do you truly believe that, if we go against whatever the humans are going to have waiting for us at the top of that mountain, we'll stand a chance without him?"

General Diren took a step towards them. "You ever seen a dragon? Real, up close, and painfully personal?"

Both shook their heads.

"Me neither," the general scowled, "and I'm not ready to wager that tomorrow morning come dawn I'll be any more ready to have that experience."

"Blay *will* fight with us!" Gwen barely recognized her own voice. "And we *will* win with his help!"

Both Gav and General Diren stared at her in disbelief.

Finally, the general sighed and straightened himself. "And if he starts to hatch there on the mountain?" he asked.

"Then I'll kill him myself."

For a moment Gwen was certain that the words had come from Gav—it certainly sounded like the sort of thing that he'd have said—but, as the elf and her centaur lover shared another stunned silence staring at her, she realized that the promise had come from her.

Blay stood on the outskirts of the village, staring up at the mountains he'd known as his only home until a short while ago. Meeting Gwen and Gav—feeling the connections he'd formed and finding himself a part of something so big—had changed things. And while he was thankful that the voice, up until that moment, had been silenced by his involvement with saving the world, he was becoming painfully aware of just how close his final day was after all the death and destruction he'd been feeding the creature inside of him.

With every fire started and every single body left in his wake, he felt himself feeling more and more right.

And right, as a dragon's egg, was very, very wrong.

*Burn it all!*

"N-no! This is… my friends are here! Families live here! They're innocent!"

*Innocent? Should one piece of kindling be seen as any more innocent as another within the fire? Why do you fight your nature? Why do you fight me?*

"Because I don't want to…" Blay shook his head—shook it from the voice and shook it from an outdated thought. It wasn't about whether he lived or died. Not anymore. "B-because my… my friends need me!"

*Friendsssss…* The voice sizzled around the word as though it were made of iron and pressing to the beast's flesh. *They already don't trust you; they already believe you to be a monster waiting to burst free and destroy them all! Why make them wait? Why not give them the gift of making their fears real? Why don't you give them a reason not to trust you?*

"That's… that's a lie!"

*Is it? Do you think you can lie to me when I'm so close to your mind I could eat it? Destroy them! All of them!*

"Stop."

*Destroy them all!*

"I said stop!"

*Destroy EVERYTHING!*

"N-no… Stop it! LEAVE ME ALONE!"

He grabbed his head and tightened his grip until he was certain he'd rip it from his shoulders and rid himself once and for all of the voice inside of it. But he didn't. Still shaking from the amount of control it was taking to subdue the beast, he shook his head of the last few whispers and forced himself to turn away from the mountain and return to the village.

He needed his rest.

Heading towards the inn, he spotted Gwen and Gav walking towards him and he gave his head one more violent shake to make sure he was rid of the voice.

He *could* do this.

He could fight!

For the cause.

*For her...* the voice gave one last taunt.

Frowning, Blay realized he couldn't argue with it.

"Yes," he agreed, "for her. Just tomorrow. Then..." he forced the voice back down into the pit of himself, "Then I'll make sure we don't hurt anybody ever again."

# TWENTY-FOUR

*T*he wind beneath her wings was once such a liberating
sensation. Whether they were carrying her out over the
ocean when the taste for fish was upon her or whether they were
guiding her through the trees of the forest to scoop up fresh meat
in her talons, flying was a thrill. The oceans' currents trembled
and the forests wore a shadow as massive as the clouds when
she and her brothers and sisters soared side-by-side. When the
dragons were flying, the entire planet knew that the owners of
those wings were the most powerful creatures to walk its surface.

But such claims are always subject to challengers…

And challengers came.

They came not on great and powerful wings nor with
any might that could change the oceans' currents or bathe
the forests in darkness. They came on small, pink legs.

But they came in great numbers.

And they came with iron.

She watched so many of her own cut down in without
any of the glory they deserved. Like a weather-beaten bear

brought down by a hive of bees, each dragon that fell at the hands of the humans and their iron was a symbol of power and savagery not bested in a battle of majesty, but one of how even enough petty insects could rob the greatest predator of its pride with nothing more than their stinging numbers.

*She hated them so much for the shame they brought upon her kin...*

*But, even greater than her hatred, was her fear of them as she realized that they'd killed every last dragon...*

*Every single one...*

*But her.*

*Though that was not for a lack of trying.*

*With their cursed blue iron buried beneath her wing, she left her home—their nesting grounds—and struggled to stay in the air as she aimed at the only nearby place she felt she might be able to safely lay her egg:*

*The mountains!*

*If only...*

*The wind beneath her wings was once such a liberating sensation, but with the humans' blue iron buried deep within her it had become an agonizing-yet-necessary means of escape. Every flap of her wings and every strain to keep them rigid enough to ride the wind was a moment of torture. But to land was to succumb to the insects, and she refused to give them that satisfaction...*

*Even if they'd already succeeded in killing her.*

*She could already feel her insides dying...*

*But maybe, with the egg waiting within her, she could leave some kind of hope for their kind.*

*Some kind of hope...*

*Blackness swept over her vision as she worked to land, stifling the urge to roar and set the world ablaze as the adjustment to her wings shifted the sword inside her. The fire in her belly wanted to get out—to destroy everything—but she knew it would rob the egg of any chance it had. And so she flew, silent and blind, until she crashed into the mountain.*

*Struggling to lift herself, she howled as the iron was wedged deeper inside of her, and, knowing she was already too close to death to seek comfort, she ignored her many broken bones and liquefied organs to commit her final act:*

*Laying her egg.*

Be strong, *she willed her legacy,* be strong, my sweet baby blaze. My sweet… baby…

*Blay…*

*Her body withered around the enchanted iron, decaying from the inside out and leaking the fire in her belly across the mountain, staining the rock that she lay upon. And when, at last, the humans' iron fell from her body, it was every bit as twisted and robbed of its glory as she…*

So is my fate, *she looked back at the single egg she was able to leave behind as sight left her forever.*

So is my fate…

Blay shot upright like a bolt fired from a crossbow, panting and sweating. The wool covers draped across his body were already beginning to singe around the edges from his fire, and he whipped them aside to keep from burning down the entire inn. Nearby, Gav snored—lying beside the bed that Gwen occupied—and Gwen…

Was awake and staring at him.

"S-sorry…" Blay wiped his sweat-drenched face. "I… didn't mean to wake you."

Gwen stared nervously back at him. "Bad dream?" she asked.

He only nodded.

"About what?"

Blay drew in a ragged breath and shook his head of the voice as it started to rise from his core.

"A mother…" he muttered, "A mother and an iron trap…"

# TWENTY-FIVE

The army of non-humans numbered in the hundreds after volunteers of various races joined with General Diren and his army. There'd been murmurs among the groups, which broke off into select clusters based on familiarity or race or background, about the general's supposed softness towards a human informant. The varying degrees of the story—ranging from a passing sympathy to a blatant declaration to serve their kind—were all short lived, however, when General Diren had arrived to lead them up the mountain. No matter the suspicions at that point, there seemed to be a rising consensus that, after the way the general had handled the human who'd come to extend Hawkes' "invitation" to them, there was little chance that there was any truth to any of it.

Either way, Gwen and the others weren't about to expose the truth of the general's kind gesture.

Continuing their march through the narrow valley and starting up the mountain, the army's mass was funneled into a long, narrow line that began a gradual slither up the mountain's lonely path. Though the sun had yet to rise, the army could already see that, with a looming set of dark, overcast clouds, they would be fighting in darkness. The darkness seemed to unnerve some more than others, but as Gwen and Gav walked in silence beside General Diren, the two heard him mutter something about the clouds being a bad omen. Whether he meant this for their side or the humans' they couldn't be certain, but neither felt driven to press him further for details.

Blay, after the nightmare that had awakened him the night before, had left the village early with only the promise to Gwen that he would be there when they arrived. The way their friend had tossed and turned, crying out in his sleep while snarling and setting small fires to the corners of his blankets, had worried her. When the call to awaken finally came and before she and Gav had left, she'd told him of what had happened. The general's concerned words from the night before seemed to echo between them, but it was finally decided that it would only do more harm than good at that point to reawaken any doubt in Diren on the day of the battle.

*"If Blay is at the top of that mountain,"* Gav finally said, reassuring her, *"then it'll be all the proof we need that he's willing and able to fight. And, if he's not, then we need to trust that he made the decision for our sake and not hold it against him."*

Seeing her lover's faith in Blay renewed her faith, as well. If Gav, the wisest soul she had ever met, had risen above the initial distrust he'd felt for Blay when they'd first met, then there wasn't a doubt in Gwen's mind that he was worthy of that trust.

That, however, only cleared her mind for the weeds of concern for his wellbeing to spread.

The three were the first to reach the summit, and as General Diren began to assess the vast, flat area and the

jagged embankment at the east-facing side of the mountain, Gwen and Gav, spotting the familiar man-sized egg at
the south-facing ledge, hurried to join their friend. It was
eerily quiet, the rhythmic taps of both Gav's hooves and
her helitrad staff connecting with the mountaintop with
her every other stop resounding over the gentle whistle of
the wind. Gwen welcomed the subtle breaks in the silence,
though, considering them a peaceful calm before the inevitable storm.

Sensing their approach, Blay unfolded himself but
remained crouched down in the middle of the mysteri-
ously stained portion of mountain Gwen recognized from
their first meeting. Nearby, just as she remembered it, was
the strange mass of twisted iron jutting from the weath-
er-stripped sword hilt. She caught Blay staring towards this
as they approached him, but something told her that it was
better to not ask what he was thinking.

"You had us worried," Gav told him, reaching out a seven-fingered hand to pull their friend up.

Blay didn't take the proffered hand.

Gwen didn't even think he noticed it.

Staring a moment longer at the twisted, dead iron, Blay
let out a sigh and finally looked downward, dragging the
fingertips of his left hand across the portion of stained rock
under his feet.

"I think I'm finally beginning to understand your need
to heal," he said, his voice low and jagged. Finally looking
up, the two took a step back.

"Your eyes…" Gwen gasped.

Blay nodded and stood, looking away again.

"Dragon tears," he said.

Gwen glanced at Gav for any explanation he might have
for such a vague response, but the centaur only shrugged.

Though he'd always had an unnatural fire in his liz-
ard-like eyes, the once orange orbs had been replaced since

Gwen had last seen him with what she was certain were burning coals. They showed completely black with a series of jagged cracks that revealed an intense, fiery glow that throbbed like the breathing of a campfire. A series of harsh, jagged cracks that seemed to splinter out from under each of his eyes and cut down the sides of his face—sharing the same fiery glow just behind the lacerated flesh—only helped maintain her concern that he'd somehow hurt himself to replace his own eyes.

"Can…" she trembled, starting to reach out towards him but then thinking better of it. "Can you even see?"

Blay looked suddenly saddened and nodded, stepping between and then past them.

"Better than I'd like to," he answered.

Turning to follow, the two saw that his back, like his face, was littered with deep, jagged gashes that let the ominous glow burning within him seep through. It was suddenly easy to see him as the dragon egg he'd always claimed to be; *painfully* easy.

"Blay!" Gav grabbed his shoulder and moved to pull so that he could turn him to face them, but he didn't budge.

Gwen gaped at this. She'd seen firsthand Gav's strength and what he was capable of, and while she didn't think he was applying his full force she was certain that the force he was applying should have been enough to turn Blay towards them if not throw him off his feet.

And yet he was able to resist the pull as though it were nothing.

Gwen whimpered, "Oh no…"

Gav let go of Blay's shoulder, giving up the effort. "You know what I'm going to say to you," he said flatly.

"That I'm prettier than ever before?" there was no humor in Blay's voice, it was as if somebody else—somebody darker; meaner—was reading from a script that Blay had left behind.

302

Gav shifted on his hooves, and Gwen caught sight of a brief twitch of his arm as he reached for his axe reflexively before stopping himself. "If you're not well enough to fight with us then—"

"Then *what?*" Blay's head turned to face them over his shoulder, but as the rest of his body remained unmoving Gwen watched a new series of cracks form and spread across his neck as his head seemed ready to rotate off his shoulders. "You'll... hurt... me?" The way he spaced out his words made it sound more like an invitation.

Gwen stepped towards him, "Blay, I don't think—" A familiar wave of heat rolled from their friend, and they spotted General Diren—still standing a long way's off with the rest of the army—turning to face the source. Swallowing her fear, Gwen walked around Blay to face him head-on. "Listen, Blay, I don't know what happened last night, and if you don't want to talk about it then nobody's about to make you, but... but we need you right now. Do you hear me? We... *need*... you! So whatever... *this* is, it needs to wait, because without your strength this war is already as good as lost. So we need you to be strong, Blay... please!"

Blay paused for a moment and looked down at her, blinking.

"Wh-what... what did you just say?" his voice once again sounded like this own.

Gwen stared, confused. She could see that something in her speech had resounded within him, but, not sure which part it could have been, she just echoed the part freshest in her mind.

*Be strong.*

The fae's lips spoke the words, but it wasn't her voice that sounded in Blay's head. Turning back, he saw Gav—every muscle tightened and ready to do something he knew the centaur didn't want to—and then, beyond him, he spotted the mangled remains of an old Winter Ray and the stained rock.

*Mother…*

Blay sighed, breathing out something dark and mean that had been welling within him all night, and rubbed a sore spot out of his neck.

"You look tense, clip-clop," he chuckled, "you getting enough fiber in your diet?"

Both of his friends seemed more relieved by his otherwise unwelcomed humor than he'd expected.

"Well you're certainly looking… dramatic," General Diren could tell that his efforts to suppress his concern were hardly vague as he caught sight of Blay as the three joined with the rest of the army. Already seeing from both Gwen and Gav that they still stood by the prior night's convictions, however, he decided not to press the issue or concern the rest of the army any more than they already were. Shrugging, he forced a smirk, "War paint was never my thing, but, on you, it works!"

"I could be wearing a tavern wench's uniform and make it work, General, you should know that by now," Blay chuckled.

"Yes, yes," General Diren rolled his eyes. "You're just as hilarious as ever. Now fall in line, soldier!" He looked over at Gwen and Gav, "You two stay with me."

Turning back to the crowd, the elf general held up his left hand and, after a short moment, the entire mountain went silent. Though she'd come to realize that he had a habit of defying expectations, Gwen was still stunned to see a single elf inspire hundreds of mixed races of non-humans to offer their undivided attention with nothing more than a single gesture. On that particular day, however, they were in desperate need for impressive and expectation-defying feats.

Almost as impressive, she came to realize, was his ability to project his voice across a mountaintop for such a massive army to hear:

"LISTEN UP AND LISTEN GOOD, BECAUSE WE'RE CERTAINLY NOT GOING TO GET A SECOND CHANCE AT THIS. MANY OF YOU ARE SOLDIERS, OTHERS OF YOU ARE FIGHTERS, AND SOME OF YOU—THE BRAVEST, I'M WILLING TO SAY—HAVE NEVER SEEN ONE END OF A FIGHT OR THE OTHER. NOW I'LL ASK THAT NONE BE BOLSTERED BY THEIR EXPERIENCE JUST AS MUCH THAT I'LL ASK THAT NONE BE DETTERED BY THEIR LACK THEREOF; WHAT I *DO* ASK IS THAT YOU RECOGNIZE THIS MOMENT, RIGHT NOW, AS THE ONE WHEN YOU ENTERED INTO A NEW CHAPTER FOR NOT JUST YOURSELVES, NOT JUST YOUR KIN NOR YOUR KIND, AND NOT JUST FOR THE WORLD…" he drew in a low breath, letting the words settle like a spell over the entire army, "YOU'RE ENTERING, HERE AND NOW, INTO A COURSE OF EVENTS THAT WILL REDEFINE HISTORY! EVERY SONG OF THIS DAY—EVERY LEGEND, EVERY RETELLING, AND EVERY WHISPER, UTTERANCE, AND THOUGHT—WILL ECHO WITH YOUR NAME BECAUSE YOU ARE STANDING ON THIS MOUNTAIN! WE ARE NOW FAMILY! CUT ALL BARRIERS IN YOUR MINDS THAT DIVIDE US, FOR WE ARE ALL YOUR BROTHERS AND SISTERS!"

Blay, though buried amidst the crowd with the other soldiers, called out, "THAT'S GOING TO MAKE FAMILY REUNIONS TOUGH TO MANAGE, SIR!"

A nervous and scattered bout of laughter passed, and even General Diren shared a chuckle, nodding.

"I'LL TRUST YOU TO BUY THE DRINKS, EGG-MAN!"

When the crowd had finally settled once again, the elf general took another deep breath. "THIS ENEMY IS UNLIKE ANYTHING YOU'VE EVER FACED! THEY'LL BE ARRIVING IN A MACHINE OF IRON BUILT SPECIFICALLY TO CARRY THEIR NUMBERS AND THEIR SUPPLIES OVER THIS MOUNTAIN! TODAY THIS MACHINE IS WITHOUT THE NECESSARY POWER TO CRUSH OUR HOMES AND DESTROY OUR WAY OF LIFE, SO UNLESS YOU'RE PREPARED TO LOSE EVERYTHING BEFORE THIS WEEK'S END I SUGGEST YOU DON'T LET THEM OR THEIR MACHINE LIVE TO SEE TOMORROW!"

The crowd erupted into cheers and hollers of agreement, raising their weapons over their heads.

General Diren nodded, smiling at the rising energy. "WE CAN ALREADY SEE THAT THIS WILL BE A DARK DAY," he motioned to the cloud-covered sky, "AND THOUGH WE MIGHT NOT SEE THE DAWN COMING, I ALREADY SEE THE SETTING OF A WINTER SUN ON THE HORIZON!"

The cheers rose again, though with greater gusto than before.

"MANY OF YOU ALREADY KNOW THE TWO TO MY LEFT," he motioned to Gwen and Gav after the cheers had died down again. "AND IF YOU DON'T KNOW THEM PERSONALLY THEN I'M CERTAIN YOU'VE AT LEAST HEARD OF THEM! MANY OF YOU ARE HERE TODAY BECAUSE OF THEM, AND OTHERS HAVE LOVED ONES ALIVE AND WELL AT THIS VERY MOMENT BECAUSE OF THEM…"

306

a premature rise of applause and whistles drowned out his words and forced him to wait for it to stifle once again. "GWEN AND GAV ARE THE REASON WE HAVE THIS CHANCE; THE REASON THAT THE HUMANS' HISTORY BOOKS WON'T INCLUDE A CHAPTER OF THE DAY THEY EFFORTLESSLY TOOK THE WORLD AS THEIR OWN! IT'S BECAUSE OF THEM THAT I BELIEVE THINGS TODAY THAT I DID NOT BELIEVE YESTERDAY! IT IS BECAUSE OF THEM THAT I'M ABLE TO SEE A DAY PAST TODAY; THAT I'M ABLE TO SEE— NOT JUST BELIEVE; NOT JUST ENVISION; NOT SIMPLY HOPE FOR; WHY I AM ABLE TO *SEE*— THAT CURSED BLUE GLOW ON THE HORIZON FADE INTO DARKNESS ONCE AND FOR ALL!

"MANY OF YOU ALREADY BELIEVE IN THESE TWO, SO WHATEVER COMES OVER THAT PASS"—he pointed off towards the northern side of the mountain—"I NEED YOU TO BELIEVE, AS I BELIEVE, THAT YOU *CAN* DEFEAT IT!"

This time, as the round of cheers and hollering and applause rose, it was with a volume and ferocity that General Diren was certain could be heard all the way back at the humans' capital.

"General…" Gwen stepped nearer to him and motioned for him to join her so she could share something that seemed to be concerning her.

Frowning, he stepped nearer to her and leaned in for her to whisper in his ear:

"It's the Winter Sun, General," she said, letting him turn towards the north to see for himself. "It isn't there…"

"How can something that massive just *not* be where it was?" Blay demanded.

With the crowd still cheering and preparing for the encroaching dawn, the four had convened. Though the general didn't seem pleased with Blay rejoining them, it was clear he was more concerned with the recent turn of events.

"Well they're certainly not ant-hilling the damn thing up the mountain," Diren muttered, shaking his head. "The glow of that hideous thing is bright enough to have been seen by now if it was getting closer."

Gwen shivered at the thought. "How could none of them have noticed that it's not there?" she asked, motioning towards the army.

Gav shrugged. "Most of them only know of its existence through what they've heard. They haven't seen it like we have. If they don't know what they're looking for, they don't know to notice that it's *not* there."

"I couldn't care less where it's *not*," Blay hissed, "I want to know where it *is* so that I can promptly place myself somewhere else!"

"Then you can skedaddle to the human capital, egg-man,' the general glared, "because at this time that's the only certain place we've got."

Gav shook his head. "Look, dawn is approaching and, more to the point, so are the humans. Obviously whatever they've got planned is also the answer to whatever's happened to the Winter Sun, so I suggest we prepare ourselves and be ready to expect the unexpected."

General Diren sighed and nodded, calling over several of his soldiers and telling them to spread the word through the ranks to prepare. Nodding, the elves were off, sprinting out in various directions to get the order delivered. Watching, Gwen saw many of the soldiers already beginning to pull out the protection elixirs they'd gotten from the mage, a few who hadn't already enchanted their weapons using that spell, as well.

Still muttering about the Winter Sun, General Diren turned to speak with a few of his lieutenants.

Pausing to make sure the elf general wasn't listening, Gav turned to face Blay.

"Under any other circumstance I wouldn't ask you to do this," he said, "but I think we're only now beginning to get a scope of the forces that are about to come down on us. I know you've been holding back your powers to not wake up the dragon, and I know that you already know the general *doesn't* want you using your powers for that very same reason, but if ever there was a time to throw caution to the wind…"

Blay frowned and shook his head. "I wish it were that simple, Gav, but the general's concerns are exactly the reason that I *can't* just set fire to whatever's coming…"

Gwen shivered at his tone. "What do you mean?"

Blay shrugged, looking back at her with his burning-coal eyes, "I mean that, if I did what you're asking, when the fire cleared it would no longer be *my* fire…"

The reality of Blay's words sank like a stone in a choppy sea, and before the two could fully come to grips with what he'd said let alone offer a response, a call rose from one of the soldiers:

"DAWN HAS ARRIVED!"

As though there was something to be seen, hundreds of heads rose in unison to the cloud-covered sky, and everyone saw what they'd already known they'd see:

Nothing.

The coverage was too thick to allow any sunlight through, and without the sunrise the coming of the dawn seemed baited with even greater possibilities of what was coming.

"HUMANS!"

As with the call for dawn, the single word ushered hundreds of pairs of eyes towards the northern side of the mountaintop, where, unlike the call for dawn, there was actually something to be seen:

Four unarmed human soldiers…

Though the army had been prepared to face anything that came over the pass, they'd all, no doubt, been expecting more. Confusion and skepticism kept the entire army motionless as the four human soldiers, dressed all in black and without a single piece of armor between them, walked at a casual-yet-steady pace towards them. Enough space had been left for whatever the humans brought to clear the pass, General Diren explaining early on that, though any other tactic would have involved blocking off their enemy's entrance, his uncertainty of what they were coming with could put any soldiers on the frontline in jeopardy. This, however…

"What in Gaia's green hell…?" the general growled. "Just what sort of stunt are they pulling?"

The four humans continued towards them, and when their advancement showed no sign of slowing the army began to arch inward, keeping the four at a distance while slowly beginning to circle around in preparation for whatever they had planned. Finally, reaching roughly the center of the mountaintop, they broke their tight side-by-side formation. The two in the rear turned back-to-back and began an even march away from the other while the two in the front started out at a diagonal, forming an ever-expanding square with each one as a point. Still the army continued to arch around them, expanding their circle and continuing to move away until they'd finally formed a large, full circle around the four. Before long, the entire mass of General Diren's army had encompassed the entire rim of the mountaintop with the four humans finally stopping, having formed a massive, evenly-spaced square in the middle of the battlefield.

Even with the space between them the humans acted in perfect sync. Still moving slowly enough to not spark an

310

attack from the surrounding army, they reached into their black sleeves and drew a small dagger. The sight stirred a series of murmurs, but Gwen could see that none believed the weapons were big enough to represent a threat on their own. Seeming to expect this, the four waited with the daggers held out for all to see long enough to settle any nerves before retrieving from their opposite sleeves a small leather satchel. These they wasted no time in dropping on the ground between their feet, letting them spill the powder they contained. Then, raising their free hands, the four humans dragged the small daggers across their palms and let the flow of blood trickle onto the contents of their dropped satchel.

The instant the first drops of blood made contact with the powder, each point erupted into a beam of light as bright as the rising sun; each beam shooting up into the sky and crashing into the dark clouds above with a force like a cannon. Though thick and relentless, the clouds spiraled around the force of the four magic beams of light and pierced through, creating a square beacon that Gwen was certain reached beyond the heavens.

Hundreds of eyes followed the spectacle, once again craning their heads as a makeshift dawn ripped past the cloud cover. Through the gap, the first few rays of the rising sun could be seen…

Along with the rising of a second sun.

A blue one.

Pride and confidence were replaced in an instant with fear and panic. Though, as Gav had pointed out, none of the other soldiers had actually seen the Winter Sun, it wasn't hard for anybody who had heard even a whisper of rumors to see the bright blue glow bleeding past the clouds for what it was.

"LAST CHANCE TO DRINK THE ELIXIR IF YOU HAVEN'T ALREADY!" General Diren's voice rose over the dull roar of the soldiers and the growing intensity of the mechanical hum of whatever was carrying the Winter Sun on the other side of the clouds.

"What is that thing…?" Gwen whimpered.

The silhouette of a painfully unnatural yet eerily familiar form shifted on the other side of the clouds. As whatever it was drew nearer, using the four beams of light as a beacon to guide its trajectory, the vague outline formed a definite shape, and a giant head swaying ahead of a massive body blocked out the view of the sky, bathing the exposed mountaintop in the light of the Winter Sun.

Blay stared up, awestruck. "… the entire planet knew that the owners of those wings were the most powerful creatures to walk its surface," he whispered.

Gwen was certain that her friend hadn't meant to say the words aloud, nor did she believe that he'd expect anyone to hear them. But she had, and she couldn't stand another moment of not knowing what her friend's revelation had told him.

Turning to face him, she demanded, "What are you talking about? What's going on?"

Gav was hesitant to turn, keeping his gaze locked on the sky as he turned his body towards them.

Blay stared at her for a long moment as the mechanical hum became a roar of machinery that reminded them of the flying machines from the military base.

And it was still so far away…

"Dragons," Blay finally said. "The humans' capital—the site that the Winter Sun was built upon—was once the nesting grounds for dragons." He looked up again, and Gwen followed his gaze. As his explanation continued, she saw that the shape of the behemoth carrying the Winter Sun was unmistakable.

"Through sheer numbers and with Hawkes' enchanted iron they were able to kill all of them…" He looked back at the south-facing peak of the mountain where she and Gav had found him earlier. "My mother flew to this spot, full of hate and fear, to leave behind their kind's last hope. She died there with a Winter Ray buried beneath wing, and… and…" he looked down as several more cracks began to form under his eyes.

Gav frowned and looked at Blay. "You're telling me that the humans killed all but one dragon so they could tame one?"

"No," Blay looked back up into the sky as the mechanical roar grew nearly too loud to hear him over. "I'm telling you they killed every last dragon so that they wouldn't have *competition* to build their own iron dragon…"

The shadow of the beast, finally centered within the four beams of light, loosed an ear-splitting whine into the air, and Gwen was reminded of the tortured gears and chains she'd heard the fae struggling with when the iron gate to the labyrinth had been raised. The army of non-humans drew back from the sound, many dropping their weapons so they could free their hands and cover their ears while others doubled over and trembled.

Then the shadowed form of wings lifted and the creature fell.

The impact was enough for the pieces of the mountain to crumble, and in an instant many of the soldiers were lost over the edges. An echo rolled outward, and Gav wouldn't have been surprised if even the fae city at the far-south could hear it past their walls. Though he wasn't sure when he'd pulled Gwen to him, he felt his lover's hand press against his chest as she arched to see through the settling dust.

"By the gods…" she whispered.

They'd seen enough of the humans' machines to recognize the ironwork and its workings, but none of it compared in sheer size to what stood over them.

It's body occupied nearly a quarter of the entire mountaintop, and, while Gav had been certain that the site of their battle with the humans would possibly be *too* large—allowing more space for the humans to work with than he was comfortable affording an enemy—he suddenly found himself wondering if the space they had left would be enough. Before he could reconsider the calculations, however, the giant, iron dragon began to stir. Trembling for a moment, it groaned under the force of its own weight as it recovered from its fall onto the mountain and then lifted itself up. As its body unfurled—reminding him of Blay's awakening process—the army was offered its first real glimpse of what they were up against:

The torso was massive and wide and supported by a pair of powerful arms that held the mechanical creature upright. The lower-half of its body seemed more bug-like, tapering off into a long "tail" with thousands of smaller "legs" that traveled nearly its full length. Gav frowned at that, trying to itemize the machine in its entirety but finding himself staring at the design of its lower half. All of the other machines, he remembered, centered on function, but if the purpose of this humongous, dragon-like war machine was mobility then they'd sacrificed a great deal of agility with a design that seemed—Gav found himself disliking the description but not finding one that was better—"fat." In fact, the full bulk of its mass seemed almost too much to lift, but with the giant machine beginning to right itself after its fall, Gav could see three sets of wings that had already folded along the length of its body. Though it was impossible to tell how long they might be when open, he could see that they were mounted at the shoulders, mid-back, and the third nearer to the base of its tail. Folded up, however, they just made the body look that much longer.

Not that it needed any help…

When it was finally upright, a set of hinged "bones" began to open from around the "head" of the iron dragon. As the hinges of its neck stretched, the screech of iron dragging against iron issued with each flexing arch, and the "face" revealed itself with the hinges swinging open. With the shield open like the protective hood Gav had seen around some lizards, a massive wolf-like head leered over them. As the creature "woke up," its eyes sparked to life and exposed themselves as giant chunks of the enchanted blue iron. Swiveling its head to "look" at the nearest group of soldiers, Gav could see the intense stare instantly work its dark magic on the poor souls; their skin beginning to blister and burn and driving them to dodge its gaze.

Gav cursed and stomped his hoof. "Damn! It's stronger than even the protective spell."

Blay sneered, "Or maybe the spell doesn't work!"

"It works," Gwen watched in horror, "but that's more of the Winter Sun iron than any of us were expecting at once."

Gav nodded. "That spell can only do so much! It's not…"

Another set of metallic screeches made the army flinch again as a secondary set of arms began to unfold from around the iron dragon's chest. The bulk of its torso extended in a pair of three-fingered claws at the end of the new arms; each having three "elbows" that, Gav guessed, allowed it a much farther reach than the primary set of arms. As the arms unfolded fully, a familiar blue glow grew brighter as they uncovered…

"The Winter Sun!" Gwen cried out, shielding her eyes as Gav hoisted her onto his back and started to gallop out of the direct range of its path.

Behind them, more of their army's soldiers cried out and then fell silent.

Continuing to navigate around the soldiers, Gav carried Gwen back to the rear flank of the iron dragon, steering clear of the Winter Sun's glow and regrouping with General Diren, who'd hurried straight into the chaos after the creature had fallen out of the sky. When he was certain she'd be safe, he set her back onto her feet.

General Diren checked them for any signs of injury before glaring back at their enemy. "WHAT THE HELL ARE YOU WAITING FOR?" he cried out. "ATTACK!"

Despite the obvious intimidation, the soldiers' resolve to win the war or die trying proved solid as their awestruck silence gave way to a rise of war cries. Brandishing their weapons, though clearly having no clear target in sight, the circle of non-humans began to close in on the beastly machine that had fallen out of the sky. As they closed in, Gav caught sight of Gwen's long ears twitching a brief moment before he heard a hollow whine of machinery, as well.

"Oh no…" Blay groaned, "What now?"

"Enough to carry their supplies *and* their army…" Gav found himself staring at the giant underbelly, once again wondering why they'd chosen such a strange design.

Then it opened up…

In an instant the mountaintop had exploded into the warzone everyone had been expecting. After only a few short minutes the non-human army had been cut down by nearly a half as a seemingly endless wave of human soldiers and machines birthed themselves from the iron dragon's stomach.

Gav hadn't wasted any time, already galloping in and shouting commands even as the massive ramp was dropping. The first half-dozen human soldiers never got to set foot off their machine before the centaur's axe passed through them. As their bodies crumpled and slowed the soldiers behind them, the iron dragon's head swiveled around to "glare" at him with its Winter Sun eyes, forcing him to sidestep the deadly rays and distance himself from the body and allowing the human army to continue its assault. Motivated by Gav's bravery, however, a squadron of Diren's elf soldiers leapt into action, climbing onto the iron dragon's back and attacking its arms and wings while others began chopping away at the many tiny legs holding its lower body.

Keeping close to Blay and General Diren, Gwen called upon her newfound fury and began to put her staff to work, though she was painfully aware from the start that her companions were doing the bulk of the work. She injured many, using the training she'd grown up with to target the human soldiers at their weakest points, but found herself unable to deliver the killing blow after incapacitating them. Fortunately, once a soldier was brought to their knees or unable to breathe properly, either General Diren or Blay weren't far behind to finish the job.

But as much as she wanted to believe her contributions were making a difference, she knew that they were already on the losing side of the battle. For every human soldier killed, they lost three of their own. And in the seconds it took to hack away at one of the iron dragon's tiny legs, a single one of the humans' armored vehicles had slaughtered another half-dozen. Gwen had tried to keep track of how many of the vehicles had emerged from the giant machine's belly, but it had been impossible. Several of them had met an explosive end with Gav using his agility and strength to steer them over the mountain's edge, but Gwen couldn't help but feel like they were drowning in an ocean that was being emptied by mere drops.

At that rate, it wouldn't be long before the humans had killed them all…

The fact that Gav had yet to get himself killed was becoming less a show of strength or agility and more a process of dumb luck that he was certain was about to run out. Being one of the biggest targets on the entire mountain for the human army, he was finding himself in the awkward position of drawing most of the enemy's attention while the dwindling non-human forces did all they could to destroy the giant iron dragon. One of the longer arms had been cut free and, after several tries, Gav was able to fool the human navigating one of the smaller machines to steer into the massive, dead iron slab and wind up dragging both the vehicle and the arm over the mountain. Satisfied with this solution, he'd used any method he could think of to send more of the vehicles over the edge.

Though it was serving to rid the battlefield of the machines, it was also making the remaining machines increasingly eager to remove him from the fight.

Eager, and desperate.

Like with any other race, Gav noticed that desperation was not far from stupidity, and being the target of multiple enemies piloting large iron machines while intoxicated with stupidity was not a good thing to be.

It was a miracle that he'd been able to dodge the first—*another moment of dumb luck*, he thought—but the second came in too fast and too soon after the first. With no other option, Gav jumped on top of the machine, feeling the iron begin to burn his lower legs as he galloped over its surface, and jumped clear as it crashed into the first. The two machines swerved and, as Gav turned on his injured legs to watch, he saw them collide with the jagged embankment at the east-facing side of the mountain. Hearing the scream of twisted metal mate with the low, angry groan of tortured rock, Gav tried to step away as the embankment cracked at the base and began to collapse over him. The burns to his hooves slowed him, however, and, realizing he wouldn't get clear in time, he dropped his axe and secured his footing, bracing himself.

318

The full weight of the collapsing boulder crashed down over him and he felt something pop in his hindquarters and fought to remain upright as the pain assaulted his body. Crying out from the exertion, he fought to hold the boulder over his head. Hearing him, several of the nearest soldiers rushed to his side and began shouldering the weight, as well, calling more to help as they found themselves at risk of being crushed as more of the supporting base crumbled.

Looking at the others, Gav came to bittersweet realization that they had just saved his life only to just as quickly put themselves at risk.

Catching sight of their predicament, several human soldiers charged at the group and cut down three of the non-humans supporting the growing weight. As the others fought to take the added burden, they stared in horror as the humans made a game of killing them one-by-one.

"Wonder how many it'll take before it crushes them," one laughed.

Another wasted no time burying his Winter Ray into another non-human, working their way down towards Gav. "Only one way to see," he replied.

"NO!" Gav roared at them, starting to jump free of the boulder but stopping when he realized none of the others would survive without his contribution.

The humans laughed; one pointing his Ray at him and shaking his head.

"Soon, centaur," he taunted, "You just wait your turn!"

Then they killed another two.

Gwen spotted Gav and several others from across the mountaintop and started towards them at a full sprint. A few humans caught sight of her path and moved to intercept her, but the first few collapsed in a flurry of arrows fired off by one of the elves she remembered from the military base before he turned his attention back to his own attackers. Another human moved to tackle her from the left, only to cry out and stumble as a dagger carved from gleaming white bone whistled by her head and buried itself in the exposed portion of his throat. Glancing over her shoulder, she spotted General Diren not far behind.

"Where's Blay?" she called.

The general motioned back towards the iron dragon. "Helping the others dismantle that thing!" he called back.

Though she was glad to hear that he was putting his efforts towards their biggest problem, Gwen found herself feeling exposed without him by her side. Despite her advancements, she'd grown used to having Blay at her side.

Forfeiting her view of Gav and shooting a glance towards the giant machine, she caught sight of him assisting several of the soldiers committed to taking out the legs, but she noticed that he was still holding back.

*Damn it, Blay, we'll never win if you don't—*

She saw a bright blue glow fill her vision and dove free before another soldier's Winter Ray could take her head off.

Rolling with the impact, Gwen skidded to a stop and scrambled to retrieve her staff, only to have the soldier kick it away from her reach. Looking up, Gwen saw the soldier silhouetted over her by the four beams of light that still fired into the sky around their iron dragon; his Winter Ray raising over his head for the final strike. Shutting her eyes as the blow was about to land, she was surprised to only feel the toxic heat of the weapon as a sharp, metallic clap resounded just over her head. Scrambling to distance herself from the soldier, she spotted General Diren staying the soldier's enchanted iron with his own sword.

"You're not dying today, fae!" the elven general grunted as he pushed back against the human. "But this one..."

Lunging forward, General Diren forced the human to withdraw in order to keep his footing, giving Gwen enough room to stand and retrieve her helitrad staff. Turning back to the skirmish, she watched, wide-eyed, as the general's sword became a blur, coming down again and again against the human's Winter Ray, knocking his iron helmet from his head in a flash of movement from the elf general's free hand. The human's face twisted as he struggled to follow the movements and hold back the attacks. But as impressive as his onslaught was, he was no more immune to the enchanted iron than any of the others, and gasped as she saw that his hands and face were beginning to blister in the glow of the soldier's Winter Ray.

"General!" she called, reaching out to him. "Get back! Stop!"

The general did neither.

"You're not dying today, fae…" he repeated as his movements grew more and more sluggish, his attacks beginning to fall more lightly and far less swiftly. "Not… today…" he trailed off as he slumped forward under the weight of his own sword, his burned and blistered hands beginning to bleed and spill blood over the guard of his weapon.

Seeing his chance, the human soldier raised his Winter Ray. "You're all dying today, monster; all of you!"

"NO!" Gwen shrieked, leaping forward and bringing the staff down on the human's exposed head.

Letting out a startled, hollow grunt, the soldier dropped his Winter Ray and stumbled as a trickle of blood rolled from his left ear. Gwen held her stance, keeping the staff held at the ready. An old, familiar part of her felt a pang of guilt start to stir, but, like a dying ember in a spent campfire, it soon burned out as she remembered how close that human had been to killing General Diren. Finally, the human toppled over with a vacant look in his unblinking eyes. After giving the body a few sharp jabs with her toe to be sure he wouldn't be trying to hurt them again, Gwen used her staff to discard the Winter Ray to a safe distance and then turning to tend to the general.

"You... you killed him," the general was still staring at the human as Gwen applied some of her soothoil to his burns.

Again the pang of guilt swelled and again she was able to forgive herself.

"I prefer to think of it as saving you, General," she said flatly, finishing with his wounds.

With the job done, Gwen hurried to her feet and closed the distance between her and Gav. As they drew nearer, she and the general spotted the human soldiers killing the unarmed group working to keep the boulder held up. A sharp whistle sounded from General Diren then, and several of his soldiers turned from their work on the increasingly tortured iron dragon.

Even from across the mountaintop, their arrows made short work of the two sadists.

Arriving at her lover's side, Gwen fought to stay strong. "You're hurt?" she could see the pain in his face—could see it was this pain that was crippling his strength—but couldn't tell where his injuries were.

"M-my... my back," Gav strained to speak past the pain and the weight of the boulder.

Nodding, she retrieved her soothoil and several of her numbing powders, hoping that it would be enough to hold the pain at bay long enough to turn the tides of the battle. Without a word, she ducked under the boulder and moved to his flank, rushing to remove the saddle from his back. With the limited lighting and the threat that the boulder might come crashing down on all of them, she was forced to work quickly, and though she was sure that the bulk of his pain still remained, she was relieved to see the centaur's vitality return as the boulder began to raise.

Blay could feel the beast within him thrashing to get out. The voice had grown so loud and so constant that there were no longer words in his head, just one, long, drawn-out growl pushing him to set fire to the whole damn mountain.

And he was running out of excuses not to.

The only thing keeping him from giving up the fight inside himself was Gwen. He'd come to grips with too many realities—the reality that she'd never feel for him what she did for Gav and the reality that he sincerely didn't expect her to being among the most painful—to be able to answer the voice's demands to know *why* it was still worth it to keep her alive if his love for her was doomed to go unrequited.

The part of him that still yearned to sit and listen in on scholars in their element knew that his unrequited love was precisely why she had to live. So long as she was breathing, he had a breath to fight for. He was a hunter who would never catch his perfect prey…

And it was that most reliable of challenges that would keep him going.

Once again stealing a glance from his efforts on the iron dragon, he let out a sigh of relief as he saw Gwen finally reach Gav and, with her magic, return the strength he needed to cast the boulder aside.

Metal shrieked over his head and he dove free of a giant sheet of iron that had once been a part of one of the massive machine's wings.

"See you fly now!" he spat up at the ugly mockery.

*If nothing else*, he thought, *we've already set their plans back several more years.*

It still didn't feel like enough, though.

Though more and more parts were beginning to fall from the humans' weapon, the non-human army was beginning to wear too thin to buy them the freedom they needed to continue. More and more human soldiers were slipping past the dwindling numbers, and it was becoming more frequent for all of them to halt their efforts just to defend themselves against a greater number of humans. The mountaintop was already littered with corpses, and the humans' soldiers just kept adding to those numbers without doing them the favor of doing their own fair share of dying.

That, however, became a distant concern as Blay and the others realized (too late) that taking all those parts off of the iron dragon was also removing a great deal of dead weight.

The shields along the side of the iron dragon's head were stripped off in one fluid motion from a roaring ogre, and as the iron slabs and mechanical boning fell to the ground the head whipped around with a greater speed than ever before and bathed many of the non-humans working along its back in its deadly glare. Diving free of the blue glow, Blay felt the burn of its gaze land on his heels and he was forced to sprint away from it, being herded towards the others.

"General!" Gav shouted a warning before pulling Gwen behind the boulder.

"GET DOWN!" General Diren called out to the other soldiers as he dove for the cover of the makeshift shield.

Many of the soldiers were close behind, but several who'd been too slow to heed the warning were incinerated by the iron dragon's Winter Sun gaze. Gav, keeping his lover held close to him, jumped as Blay slid past the boulder before scrambling back to join them as the ground he'd just been occupying shone with the cold and unforgiving blue light.

Then the mountain began to shake as the iron dragon started towards them. Glancing around the boulder, they watched in horror as the scorching gaze and toxic fangs went to work on anything and everything it came across. A new breed of fury seemed to drive the mechanical creature as the line dividing sides vanished, the human soldiers became just as expendable in the eyes of the pilot. Gav narrowed his eyes at the carnage, already having a good guess who was behind the controls. The only remaining secondary arm shot out with lightning-fast ferocity and snatched one of the smaller machines in its claw before hurling it through the air towards them.

"MOVE!" Gav shouted, sparking the group to move away from the boulder as the machine burst against the opposite side and sent the chunk of rock rolling towards them, crushing several more of those too slow to heed the warning.

"Dammit," General Diren hissed, "they're killing us!"

"Tell us something we don't already know, General," Blay scoffed.

"Listen here, egg-man, I've got a right mind to—" the general's threat silenced itself as he made eye contact with him. "By Gaia's green hell…" he gasped, "It's already happening, isn't it?"

Blay only shook his head violently.

More screams—even closer—echoed as the iron dragon continued its murderous rampage towards the group, taking out every living thing in its way.

Gwen whimpered and shivered. "I can't believe he'd go to these sorts of lengths," she could no longer hold back her sobs.

Blay scoffed at that and it evolved into a rolling chuckle which exploded into laughter. All the survivors hiding behind the boulder looked up at him with growing concern, the question of whether or not to risk the iron dragon just to distance themselves from the unstable dragon's egg flashing in many of their eyes.

And Gav couldn't blame them.

Blay's body was shimmering from a combination of his sweat and others' blood, and every muscle seemed to be strained against the surface of his skin. It looked as though his own body had become too much for his skin to contain.

Still cackling, Blay looked up at her, his eyes flaring like twin flames that chipped away the edges of his face. "They spent centuries—*centuries!*—crawling in the mud and cutting down their own kind for the biggest mound! Your whiny fae buddy hasn't taught them a damn thing, he's just grown as savage as them, and now they're all watching everything they've been working for slip away and they're doing what they do best: they're going on a killing rampage to salvage whatever they can claim!" He scoffed and shook his head, "You can't believe *this*, Gwen? There's *a lot* more to lose now than just a mound of mud. You'd better start believing!" he finished just as another wave of laughter took him, splitting several more fresh cracks across his body and causing him to cry out in pain.

Gav glared at him. Every passing second was bringing them closer to certain death and the only potential means of saving them was spitting taunts at his lover and fighting to hold it all back. Unable to tolerate it any longer, he closed the distance between him and Blay before stomping his hoof when there was no more distance left to close.

"THEN HELP US!" he roared in the dragon egg's face. "YOU HAVE THE POWER, BUT INSTEAD YOU—"

"Gav..." Gwen laid a hand on the centaur's shoulder to relax him. "We don't know what could happen if he did. The dragon inside of him could just as easily turn on us as them. We just don't know."

Gav frowned and looked back at her, nodding. "That's the point, Gwen, we don't know what will happen if he lets it out... but we all already know what will happen if he doesn't."

His words sank into all of the survivors as the reality of what had to be done set in.

Gwen whimpered, her lower lip trembling. "Gav..." she cast a tear-filled gaze at Blay and shook her head. "B-Blay," she ignored the heat spilling out from the cracks of his body as she draped her arms around her friend. "I... I don't want it to end like this!"

Blay's body trembled at the fae's embrace and his arms slowly moved to hold her, his eyes shimmering as he looked up at Gav.

"I know you don't, Gwen," he said without looking away from Gav, "but it's what has to be." Pulling away, he looked down at her, cupping her hands in his. "Just... please believe in me. I... I need to know that you'll be thinking of me as you've known me when I let it out..."

Sobbing, Gwen could only nod.

Gwen's vision was growing blurry as the rock they'd been hiding behind trembled and began to lift. Looking up, she could make out the shadow of the iron dragon as it hoisted the boulder, robbing them of their shield and brandishing it as a weapon.

Then she heard a sound that reminded her of clumps of ice falling from her old house's roof during the spring thaw. Clenching her eyelids and wiping away the tears, she looked back at Blay in time to see several of the last eggshell shards his skin had become fall away and expose a man-shaped womb of fire and magma. The sizzling cocoon throbbed and shifted for a long moment—the boulder still lifting higher above them—before it finally tore open.

*Years!* Hawkes seethed from within the heart of his creation. *Years of suffering! Years of working! Years of planning!*

*And the one who was owed to me for my commitment* defies *me?*

He roared within the claustrophobic confines, working the controls to keep Gwendolyn and the beasts she'd sided with out of the Winter Sun's beautiful glow. He wouldn't allow them the honor of perishing under its light! He would crush them like the bugs they were! He would...

As his field of vision was clear of the boulder, he caught sight of nothing but shadow.

"What?" he strained to see.

Nothing...

Howling in a rage, he slammed the controls to smash the boulder down blindly. He no longer cared if he saw them die, so long as they did die!

The lever moved halfway and then jammed, refusing to let the weight of the boulder drop any further.

"What?" he found himself repeating himself.

And then he saw the fire...

In a whirlwind of silver scales and fire Blay erupted into his true form. Gwen had hoped that she could keep her final promise to her friend—had wanted nothing more than to be able to hold onto the belief that what he'd become *was* still him—but she hadn't had to. What she'd always thought would be a violent or visceral scene had been one of the most magical and breathtaking things she had ever witnessed. And when it was over, Blay stood over them, a towering creature with silver scales and wings as white as fresh snow, and clutched the boulder in an ivory grip that had Hawkes' iron dragon groaning from strain.

He didn't set fire to them.

He didn't look upon them menacingly or without recognition.

His eyes were still his own beautiful orange orbs.

"It's you," she couldn't hold in the wave of laughter and tears. "It's really you, Blay!"

Hearing his name, the dragon offered a single, solemn nod.

And then he fought for them.

Slamming the boulder outward, they watched as the chunk of mountain crashed against the iron dragon's chest—straight into the Winter Sun, shattering the machine's arm and eclipsing the toxic light in the process—before heaving a wave of fire into the iron dragon's face. The machine thrashed its head before trying to turn its blue gaze upon its enemy, only to have Blay roar and catch it by its iron throat. The skin of his clawed hand sizzled against the iron, and he roared again before yanking the neck outward again and again and again. With each tug, the mountain seemed to tremble with the force and more and more bits began to break free from the iron dragon before…

"WATCH OUT!" Gav scooped her up and galloped out of the way as the iron dragon's severed head crashed onto the mountaintop.

Though she half expected the mechanical creature to die at that moment, she quickly saw the foolishness in that as the body continued to fight back against Blay's relentless advancements. Fresh waves of fire enveloped what remained of the machine—earning a fresh set of mechanical whirrs and blind thrashing—as he continued to strike against the Winter Sun with the boulder. Though the enchanted iron refused to die—refused to go cold and lifeless—the iron-work around it began to crumple.

"Gwen," Gav pointed, "look!"

There, past a panel of folded iron, was a wooden panel. Remembering the wooden case Hawkes had kept his iron knuckles in, Gwen nodded.

"He's in there!" she said, certain it was true.

Gav nodded, setting her on his back and hoisting his axe.

"Just be ready," he whispered.

*Could you kill him to heal the world?*

*Would you kill him to save them all?*

"I will be," she promised.

Blay was always a clever fighter. It was one of the qualities Gav had always admired him for. For all his bad jokes and savage approaches, he had never been one to fight without flexing his brain before his muscle. Gav had worried that, upon hatching, they'd be faced with something that, solely for the sheer increase in muscle, didn't rely on wit as much as they'd come to expect.

Gav's worries had been wasted.

He watched, waiting for the best moment to put an end to it all, and marveled as the giant silver creature their friend had become delivered hit after hit. More and more the chest of the iron dragon began to crumple away, and with every hit his enemy landed, Blay was quick to recover, return several more of his own, and be ready for the next attempt.

Hawkes was running out of moves, and he was running out of pieces. Even worse for him, however, was the time he was running out of.

Gav was certain that Blay wouldn't even need their help to kill the vagrant fae…

Until Hawkes, in a desperate attempt to put down the creature that was turning the tides of the battle, did just that…

Sacrificing its own weapon, the iron dragon grabbed the portion of crumpled iron from its chest and tore it all off, Winter Sun and all, exposing the enchanted wood barrier where Hawkes was controlling the mechanical creature.

Then, rolling free of the boulder Blay had been keeping between them, he struck the silver dragon again and again and again…

The massive orb of enchanted iron roared and sizzled with each impact, and the beautiful silver scales and white wings were soon stained with red and bathed in the toxic blue glow.

"Gav!" Gwen gasped, "He's going to kill him"

Nodding, he began to map out a plan.

"Can you get past that barrier?"

"I'll find a way! Just do something!"

It wasn't like Gav to not think something all the way through. As a *vernunt* it simply wasn't in his nature. But Gwen had taught him a great deal about faith, and there was nothing and no one he had more faith in than her. With barely enough time to consider his aim, Gav hurled his axe and took off at a full gallop straight towards the iron dragon with his lover poised and waiting at his back.

The iron dragon moved to bring the Winter Sun down on Blay once more, but the axe found its mark within the shoulder it clutched the weapon in. Metal screeched and struggled against the jammed mass of the giant stone blade before the mechanical limb let out a loud pop and dropped the Winter Sun on top of the spark-spitting void where its head had once been. With the weight of the iron crashing down on the enchanted wooden barrier, the fae-centaur lovers watched as the machine began to crumple in on itself; the wood beginning to split and splinter under the immense weight.

"Help Blay," Gav instructed as they neared the heaving dragon.

Gwen nodded and braced herself, hoping that she wasn't already too late.

N

Without slowing, Gav let Gwen leap from his back and roll to her feet in a desperate sprint to get to Blay. Uncertainty racked her mind as she looked at the dying dragon, unsure if she would be able to do anything for a creature of that size.

But if everyone had been willing to put all their faith in her up until that moment, maybe it was time she tried doing the same.

Kneeling beside the dragon's head and staring into the fading light of its eyes, she began to go through the familiar motions:

"Faithmist for stillness... Sootheoil for clarity... And the flesh... and the... no..."

The light was already gone from Blay's eyes...

She was too late.

It hadn't taken long for Gav to tear Hawkes through the enchanted barrier, but the exposure to the Winter Sun, no matter how brief, was enough to make him feel the scalding grip of an iron death drawing near.

But he had the only other surviving vagrant fae in his grip, and his enchanted iron and every unholy weapon he'd created from it was about to meet the fate of its maker.

"I'm only sorry that I can't do this in the labyrinth, *vagrant*," he snarled, taking his throat in one of his hands and beginning to do what was several years overdue.

Gwen was sobbing over the body of her friend, letting herself ramble as she buried her face into the silver scales.

She spoke of her life in the fae city and everything she'd dreamed of.

She spoke of the mistake that had marked her a vagrant to her people; the mistake that had started her on a spectacular journey.

332

She spoke of saving others.

She spoke of saving herself.

She spoke of all the things she'd dreamed and all the possibilities that a world without pain and suffering and death might bring.

She spoke so randomly and so fast that the words stopped having any meaning at all. But still she spoke, finding the words losing more and more purpose but somehow gaining more and more meaning.

Eventually she found herself calling upon words that were not words and singing a song that no other knew how to sing.

And it wasn't until the massive chest of the first dragon to grace those mountains in years rose with a new breath that Gwen realized it…

She'd discovered her *sparadikt*!

"Do you really think it's over, General Diren?" Gwen asked, looking hopefully at the newly decorated elf general from across their booth at the village pub.

With the pad of his thumb still absently rubbing the surface of his newest medal, the elf general sighed and shook his head, giving Gav a look. "Will she ever start calling me 'Fynn' like I've asked?"

Gav chuckled and took another sip from his pint. "Will you ever stop rubbing your new award?" he asked back.

General Diren stared down at it, not missing a beat as his thumb made another pass over its surface.

"Answers that question," Gwen giggled.

"Don't wear that thing down before your kid has a chance to be born," Gav smirked. "I'm sure you'd like it to have some of its luster while you bore poor baby Diren to tears with this tale."

"Bore?" he shook his head, smirking, "A pair of vagrant faes on opposite sides? A Winter Sun on the horizon of a dead world? Passionate romance? The only fae healer to ever achieve a resurrection?"

Gwen giggled, "I'm sure they'll be happy just hearing about the epic battles and a dragon flying off into the sunset."

General Diren nodded, giving his medal one last rub before pinning it back to his uniform. "I suppose it's worth it to keep pristine for the family," he nodded before rising to his feet. "Speaking of which, I think I've earned some much needed time with my wife-and-soon-to-be-mother of my child."

Gwen frowned and looked up after him. "You didn't answer my question, General: do you really think it's over?"

The elf general paused and stared off for a long moment, immersed in his own thought. Then, smiling, he shook his head.

"No, Gwen, I don't. I don't think it will ever be over. And that's okay, because it's when trouble like that rears its ugly head that heroes like you two show up and change the world." He smirked and patted the two of them on their shoulders, "And what fun would the world be without heroes and changes they bring?"

Gwen couldn't help but smile at that. "Thank you, General… for everything."

Gav smiled and raised an eyebrow at her once the general was gone.

"I take it you like the idea of being a hero?"

Blushing, she shrugged. "I guess I'm not really thinking about that right now."

"Oh?" Gav smirked and gave her a coy grin, "And what are you thinking about then?"

Moving to sit against him, she gave him a long, passionate kiss, once again feeling right in his embrace.

"Right now," she admitted, "I'm happy just thinking of this moment and whatever moment we'll share next."

Wrapping his arms around his fae lover, Gav found himself thinking the same thing.

# EPILOGUE

*Like maple leaves during the Autumn Equinox…*

Le told her, because she loved hearing him say the words and because he loved saying it, that her hair was the color of maple leaves during the Autumn Equinox.

It was like looking back at a nightmare now, as though everything before that moment—all of the lies and the fear and the hatred and the death—had all just been some terrible scene pulled from the recesses of a madman's mind. He wanted so badly to convince himself that none of it had been real; that it truly had just been a bad dream and, as he looked into the beautiful fae's eyes and pictured a life together with her, that none of it mattered. Knowing that the danger might still linger was what kept it real, though. In his mind, a mind that was never done galloping at full speed, he knew what his heart wanted to forget, that in order to keep her—to continue holding her like he was— they needed to be ready for anything. They'd stepped into the world as nothing more than a healer and a thinker, but they'd stepped out of the dying of the Winter Sun as so much more. Like the beautiful fae's spells or one of his thoughts, the swirling chaos had come to rest with something beautiful and far stronger than its parts. Eventually the world might begin to move past what they'd done, and perhaps even come to forget it all as nothing but an epic tale of bravery and strength saving the world. That, more than anything else, sang as a bittersweet melody in his mind. He'd set out to do right, to be honorable in an otherwise dishonorable world, and he and his lover had come out of it with more than they'd bargained for. Because until that day came when children stopped asking yet again to hear the story of Gwen and Gav: the fae-and-centaur lovers who defied all odds and united a world to save itself, they had a far greater role than any could have imagined:

That role of heroes.

He told her again and again that her hair was the color of maple leaves during the Autumn Equinox, because, try as he might to pretend they could exist in that moment as lovers forever, Gav knew that the day would come when they needed to be so much more once again.

# ABOUT THE AUTHORS

*Megan J. Parker* lives in upstate New York and is normally found lounging in the writing office with her husband and fellow author, Nathan Squiers.

Since the debut of her first novel, *Scarlet Night*, Megan J. Parker has gained international recognition and has been a bestseller in paranormal romance and dark fantasy. Her first novel, *Scarlet Night*, also was a runner up for 2013's Best New Series Award on the blog, Paranormal Craving. In 2016, she became a *USA Today* Bestselling Author and since then, has been on the list three times.

On her down time, she likes reading and designing new logos and videos. Her passion for telling stories is portrayed in all her work and when there's a story to tell, you can be sure she'll tell it to its full extent. She is finally fulfilling her dream of owning a design company along with her literary career at EmCat Designs.

*Nathan Squiers*, along with his loving wife & fellow author, Megan J. Parker, two incredibly demanding demons wearing cat-suits, and a pair of "fur baby" huskies, is a resident of Upstate New York. When he isn't dividing his time between writing or "nerding out" over comics, anime, or movie marathons, he's chasing dreams of amateur body building. If he can't be found in a movie theater, comic shop, or gym, chances are "the itch" has driven him into the chair at a piercing/tattoo shop... or he's been "kidnapped" by loving family or friends and forced to engage in an alien task called "fun."

Made in the USA
Middletown, DE
13 September 2022

72803260R00205